Praise for Susan Rieger

The Divorce Papers

"Brims with brio and wit."

—*Entertainment Weekly*

"It's in the personal correspondence that [Rieger] really shows a story-teller's imagination. . . . Rieger's literary feat: finding entertainment and compassion in the wreckage of a failed happily ever after."

—Emily Giffin, *New York Times Book Review*

"In this comedy of manners, Sophie Diehl, a criminal-law associate . . . not only learns to navigate the ecosystem of a high-society divorce, but also reassesses her own divorced parents and her ideas about love and loyalty."

—*New Yorker*

"[Rieger] uses office politics and legal clashes to brilliant and scathingly funny effect. Think *The Good Wife* but funnier and, in the end, more poignant."

—*Christian Science Monitor*

"Whip smart . . . The characters are hilarious and brilliant."

—*Lucky*

"Fresh and lively . . . smart and wonderfully entertaining . . . The power and canniness of this bittersweet work of epistolary fiction pulls you along."

—Alan Cheuse, NPR

THE DIVORCE PAPERS

THE DIVORCE PAPERS

A NOVEL

From the Files of Sophie Diehl, Esq.

SUSAN RIEGER

B\D\W\Y
BROADWAY BOOKS
NEW YORK

Copyright © 2014 by Susan Rieger
Reader's Guide and Author Q&A copyright © 2014 by Random House LLC

All rights reserved.
Published in the United States by Broadway Books, an imprint of the
Crown Publishing Group, a division of Random House LLC,
a Penguin Random House Company, New York.
www.crownpublishing.com

BROADWAY BOOKS and its logo, B \ D \ W \ Y, are trademarks of Random House LLC.

"Extra Libris" and colophon are trademarks of Random House LLC.

Originally published in hardcover in slightly different form in the United States by Crown Publishers, an imprint of the Crown Publishing Group, a division of Random House LLC, New York.

"A Reader's Guide" was previously published online at RandomHouse.com in 2014.
"A Conversation with Susan Rieger" was previously published online at Amazon.com in 2014.
"Recommended Reading" was previously published in slightly different form online at ReadItForward.com in 2014.

Grateful acknowledgment is made to HarperCollins Publishers and Carcanet Press Limited for permission to reprint the poem "Telemachus' Detachment" from *Meadowlands* by Louise Glück. Copyright © 1996 by Louise Glück. Reprinted by permission of HarperCollins Publishers and Carcanet Press Limited.

Library of Congress Cataloging-in-Publication Data
Rieger, Susan, 1946–
The divorce papers : a novel / Susan Rieger. — First edition.
pages cm
1. Divorce—Fiction. 2. Domestic relations—Fiction. 3. Women lawyers—Fiction.
4. Divorce settlements—Fiction. 5. Domestic fiction. I. Title.
PS3618.I39235D58 2014
813'.6—dc23
2013027552

ISBN 978-0-8041-3746-1
eBook ISBN 978-0-8041-3745-4

PRINTED IN THE UNITED STATES OF AMERICA

Book design by Jaclyn Reyes
Cover design by Ben Wiseman

10 9 8 7 6 5 4 3 2 1

First Paperback Edition

For Maggie Pouncey,
no writer could ask for a better reader,
no mother a better daughter

THE DIVORCE PAPERS

How these papers have been placed in sequence will be made manifest in the reading of them. All needless matters have been eliminated, so that a history...may stand forth as simple fact. There is throughout no statement of past things wherein memory may err, for all the records chosen are exactly contemporary, given from the standpoints and within the range of knowledge of those who made them.

—BRAM STOKER, *Dracula*
1897

1/1/99

My Durkheim File

I. INTAKE

1999

HAPPY NEW YEAR

DANIEL, MARIA & JANE DURKHEIM

Dear Poppa,

I wish you were here. Mommy and Daddy are very cranky. Is 1999 going to be a good year? What's a millennium? And what's Montezuma's revenge? Daddy has it. Mommy says I have an iron stomach.

xoxoxoxoxoxoxoxoxo

Jane

MARIA DURKHEIM
404 ST. CLOUD STREET
NEW SALEM, NA 06556

February 1, 1999

Dr. Stephanie Roth
211 Central Park West
New York, NY 10024

Dear Stephanie:

I need your help. Life is falling apart here. I'm sure you've heard our news. Daniel has asked for a divorce. It's so wrong, for him, for me, for Tom, most of all for Jane. Our marriage has its problems, God knows, but there's life in it yet, and I cannot bear the thought of putting our daughter through a divorce. You've been a close friend of Daniel's since medical school; he listens to you and trusts your judgment. Would you ask him to slow down, talk things through, maybe give marital counseling a shot? We've been together 18 years; he shouldn't throw it all away.

I'd be grateful for anything you could do. Thanks.

Yours,

Mia

February 6, 1999

Maria Durkheim
404 St. Cloud Street
New Salem, NA 06556

Dear Mia:

I am truly sorry you're taking the divorce so hard but I can't help you. Daniel's decision wasn't made on the spur of the minute. He has been unhappy in the marriage for years, and you have been too, if you could be honest with yourself. He is, of course, sad about the affect of the divorce on Jane, but he is confident she will be much better off in the long run. It's not good for a child to grow up in a home where the parents don't love each other and can't get along. I believe in my heart he has made the right decision, for everyone's happiness, including yours.

You should think about the future and all its myriad possibilities. Don't cling to the past. Put the bad times behind you and move on. Honestly, this is the best thing that could happen. You'll see.

I wish you well in all your future endeavors.

Yours,

Stephanie

February 11, 1999

Dear Stephanie,

Fuck you, too.

—Mia

February 15, 1999

Dan—

You are a complete and utter asshole. Whose idea was Golightly's? Yours or that scumbag lawyer you hired?

You shouldn't play these games with me; I'm better at them than you. Here's the current plan. I'm going to have my answer delivered (wrapped around a dead fish) at the annual Ped/Onc meeting next month, by the High Sheriff of the Commonwealth of Massachusetts, all decked out in his dress whites. (My father has supported his campaigns over the years.) I looked it up: the meeting is on March 11, in Boston, at the Ritz-Carlton, and you're speaking at 2 pm in the main ballroom.

M.

UNITED STATES COURT OF APPEALS
THIRTEENTH CIRCUIT

CHAMBERS OF
JUDGE ANNE HOWARD

185 CHURCH STREET
NEW SALEM, NA 06555
(393) 875-5511

February 28, 1999

David Greaves
Traynor, Hand, Wyzanski
222 Church Street
New Salem, NA 06555

Dear David,

Thank you for hosting my retirement dinner. I love getting together with my former clerks (I was going to say "old" clerks, but Sophie hardly qualifies under that heading). You're such a smart, interesting, decent bunch. And I was so pleased that Jared came up from D.C.

The upside of senior status is the lighter docket, and I'm ready for that; the downside will be the diminishing quality of my clerks. I have to face it (without complaining): I'll no longer get the very best. I shall miss that. I loved working with you, the original who set the standard, and all your descendants down through Sophie, and I've taken pride and pleasure in my role as a Supreme Court feeder. At last count (and I do count), I've sent 10 on to clerk for the Court. Ruth will still take my calls, no doubt, but the others are likely to plow greener pastures. I don't blame them. I've had a great run.

Sophie seems at sixes and sevens. She and I have lunch once a month. We take turns treating each other at Golightly's. It was her idea. "I'm a tonic for you," she said when she first called. "Clerks are worshipful, and if not worshipful, then calculatingly sycophantic. Lawyers, they're toadies. Which explains, of course, why judges are tyrants, looking down, literally, on everyone in the room. You need a little roughing up now and again, a little humbling." Does everything she thinks come out of her mouth?

I wonder what she'll end up doing. I had her pegged as a professor, like her father, but when I said that once, she looked at me as though I were out of my mind: "Can you imagine anything worse than reading and writing all day, and then only being allowed out to lecture to a class of entitled, fledgling Gordon Gekkos who expect an A for showing up? Whose parents call when they don't get one? I'd rather defend meth heads. Which I do." I'm glad she's under your wing while she tries to figure out what she wants. She's so quick, so lively. Prickly too, of course. She told me she regularly goes down to your office at the end of the day, to "take off my shoes and take down my hair—metaphorically." It was good work I did, making this connection—for you both. You missed out on a daughter, with those fine, handsome, brainy sons of yours, and now a grandson. And she missed out on—well, you'll figure that out, if you haven't already.

The oysters were wonderful, especially with the Champagne. Why eat anything else, as Isak Dinesen believed. A splendid feast in all respects. My best to Mary.

Fondly,

Anne

Crankiness Abides

From: Sophie Diehl

To: Maggie Pfeiffer <mcp15@mather.edu>

Date: Mon, 1 Mar 1999 1:30:07

Subject: Crankiness Abides

3/1/99 1:30 AM

Dear Mags,

I will turn 30 in 6 months and I don't know what I should be doing. You know what you want to do; Matt knows what he wants to do; my sibs know what they want to do, except of course Francoise, who just likes kicking around the world. But still, that's something. I'm treading water. Do you remember swim class at Brearley, the 30 minutes of drown-proofing, as if we might find ourselves one dark night floating on a mahogany plank in the Atlantic with Leonardo DiCaprio?

I know I shouldn't write emails after midnight, but I can't fall asleep; I drank too much tonight and I'm feeling sorry for myself. (I promised myself I wouldn't gripe to you before I sat down at the computer, but as you know better than almost anyone, I can be a self-pitying drunk, which is a step above a mean drunk, but not much. I apologize.) I will pull up my socks in proper Diehl fashion and try to find the silver lining. One bit of news: I saw Andrew Bellow on the street on Friday with the chickie he's taken up with, looking tired and unhappy. Chickie wasn't looking so good either. Roots showing, black tights with a run. I can't say my spirits lifted at the sight of them (Andrew smiled brightly and said hello as we passed. I nodded.), but I may have walked on with a lighter step. I updated my bad boyfriend list earlier: Andrew makes 5.

I did have a good time tonight, though it's triggered all these anxieties. David had a dinner party for Judge Howard and her clerks. She's retiring. Great food (oysters, lobster, the finest trayf in the land), great stories, great toasts. The judge was so happy with the occasion and all of us. As a group, they seem pretty happy with their lives and work. They're also pretty impressive, a deputy U.S. AG, the New York State AG, the deans of Mather and Narragansett Law, the managing partner of THW (and these were just the locals). David got us all T-shirts, with the Judge's great line from *Ernest v. Farago*: "What has become of us? When did we start fencing unicorns and foddering wolves?" Judge Howard is wonderful in every way. I worship her. Truth be told, I want to be federal circuit judge ("Decroche la lune," as Maman always says) but I can't say that to people (except you, of course) and I don't know how to get from here to there. (Give piles to the Narragansett Democratic Party?) Geez, it is 1:30. I will settle now for getting from here to bed.

Love,
Sophie

TRAYNOR, HAND, WYZANSKI

222 CHURCH STREET
NEW SALEM, NARRAGANSETT 06555
(393) 876-5678

MEMORANDUM
Attorney Work Product

From:	David Greaves
To:	Sophie Diehl
RE:	Mrs. Maria Durkheim
Date:	March 15, 1999
Attachments:	

I'd like you to interview a prospective client in a divorce case this Wednesday. I know you haven't done a matrimonial, but the situation calls for white-glove service and there's no one else available that day. Fiona is out of the office this week, Felix will be in court, and I'm trying to close the Pericles deal. The downside of a boutique firm. But the upside too; we all become utility infielders.

The client's name is Maria Durkheim. She is Bruce Meiklejohn's daughter. She's coming in at 10:30 a.m. He called me last night to ask us to talk to her. He'd like us to take her case. He said he thought his daughter needed "heavy artillery." I know what *he* means, but I don't know what *she* wants. The husband is a big star at Mather Medical School, an oncologist, chaired professor, department head, Freeman Prize winner. Meiklejohn doesn't like him one bit, and he made it clear he's glad they're breaking up. He said the marriage was a mistake from the start—"water and oil," he called it, using standard Meiklejohn-speak for "Jew and Gentile." He described Dr. Durkheim as "one of those people, you know the kind, overly aggressive and ambitious, striving, someone who tries too hard to fit in." Bruce Meiklejohn is straight out of the Darien of *Gentleman's Agreement*. I once heard him say, "Mather College was never the same after the GI Bill." Too many physicists? Anyway, I want to give you a heads-up. I have no reason to believe the daughter subscribes to any of this, but Meiklejohn says the divorce could be ugly. There's a child, a ten-year-old girl,

Jane. She was uppermost in Meiklejohn's mind. "Now, hear this, Greaves, you look out for my granddaughter, Jane." I don't know if the ugly part involves money or Jane, or the couple's dynamic. Probably all three, if experience means anything.

Let me know if you're free Wednesday morning. It's only a couple of hours of your time, and you might even enjoy it. Divorcing couples harbor murderous thoughts; they just have better impulse control than your regular clients.

TRAYNOR, HAND, WYZANSKI

222 CHURCH STREET
NEW SALEM, NARRAGANSETT 06555
(393) 876-5678

MEMORANDUM
Attorney Work Product

From: Sophie Diehl
To: David Greaves
RE: Mrs. Maria Durkheim
Date: March 15, 1999
Attachments:

I'll do the interview, of course, if you need me to do it, but I can't believe you don't have better choices. Proctor? Virginia? I have two serious deficiencies, both of which make me a lousy candidate for the job.

1st. My rank inexperience as a lawyer who's never done a civil case, let alone a divorce, should stop you in your tracks. I put into evidence Sophie Diehl's CV Lite:

1969:   Sophie is born
1987–91:   Sophie attends college
1991–92:   Sophie spends the year paralegaling at the Southern
               Center for Human Rights
1992–95:   Sophie attends law school
1995–97:   Sophie clerks on the 13th Circuit
1997–   Sophie begins working at THW doing criminal defense
               work (1½ yrs! That's it.)

2nd. If, despite the clear and convincing evidence presented above, you persist in your request, I would ask for an ironclad dispensation from anything beyond the intake interview. I cannot do a divorce. I am not only ill equipped legally; I am ill equipped temperamentally. (i) I don't like client contact. I suspect it's why I settled on criminal work. I like that most of my clients are in jail. They can't get to me; I can only get to them. (ii) I don't like divorcing parents. I had my very own set, both of whom behaved very, very badly in ways that would make your hair stand on end.

How's this for a rewrite of *Anna Karenina*: "Every divorcing family is unpleasant in its own way." Poor Anna K, so heartbreakingly 19th century. No one dies for love anymore; only love dies and then they get a divorce. Perhaps I'll write the modern update of *Anna*; she gets divorced and loses custody, but she has visitation every other weekend. Then she goes back to school and gets an MSW and works with troubled children. She doesn't throw herself under the train; she simply takes the subway. (She can't afford a cab: bad settlement.) Could that be Mrs. Durkheim's story? Is there a Vronsky? Do I have to find out things like that, for damage control? What else do I need to find out? Is there a checklist? Do I interview or do I just listen? What do I do? (Do you hear the anxiety in my voice as I write, rising to a near screech?)

Gentleman's Agreement?

TRAYNOR, HAND, WYZANSKI

222 CHURCH STREET
NEW SALEM, NARRAGANSETT 06555
(393) 876-5678

MEMORANDUM
Attorney Work Product

From:	David Greaves
To:	Sophie Diehl
RE:	Maria Durkheim
Date:	March 16, 1999
Attachments:	*Divorce Work Sheets*
	Narragansett Code, Sections 801ff., Title 33
	Divorcing USA excerpts

Data: There is a *Divorce Work Sheet*. I am attaching a copy to this memo. It asks about income, deductions from income, assets, liabilities, and monthly expenses. If you think she's up to it, send it home with Mrs. Durkheim to fill out. It's long—four densely packed pages—but a divorcing person needs to think about all these things, especially if she doesn't have any independent savings or income, which I suspect is the case here. The first page, Income & Deductions/Assets & Liabilities, is a snapshot of the marriage's wealth, the resources to be divided by the couple. The next three pages itemize monthly living expenses, providing a basis for spousal and child support. Other things to do in preparation:

(i) Get from the library copies of the *Divorce Work Sheet: Summary Biographies,* and fill one out for both Durkheims during the interview.

(ii) Take a look at a negotiated settlement; I recommend the Haberman divorce; it will give you an idea of how the upper-middle classes divide the spoils.

(iii) Cast an eye over Sections 801ff., Title 33, of the Narragansett Code, the Narragansett divorce and custody statutes. I've made a list of the most relevant sections. I'm assuming you took a course in Family Law at law school, yes? And you must have taken Civil Procedure.

Intake: As to what to expect at the intake interview, in my experience, women who've been left or betrayed (and I'm not being sexist, merely observant) spend the hour venting—he's the most selfish man in the world (or New Salem)—or crying. The wives who do the leaving are another story; they're racked with guilt. They'll offer to give up everything but the children. I've attached a handout, excerpts from an article in *Divorcing USA* (awful name) that Fiona has given to clients on the psychology of divorcing. It's basic but accurate. (I have vowed I'll never get a divorce no matter how awful things get; I'll shoot myself—or Mary— first. I have no interest in finding out how loathsome I can be. Or Mary, for that matter.)

Your job is to think and listen like a lawyer but talk to her as a kind acquaintance, someone who doesn't know her well but is nonetheless warmly disposed toward her. (You've got to drop the criminal lawyer's skeptical demeanor.) Prompt her, encourage her to answer your questions, but don't press. It may take an hour; don't let it go much beyond that. Nothing new will be said after that. (Shrinks stop after 45 minutes, on the same basic theory, I believe, and they do it with a level of ruthlessness that is the envy of appellate judges.) Take notes, of course; there's no other way to remember the details (wherein God and the Devil reside). Then write it up. Or you can tape it. You'll be off the case after that.

Fees: You'll need to talk money with her, not something you do with your clients. The usual retainer for a divorce with children is $6,000, which covers the first 40 hours (at $150/hour), not including costs. She may wish only to consult, in which case you should bill her at $150/hour for the time you actually spend with her. If she decides to sign on, we'll add the write-up to the bill; if she's just shopping, we'll eat it.

Client Conduct: Yes, find out if there's another man or woman, for both Durkheims. We're a no-fault divorce state, but if the case goes to trial, the judge can consider fault, and in custody fights, even the kitchen sink comes in. It's always better to know what they've done—though of course, they always lie to you.

You might see if she has been acting out. It's not unusual for one or both of the divorcing parties to misbehave, create scenes in public, make extravagant purchases with the joint credit card, slash tires, bug a phone or bedroom, in short, do things they'd never do in normal life. Judges don't like really really bad behavior, and if it's going on, it's good (if possible) to nip it in the bud.

One last thought, which is not, strictly speaking, relevant but is nonetheless interesting. You might find out if Dr. D's parents are dead. I've found that people are more likely to seek divorce—and do it more cold-bloodedly—after their parents are gone. I get the sense that Dr. D is the one pushing for divorce. Meiklejohn didn't say this outright, but he mentioned his daughter's reluctance to speak to an attorney. She felt it was too soon.

VIP Clients: The Meiklejohns and the Mathers (distaff side) are long-time clients of the firm. Proctor's grandfather was the executor of Mrs. D's great-grandfather's will, and Proctor is the executor of her mother's. Mrs. D's mother (née Maria Mather) died more than 20 years ago. Ten months later, her father remarried. The current Mrs. Meiklejohn, Cindy, is, as you know, Society (if you can say there is any Society left in New Salem. Everyone—except you, of course—belongs to the Cricket Club these days: no more inherited memberships). She's a good deal younger than her husband but more than ½ HA +7. My guess is she doesn't care what happens with the Durkheims—except insofar as their behavior upsets her husband. She doesn't like to see him unhappy. I'm with her on that. Good luck—and again, thanks.

Miscellany: *Gentleman's Agreement* is a movie about anti-Semitism from the late '40s, with Gregory Peck playing Jewish. You need to bone up on your movie backlist, Sophie. You have seen *The Third Man*, haven't you?

TRAYNOR, HAND, WYZANSKI

222 CHURCH STREET
NEW SALEM, NARRAGANSETT 06555
(393) 876-5678

Divorce Work Sheet: Income & Deductions and Assets & Liabilities
Attorney Work Product

INCOME & DEDUCTIONS

Sources of Income (gross)
Salary
   Employer 1
   Employer 2

Other Sources
   Self-Employment
   Bonuses
   Interest
   Dividends
   Royalties
   Gifts
   Trust Disbursements
   Spousal Support
   Other

TOTAL INCOME

Deductions from Income
Fed Tax _____ (#) exemptions
State Tax _____ (#) exemptions
FICA
Medicare
Other

TOTAL DEDUCTIONS

ASSETS & LIABILITIES

Assets (fair market value)
Real Estate
Motor Vehicles
Personal Property
Retirement/Deferred Plans
   Pension
   IRAs, 401(k)s
   Other
Bank Accounts
Stocks, Bonds, Mutual Funds
Other

TOTAL ASSETS

Liabilities
Mortgages
Loans
   Automobile
   Home Equity
   Personal
Credit Card
Education Loans
Other

TOTAL LIABILITIES

Divorce Work Sheet: Monthly Living Expenses
Attorney Work Product

HOME
    Mortgage
       Principal
       Interest
    Real Estate Taxes
    Rent (or co-op/condo minimum maintenance payment)
    Insurance
    Home Maintenance Including Allowance for Major Home Repairs
    Grounds Maintenance (gardens, snow removal, lawn mowing, tree
       trimming)
    Utilities (heating, gas, electricity, water, sewer)
    Phone
    Domestic Help
    Furnishings
    Other

FOOD
    Groceries
    Children's School Lunches
    Other

CLOTHING
    Clothes & Shoes
    Dry Cleaning & Laundry
    Other

PERSONAL CARE AND MAINTENANCE
    Hairdresser
    Hygiene Products
    Other

Divorce Work Sheet: Monthly Living Expenses (cont.)
Attorney Work Product

TRANSPORTATION
Automobiles
    Loan Payment
    Gasoline
    Maintenance & Repairs
    Insurance
    Excise Tax
    Parking
Other Transportation

EDUCATION
Tuition & Fees
Loan Repayment
Other

CHILD CARE
Day Care
Child Support Obligations
Other

MEDICAL
Insurance
General Practitioner/Pediatrician
Gynecologist
Psychological Counselor
Physical Therapist
Dentist/Orthodontist
Eyeglasses
Prescription Drugs
Other

DEBT AND OTHER FINANCIAL OBLIGATIONS
Credit Card
Personal Loans
Alimony Payments
Other

Divorce Work Sheet: Monthly Living Expenses (cont.)
Attorney Work Product

PAYMENTS TO SAVINGS
Pensions & Retirement Accounts
IRAs, 401(k)s, etc.
Savings Accounts & Investments
Other

INSURANCE
Life
Disability & Long-Term
Other

LEISURE AND ENTERTAINMENT
Movies, Theater, Concerts, Sports Events, etc.
Sports Activities
    Lessons, Fees & Programs
    Clothes & Equipment
Eating Out
Parties & Other In-Home Entertainment
Vacations
Books, Magazines, Newspapers
Gifts
Entertainment Equipment (VCR, TV, computer, etc.)
Household Pets
    Food & Supplies
    Veterinary Expenses
Other

CHARITABLE CONTRIBUTIONS

MISCELLANEOUS EXPENSES (Specify)

TOTAL MONTHLY EXPENSES

Narragansett Statutes
Title 33 of the Narragansett Code, Sections 801ff.
Dissolution of Marriage, Annulment, and Legal Separation

Table of Contents [Redacted]

DIVORCING}USA

Breaking Free Without Breaking Down:
A Psychological Portrait of Divorce
Patricia Lahey
April 1997
Excerpts, pp. 37–39

People who get divorced are still attached. Separating is hard, even when husband and wife agree it's the right thing. And usually they don't agree on that any more than they agree on custody, alimony, or child support. They have to despise each other to go through with it. Otherwise, they can't do it; they don't have the stamina. They demonize the other person so that they can justify their delinquencies, their selfishness. And every party's the injured party. Often the person who initiates the divorce is the angrier, the more self-righteous, the more vindictive. Not in the beginning necessarily. Guilt has a part but usually only in the early stages. People want to be right but never so much as when they're divorcing. . . .

In my experience, men rarely leave, no matter how unhappy they are, unless there's another woman. They find someone, then they leave. They don't like being alone; they don't do it well. The woman may not be someone he wants to marry; she may simply be a transitional object, someone to get him over the hump. The obverse doesn't hold. If the woman is the one who is asking for a separation, there may not be anyone else. A lot of women simply want out; they fantasize about being alone, sitting in a white room with no phone.

TRAYNOR, HAND, WYZANSKI

222 CHURCH STREET

NEW SALEM, NARRAGANSETT 06555

(393) 876-5678

MEMORANDUM
Attorney Work Product

From:	Sophie Diehl, Divorce-Attorney-For-A-Day
To:	David Greaves
RE:	Matter of Durkheim: Intake Interview Cover Memo
Date:	March 17, 1999
Attachments:	*Fee Agreement*
	Intake Interview Transcript
	Divorce Work Sheet: Summary Biography:
	Maria Meiklejohn Durkheim
	Divorce Work Sheet: Summary Biography:
	Daniel Edward Durkheim
	Domestic Relations Summons
	Complaint for Divorce

You won't believe this. Mrs. Durkheim's husband's lawyers (K&B! Get out the shovels) had her served with the divorce summons while she was having lunch with a friend at Golightly's. I almost fell off my chair. I would have been less surprised if one of my regular clients told me he had offed someone during lunch at Golightly's.

Down to business. I met with Mrs. Durkheim this morning at 10:30. I think I did okay; at least I didn't bungle it, which was a possibility given my deficits, legal and human. Mrs. Maria (Mia) Mather Meiklejohn Durkheim has retained the services of the firm (but not me, as I explained to her) to represent her in a divorce action against her husband, Dr. Daniel E. Durkheim. She signed the *Fee Agreement* on the spot, barely glancing at the terms. I advised her against this but met stubborn resistance. The interview took an hour, the discussion of the laws and the retainer another hour, and the form-filling a half hour. (I billed her account $375, for two and a half hours of work, a first for me. Not my usual $50 plus costs.) I taped the interview and asked Hannah to transcribe it so Fiona (Felix? you?) won't have to start all over again. It gave me a taste of how your generation of lawyers works, dictating into a machine and then having the secretary transcribe it. Associates type their memos and their briefs, too, and even do all the formatting. (I'm not being ageist, merely observant.)

My box of tissues went unused. Mrs. Durkheim did not vent. She was composed, collected, articulate. While she answered questions willingly, easily, she expected me to take the lead in the interview. She asked me to summarize the law and explain her options. I came clean early on and told her I was pinch-hitting for the firm's ace divorce lawyer, who was out of town. She seemed fine with that.

I asked her questions about her marriage, the family's finances, her daughter. She was very knowledgeable, no baby-wife she. I was able to pull together a rough chronology, synchronizing salary history and marital history. (See the **Divorce Work Sheet: Summary Biographies** for both Durkheims.) I explained Narragansett's no-fault/fault statute and the principle of equitable distribution in dividing property and awarding support. I told her she could not effectively contest the divorce or refuse to cooperate. The parties do not have to agree to a divorce; if one of them wants out, she can get out. ("Not like a get," she said.) I said it was in her interest to cooperate. A divorce, I explained, is simply a civil action which dissolves a civil union and allocates property, obligations, and progeny; it does not provide "closure" or any other cathartic function. ("I get it," she said. "It's all—it's only—about money.") I gave her a brief rundown on custody (best interest of the child) and explained the difference between joint and sole, legal and physical. I told her that most divorces were settled by negotiation, not trial, and that the parties could make any agreement they wanted so long as it wasn't against public policy. I did my reading but reading isn't experience. (By the way, I didn't bill for the 2+ hours I spent doing homework last night; it didn't seem right. A real divorce lawyer would have known it all.) If anything I said was incorrect, Fiona can set her straight.

I told her she had two options: she could wait until her husband made her an offer, or she could make an offer to him. I gave her a copy of the **Divorce Work Sheets** and told her to take a stab at pulling together a projected annual budget, post-divorce, for herself and her daughter. She said she would do whatever was necessary.

She was wonderfully clearheaded throughout. She's very smart and she understands what she needs to do. She had even called a Realtor before coming in to get a new valuation on the family home. Can you believe she had the presence of mind to do that? The rich *are* different—and she knows it. She's angry at her husband but her anger hasn't clouded her judgment. She's not out to fleece him. For one thing, she has, if not money of her own, then access to money; for another, though money is not nothing to him, he wants success more. And on that point, she doesn't wish him well. She's put a proper Sicilian curse on him.

Mrs. Durkheim *has* acted out a bit, though nothing too extreme. She conducted a brief, unpleasant correspondence with the woman she believes is her husband's new lover. She brought copies with her and gave them to me. I've put them in the file, along with the note she wrote her husband after she had been served the summons at Golightly's. Her epistolary style, as you will see, is very much to the point.

Mrs. Durkheim is 41 years old but looks younger. She's tall (my height) with blond hair, straight black eyebrows, and eyes that look black. Although her Christian name is Maria, she goes by Mia and always has. She was named for her mother, who was called by her full name. Since her mother's death, her father sometimes calls her Maria. She doesn't think he does it out of sentiment, only carelessness.

I like Maria Durkheim. She still has a sense of humor (which was the first casualty of my parents' divorce), and she loves her child. She probably sounds harder in the interview than she actually is. I don't think her brave talk is all bravado—maybe half. She is determined not to feel sorry for herself, at least not publicly. Good for her. Dr. Durkheim's father died in 1992, his mother in September, 1998. He inherited a small amount of cash and a 10-year-old car.

TRAYNOR, HAND, WYZANSKI

222 CHURCH STREET
NEW SALEM, NARRAGANSETT 06555
(393) 876-5678
ATTORNEYS AT LAW

FEE AGREEMENT

I, **Maria M. Durkheim**, the "Client" of **404 St. Cloud Street, New Salem, NA,** hereby retain the firm of Traynor, Hand, Wyzanski, the "Attorneys," in connection with: **divorce proceedings** and such other work as may from time to time be performed by the Attorneys on the Client's behalf.

1. The Client shall pay to the Attorneys **$6,000.00** as an initial retainer in this matter, and, in consideration of this payment, the Attorneys agree to perform legal services as herein provided.

2. The initial retainer paid by the Client shall be applied against legal services actually performed for the Client by the Attorneys (as well as any attorneys working under their direction). There shall be no minimum fee. The services shall be charged at the hourly rate of **$150.00**.

3. Hourly time charges for legal services performed include but are not limited to: court appearances; office conferences; telephone conferences; legal research; depositions; review of file materials and documents sent or received; preparation for trials, hearings, and conferences; and drafting of pleadings and instruments, correspondence, and office memoranda.

4. The Client shall in addition pay for all out-of-pocket disbursements incurred in connection with this matter, including but not limited to: filing fees, witness fees, travel, sheriff's and constable's fees, expenses of depositions, toll calls and faxes, and investigative expenses. The Attorneys agree to obtain the Client's prior approval before incurring any disbursement in excess of **$150.00**.

5. The Client shall pay the initial retainer to the Attorneys no later than: **April 1, 1999**. The Attorneys shall provide the Client with an itemized statement of services and out-of-pocket disbursements on **July 1, 1999**, and every **three** months thereafter. In the event the time charges and/or out-of-pocket disbursements of the Attorneys exceed the initial retainer, the Attorneys shall submit additional itemized billings on the first business day of the month, payable by the Client within 30 days of the billing date.

6. Accounts not paid by their due date shall be subject to interest at the rate of 1.5% per month until paid. Failure to pay billings promptly will permit the Attorneys after notice to the Client to terminate the Attorneys' representation of the Client, and the Attorneys shall be entitled to file a notice of withdrawal in any pending judicial action.

7. If the total cost of the legal services performed by the Attorneys shall be less than the amount of the initial retainer paid by the Client, the balance shall be refunded to the Client.

8. The Court may award counsel fees to one party and order the other party to pay the amount awarded. Alternatively, the parties, to avoid a contested trial, may agree by settlement contract to provide that one of the parties will contribute an agreed amount toward the other party's legal expenses.

   a. No representation is made in this Agreement that any contribution by the other party will be obtained toward the Client's legal expenses.

   b. In the event a contribution is obtained from the other party for the benefit of the Client, the amount in question shall be credited against the Attorneys' final bill to the client.

9. This Agreement represents the full and complete agreement between the Attorneys and the Client as to the terms of the Attorneys' representation of the Client in the matter described. There are no exceptions.

THIS IS A LEGALLY BINDING CONTRACT. IF THE CLIENT DOES NOT UNDERSTAND THE TERMS AND CONDITIONS OF THE CONTRACT, THE CLIENT IS URGED TO SEEK INDEPENDENT COUNSEL.

We, the Client and the Attorneys, have read the above Fee Agreement and understand and accept its terms. Both have signed it as their free act and deed, and the Client acknowledges receipt of a copy of the Agreement.

Signed this **17th** day of **March, 1999.**

Traynor, Hand, Wyzanski

By:

Client Maria M. Durkheim   **Attorney** Anne Sophie Diehl

Maria Durkheim   *Anne Sophie Diehl*

Traynor, Hand, Wyzanski
222 Church Street
New Salem, Narragansett 06555
(393) 876-5678

Intake Interview

Interview Subject: Maria Meiklejohn Durkheim
Interviewer: Anne Sophie Diehl
Date: March 17, 1999
RE: Legal Separation and Divorce

Transcription by: Hannah Smith
Date: March 18, 1999

1	Q. Good morning. I'm Sophie Diehl. David Greaves, your
2	father's lawyer, asked me to meet with you this morning. I am
3	an associate with the firm.
4	A. Hello, I'm Maria—Mia—Durkheim, née Meiklejohn.
5	Thank you for seeing me on such short notice.
6	Q. Not at all. I would like to tape this interview, if that's all
7	right with you, to have an accurate record.
8	A. That's fine.
9	Q. How can I help you?
10	A. On February 15th—here are the papers—my husband,
11	Daniel Durkheim, Dr. Daniel Durkheim, had his lawyers,
12	the scumbag firm of Kahn & Boyle, serve me with a summons
13	for divorce, I think that's what it's called, while I was having
14	lunch at Golightly's on Cromwell. I can't believe that's
15	standard practice, no? The University Club perhaps, maybe
16	the Plimouth or the New Salem Cricket Club, but Golightly's?
17	Your grandmother's restaurant. That cozy bastion of linen
18	tablecloths, padded booths, hotel silver plate. I was with
19	a colleague, not even a friend, when this damp, cringing
20	person sidled up to me and asked if I was Maria Meiklejohn
21	Durkheim. I said I was. He handed me the summons, then
22	backed away. I thought at first, stupidly, it was the wine
23	list. When I saw what it was, I almost fell into my Niçoise.
24	I thought I'd black out. Pulling myself together, I realized
25	my colleague was staring at me. Other people too. I sat up
26	straight, called the waiter over, and ordered a bottle of Pouilly-
27	Fuissé. "I feel like celebrating," I told my colleague. "My
28	treat." It was an extreme test of my savoir faire. Even now it
29	makes me catch my breath. Can you believe it?
30	Q. I can. I'm a criminal lawyer. Bad behavior doesn't
31	surprise me. But I've never heard of anyone else being served
32	at a restaurant.

1   A.   I got served at a restaurant. Ha. I suppose I should return

2   service on a squash court. The Cricket Club. I wouldn't

3   mind smashing him—or those scumbag lawyers. What do

4   I do now? It's been at least a month. I didn't say anything

5   to my husband for several days, then I wrote him an acid

6   note, threatening to have him served during a speech he was

7   planning to give at the annual Pediatric Oncology conference

8   in Boston. I have a copy. Would you like it?

9   Q.   Yes, I would. Did you actually carry out the threat?

10   [Note to Hannah: I'm placing the letter in the file.]

11   A.   Oh, no. It's been my experience that there's no need to

12   carry through on a well-crafted threat with upper-middle-

13   class types. The purpose is to wrong-foot them, raise their

14   blood pressure, gin up their anxiety level. I kept imagining

15   him looking up all the time as he was reading his paper, to see

16   if a sheriff's deputy was closing in on him. I thought I had a

17   good chance of ruining the conference for him. I think I may

18   have. Of course, he never said anything. Nor did I.

19   Q.   Is it only on the upper-middle classes that threats alone

20   work?

21   A.   I can't say for everyone, but with the rich, you have to

22   carry through or they don't take you seriously. My father

23   would tell you that.

24   Q.   Other than the threats, have you done anything?

25   A.   What do you mean by "done"?

26   Q.   Have you responded more formally?

27   A.   No. That's why I came in today. I'm guessing I need to

28   make some sort of response. What should I do now?

29   Q.   Ah. The usual next step is to retain a lawyer to represent

30   you. You may wish to consult more than one, to determine

31   who will provide you with the services you need for a fee you

32   judge reasonable.

1	A. When it comes to lawyers, I trust my father, and he says
2	Traynor, Hand is the best there is. Consider yourself retained.
3	Tell me what your fee is. I'll pay it.
4	Q. Oh, I am not the lawyer you want to retain. David asked
5	me to fill in this morning for Fiona McGregor, who's on
6	holiday. We have terrific divorce lawyers in the firm. Besides
7	Ms. McGregor, there's Felix Landau, who is in court today,
8	and David, too, because he can do anything. I've never done
9	a divorce.
10	A. Somehow, I find that reassuring. It's my first divorce too.
11	Q. But I'm a criminal lawyer.
12	A. Just what I need for Ray Kahn.
13	Q. Don't worry about him. 90% blowhard. Let's look at
14	these Divorce Work Sheet: Summary Biographies. We can go
15	over them together, and I'll explain Narragansett divorce law
16	as best I can. But why don't we start by my asking you some
17	questions about you, your husband, your marriage, and your
18	daughter, yes?
19	A. Shoot.
20	Q. How old are you? How old is your husband? How long
21	have you been married?
22	A. I'm 41. Daniel is 52. We've been married for 16 years,
23	since 1982. But we lived together for 2 years before that.
24	Daniel was married when I met him, to Helen Fincher. They
25	were married in 1974, separated in 1980—there was a bit of an
26	overlap, I'm afraid, with Helen and me, tacky, I know—and
27	divorced in 1982, a New York record, I believe. She has so
28	much family money, it wasn't an issue, and then she couldn't
29	stand him. I didn't understand that; I thought he was the most
30	wonderful person I'd ever met. Our opinions are probably
31	more aligned now.
32	Q. Were there any children from your husband's first marriage?

1   A.   Sorry, yes, a son, Thomas Maxwell Durkheim. Tom.
2   He's 22 now. He was born in 1976. An Amherst grad.
3   Lovely boy, much easier, kinder, sweeter than his father, or
4   his mother for that matter. Bad asthma, bad lungs since he
5   was a baby. Premature. He's working now on Wall Street, at
6   Fincher & Morgan, his grandfather's firm. Daniel paid no
7   alimony to Helen, only child support, $15,000/year, until
8   Tom was 18. It stayed the same throughout. Then he paid for
9   college. Theoretically. Mather pays 50% of college tuition for
10   its employees, which with Amherst, I think its tuition was
11   $24,000; he only had to pay $12,000, plus room and board,
12   another $8,000. Not much for a man making $300,000 plus
13   a year. [Pause] I'm sounding bitter—and common. I'll pull
14   myself together.
15   Q.   Did Thomas live with his mother? Or with you and your
16   husband?
17   A.   He grew up in New York City and lived with his mother.
18   When we lived there—we moved to New Salem in '91,
19   when Daniel was appointed Chair of the Pediatric Oncology
20   Department here at Mather Med—we saw a lot of him. We
21   saw less of him after we moved. He was 14. Daniel is a bit
22   rough on him. Tom wants his dad's good opinion, but also
23   thinks Daniel can be a prick. Can I say something like that?
24   You don't mind, do you? You must have heard worse. I don't
25   think they've seen each other since Christmas. I don't know
26   what Daniel has said to Tom about our separation. I asked
27   him last week how Tom was taking it. "Taking it?" he asked.
28   "You're not his mother. What difference should it make to
29   him?" Eighteen years, since he was three, and his father
30   thinks it means nothing. [Pause] I don't know what Tom
31   is thinking. I've spoken to him twice now. He doesn't give
32   anything away. He doesn't want to talk about himself, only

asks how Jane and I are doing. He's stoical and doesn't expect
too much of his parents. Helen's got a leg up on Daniel. She's
already married to her third husband.

Q.   Can you give me some financial history of the marriage?

A.   When we met in 1980, I was working as an assistant
editor at *Femina* magazine. Do you remember *Femina*? It
believed in good clothes, good haircuts, and good books. I was
making $28,000, which wasn't bad for that kind of job. Daniel
had finished school; he has an M.D./Ph.D. from Columbia
but was only making $23,000, as a resident, working 90 hours
a week at Presbyterian Hospital. All of his salary, after taxes,
went for child support. But at least he had no med school
debt. M.D./Ph.D.'s are fully funded. Our rent was $325;
we had a Columbia apartment, on baja Claremont. It was a
serious comedown for him. When he was married to Helen,
they lived off Central Park West on West 69th. But he was
never home, and I didn't mind it. My father might have given
us some money, but his money always comes with strings;
I didn't think it was worth it. Except, he did give us each
$10,000 a year as a gift once we married. And then after Jane,
our daughter, was born, he gave her $10,000 a year too.

Q.   Tell me about Jane.

A.   She's perfect. She's 10 years old, almost 11. She goes to the
Peabody School, where I went and everyone in my family went,
back to the egg. My mother was a trustee and her mother and
her grandmother were trustees. We are old, old New Salem.
My mother was a Mather and Granny was a Peabody. I don't
remember what Great Gran was—I never knew her—but
she was a Maria. We are all Marias, from mother to daughter,
back to my Great Great Great Gran, whose mother's first
name was Humility. The family was, is, horribly ingrown. Up
through my mother's generation, you couldn't marry outside

the magic circle. My father didn't really belong; his family
were latecomers, upstart 19th-century immigrant Scottish
merchants, but they'd gone to the right schools and weren't
Catholics. My mother's full name was Maria Maple Mather
Meiklejohn. Her family nickname was 4M. My full name is
Maria Mather Meiklejohn. [Pause] Durkheim. I need to ditch
that. In school, I was called 3M or Scotch, for Scotch Tape.
Daniel used to say my family went back to the *Mayflower* and
his to the ark. I never imagined I'd be back in New Salem. I
thought I had escaped. I was working on becoming—rather
successfully, I thought—a New York Jewish intellectual. Here,
I'm seen as part of the cotillion crowd.

Q. Are you working?

A. I'm a writing tutor at Mather. I decided to get my Ph.D.
in American studies when we moved here. The only publisher
in town is the Mather Press, and I wasn't interested in
publishing foreign-language translations, which is what they
mostly do. Their big project now is a complete translation by
a French/American couple of *Remembrance of Things Past*.
Did you know no one has ever finished translating all seven
volumes? They all die mid-series; it's like a curse. Have you
read Proust?

Q. No. My mother is French, and if I ever read it in English,
instead of French, which would do me in, she would be very
disapproving. So I don't read it at all. You?

A. I've read the third book, *The Guermantes Way*. Bill
Pritchard, Tom's English professor at Amherst, said to start
there, then go backward. But I couldn't.

Q. Are you making progress with your Ph.D.?

A. I finished my course work in 1996. For my thesis, I'm
working mostly on Jacob Riis but also on other late 19th-/
early 20th-century American journalists, photojournalists,

muckrakers. This divorce thing has thrown me off. I can't see
making much progress this year. Some days, getting out of
bed is a serious challenge. I do manage to do my job, but it's
a struggle, and it's only four afternoons/evenings a week, 16
hours altogether.

Q.   Do you make a living wage as a writing tutor?

A.   Oh, no. I make $14,000, which is a scant $1,000 more
than Jane's tuition. Last year Daniel made $370,000, 25 times
as much as I. These are things I think of when I think about
divorce. My lack of resources. I don't worry about it exactly—
my father won't let Jane and me starve—but I would hate
having to ask him or Daniel for money. Too humiliating to
have to keep going back to the trough.

Q.   You said your husband was in oncology?

A.   He's chair of the Department of Pediatric Oncology,
which is one of Mather Medical School's great departments,
and Dowling Professor. He's a big star, both as a clinician and
a researcher, and he's very ambitious. He won the Freeman
Prize, and was nominated for the Lasker. I'd guess he's
gunning for a MacArthur and, in his late-night fantasies, a
Nobel. His specialty is brain tumors. He's the best there is,
even though most of his patients don't make it. They just
make it longer than other docs' patients. It's given him a Jesus
complex. He's so used to being admired, starting with his
parents, that he expects it from everyone, even Jane and me.
Mather recruited him very heavily; so did Harvard, Stanford,
and Yale. He's been generously funded by NIH for the last
13 years, and his current grant has 4 years to run. When
he left Columbia, he brought his grants and lab with him,
including four researchers. I was wretched about the decision.
Who with any sense would live in New Salem when they
could live in New York? I had close friends, a nice social life,

1   a good job. I didn't want to be a chair's wife. I didn't want to

2   be unemployed, I didn't want to come back to New Salem. In

3   '88, I'd left *Femina* and gone to work for Monk's House as a

4   nonfiction editor, and I loved it. I wanted him to turn it down,

5   but he said the offer was one he couldn't refuse and I thought

6   he'd never forgive me if I didn't go along. As it turns out, he

7   didn't forgive me anyway. Though he's not said so outright,

8   he's not happy at Mather. Too much management and not as

9   great a variety of cases as in New York. So my unhappiness, of

10   course, is intolerable, a reproach.

11   Q.   Who looks after Jane most of the time?

12   A.   I look after her. It's one of the reasons I'm a writing tutor.

13   It's part-time. I can be home with Jane after school and on

14   holidays. We do have a housekeeper, Luz Garcia. She comes

15   in every day. We need someone full-time; she works 40 hours

16   a week for us, though not on an 8-hour-a-day schedule, and we

17   pay her Social Security—in case Daniel wants to head NIH

18   someday. Just kidding; I'd pay it anyway. This is being taped,

19   right? Luz is a resident alien. We helped her get her green

20   card. She's wonderful. I have a younger sister, Cordelia, who

21   has Down's and lives in Philadelphia, in a halfway house. I

22   visit her twice a month, sometimes more. I stay over in Philly,

23   Tuesday to Wednesday—that way I see her two days on each

24   visit—and Luz stays over in the house with Jane. It's too

25   hard to rely on Daniel, though he makes a huge effort to have

26   dinner with her every night, and especially on Tuesdays when

27   I'm away. He works 90 to 100 hours a week, resident's hours.

28   On weekends, which look like weekdays for him, he always,

29   or almost always, spends part of Saturday or Sunday doing

30   sports with Jane. Right now, he's teaching her squash. Jane's

31   a great athlete and Daniel's a dogged one. Very competitive,

32   needless to say. He won't fight me for custody—if that's where

you're going. He doesn't have time, and he thinks, I think, I'm
a pretty good mom, or at least a devoted one. Since she was
born, I've loved her more than anyone else. [Pause] Well, that
says it all, doesn't it. Well, maybe not all. In some way, it's
been self-protective. Daniel has always needed "his children,"
those terribly sick and dying children, more than he needed
me or Jane. [Pause] But I'm not being fair. He adores Jane. He
calls us, or used to call us, the Three Musketeers. If we were
going somewhere, out to dinner or maybe a movie, the two
of them would go through this silly ceremony of departure,
a kind of Monty Python changing of the guard. I was the
audience. It started when Jane was about 3. He'd stand at
the side door and shout out, "Musketeers on the forecastle."
Hearing those words, from wherever she was, Jane would fling
herself down the stairs to join him. When she got there, he'd
hold out his right hand and say, with a very solemn face, "All
for one." Jane would high-five him and answer with an equally
solemn face, "And one for all." Then he'd scoop her up, throw
her over his shoulder, and carry her out to the car. Jane was
in heaven in those moments; I think he was too. [Pause] The
Musketeers have disbanded.

Q.   Was your husband's decision to start divorce proceedings
a surprise to you?

A.   No. Yes. He told me on January 3rd, three days into
the New Year, that he wanted a divorce. It threw me into
a tailspin. I thought we'd live unhappily ever after. I never
thought he'd go through with a second divorce. I asked him
if there was another woman. He said no but I don't believe
him. I know his modus operandi, after all. I think he's been
messing around with Dr. Stephanie Roth, a dermatologist
with a private practice in New York. They were in med school
together, and they've been intermittently in touch since.

She's apparently *the* person to see for wrinkles in the City. Her bread and butter is rejuvenating work, Botox, dermal abrasions, and the like. She had a write-up once in *Harper's Bazaar*. Her face looks like it's been ironed. [Pause] Do you remember that scene in *A Man for All Seasons,* when More confronts Richard Rich for betraying him in exchange for being made Chancellor of Wales? More says to him, "I can understand a man giving up his soul for the world, Richard, but for Wales?" That's how I feel. I can understand Daniel leaving me, but for Stephanie Roth?

Q.   You seem very composed now.

A.   Xanax. I took 3 mg. before I came. I've been seeing an analyst from Northeastern Psychoanalytic, for 6 years. Isabel Stokes. Over the years, she's prescribed for me a variety of antidepressants. Right now I'm on Wellbutrin. I've been depressed since I was 10. I'm a pretty high-functioning depressive, but a depressive nonetheless. Daniel hates it; he takes it personally. I can't blame him altogether. Depressives are downers. Dr. Stokes gave me Xanax back in January. I was so anxious, I couldn't read, I couldn't sleep, I couldn't eat. I took it pretty regularly in January and February, but now I only take it when I think an occasion calls for it. Like this. When I was given the summons at Golightly's, I almost passed out. Since then, I never travel without the Xanax. I still haven't gotten over it. I can't believe Daniel would have agreed to that, but maybe I'm being naïve. He might say in his defense that I had provoked it. It was all my fault, as was everything.

Q.   What do you mean by provoking it?

A.   I had a brief correspondence with Dr. Stephanie, which may have stirred the pot.

Q.   Could you be more specific?

1	A. I brought copies. I wrote to her; she wrote back; I wrote
2	back. Here.
3	[Extended pause. Note to Hannah: I am placing the three
4	letters in the file.]
5	Q. I see. Anything else?
6	A. Yes. About a week after he told me he wanted a divorce,
7	I asked him to rethink his decision or at least consider
8	mediation or counseling. He wasn't interested. I then asked
9	him to hold off doing anything definitive, such as hiring a
10	lawyer, until I had gotten more used to the idea. He agreed.
11	He saw how upset I was. We talked about telling Jane. I asked
12	him if we could consult a therapist to find out the best way of
13	telling her. He agreed very quickly, and two days later we had
14	an appointment with Dr. Rachel Fischer, a child psychiatrist
15	at the Mather Child Study Center. I don't know where he
16	found her; he's very anti-shrink, thinks psychiatry is voodoo.
17	He believes in willpower—it's the Ayn Rand in him—and he
18	disapproves of mental illness. Also obesity. He thinks of them
19	as mental slovenliness. Anyway, we went to see her on January
20	25th. She gave us some pointers, nothing surprising. She said
21	we should speak to her together and reassure her that we were
22	only divorcing each other, and not her. She advised holding
23	off telling Jane until I could talk about divorce without crying.
24	Even Xanaxed up the wazoo, I was a wreck the first two
25	months, on or over the verge of tears all the time.
26	Q. Have you told Jane?
27	A. There's a story. Two days after I was served at
28	Golightly's, when I was in Philadelphia visiting my sister, I got
29	a call at 8 p.m. in my hotel from Jane. She was sobbing. Daniel
30	had told her we were getting a divorce. He got it into his head
31	that she knew somehow, and he thought he should reassure
32	her. I drove home immediately. Jane was a mess. And I didn't

get to see Cordelia the next day, which was her birthday, and
which was very upsetting to her and to me. What a prince,
what a perfect prince. [Pause] The next day I told my father,
who encouraged me to consult his lawyers. A month later,
armed with meds, here I am.

Q.   Are you both living in the same dwelling?

A.   Dwelling, I like that. Yes, we're in separate bedrooms
in our house. It's a new house, 404 St. Cloud. We built it two
years ago, probably to ward off divorce. Isn't that what people
do? They have a baby or build a new house. It's a nice house,
modern, horizontal, clean-limbed, wood and windows, very
un–St. Cloud, which is a stew of English Tudor, American
Craftsman, and Tuscan Villa. Neighbors objected at first, but
we planted some full-grown trees in the front, and they subsided.
Daniel worked on the designs with the architect. He had thought
of becoming an architect at one point; in college, he went to
Columbia, he double-majored in chemistry and art history.

Q.   Do you have a mortgage? Do you know its value?

A.   I'm good about money. I pay the bills, I keep the tax
records. The house cost $375,000, more or less, including the
land and our very expensive Mather School of Architecture
architect. Its current value is about $525,000. I called a
Realtor, Laura Bucholtz, yesterday, to get a quick estimate.
She was the agent on the land sale and knows St. Cloud Street
from Germyn Street to Allerton. We have a 30-year mortgage
for $250,000 at 8%. Carrying costs, including local taxes but
not utilities, are about $3,500 a month. Daniel will want to
keep the house. I suppose that gives me some leverage?

Q.   It may. Is there any other real estate?

A.   My father and I own a house on Martha's Vineyard,
on the water in Aquinnah. It was my mother's house, and
she left it to us in a trust; the survivor gets it all. There's a

special name for that. This creates problems for my father. Of course, he doesn't want me to predecease him, but his wife, my stepmother, Cindy, would like to be able to use it and to decorate it. The house is a wreck. Nothing's been done to it since 1920, except the bare minimum to keep it from falling down, and the Vineyard in those days wasn't what it is today. It has no inside toilets, only an outhouse with a row of 4 WCs off the back porch. And my father and I have to agree on any changes because we own it together, and we can't so we don't. [Pause] We don't agree on much, except Jane.

Q.   Do you know what it's worth?

A.   When my mother died in 1979, it was valued at $90,000. It's probably worth $3 million now. Maybe more. The land, not the house. The site is spectacular.

Q.   Do you use it? Does your father?

A.   My father never goes up. He finds the toilet situation unacceptable. Oh, and there are no showers, only bathtubs. I go up at least once a year with Jane, who loves it. When she was smaller, she thought the outhouses were great fun, but now she'd like a proper inside toilet. I think she's been lobbying my father. My father wants to fix the whole place up, make it an Edgartown kind of house. That or nothing. I want inside toilets and a shower and a dishwasher and cable, but I want to keep the house's essential character. It's all I have left of my mother. Daniel went up once, never again. He is hugely resentful that I haven't put him on the deed. I keep explaining that I can't, but he refuses to understand, seeing it as a deliberate act on my part. And he, too, hated the toilets. I think in some ways men are more fastidious than women.

Q.   Any other property?

A.   The usual detritus of middle-class acquisitiveness. The only things I think we'd argue over are a Persian rug, which

was a wedding present from my grandparents, an early Cindy
Sherman photograph, and a Jenny Holzer sign, "Abuse of
power comes as no surprise." They're the only things we'd
both want.

Q.   Are you likely to inherit any money, property?

A.   I suppose I'm likely to inherit money from my father
when he dies, if he dies, but I can't count on it. For one thing,
I might easily predecease him. My mother died young, 46,
and so did her mother. For another, he's only 68, and the
Meiklejohns live forever. He's got a brother who's 87 and
still sits on the federal bench. Both his parents died in their
90s. For a third, he's controlling. And he's always rewriting
his will. Ask his lawyer, Proctor, as in *The Crucible*. He's a
member of your firm. I think he does a new one every three
months. He recently said he created a trust for Jane and me,
but he's the trustee. What does that mean? He won't tell me
anything else. This may change with the divorce. He doesn't
like Daniel. He doesn't exactly think he married me for my
money, but he doubts he would have married me without
it. But that could be said for my looks as well. Daniel likes
tall blondes with irregular features, bluestockings with trust
funds. Helen, his first wife, had serious money. Do you know
the Fincher Galleries at the Fine Arts Museum? A gift of her
grandparents. Dr. Stephanie is a bit of an outlier, not a WASP,
no family money, too short. Her dad was only a doctor, also a
dermatologist. But he was frugal and he believed in real estate.
He left her, free and clear, two apartments in the Beresford.
She lives in the smaller one, eight rooms. [Pause] I'm not sure
she'll get to walk down the aisle. [Pause] You shouldn't think I
was brought up to talk about money. I wasn't. My mother, who
was a rigorously honorable, straightforward person, imposed
an absolute embargo on money as a subject of conversation;

she thought talking about money was common. It offended
her, the way Nixon's hate list and anti-Semitism offended her,
as a sign of bad breeding. I was never allowed to say how much
anything cost. I must have looked an idiot. I went to school
with the children of professors and lawyers. They knew what
everything cost, including their parents' psychiatrists. [Pause]
I don't talk about the price of things, that lesson has stuck,
but I am prepared to acknowledge certain obvious facts about
my life and my upbringing. I was brought up rich and I have
the exaggerated sense of entitlement that money confers. I
don't always get what I want, but not because of money. That
makes me very different from most other people, including my
husband. He never had money until recently. He likes it, having
it and spending it, but success is more important to him.

Q.   What about other assets? Savings and the like?

A.   Daniel makes the money, and he handles the
investments. I don't think he's hiding anything. He has
retirement funds with TIAA-CREF in the neighborhood
of $600,000. He also has a 401(k) plan with approximately
$300,000 in it. Other assets include about $700,000 in stocks,
$90,000 in treasury bills, and $80,000 in a savings account.
He does a quarterly accounting; I got the figures from the one
he did in early October.

Q.   Any insurance policies?

A.   Daniel is insured for $1.5 million; I'm insured for
$200,000—to pay Luz's salary in case I conk. He'd need
somebody.

Q.   Could you provide a salary history? And a few other
particulars? [Note to Hannah: I handed Mrs. Durkheim
copies of the Divorce Work Sheets: Summary Biographies for
her and her husband.]

A.   Of course.

1   Q.   Does your husband have any separate assets? Any
2   inheritances?
3   A.   Daniel's an orphan. His father died in 1992, his mother
4   in 1998. He inherited a 1989 Honda Accord and $16,000.
5   His parents owned a printing business. They never made
6   much money, but they saw that their son, their only child,
7   was well educated. And praised, praised for everything
8   he did, every bowel movement, every report card, every
9   titration. They didn't much care for the grandchildren. They
10   couldn't hold a candle to their father. And they certainly had
11   no use for me or Helen. We weren't worthy of him; we didn't
12   appreciate how extraordinary he was. If I made them dinner,
13   they thanked Daniel; if he didn't visit them, it was my fault.
14   They made sure they didn't die in debt. They were fierce
15   about not saddling Daniel with nursing home costs and the
16   like. They had long-term-care insurance for nurses and that
17   sort of thing, and they belonged to burial societies and had
18   prepaid their funerals, coffins, headstones, plots, even the
19   cantor. God, my father never prepays anything. You lose the
20   float.
21   Q.   Have you begun to think about what you want out of this
22   divorce?
23   A.   I will need support for a while, but I don't want to take
24   him to the cleaners. I don't have bag-lady fears, at least not
25   acute ones. After all, I've got the Bruce Meiklejohn safety
26   net. My wishes are personal, not financial. I want to come
27   out of this with my ego intact. And I'd like it if Daniel's took
28   a beating. I don't want anything really bad to happen to
29   him. No fatal diseases, no malpractice cases, no accusations
30   of scientific fraud. He is, after all, my daughter's father. But
31   I don't want anything good to ever happen to him either.
32   I want nothing to happen to him. I want him to die of

1 disappointment, after a long, lonely, cheerless life that ends
2 with bedsores and tubes up the nose, in a nursing home.
3 Q.   You have thought about it. Your husband seems to want
4 to move quickly. Will you be able to do that?
5 A.   I don't know. He's got a mean temper. He blows up easily
6 and horribly if he feels thwarted in any way. He thinks he's
7 always right, and when people disagree with him, he invariably
8 regards them as stupid or envious or malignant. He was
9 arrogant when I met him, but tolerably so; then, it seemed to
10 me he just knew how good he was. Now, he's too important to
11 take out the garbage, or telephone when he's going to be late,
12 or remember my birthday. I think the Freeman Prize did it.
13 He was the youngest recipient ever. That's a long answer. I just
14 don't know how awful he'll be. Of course, I can be awful back.
15 I've learned how to do that. God, I hope Jane survives us.
16 Q.   Do you have any questions for me?
17 A.   Could you tell me about Narragansett divorce law?
18 What next?
19 Q.   Let's fill out the Divorce Work Sheet: Summary
20 Biographies. Then I'll tell you what I know about the law and
21 show you a copy of our retainer agreement. I'll also set up an
22 appointment right now for next week for you to meet with
23 Fiona McGregor.
24 A.   I was dreading this unnecessarily. Thank you. Thank
25 you so much. Is it really true you've never done this before?
26 You're a natural.
27 [Note to Hannah: I set up an appointment with Fiona for
28 Tuesday, March 23, at 10 a.m.]
29 [End of Transcript]
30
31
32

TRAYNOR, HAND, WYZANSKI

222 CHURCH STREET
NEW SALEM, NARRAGANSETT 06555
(393) 876-5678

Divorce Work Sheet: Summary Biography
Attorney Work Product

From:	Sophie Diehl
To:	Files
RE:	Matter of Durkheim
Date:	March 17, 1999

Maria Meiklejohn Durkheim: Wife

Date of Birth:
July 14, 1957, Age 41

Marriages and Divorces:
Daniel Durkheim, married June 21, 1982

Children:
Jane Mather Durkheim, born April 23, 1988

Education:
B.A.	University of Chicago 1979
M.Phil.	Mather University 1995
Ph.D.	Mather University, expected 2001

Employment History:

Femina Magazine

Assistant to the Features Editor, June 1979 to June 1981	$ 19,000
Assistant Features Editor, July 1981 to July 1983	$ 28,000
Features Editor, July 1983 to October 1988	$ 42,000

Monk's House (Publishing Company)

Editor, Nonfiction, October 1988 to July 1991	$ 47,000
Freelance Editor, August 1991 to August 1992	$ 23,000

Mather University

Teaching Assistant in English, August 1993 to August 1995	$ 4,000
Writing Tutor, English Instructor, August 1995 to present	$ 14,000

TRAYNOR, HAND, WYZANSKI

222 CHURCH STREET
NEW SALEM, NARRAGANSETT 06555
(393) 876-5678

Divorce Work Sheet: Summary Biography
Attorney Work Product

From:	Sophie Diehl
To:	Files
RE:	Matter of Durkheim
Date:	March 17, 1999

Daniel Edward Durkheim: Husband

Date of Birth:
March 14, 1947, Age 52

Marriages and Divorces:
Helen Maxwell Fincher, married December 7, 1974, divorced June 7, 1982
Maria Mather Meiklejohn, married June 21, 1982

Children:
Thomas Maxwell Durkheim, born November 1, 1976
Jane Mather Durkheim, born April 23, 1988

Education:
B.A.	Columbia College, Columbia University 1969	
M.D.	College of Physicians and Surgeons, Columbia University 1978	
Ph.D.	Columbia University Graduate School of Arts and Sciences 1980	

Post-Degree Education and Training:
Postdoctoral Fellow, Columbia University, 1980 to 1981	$ 18,000
Intern, Pediatrics, Presbyterian Hospital, 1981 to 1982	$ 20,000
Intern, Oncology, Presbyterian Hospital, 1982 to 1983	$ 22,000
Resident, Pediatric Oncology, Presbyterian Hospital, 1983 to 1986	$ 24,000
Chief Resident, Pediatric Oncology, Presbyterian Hospital, 1986 to 1987	$ 30,000

Employment History:

United States Army, Vietnam, 1969 to 1971, Medic $ 8,000

College of Physicians and Surgeons, Columbia University

    Assistant Professor, 1987 to 1988 $ 80,000

    Professor, 1988 to 1991 $ 150,000

Mather Medical School and Mather Medical Center

    Professor, 1991 to present

    Chief, Department of Pediatric Oncology, 1992 to present $ 370,000

Commonwealth of Narragansett
Family Court

County: Tyler   **Docket No:** 99-27

Domestic Relations Summons

Daniel E. Durkheim   **Plaintiff**

v.

Maria M. Durkheim   **Defendant**

To the above-named defendant:

You are hereby summoned and required to serve upon plaintiff's attorney: Ray Kahn

whose address is: 46 Broadway, New Salem, Narragansett 06555

a copy of your answer to the complaint for: divorce

within: 20 days of service of this summons

If you fail to return service, the Court will proceed in 90 days to the hearing and adjudication of this action without you.

You are also required to file your answer to the complaint in the Office of the Registrar of the Family Court at: New Salem, NA

At: New Salem, NA

Date: February 15, 1999

Registrar of Family Court: Paul McIntyre

Acceptance of Service

I, the above-named defendant: Maria M. Durkheim accept service of this summons and understand that judgment may be rendered against me in accordance with the complaint, a copy of which I have received this day:
Date:
Signature of defendant:

_____

The above-named defendant: Maria Durkheim
swears that the acceptance of service was his free act and deed.
Date:
Notary Public:
Signature of Notary Public:
Commission Expiration Date:

Commonwealth of Narragansett
Family Court

County: Tyler   Docket No: 99-27

Complaint for Divorce

Daniel E. Durkheim   **Plaintiff**

v.

Maria M. Durkheim   **Defendant**

1. Plaintiff who resides at: 404 St. Cloud Street, New Salem, NA 06556
    is lawfully married to the defendant
    who resides at: 404 St. Cloud Street, New Salem, NA 06556
2. The parties were married at: New York, NY on: June 21, 1982
    and last lived together: currently at: 404 St. Cloud Street, New Salem,
    NA 06556
3. The minor child of this marriage is: Jane Mather Durkheim
    who was born: April 23, 1988
4. Plaintiff certifies that no previous action for dissolution, divorce,
    annulment, separation, support, desertion, custody, or visitation has
    been brought by either party against the other: none
5. On or about: January 3, 1999 the plaintiff determined that:
    there was an irretrievable breakdown of the marriage that continues to
    the present time.
6. The plaintiff requests that the Court
    a. grant a divorce for: irretrievable breakdown of the marriage
        (33 N.C.A. §801ff.)
    b. grant custody of the above-named child: joint
    c. order a suitable amount of support for the above-named child: yes
    d. order exclusive use of the family home to: Daniel E. Durkheim
    e. order spousal support: no
    f. order equitable distribution of the marital assets: yes

Signature of attorney: Ray Kahn, Kahn & Boyle
Name of attorney: Ray Kahn, 46 Broadway, New Salem, NA 06555
Date: February 15, 1999

Narragansett Statutes
Title 33 of the Narragansett Code, Sections 801ff.
Dissolution of Marriage, Annulment, and Legal Separation

Sec. 801. Grounds for dissolution of marriage; legal separation; annulment.

(a) A marriage is dissolved only by

(1) the death of one of the parties or

(2) a decree of annulment or dissolution of the marriage by a court of competent jurisdiction.

(b) An annulment shall be granted if the marriage is void or voidable under the laws of this state or of the state in which the marriage was performed [e.g., same sex marriage].

(c) A decree of dissolution of a marriage or a decree of legal separation shall be granted upon a finding that one of the following causes has occurred:

(1) the marriage has broken down irretrievably;

(2) the parties have lived apart by reason of incompatibility for a continuous period of at least eighteen (18) months immediately prior to the service of the complaint and there is no reasonable prospect that they will be reconciled;

(3) adultery;

(4) fraudulent inducement;

(5) wilful desertion for one year with total neglect of duty;

(6) seven (7) years' absence, during all of which period the absent party has not been heard from;

(7) habitual intemperance;

(8) intolerable cruelty;

(9) sentence to imprisonment for life or the commission of any infamous crime;

(10) legal confinement in a hospital or hospitals or other similar institution or institutions, because of mental illness, for at least an accumulated period totaling five (5) years within the period of seven (7) years preceding the date of the complaint;

(11) bigamy.

Sec. 804. Service and filing of complaint.

A proceeding for annulment, dissolution of marriage, or legal separation shall be commenced by the service and filing of a complaint in the Narragansett Family Court for the judicial district in which one of the parties resides.

Sec. 805. Stipulation of parties and finding of irretrievable breakdown.

(a) In any action for dissolution of marriage or legal separation, the court shall make a finding that a marriage has broken down irretrievably where both parties so stipulate and have submitted an agreement concerning the custody, care, education, visitation, maintenance, or support of their children, if any, and concerning alimony and the disposition of property. The testimony of either party in support of that conclusion shall be sufficient.

(b) In any case in which the court finds, after hearing, that a cause enumerated in subsection (c) of section 801 exists, the court shall enter a decree dissolving the marriage or granting a legal separation. In no case shall the decree granted be in favor of either party.

MARIA DURKHEIM
404 ST. CLOUD STREET
NEW SALEM, NA 06556

March 19, 1999

David Greaves, Esq.
Traynor, Hand, Wyzanski
222 Church Street
New Salem, NA 06555

Dear Mr. Greaves (David?):

I want to thank you for Wednesday's consultation with Anne Sophie Diehl. She was a brilliant pinch-hitter, exactly what I needed. I think I'd have fallen into silence and hostility if I'd had to talk with a real, 14K professional divorce lawyer, and I certainly wouldn't have handed over my correspondence with Daniel or Dr. Roth, who by the way writes like a dog and can't spell. Ms. Diehl made it all easy, or at least easier. It wasn't that she was unlawyerlike or unprofessional, but she never pulled rank. She never acted as though she was master of an arcane set of rules I was too ignorant to understand. She didn't patronize me; she didn't say I should leave it all in her hands. She made everything clear; and she told me what *I* had to do. I haven't felt very good in the last few months. My husband's leaving me—or wanting to leave me—has undone me at the seams. Ms. Diehl made me feel competent and capable. And she laughed at my jokes. And she knew she should have at least tried to read Proust.

My father always spoke well of you, of your discretion, intelligence, judgment, tact. He was right.

And now, to the point. Freud says that the most important part of any letter is usually the P.S. (I'm trying to be more up front; the third paragraph shows emerging mental health.) I'd like Ms. Diehl to act as my lawyer. I know she's not an experienced divorce lawyer, but she's smart and I don't think she'd be cowed by the thugs at Kahn & Boyle. (I can't believe Daniel hired them. I didn't think they represented anyone who'd actually filed an income tax return.) The expert you have could help her out—I'll cheerfully pay double if that's what it takes. I don't think our situation is all that complicated; I can't imagine we'll have to go to court. I'm not out for blood. Well maybe blood, but not bone.

Is it possible to have Ms. Diehl take my case? I would like it. I told my father what a great lawyer I thought she was. He was very pleased; he liked that I liked his lawyers. He and I usually don't agree about people—my mother and Jane being the exceptions. His judgment may be better than I thought. Could it be he was right about Daniel all the time?

I hope you'll forgive the casualness of my tone. My father has spoken so often about you, I feel I know you. I look forward to hearing from you. Thank you for your consideration.

Yours truly,

Mia Durkheim

P.S. I've just reread this letter. "Casualness of tone" hardly does it justice. It is downright garrulous and indiscreet. I'm not quite myself these days. I *know* better. I just can't seem to *be* better.

TRAYNOR, HAND, WYZANSKI

222 CHURCH STREET
NEW SALEM, NARRAGANSETT 06555
(393) 876-5678

MEMORANDUM
Attorney Work Product

From: David Greaves
To: Sophie Diehl
RE: Matter of Durkheim: Attorney Reassignment
Date: March 23, 1999
Attachments: Maria Durkheim's Letter of March 19, 1999

Sophie—

I'm going to have to go back on my word. I need you on the Durkheim divorce. Maria Durkheim wrote me a letter, requesting you to act as her lawyer in the divorce. She liked you. I've attached a copy of her letter with this memo. She knows you aren't a pro. She's offered to pay for two lawyers to have you. It's a serious compliment, though, understandably, you may not be able to see it that way.

I'll work things out with the boys in the back room. And I'll see that there's extra remuneration for the work you put in on this case.

David

Advice Sought

From: Sophie Diehl   3/24/99 2:31 PM
To: Maggie Pfeiffer <mcp15@mather.edu>
Date: Wed, 24 Mar 1999 14:31:39
Subject: Advice Sought

Mags—

I am so angry I can't think straight. The firm is doing a divorce. Fiona was out of town when the client (female) came in for intake. David asked me to do the interview. He promised that was all I'd have to do on the case. The client then turns around and asks for me to act as her attorney (she "liked" me, David said, calling her request "a serious compliment"), and he now says I'm to do it. I am beside myself. Did I mention that the client is the daughter of a Very Important Client?

What really galls me is the way he asked. He didn't ask. He just said I was on the case. Do you remember how my mother used to ask my sibs and me, when we were little, to do something? "Est-ce que tu veux le faire maintenant, ou plus tard?" As if she was giving us a choice. Maybe that's David's attraction for me. He's like ma chere Maman, only less ruthless, no subterfuge. I could quit, of course, and go work for the Legal Defender, but then I'd have to represent wife beaters and shoplifters, instead of major felons. I can't believe David's doing this to me. I thought he was a pal, my rabbi.

And then there's Fiona. She will not be pleased. Oh, well. I'm already in her bad book. Ever since she found out I clerked for Judge Howard, she's been so unpleasant, as though I did it simply to one-up her.

Love,
Sophie

Re: Advice Sought
From: Maggie Pfeiffer   3/24/99 3:26 PM
To: Sophie Diehl <asdiehl@traynor.com>
Date: Wed, 24 Mar 1999 15:26:43
Subject: Re: Advice Sought

Sophie—

I can't believe you're disappointed in DG, or surprised. (Anger, I accept.) What did you expect him to do? He's your boss, for Lord's sake, at a firm that makes a lot of money and, not incidentally, pays you a bigger salary than anyone else I know. Matt won't make as much as you until he's 60, if then. Do you know how much a second-year associate architect makes?

As I recall, you always decided to do what your mother wanted "plus tard." "Who knows," you'd say, "I could be dead later and not have to do it."

How about coming around the drama school Friday night and watching *The Real Thing* rehearsal? We can get a drink after. I'd like you to meet the director, Harry Mortensen. He's third-year and very talented. Everyone wanted to work with him. He's also dark and brooding and smart and witty. If you fell for him, he could just break your heart. Right up your alley, sweetie.

Love and kisses,
Maggie

TRAYNOR, HAND, WYZANSKI

222 CHURCH STREET
NEW SALEM, NARRAGANSETT 06555
(393) 876-5678

MEMORANDUM
Attorney Work Product

From: Joe Salerno
To: Sophie Diehl
RE: Request from David
Date: March 24, 1999
Attachments:

Sophie—

David has asked to borrow you for 5–15 hours a week for the next several months. He said it was an important case, and he wouldn't ask unless it *was* important, would I mind? I don't see why he put it to me as a request. We're usually not so punctilious with each other. But do you mind?

I know you'll get all your work for us done, and I won't assign you a new case without first discussing it with you. I got the sense from David's testiness that perhaps he didn't have that kind of discussion with you. But a managing partner has to manage. I don't envy him his job.

Love,
Joe

Matter of Durkheim

From: Sophie Diehl   3/24/99 6:26 PM
To: David Greaves <dagreaves@traynor.com>
cc: Hannah Smith <hsmith@traynor.com>
Date: Wed, 24 Mar 1999 18:26:22
Subject: Matter of Durkheim

David—

I'll need help with the Durkheim divorce. Will you do it? Felix?
I don't think Fiona would want the job, but I may be wrong.
What are the next steps?

Sophie

TRAYNOR, HAND, WYZANSKI

222 CHURCH STREET
NEW SALEM, NARRAGANSETT 06555
(393) 876-5678

MEMORANDUM
Attorney Work Product

From: David Greaves
To: Sophie Diehl
RE: Matter of Durkheim: Attorney Assignment; Use of Email;
            Meeting
Date: March 24, 1999
Attachments:

Hannah printed out your email. I'll work with you on the Durkheim case. Felix is up to his ears in divorces at the moment, and, as you wrote, Fiona is not a good choice. It wouldn't work well, a junior associate taking the lead over a junior partner. I'll explain it to her.

We should meet this Friday to talk about the case. (I'll be out of the office tomorrow.) What about 3 p.m. in my office? In the meantime, look over some of the separation agreements we have in the files. In addition to the Habermans', I recommend the Colliers', Jason and Rebecca Peele's, the Crawfords', and the Goldsteins'. And, most important, the Peele file, in its entirety. Kahn & Boyle were the attorneys for Jason Peele. They play by their own rules. You should know what you're up against. They're not good lawyers, only mean ones, but the latter often passes for the former.

In the future, please do not use email to discuss a case, no matter how insignificant the information you are conveying may strike you. I have thought about this a good deal; I am not simply being a Luddite. I recognize email's uses, but I persist in thinking that most communications between attorneys and between attorneys and their clients should not be transmitted electronically. It's too easy for email to be misdirected, forwarded, hacked into. There is always the risk that someone other than the designated recipient will read your email. I worry not only that confidentiality will be broken but that by using email, we are playing fast and loose with the lawyer-client privilege and possibly forfeiting claims to protected attorney work product. Have you been following the Microsoft antitrust trial? Microsoft was hoisted on its own petard. There was a mountain of incriminating emails. Fitting in that case, perhaps, but not ours. I recognize that your message could compromise no one, but I would prefer that we stick to interoffice memoranda.

Re: Re: Advice Sought
From: Sophie Diehl   3/24/99 6:36 PM
To: Maggie Pfeiffer <mcp15@mather.edu>
Date: Wed, 24 Mar 1999 18:36:57
Subject: Re: Re: Advice Sought

Oh, Maggie,

I can't believe I ever had a crush on that man. What a skunk. Boy,
did he have me snookered. I sent him an email saying I'd take
on the case and got back a lecture on emails and the threat they
pose to the attorney-client privilege. It was so infuriating. I know
the rules—and the risks. There was nothing in my email that
compromised anyone or anything. (Just my luck, he'll intercept
THIS email.) And, he never said "Thank you," or "I know this is not
something you signed on for." Of course, if he doesn't recognize
a debt to me, then it doesn't exist. And then there's Fiona; she's
not going to take this well. I can hear her now: "You Yale Law grads
knock me out. There's nothing you can't do. Habeas corpus with
the right hand, alimony with the left." She'll no doubt accuse me
of poaching her case. This is a royal screwing.

I'll drop by your rehearsal around 9:30 on Friday. I can't wait to
meet this Harry fellow. Is he more Rochester or Heathcliff?

Love,
Sophie

P.S. Would I have had a crush on DG if he didn't look like Jeff
Bridges? (Rhetorical question. Don't answer. My chronic weakness
for sturdy men. And Starman Bridges NOT Lebowski.)

Join the E-Generation

From: Sophie Diehl   3/25/99 10:10 AM
To: David Greaves <dagreaves@traynor.com>
cc: Hannah Smith <hsmith@traynor.com>
Date: Thu, 25 Mar 1999 10:10:16
Subject: Join the E-Generation

Dear David—

Millennium Approaches. I think it's time you bit the dumdum and entered the electronic age. We don't need to be bombarding each other with constant streams of memoranda—like 18th-century courtiers sending notes round by hand. All that letterhead paper, filing, etc. I will make a promise. I will never send you an email that couldn't be read by either opposing counsel or your mother. (The two negatives make an intended positive.) Email is very useful for making appointments, sending reminders, and the like. And if you want to make an email part of the record, you can print it out and have Hannah file it.

I won't be able to make the Friday appointment. I'll be out of the office all day, interviewing possible witnesses for the Trilling case. How about Monday morning? I can do anytime until 1 pm when I've got to leave for an evidentiary hearing.

I'm cc'ing Hannah so she can check your calendar.

Yours,
Sophie

P.S. Atticus as Jewish. I need to see that. I have seen *The Third Man*. It's my mother's second-favorite movie after *Smiles of a Summer Night*. I've also seen *Paths of Glory*, which is my father's favorite movie, not counting *Chariots of Fire*, that great British weeper. So, do you watch *The Simpsons*?

Mr. Watson, Come Here

From: David Greaves   3/26/99 6:32 PM
To: Sophie Diehl <asdiehl@traynor.com>
Date: Fri, 26 Mar 1999 18:32:11
Subject: Mr. Watson, Come Here

Dear Sophie—

I hope your Trilling interviews went well. I've slotted you in at 9:30 Monday. Do you check your email over the weekend?

What do you think of my maiden email? I was taken by your lavish style—especially after that first terse, unfriendly (probably, deservedly so) message. What with the courtiers, the dumdums, and the bombarding streams, I was immersed in a soup of metaphors. Will email do this to me, too?

You might be interested to know that my mother is not a prig; I can't imagine anything you'd say in your most indiscreet moments that would shock her. She's like Grace Kelly's mother in *To Catch a Thief*, very down-to-earth, a bourbon drinker. You'd like her. She'd like you. My starchiness can't be laid at her feet.

I am sorry you've been roped into this matter. I know I promised. At the very least, I should have asked you in person.

David

P.S. I know who the Simpsons are. I have sons, remember.

P.P.S. Don't think I didn't catch the Tony Kushner reference. I think *Angels in America* is the great American play of the second half of the 20th century. First half: *A Streetcar Named Desire*.

Men

From: Sophie Diehl   3/27/99 11:32 AM
To: Maggie Pfeiffer <mcp15@mather.edu>
Date: Sat, 27 Mar 1999 11:32:54
Subject: Men

Mags—

I am wiped out. I crawled in at 4 a.m. I haven't stayed out, let alone
up, that late since your wedding. What can I say? Harry is terrific.
I could fall for him, heavily and physically. I didn't see any of his
dark, brooding side. Probably blinded by those shoulders. He was
funny, smart, interesting—and interested. He liked my client stories,
especially the Trilling saga; but then what's not to like about a case
where a sociopath kills his neighbor because his Pekinese shat on his
lawn? I'm seeing him again tonight after the rehearsal. My fantasy
life may start taking a backseat to my real one. Although that has
been resurrected. I've resumed my crush on DG. He wrote me an
email in his old unconsciously (?) flirtatious way. Or, maybe not.
Maybe he was just being teasing and playful.

I have to go into the office this afternoon to work on the Trilling case
and tidy up my regular workload, since on Monday I begin divorce
detail. I'll see you this evening. I'll come by at the end of rehearsal
to watch the last act. I think the play will be a great success and you
are wonderful as Annie, though not very likable. It's interesting that
a play about love is about adultery. I know you can't do a marriage
play without adultery—no plot—but there are less cruel ways of
doing it (though no doubt less dramatically interesting). Perhaps for
Stoppard, only the love for children is the real thing. My favorite bit
is the second scene, where the playwright's first wife says about
him and their daughter: "He's in love with his [daughter]." (I'm
improvising.) And you (second wife) say: "Isn't that normal?" And
the ex-wife says: "Normal is the other way round." I wonder why he

picked this play? Does it resonate with anyone who wasn't divorced or whose parents weren't divorced? I'm thinking I should send my new client and her husband (and his new sweetheart) complimentary tickets to your play. I'm also thinking I should stop fantasizing about Mrs. Greaves's husband. God, he's as old as my father. I am disgusting.

But then there's Harry. Do you know when I saw him, I could feel the hairs on the back of my neck bristling? I haven't felt that way since 11th grade when I sat across the aisle from Jack in the theater class at Collegiate. I used to think I'd fall off my chair. I'd lost all will; I was pure desire—and desire couldn't sit up straight or pay attention to *Joe Egg*. Do we ever feel that intensely again? No. Only teenagers kill themselves for love; Maman says, Anna threw herself under the train not because she lost Vronsky but because she lost her son. There we are again: the love for children.

I need more sleep.

Kiss Matt for me. Love,

Sophie

Hello

From: Harry Mortensen   3/27/99 3:01 PM
To: Sophie Diehl <asdiehl@traynor.com>
Date: Sat, 27 Mar 1999 15:01:53
Subject: Hello

Sweet Sophie—How are you feeling? Did you get any sleep? I'm wrecked. And you did it. You are coming by rehearsal tonight, aren't you? It should be over by 12:30, but you're welcome anytime.

Harry

TRAYNOR, HAND, WYZANSKI

222 CHURCH STREET
NEW SALEM, NARRAGANSETT 06555
(393) 876-5678

MEMORANDUM
Attorney Work Product

From: Sophie Diehl
To: David Greaves
RE: Matter of Durkheim
Date: March 29, 1999
Attachments:

At our meeting this morning, we discussed the next steps to be taken in the Durkheim case. In the next few days, I shall attend to the matters that need attending to and do more reading and research. You will deal with Fiona in a way that will mitigate any ill feelings this assignment may have inadvertently engendered.

Matters That Need Attending:

1. **Letter to Mrs. Durkheim/Addendum to the Fee Agreement**

   I shall write Mrs. Durkheim today explaining the conditions under which I will represent her. I shall advise her against using me and give her many cogent reasons why you or Fiona would better serve her (never mentioning my own disinclination). I shall say that if against advice of counsel, she still wants me to represent her, I will do my best. I will also say that because of my inexperience, I will regularly consult with you to make sure that she is getting the best legal advice. If she chooses to retain me, I shall ask her to sign an *Addendum to the Fee Agreement*, which spells out that she will be charged for your time as well as mine. We agree that it is better that I write the letter. Mrs. Durkheim might interpret a letter from you to that effect as patronizing, insensitive, and dismissive. ("Father's Lawyer Knows Best.")

2. **Notice of Appearance; Acceptance of Service; Answer to Complaint**

   We need to accept service and file a Notice of Appearance with the Court and K&B; we should also answer the complaint: nothing too specific, boiler-plate.

3. **Discovery**

    After the matter of representation is fixed, we need to begin discovery. Mrs. Durkheim is in the process of assembling a financial history of her marriage and a proposed post-divorce budget for herself and her daughter. She does not believe it will be difficult to assemble the information and supporting documentation. She handled the family finances, kept the books, paid the bills. She doesn't believe her husband has any hidden assets. Is she being naïve? Doesn't she know about the Caymans? When we have a better idea of income and expenses, assets and liabilities, we can begin to formulate an offer.

4. **Motion for Temporary Support**

    Mrs. Durkheim's current income will not support her and her daughter. While her father would no doubt help her out until a settlement is reached, we should probably begin to think about making a motion for temporary support. In the Peele case you had me read, Jason Peele (a K&B client) closed the joint checking account, canceled his wife's credit cards, and emptied out the safe deposit box—a week after the summons was served. And she had no job at all.

5. **Continued Residence in the Family Home**

    Even if she doesn't want to, Mrs. Durkheim needs to stay put in the family home until a settlement is reached. It can't look as though she's abandoned him. Also, since he's so attached to the house, it may provide us with some leverage in the negotiations. We need to be vigilant here. Before he made any kind of offer of settlement, Jason Peele made a motion to exclude his wife *and children* from the family residence and changed the locks.

Narragansett Statutes
Title 33 of the Narragansett Code, Sections 801ff.
Dissolution of Marriage, Annulment, and Legal Separation

Sec. 833. Temporary alimony and support and use of family home or other residential dwelling.

At any time after the return day of a complaint, temporary alimony and child support may be awarded to either of the parties. In making an order for temporary alimony, the court shall consider all factors enumerated in section 832 (permanent award of alimony). In making an order for temporary child support, the court shall consider all factors enumerated in section 834 (permanent child support). The court may also award exclusive use of the family home or any other dwelling that is available for use as a residence prior to dissolution of the marriage, legal separation, or annulment to either of the parties as is just and equitable without regard to the respective interests of the parties in the property.

TRAYNOR, HAND, WYZANSKI

222 CHURCH STREET
NEW SALEM, NARRAGANSETT 06555
(393) 876-5678

MEMORANDUM
Attorney Work Product

From: Fiona McGregor
To: David Greaves
RE: The Meiklejohns
Date: March 29, 1999
Attachments:

What is going on? I go off to Ireland for two weeks and return to find that Sophie Diehl is doing a Meiklejohn divorce. I had barely sat down at my desk this morning when Jennie burst in to tell me the news. (She was all wide-eyed, breathless; you'd think we'd been retained by Jerry Hall.)

It is irresponsible, not to say insulting to the divorce practice partners of the firm; an embryonic criminal lawyer who knows nothing about family law and who has been practicing law for 10 minutes is assigned the firm's biggest, most important divorce case in years, and I am not consulted or even notified. How did this happen? Is it now firm policy that only Mather or Yale Law School graduates can represent the likes of the Meiklejohns? I can't believe this is the way to run a law firm. I am stunned. There's no other word.

cc: Jason Bell
       William Frost
       Proctor Hand
       Virginia Ladder
       Felix Landau
       Frank O'Keefe
       Joseph Salerno
       Katherine Sales
       John Wynch

TRAYNOR, HAND, WYZANSKI

422 CHURCH STREET

NEW SALEM, NARRAGANSETT 06555

(393) 876-5678

MEMORANDUM
Attorney Work Product

From: David Greaves
To: Fiona McGregor
RE: In the Matter of Durkheim: Legal Representation
Date: March 29, 1999
Attachments:

At my request, Sophie did the intake interview because you were out of town. A few days later, Maria Durkheim wrote me, asking for Sophie to represent her in the divorce. If you'd like to read Mrs. Durkheim's letter, ask Hannah for a copy. You couldn't be more unhappy than Sophie, who has no interest in doing divorces, not even a Meiklejohn's.

When a client asks for a specific lawyer, the client gets that lawyer. That's how this firm is run.

cc: Jason Bell
William Frost
Proctor Hand
Virginia Ladder
Felix Landau
Frank O'Keefe
Joseph Salerno
Katherine Sales
John Wynch

All About Eve

From: Sophie Diehl   3/29/99 4:14 PM
To: Maggie Pfeiffer <mcp15@mather.edu>
Date: Mon, 29 Mar 1999 16:14:55
Subject: All About Eve

Dear Mags—

That divorce I've been roped into doing is heating up—not between
the unhappy couple, as you'd expect, but in the office. Fiona is hopping
mad. She wrote a memo to DG that was bristling with indignation and
sent cc's to all the partners. Four of them went out of their way to show
it to me. Joe said it was *All About Eve* with the gloves (white or boxing?)
off. I haven't seen him so cheerful since we won the big WMU case.
Needless to say, I am an object of her wrath—though DG got a dose of
it as well. I don't know why she dislikes me so much. She made a crack
about Yale and Mather lawyers, but then everyone does. We can't pass
the bar, but we know our Rawls. I need to talk to my mother. She'll tell
me it will all be all right.

Sophie

TRAYNOR, HAND, WYZANSKI

222 CHURCH STREET
NEW SALEM, NARRAGANSETT 06555
(393) 876-5678

MEMORANDUM
Attorney Work Product

From:	Sophie Diehl
To:	David Greaves
RE:	In the Matter of Durkheim: Legal Representation
Date:	March 29, 1999
Attachments:	Letter to Maria Durkheim

Attached is a draft copy of my letter to Maria Durkheim. It is perhaps not strictly correct for a legal document, but in its way it is responsive to Mrs. Durkheim's and she will, I believe, take it in the spirit in which it is offered. Let me know what changes you think I should make.

I've asked all the Catholics in my family to light a candle to Saint Jude.

TRAYNOR, HAND, WYZANSKI

222 CHURCH STREET
NEW SALEM, NARRAGANSETT 06555
(393) 876-5678
ATTORNEYS AT LAW

March 29, 1999

Maria M. Durkheim
404 St. Cloud Street
New Salem, NA 06556

Dear Mrs. Durkheim:

I am writing in regard to your request that I represent you in your divorce. I will be absolutely straight with you. I'm not the best person for this job. I am a criminal lawyer. I am not only ill prepared to act in a matrimonial case, I am barely on speaking terms with the rules of civil procedure. I have never litigated a civil action; I have never drafted any of the relevant documents or negotiated a separation and custody agreement.

I can understand the impulse that drove you to ask for me. You don't want to have to tell your story over again. I think the same impulse makes therapy patients stick with a therapist no matter how useless or damaging the treatment. The operating—and pessimistic—theory seems to be that the devil you know is better than the devil you don't. Don't make that mistake in this instance. You have much better options. (And you won't have to retell your story; the taped and transcribed versions of your interview are in your file at the firm.)

There are in our offices three attorneys who are knowledgeable and experienced in matrimonial law, all of whom would do an excellent job for you: Fiona McGregor is a recognized authority who has written articles for *The Narragansett Lawyer* and taught the state bar review sections on divorce and dissolution; Felix Landau has been practicing matrimonial law for 25 years and is an ace negotiator; David Greaves, our managing partner, is a superb litigator and one of the most respected lawyers in the state. My best legal advice to you is to choose one of them. You want a lawyer who is known in the legal community as an expert and won't be patronized or bullied by Ray Kahn. You want a lawyer who has credibility with the judges in Family Court. I am not that lawyer. I've never even been in Family Court. There is also the financial aspect of my representation. I am not only the least competent divorce lawyer in our firm but also the most expensive, since you will have to pay for the services of a second lawyer, someone who actually knows what he or she is doing. Frankly, I'm not worth it.

I know you will take this letter in the spirit in which it is intended. If I was less direct, I would be derelict in my responsibility, not only to you but to my profession. I am asking you to reconsider your decision. At such a vulnerable juncture in your life, you need to have the best legal representation available.

In the event you are sued for murder instead of divorce, I am the lawyer for you. As things stand now, I am not. I look forward to hearing from you.

Yours,

Anne Sophie Diehl

Anne Sophie Diehl

cc: David Greaves
        Felix Landau
        Fiona McGregor

TRAYNOR, HAND, WYZANSKI

222 CHURCH STREET
NEW SALEM, NARRAGANSETT 06555
(393) 876-5678

MEMORANDUM
Attorney Work Product

From: David Greaves
To: Sophie Diehl
RE: In the Matter of Durkheim: Legal Representation
Date: March 29, 1999
Attachments:

"Not strictly correct" is putting it mildly, but as you observe, she will take the letter in the proper spirit. You realize, of course, it won't work; in fact, it will only confirm her decision. What she likes is your sensibility; that's what she's buying. The only way I see for you to get out of it is to say that you don't want to do it, that you hate civil cases, and I would be extremely reluctant to have you say that flat out—especially in print. You can understand; we don't want to be known as a law firm with uncivil anti-civil law lawyers.

You can let the letter go as it is—or you could rewrite it in so formal, legalistic, and stilted a style that Mrs. Durkheim would not find you so appealing, so charming. I'm not sure it would work, but it might have a better shot. I leave it to you.

II. ORDERS/DISCOVERY

April 2, 1999

Anne Sophie Diehl
Traynor, Hand, Wyzanski
222 Church Street
New Salem, NA 06555

Dear Ms. Diehl (Sophie?):

It used to be my mail consisted entirely of bills, catalogues, and *The New Yorker*. Yesterday's post brought your letter, a letter from your colleague Ms. McGregor, and a letter from Ray Kahn of K&B, which includes a Notice of Automatic Court Orders. I enclose for your information (and edification) Ms. McGregor's letter (a follow-up on yours) and the K&B letter. Apparently I was supposed to respond to his summons and complaint on or before March 8 (20 days after the summons). Because I didn't do that, Daniel is closing out our joint checking account.

You will already have grasped that I want to stick with you as my attorney—so long as you are willing, or not completely unwilling. I know you'd rather do your murders, but my case shouldn't take that much of your time. I don't care that you're inexperienced. I know the firm will see that I am well represented; and as I said earlier, I don't mind paying double if that's what it takes. (I suggest David Greaves over Ms. McGregor, but it's your call.)

Do I need to see you next week, or can you respond to the K&B letter without my input? (Apropos the Automatic Court Order #1, can I sell Daniel's Audi to pay your attorney's fees?) I am putting together the financials you asked for. Jane and I are planning to go away the week of April 11 to visit friends in Hawaii, unless you advise against it. I don't think Dan would change the locks on us. He loves Jane, and he doesn't want to look bad. If he locks us out, he knows my father will call the dean of the medical school and the president of the hospital and maybe even the director of the NIH. He never liked Daniel but he held his dislike in check. No longer. I'm holding him back now. I haven't told him about this second grenade from K&B. I don't want to bring him in unless (until?) I need to.

Dan said he didn't tell K&B to serve the summons at Golightly's; it was their idea. "But they're *your* lawyers," I said. He shrugged. We are barely talking to each other; instead we leave notes. My latest is in the packet. He has set himself up in a guest bedroom and put in a new phone line to that room. I think it's for calls to Dr. Stephanie. I picked up the receiver once when he was out, and the party on the other end hung up. Where does love go?

I took your letter in the spirit you intended it.

Yours truly,

Mia Durkheim

Mia Durkheim

cc: David Greaves

TRAYNOR, HAND, WYZANSKI

222 CHURCH STREET
NEW SALEM, NARRAGANSETT 06555
(393) 876-5678
ATTORNEYS AT LAW

March 31, 1999

Maria M. Durkheim
404 St. Cloud Street
New Salem, NA 06556

Dear Mrs. Durkheim:

I am following up on Sophie Diehl's letter to you on the subject of legal representation by Traynor, Hand, Wyzanski. She sent me a copy. As you know, Sophie was standing in for me at the intake interview. I was in Ireland, visiting my grandparents.

Sophie is not being falsely modest when she advises you to choose another lawyer in the firm. She is a competent criminal lawyer, but she knows nothing, as she herself admits, about civil law and civil procedure, let alone the ins and outs of matrimonial law. I join her in urging you to go with a more experienced practitioner. I've read Sophie's write-up of your interview, and I anticipate problems. Your husband's decision to retain Kahn & Boyle must be seen as a very hostile, very aggressive move; K&B regards any settlement that provides for alimony or child support for children over the age of 18 as a case of bad lawyering.

I stand ready to help in any way I can, as of course do Felix Landau and David Greaves. All three of us have extensive experience with separation, divorce, and custody actions. If you'd like to discuss the subject of your representation, I'd be happy to speak with you.

Sincerely yours,

Fiona McGregor

Fiona McGregor

March 30, 1999

Mrs. Maria Durkheim
404 St. Cloud Street
New Salem, NA 06556

Dear Maria:

On February 15, this law firm, on behalf of your husband, Dr. Daniel Durkheim, served you with a Summons and Complaint for Divorce with a Return Date of 20 days, calculated as March 8, 1999. It is now March 30 and we still have not heard from you or your lawyers. Would you please acknowledge receipt of the Summons and Complaint? For your information, we enclose a Notice of Automatic Court Orders and inform you that they have been in effect since the day you were served, a fact independent consultation with counsel will confirm.

We are in the process of drafting a separation and custody agreement. Your husband wishes to conclude the agreement within the statutory 90 days of the Return Date, so that the Interim Decree may issue on day 91, June 7, 1999, and the final decree, the Decree Nisi, may issue 90 days later, on September 6, 1999. Given the substantial economic resources of both you and your husband, we do not anticipate either protracted negotiations or a trial.

In the interest of promoting an early disposition of this matter, Dr. Durkheim is closing your joint checking account as of April 1. Other measures indicating a separation of property may be taken shortly.

We look forward to hearing from you or your attorney.

Sincerely yours,

Ray Kahn

Ray Kahn, Esq.

Commonwealth of Narragansett
Family Court

County: Tyler   **Docket No:** 99-27

Notice of Automatic Court Orders

Daniel E. Durkheim   **Plaintiff**

v.

Maria M. Durkheim   **Defendant**

The following Automatic Orders shall apply to both parties where the plaintiff has filed a complaint of dissolution, legal separation, or annulment against the defendant. The Automatic Orders shall be effective with regard to the plaintiff upon the signing of the complaint and with regard to the defendant upon service and shall remain in place during the pendency of the action, unless terminated, modified, or amended by further order of the courts upon motion of either of the parties. The Return Date for Service in this proceeding is: **March 8, 1999**

1. Neither party shall sell, transfer, encumber, conceal, assign, remove, or in any way dispose of any property individually or jointly held by the parties without the consent of the other party in writing or an order of the court, except in the usual course of business or for customary and usual household expenses or for reasonable attorney fees in connection with this action.
2. Neither party shall incur unreasonable debts hereafter, including but not limited to further borrowing against any credit line secured by the family residence, further encumbrancing any assets, or unreasonably using credit cards or cash advances against credit cards.
3. The parties shall each complete and exchange sworn financial statements by: **April 7, 1999** (or 30 days after the Return Date). The parties may thereafter enter and submit to the court a stipulated order allocating income and expenses, in accord with the Uniform Child Support Guidelines.

4. The Case Management Date for this case is: **May 7, 1999** (no earlier than 60 days after the Return Date). If custody or visitation is contested or if any financial issues are disputed, the parties must agree to a schedule of discovery deadlines or appear with their attorney in court on the Case Management Date.

5. Neither party shall permanently remove the minor child or children from the Commonwealth of Narragansett, without written consent of the other or order of the court.

6. The parties, if they have a minor child or children, shall participate in the Parent Education Program before: **May 7, 1999** (60 days of the Return Date).

7. Neither party shall cause the other party or the children of the marriage to be removed from any medical, hospital, and dental insurance coverage, and each party shall maintain the existing medical, hospital, and dental insurance coverage in full force and effect.

8. Neither party shall change the beneficiaries of any existing life insurance policies, and each party shall maintain the existing life insurance, automobile insurance, and homeowner's or renter's insurance policies in full force and effect.

9. If the parties are living together on the date of service of these orders, neither party may deny the other party use of the current primary residence of the parties, whether it be owned or rented property, without court order.

10. If the parents of minor children live apart during a divorce or dissolution proceeding, they shall assist their children in having contact with both parties, which is consistent with the habits of the family, personally, by telephone, and in writing.

By Order of the Court

Failure to obey these Orders may be punishable by contempt of court. If you object to or seek modification of these orders during the pendency of the action, you have the right to a hearing before a judge within a reasonable time.

Filed: **February 15, 1999**

4/2/99

Dear Danny—

I got a letter yesterday from that pig of a lawyer you've hired. Was it Mr. Kahn's idea to close the checking account, or did you think of that all by yourself? You're in a great hurry to be rid of me. I have hired lawyers and you shall hear from them shortly.

In his letter, Mr. Kahn addressed me as Maria. If he does it again (or calls me Mia), I won't sit down in a room with the two of you and negotiate. I am perfectly willing to go to trial. Do you know how long the backlog is? 26 to 30 months, I was told.

Jane and I are going to Hawaii next week.

In faithful abidance of the Automatic Orders.

M.

TRAYNOR, HAND, WYZANSKI

222 CHURCH STREET
NEW SALEM, NARRAGANSETT 06555
(393) 876-5678

MEMORANDUM
Attorney Work Product

From:	Sophie Diehl
To:	David Greaves
RE:	Matter of Durkheim
Date:	April 5, 1999
Attachments:	Acceptance of Service (draft)
	Notice of Appearance (draft)
	Answer (draft)
	Certificate of Service (draft)
	Letter to Maria Durkheim from Ray Kahn
	Notice of Automatic Orders
	Note to Daniel Durkheim from Maria Durkheim

I've drafted the official documents (the Acceptance of Service, the Notice of Appearance, the Answer, and the Certificate of Service) using office forms. At the end of the Answer, I ask the Court to dismiss the action? Is that right? What does that mean? In a criminal case, if the case is dismissed, the prisoner goes free—until they re-indict. In a divorce, if the case is dismissed, the parties remain incarcerated. I will never get the hang of this.

Mrs. Durkheim forwarded to me a letter, dated March 30, from her husband's shyster lawyer, Ray Kahn. It included a belated copy of the Notice of Automatic Orders, which should have gone out with the summons and complaint, and legal advice, which he shouldn't have given to his client's wife, on the effect of those Orders. Can I tell Mr. Kahn that his deadlines all have to be pushed back because Mrs. Durkheim didn't receive the Orders until April 1? Can I tell him he shouldn't give her legal advice?

On April 1, Dr. Durkheim closed out the checking account he had with his wife. By my reading of Automatic Order # 1, he shouldn't have done that without her written consent. Do I make a fuss about it? (Mrs. Durkheim didn't sound upset about it—though she did send her husband a saber-rattling note in return. I didn't know American WASPs were so explosive. There might be an audience out there for her Collected Letters.)

What I don't get about civil litigation is the relative importance of things. In a criminal case, we fight tooth and nail over everything. It's all trees, no forest. You never know what will persuade the jury or the judge to go your way. Is it the same here? Do I challenge everything the other side does? Do I bury them in motions and contempt orders? What do I let slide? What do I insist on?

Dr. Durkheim's strategy seems to be to starve his wife into submission, so to speak, by closing the checking account and generally shutting off the funds. Should we make a motion for temporary support? Should I garnish his salary? Can you imagine how enraged he would be if we got a court order against him withholding temporary child support and alimony from his hospital salary? The thought of it makes me light-headed and giddy.

Kahn says in his letter that he is preparing an offer. Isn't that a bit premature? Formal discovery hasn't begun. Is Kahn assuming that he can proceed because Mrs. Durkheim has handled the family finances during the marriage? What do we do about possible hidden assets? Do we need to hire a private investigator? (Query: Are men who mess around more or less likely to hide assets than men who don't mess around? Are the two pathologies related?)

Kahn also says in his letter that he doesn't expect the negotiations to be complicated or protracted in light of both parties' "substantial economic resources." Is that code for no alimony? I can understand a marriage ending; what I can't understand is the way people end it. Doesn't the doctor recognize any obligation to his wife? She left New York and gave up her job, her friends, her 4 rms riv vu so he could take his great big job at Mather. My mother always says, never make sacrifices for your husband or children; they hold it against you forever. I say we ask for seven fat years of alimony, to compensate for the seven lean years she spent in New Salem. This may be known as the Pharaoh's Dream doctrine of divorce.

Mrs. Durkheim says her husband wants the St. Cloud Street house. I anticipate he will offer to give up any claims he might have to the Martha's Vineyard house in return. That strikes me as untenable. He has no claim to the Vineyard house. First of all, Mrs. Durkheim inherited her share of the house before her marriage. Second, she and her father hold the house in trust as tenants in the entirety, which means neither can sell or otherwise transfer his or her share to anyone else; the survivor takes all. If the doctor wants a share, he'll have to stick it out until his father-in-law dies. Correct?

Commonwealth of Narragansett
Family Court

County: Tyler   **Docket No:** 99-27

Acceptance of Service
Domestic Relations Summons

Daniel E. Durkheim   **Plaintiff**

v.

Maria M. Durkheim   **Defendant**

I, the above-named defendant: Maria M. Durkheim accept service of this summons and understand that judgment may be rendered against me in accordance with the complaint, a copy of which I have received:
Date: April 5, 1999
Signature of Defendant: Maria M. Durkheim

The above-name defendant: Maria M. Durkheim
swears that the acceptance of service was his free act and deed.
Date: April 5, 1999
Notary Public: Hannah Smith, Traynor, Hand, Wyzanski
Signature of Notary Public: Hannah Smith
Commission Expiration Date: November 1, 2001

Notice of Appearance
Complaint for Divorce

The above-named defendant: Maria M. Durkheim has retained as attorneys in this action:

David Greaves and Anne Sophie Diehl
Traynor, Hand, Wyzanski
222 Church Street
New Salem, NA 06555

Date: April 5, 1999
Signature of defendant: Maria M. Durkheim
Signature of attorney: Anne Sophie Diehl

Commonwealth of Narragansett
Family Court

County: Tyler   **Docket No:** 99-27

Answer to Complaint for Divorce

Daniel E. Durkheim   **Plaintiff**

v.

Maria M. Durkheim   **Defendant**

Now comes defendant Maria M. Durkheim **by her attorneys, and answers plaintiff's complaint for divorce, dated** February 15, 1999 **as follows:**

1. Defendant admits the allegations contained in Paragraphs 1, 2, 3 and 4.
2. Defendant does not have sufficient information to admit or deny the allegations contained in Paragraph 5 and leaves plaintiff to his proof.
3. Wherefore, defendant requests that this Court dismiss plaintiff's complaint and order plaintiff to pay her attorney's fees and costs necessitated to defend this action.

The defendant, by her attorneys,
Traynor, Hand, Wyzanski
222 Church Street
New Salem, NA 06555
(393) 876-5678

Signature of Attorney: Anne Sophie Diehl, Traynor, Hand, Wyzanski

Date: April 5, 1999

Certificate of Service

I, Anne Sophie Diehl, Esquire, **hereby certify that on the** 5th **day of** April 1999, **I caused a copy of the foregoing defendant's answer to plaintiff's complaint for divorce to be served on plaintiff's attorney by mailing a copy, first class, postage prepaid, to:** Ray Kahn, 46 Broadway, New Salem, NA 06555.

Signature of attorney: Anne Sophie Diehl, Traynor, Hand, Wyzanski

TRAYNOR, HAND, WYZANSKI

222 CHURCH STREET
NEW SALEM, NARRAGANSETT 06555
(393) 876-5678

MEMORANDUM
Attorney Work Product

From: David Greaves
To: Sophie Diehl
RE: Matter of Durkheim
Date: April 5, 1999
Attachments: *Martins v. Martins*, 224 Nar. 887 (1955)

Sophie—

The good news is: you're hooked on the case; you're asking the right questions; you're thinking like a divorce lawyer. Also, you did an excellent job with the intake. That's the good news.

The bad news is: you're free-associating in your memo, if you can call it a memo; you may be thinking like a lawyer, but you're writing like a self-indulgent alternative-newspaper feature writer. I understand that you are looking for help; this is all new to you. But you aren't a legal neophyte. You can ask questions in an orderly way. You need to get a grip, Sophie.

Re ¶1. The official documents are fine. The reason you ask the court to dismiss the action in the Answer is because (1) Mrs. Durkheim didn't concede that the marriage was irretrievably broken; and (2) you didn't file a cross complaint on behalf of Mrs. Durkheim against her husband. The logical conclusion, then, is that she doesn't want a divorce, on either his terms or hers. Hence, she wants the marriage to continue. Of course, the marriage can't continue if her husband is determined to get a divorce, so her Answer asking for a dismissal is a combination stalling action and warning shot to the other side.

Re ¶2. In your letter to Kahn, you could mention that the Notice of Automatic Orders should have been sent with the summons, but I'm not sure how much mileage you can get out of it. I don't think you can push back the deadlines, since Mrs. Durkheim was instructed to respond to the summons and complaint by the Return Date and the Return Date is the date that triggers the deadlines. As for the legal advice he offered on the effect of the Automatic Orders, instead of reprimanding him, you might point out that they apply to his client as well. See notes below to ¶3. You can tell him that in the future, all correspondence should be sent to you and not to Mrs. Durkheim.

Re ¶3. Although he could simply have withdrawn all the funds or stopped making deposits, Dr. Durkheim should not have closed out the bank account without his wife's consent. You should tell Mr. Kahn that if Dr. Durkheim does anything like that again (Kahn says in his letter that his client will take "other measures indicating a separation of property"), you will bring a contempt motion. This threat will let K&B know that you will not be pushed around. A contempt motion, even if it failed, would slow things down. And slowing things down is a way for Mrs. Durkheim to exercise leverage. Also, if Dr. Durkheim continues to take "measures indicating a separation of property" as a way to spur his wife on, he puts himself in the wrong in the event negotiations break down and the case goes before a judge. Our judges don't like it when parties flagrantly violate the Automatic Orders. Mrs. Durkheim's note to her husband doesn't surprise me. Haven't you read Cheever? We WASPs are perfectly capable of behaving badly, explosively, especially when we're drunk but not exclusively.

Re ¶4. In a divorce, the lawyer's job is to get the best agreement she can for her client. This means that you and Mrs. Durkheim must sit down and decide the bottom line. What does she need or want in terms of spousal support, child support, savings, property, etc. What is the least she will accept. What will she give up in exchange for other things she wants or needs. In many divorces, the parties fight over very small things—the talismans of the relationship. Keep your eye on the big picture, the forest. Your greatest advantage is Dr. Durkheim's sense of urgency. He wants it done with. He also, apparently, wants the house, which gives you another strong negotiating tool.

Re ¶5. You might ask Mr. Kahn what arrangements Dr. Durkheim, as the family's primary breadwinner (so old-fashioned a term these days), has made for paying household and other expenses, such as his daughter's school fees, credit card debt, and the like. As things now stand, Dr. Durkheim doesn't have to give his wife an allowance or any spending money, though she can withdraw funds, as can he, from their joint and separate accounts. Until one of them moves out or Mrs. Durkheim makes a motion for temporary support, Dr. Durkheim's obligation is solely to provide the necessities. I refer you to *Martins v. Martins*, 224 Nar. 887 (1955), which despite its advanced age still provides the governing rule *so long as spouses are living together, even if they are sleeping apart*. I attach a copy of that case. I suspect that Dr. Durkheim's next move, on advice of counsel, will be to close the joint credit card accounts and dismiss the housekeeper. This will serve two purposes: (1) it will, as you say, "starve her out"; and (2) it will establish a low threshold of support, one that includes only the necessities. If he does that, you will have to bring a contempt motion, to let him know that you will not allow him to dictate terms this way. You might want to begin drafting such a motion, to have it on hand to wave in front of Kahn. You might also contemplate making a motion for temporary support—or at least let Kahn know you are contemplating such a motion. Kahn is a bully and a coward, and he hates to lose. He won't go to court unless he thinks he will win—or unless his client insists. If you are very clear in your first letter about what you will and will not accept, he will get the message. His manner will remain aggressive and offensive, but his position will be flexible—if only so as to insure that at the end he will look like he's won. Throw him a sop; give him a small victory at a crucial juncture, like the house perhaps. Lose a battle, win the war.

Re ¶6. My guess is Kahn is preparing a lowball offer, his idea of a warning shot. He is free to do it anytime he wants to, and we are free to ignore it until discovery is completed, which we may or may not want to do. We may have to bring in a private investigator but not yet. Let's wait and see what information they turn over during discovery. The firm has one on retainer. (You'll like him; he's out of Damon Runyon, the kind of man a criminal lawyer properly appreciates. And he'll love you. Civil law cases pay his bills; criminal cases make his heart race.) (Answer to Query: In my experience, adulterers do not hide assets more than other men. And only hiding assets is pathological; adultery is normal.)

Re ¶7. Of course, Mrs. Durkheim should ask for alimony, or spousal support as it is also called. The law does not expect the wealthy parents of a woman to support her after divorce. Your seven-year figure has a kind of compelling logic; by accompanying her husband, she lost not only sub-stantial income but also the opportunity for career and salary advance-ment. In her current state, with an M.Phil., she is not readily employable as a university instructor, and her current salary, after taxes, wouldn't even pay the rent of a two-bedroom apartment in New Salem. The ques-tion is: How much money does she have? I'm relying here on the intake interview, so the figures are rough. Both she and her husband have been receiving $10,000/year from her father. After 16 years, that should be with interest at least $300,000 each. Kahn might propose transferring to her Dr. Durkheim's gift fund, which would give her a total of $600,000+ (I'm guessing here; there's probably a good deal more), and forgoing alimony. At a conservative 8% a year, she would have $48,000/year, which the court, with child support, might consider adequate, though not at the level she was accustomed to. There's $900,000 in their various accounts (not including his pension or the 401[k]), so if she got back her father's money, he'd still have some savings. I'm not recommending this—but identifying it as a possible bottommost bottom-line position. Of course, she should get half the pension fund and half the 401(k) in addition.

The thing about alimony, which Dr. Durkheim might find attractive, is that it's tax deductible to him, the payer, and taxable to his wife, the payee. Child support, on the other hand, is not tax deductible to the payer and in essence constitutes tax-free income to the payee. Prepare yourself for an offer with a low child support payment and some alimony to make up the difference. I can see them offering, say, $3,000/month in child support and $3,000/month in alimony. Mrs. Durkheim would do better with all $6,000 in child support, not only because of the tax considerations but also because of the later cutoff date. Dr. Durkheim will probably offer alimony only for three years, long enough for Mrs. Durkheim to get her Ph.D. Child support would run at least seven years, until Jane was 18. One last thing, the more money Mrs. Durkheim gets up front, the better off she is. Something like 70% of ex-husbands stop paying some if not all of their alimony and child support obligations at some point, and very, very few pay to the end. Ex-husbands don't like paying their ex-wives, even if the money is for their children.

Re ¶8. Under Narragansett law, the Vineyard house is considered separate property. Mrs. Durkheim acquired it prior to her marriage. It is hers and hers alone, whether the tenancy is joint, in common, or in the entirety, whether it is owned in trust or outright. Mrs. Durkheim could of course voluntarily transfer an interest to her husband upon her father's death, but no court would compel her. A legacy received during a marriage, such as the Honda Dr. Durkheim inherited on the death of his parents, is also considered separate property, though the rule is not so ironclad. We can be sports here. We'll let him keep the car and also the $16,000 his parents left him. At this point, we should not bring up the Vineyard house. Let them bring it up. And they will.

Mrs. Durkheim cc'ed me on her letter. I shall speak to Fiona.

I have spent the last hour dictating this memo; it will probably take Hannah another 30 minutes to type it up. Then I'll have to proof it; that's another 15 minutes. We—I, that is—may have to swallow some of the cost. I shall see you are fully credited for the time you spend on the case. Since your time is cheaper than mine, think things through before committing pen to paper. The more disorganized your memos, the longer it will take me to respond to them.

No. 55-228
Martins v. Martins
Supreme Court of Narragansett
224 Nar. 887 (1955)

Cutler, Ch.J., delivered the opinion of the Court.

The issue before this Court goes to the heart of marriage and to the proper role of the State in regulating domestic relations between a husband and his wife. We have been asked by the parties here to determine the support obligations a husband owes the woman he is married to and living with. It is an issue with enormous ramifications bearing on the autonomy of the marital household and the privacy of the marital relationship.

Leo and Letitia Martins have been married for 39 years. They live three miles outside Pemberton in Berks County. Mr. Martins is 68 years old, his wife is 62. They have two grown children who are married and living in other states. Three years ago, Mr. Martins retired from National Construction, where he worked for 44 years as an electrician. Mrs. Martins has never worked outside the home. Mr. Martins receives an annual pension of $5,200 from National and an additional $2,600 from the Social Security Administration. His savings account at the Central Bay Bank has $9,000, earning 3% annual interest.

The Martins live in their own home purchased for $3,000 the year they were married. Title is in Mr. Martins's name. He owns it free and clear, the mortgage having been paid off more than 15 years ago. Built in 1905, it is a two-story dwell-ing with an erratic coal furnace and an outside latrine, both of which are original to the house.

Most of the features of the house date to its construction, the notable exceptions being electrical lighting on the first floor and hot water, which is heated by a wood-burning kitchen stove, purchased at a sale close-out in 1930, six months after the Crash. There are no electrical outlets. They do not have a refrigerator—they have an icebox, perhaps the last extant one in Berks County—and their only radio is a shortwave radio constructed by their son for a Boy Scout badge. By current American standards, the house is primitive. Its current value, owing to its state of disrepair, is less than the original purchase price, though the land it sits on, 17 acres of prime farmland, was recently valued at $8,500.

The Martins do not farm the land but rent out the larger fields to a neighboring farmer. The rents bring in an additional $1,200 a year. Mrs. Martins raises chickens for their eggs, which she sells from a farm stand on the property. Her monthly net earnings from the eggs are approximately $20, which constitute her only discretionary income. Over the years, she has saved $1,400, which she keeps in a savings account, earning 3.5% interest, at Union Bank.

The furnishings are in keeping with the house. The marital bed, now occupied only by Mr. Martins, was purchased by the couple the year they married. The other furnishings were bought at fire sales and local auction houses during the Depression.

In 1952, Mrs. Martins underwent abdominal surgery, which was paid for under Mr. Martins's Major Medical Blue Cross policy. Through his union, the International Brotherhood of Electrical Workers, Mr. Martins pays $10 a month for this policy, which covers both him and his wife. Their other expenses for medical care, except for their spectacles, which Mr. Martins buys for both of them, have been negligible. Neither of the Martinses has visited a dentist in the last 15 years.

Mr. Martins owns a 1940 Buick. He does the maintenance on the vehicle. On Sundays, he drives Mrs. Martins to Bethesda Methodist Church for Sabbath worship. Twice a month, he drives her to the local A&P to buy groceries. At Christmastime, he drives her to Massachusetts so that she can visit with their daughter and son. She stays a week with each. Mr. Martins does not participate in these visits, not being on speaking terms with either of his children.

Other than her egg money, Mrs. Martins has no income of any sort of her own. For the last several years, during her annual visit to Massachusetts, her daughter has bought her either a pair of shoes or a dress. Mrs. Martins owns one coat, which is more than 15 years old, and one purse of indeterminate vintage. Twice a year, winter and summer, Mr. Martins gives Mrs. Martins $20 and takes her to the Salvation Army Thrift Store to purchase clothes, including undergarments and sleepwear.

Mrs. Martins moved out of the marital bedroom five years ago and now sleeps in the bedroom formerly occupied by their children. She has repeatedly asked her husband to make improvements in the house and to buy her clothes. He has consistently refused. They have not been to a motion picture or other entertainment palace in more than 12 years. They have not taken a vacation in 25 years. They do not belong to any clubs or benevolent associations and do not visit with friends or entertain in their own home but appear to live parallel, solitary lives.

Mrs. Martins is a conscientious housekeeper and homemaker. Her domestic duties are heavy and onerous, owing to the absence of such modern conveniences as a washing machine, clothes dryer, and vacuum cleaner. Despite a bad back, she spends more than 50 hours a week cleaning and cooking, and it is only through her efforts, which might be fairly likened to Hercules's labors in the Augean stables, that the couple is kept from living in absolute squalor. Mr. Martins does no work at all around the house or garden, having declared to his wife that he is in retirement.

In September 1953, Mrs. Martins, at the urging of her children, brought suit against her husband in Narragansett Superior Court to compel him to buy a new furnace, install an inside toilet, and purchase for her a new coat, hat, scarf, and overshoes. She also asked the Court to order him to pay her an allowance of $20 a month for personal items and expenses. The Superior Court granted her request and ordered Mr. Martins to pay his wife a single lump sum of $1,500 for the purchase and installation of a new furnace and toilet and $4 a week spending money. The Appellate Court affirmed. We reverse.

In *Dupuis v. Dupuis*, 202 Nar. 576 (1933), a wife sued her husband for failure to provide her with household goods and amenities. Although the circumstances of her existence were not so grim as those recounted here, they are similar enough for us to recognize its ruling as the governing precedent. Mrs. Dupuis wanted money to install a new refrigerator in place of a 19th-century icebox, to purchase new bedclothes and linens, and to buy a new sofa, the old one having collapsed. She also asked the Court to order her husband to repair the family automobile, which had two missing side windows and a broken heater. The Court rejected her suit and set out the rule, which today we apply again.

> However much we might deplore the miserliness of Mr. Dupuis, we cannot do what his wife asks. A husband is obliged to provide the necessities of existence, which the law defines as adequate food, clothing, and shelter and reasonable medical attention. He need not provide more, no matter his income or savings. It is not the Court's business to dictate the appropriate standard of living, only the minimum below which no woman should be expected to live. Where the husband has met this minimal standard and where the marriage bond between the couple is maintained and he has not abandoned her or she him, the Court will not substitute its judgment for that of the household. *Dupuis v. Dupuis*, 202 Nar. at 580.

As in *Dupuis*, we too deplore the miserliness of the husband/breadwinner, but personal feelings cannot provide the governing standard. While Mrs. Martins has fled the marital bedroom, she has remained beneath the marital roof and expressed no wish or interest in obtaining either a legal separation or divorce. Nor for that matter has Mr. Martins, and there is no evidence that conjugal rupture is the reason for his iron grasp on the purse strings or her suit to loose it. Minimal as it is, Mr. Martins has provided his wife with adequate food, shelter, and clothing and reasonable medical care. So long as their marriage continues and so long as he continues to provide to his wife these bare "necessities of existence," the Court will not interfere with their domestic financial arrangements. In accord *Commonwealth v. George*, 358 Pa. 118, 56 A.2d 228 (1948); *McGuire v. McGuire*, 157 Neb. 226, 59 N.W.2d 336 (1953).

There is hardly a married couple in this country who does not have disagreements over money. In the absence of proof of neglect or desertion, the Court must leave them to their own devices. The sanctity of marriage demands no less; as the State will not intrude into a couple's bedroom or bathroom, so it must not take over the checkbook. The case is reversed and remanded.

Parisier, J., Lawler, J., Bauer, J., Pritchard, J., Gordon, J., and Cabolis, J., join this opinion.

* * *

Narragansett Statutes
Title 33 of the Narragansett Code, Sections 801ff.
Dissolution of Marriage, Annulment, and Legal Separation

Sec. 832. Alimony (also known as Maintenance or Spousal Support).

The Narragansett Family Court may order either of the parties to pay alimony (also known as maintenance or spousal support) to the other. In determining whether alimony shall be awarded, and the duration and amount of the award, the court shall consider the length of the marriage, the causes for the dissolution, legal separation, or annulment of the marriage, the age, health, station, occupation, earning capacity, amount and sources of income, vocational skills, employability, property, liabilities, and needs of each of the parties, and the opportunity of each for future acquisition of capital assets and income.

Sec. 834. Parents' obligation for maintenance of minor child.

(a) The parents of a minor child of the marriage shall maintain the child according to their respective abilities.

(b) If there is an unmarried child of the marriage who has attained the age of eighteen (18), is a full-time high school student, and resides with a parent, the parents shall maintain the child according to their respective abilities until the child completes the twelfth grade or attains the age of nineteen (19), whichever first occurs.

(c) In determining the respective abilities of the parents to provide maintenance, the court shall consider the age, health, station, occupation, earning capacity, amount and sources of income, property, vocational skills, and employability of each of the parents, and the age, health, station, occupation, educational status and expectation, amount and sources of income, vocational skills, employability, property, and needs of the child.

Chagrin

From: Sophie Diehl   4/5/99 5:54 PM
To: Maggie Pfeiffer <mcp15@mather.edu>
Date: Mon, 5 Apr 1999 17:54:22
Subject: Chagrin

Maggie—

I am so embarrassed. I wrote a rambling, incoherent memo on the
divorce to David, and he blasted me for "free-associating." He told me
to "get a grip." I don't know how I'm going to face him. I feel like such
a jerk. I'm so used to writing to Joe, who's tolerant of my style—his
own being not so different. Joe and I write memos that are the written
equivalent of thinking aloud. It works for us. David actually said I should
think before I write. Another reason to hate civil litigation. I imagined
this assignment would be demoralizing but not in this particularly
humiliating way. Every time I think about it, my stomach turns over.

I've only seen Harry once in the last week, and only for a quick coffee
on Wednesday; our schedules are not compatible—no one's schedule
is compatible with mine at the moment. He did send me an email,
however. There is a fabulous economy to his wooing style. It works
for me. The Trilling case is taking all my time, but I still have to do this
damn divorce. (That free-association memo took over an hour, whatever
David thinks.) I billed 70 hours last week. (I actually worked 85 hours
last week—it's never all billable—and last Thursday I put in 20 hours.)
If I keep up at this level, I'll bill 3,000 in the year. This has to stop. This
is New Salem, for heaven's sake, not New York.

I've emailed Joe and David to say I needed the coming weekend off.
I begin to regret I introduced David to email. Last weekend he sent me
two. My plan is to go to your opening on Friday and then sleep for the
next two days—or at least stay in bed. I wonder if I'll have a sleepover.
Another thing to give me a jittery stomach. It must be nice to be
married. Is it?

THE DIVORCE PAPERS (Page 105)

Maman's coming in Thursday night, by herself. Jake has to work Friday, patients. I understand: I'd be annoyed if my shrink took off for a long weekend. All of August is bad enough. He sends his regrets. I'm thinking of inviting David to have lunch with me and Maman on Friday, instead of apologizing. What do you think? I don't think he knows who she is. He's never said anything. Maybe he's never heard of her. (Is that possible?) He probably doesn't read mysteries—though I thought everyone smart read mysteries.

What do you think?

Love,
S.

Hello

From: Harry Mortensen   4/4/99 3:01 AM
To: Sophie Diehl <asdiehl@traynor.com>
Date: Sun, 4 Apr 1999 3:01:22
Subject: Hello

Sweet Sophie—Where are you? Why aren't you here?

Harry

From: Maggie Pfeiffer   4/5/99 11:33 PM
To: Sophie Diehl <asdiehl@traynor.com>
Date: Mon, 5 Apr 1999 23:33:19
Subject: Re: Chagrin

Dear Sophie—

Just apologize to David, straight out. Tell him you're sorry about the
memo. Explain it as a bad habit you've fallen into doing criminal
law. Tell him all the cowboys do it. Tell him it's another reason you
shouldn't be doing this divorce. Then swear it will never happen again
and it will be behind you. From everything you've ever said about
David, he's already moved on.

You should invite David to lunch with your mother. I'd like to see
those two together—the gods of your life squaring off. Maybe they'll
spontaneously combust in each other's presence.

The cast party will be at the Rink. Bring your mother—or not. Maybe
not. Drama students tend to misbehave dramatically. There might be
some things going on that she should be shielded from—for your sake,
not hers. It's an insider's party. And I don't think you want to introduce
her to Harry quite yet.

I can't say I'd recommend marriage across the board—having seen
some pretty rotten ones—but being married to Matt is better than
anything I can think of, anything I can imagine. He's wonderful. He
not only puts up with me—and I know I'm a piece of work—he loves
me the way I am. I'm crazy about him. Caveat: he is not perfect, but
I never have wanted to shoot him more than once a week. That may
change; after all, we're still newlyweds.

I'm so tired. I couldn't remember my lines tonight. I've heard that some
NY people will be in the audience on Friday, including Juliet Taylor,
Woody Allen's casting agent. Talk about stomach problems. I haven't
eaten in two days.

Courage, ma chere.
Love,
Maggie

TRAYNOR, HAND, WYZANSKI

222 CHURCH STREET
NEW SALEM, NARRAGANSETT 06555
(393) 876-5678

MEMORANDUM
Attorney Work Product

From:	Sophie Diehl
To:	David Greaves
RE:	Mrs. Maria Durkheim: New Information About the Marriage
Date:	April 6, 1999
Attachments:	Letter

I am writing this on the fly. I've got a ton of things to get done by the end of the day, but I thought you should be informed of some late-breaking developments in the Durkheim divorce. I shall try to be orderly.

Vronsky made his appearance! Late yesterday afternoon, about 5 p.m., a visibly distraught Mia Durkheim appeared in my office, clutching a letter. She said she needed for me to read it right then, in her presence. Of course, I did. I've enclosed the letter with this memo. I was reassuring and told her not to worry; we'd pull out all the stops and protect her and her interests. I told her that divorces get ugly at times—she had to expect that—and that threats, veiled or open, were part of the negotiating process. I did my best to calm her down and send her home in a moderately composed state of mind.

Did I say the right things? I believed them when I said them. Do you think Dr. Durkheim would actually follow through? Or is she panicking needlessly? She had been up the night before writing the letter and only fell asleep after Jane left for school this morning. When she woke up at 4:30, she decided she had to speak with me immediately. She looked so different from the way she had at the interview: older, haggard, depressed, sad, anxious. I felt so bad for her. I hate divorces.

She lied to me during the intake interview, or rather, she left out things she should have told me. I should have known; I never believe my criminal clients—they're always innocent—but she seemed so sane and so frank. I don't think her confession changes anything (does it?), but I'm glad she came clean. I don't like surprises. Do I need to wait for the other shoe to drop? Will there be more confessions, more surprises?

MARIA DURKHEIM
404 ST. CLOUD STREET
NEW SALEM, NA 06556

April 5, 1999

Anne Sophie Diehl
Traynor, Hand, Wyzanski
222 Church Street
New Salem, NA 06555

Dear Sophie:

I was not altogether straight with you at our interview, and now that you are officially my lawyer, I think I have to come clean. My sin is one of omission. I didn't lie to you; I just left something out that probably bears on the case. You asked me if there was another woman in Danny's life, but not if there was another man in mine (were you being kind? or discreet? or did you think I wasn't the sort?)—and so I didn't volunteer the information I will now disclose.

The summer before Danny and I got involved, I was involved with another married man, a French one, considerably older than I, named Jacques Valery, who was a sportswriter at the *New York Globe*. (His marriage was badly frayed—aren't they all?—and I was young, self-centered, and a bit wild.) I broke it off the day after Danny and I went out for the first time. I was already madly in love with him and could see a future for us. There was none with Jacques; he was too old and too encumbered with wife, children, mortgage, cat, the usual suburban flotsam of married life. And he wasn't interested in starting over. He was pure affair material, right down to the accent. In the spring of 1993, about a year and a half after the move to New Salem, I discovered that Jacques was working in Philadelphia for the *Chronicle*. I was wretchedly unhappy and decided to look him up during one of my visits to my sister, Cordelia. He had gotten divorced and remarried, but the new wife was living in New York; he was commuting and, during the three days he stayed in Philly, at loose ends. We had dinner a few times, and then one night we went back to my hotel for a drink. One thing led to another, and before too long, we had resumed the affair. It lasted almost five years. I gave it up last winter; Danny and I were getting along horribly, and I thought perhaps he had gotten wind of it. I now think I sensed Danny was fooling around and I got scared that we would break up. (I was right; it turns out he was starting up with Dr. Stephanie just as I was breaking off with Jacques.)

Danny and I were very happy in the beginning (I have to keep reminding myself of that). I loved listening to him; I loved the way his mind worked, and no one has ever made me laugh the way he did, and probably still could. He could be the best company. Even now sometimes, when I'm reading a book or watching a movie, I'd like to know what he thought about it.

Things started going off after Jane was born. We couldn't seem to make each other happy. I don't know what happened. I think now Danny was jealous of Jane, or of the way I felt about her. I fell in love with her, and he felt displaced, supplanted. He was so used to my admiration, almost as fawning as his parents'. Nancy Reagan had nothing on me.

Do you know that bit from *A Room of One's Own*, where Woolf talks about women serving as looking-glasses with the "magic and delicious power of reflecting the figure of man at twice its natural size." That was my job in the marriage—worship—and for the first ten years, I did it effortlessly, wholeheartedly. I was mad about him. Then I grew up, had a baby, and wanted a marriage with two normal-sized people. Isn't ten years of adoration all a reasonable narcissist has any right to expect from a wife? You'd think the parents of his patients would take up the slack. I saw one of them actually kiss his hand, as if he were the pope. Then there are the letters he gets regularly from them, thanking him for all he does for their children. I'll show you the most recent. He left it on the counter for me to see (no doubt as a rebuke), and Jane too. She cried when she read it. To my credit, I didn't crumple it up and toss it out. I'm inured to these outpourings. I know I shouldn't be so mean and petty about all this. Those parents are utterly sincere, heartbreakingly grateful. And he is truly a first-rate doctor. If only he weren't a third-rate human being.

The last years of our marriage were awful, just awful. After I broke with Jacques, I became terribly depressed and gained 30 pounds. I began to hate Danny. I'd have fantasies when the phone rang late at night and he wasn't home that it was the police calling to say they'd found him in his car wrapped around a telephone pole. I wanted him so much to change, to be what I needed, but there was no way that would happen. He grew to hate me too, I think. He hated living with a depressed woman. If only he could have said to me how much he appreciated what I had done for him, moving to New Salem and putting his life and career first, maybe I could have rallied. But he didn't. And I didn't.

I'm getting scared now that he may decide to go for custody. We had a set-to last night; we ran into each other in the kitchen. I was eating ice cream out of the container and weeping to myself. He looked at me with such disgust. "This isn't good," he said. "Pull yourself together. Stop feeling sorry for yourself. Do you ever think that your self-pity has no effect on Jane? No child should have to grow up under that kind of baleful influence." Baleful! God, he can be so devastatingly mean. Could he win custody? I couldn't bear it.

You've got to help me. I've made a mess of things, but I love Jane more than I can say, and I'm the parent who's raised her. What if he knows about the affair? Could that hurt me in court? I'll give up anything, everything to get custody. Am I being hysterical (it's 2 a.m. and I'm never at my most rational after midnight)? I'll probably feel saner in the morning if I can manage to get some sleep, but at the moment, I'm feeling desperate and so, so scared.

I couldn't have written this to Fiona. Thank you for taking my case.

Yours,

Mia

March 22, 1999

Dear Dr. Durkheim,

When we first saw you in 1996, we had practically given up all hope. All the other doctors told us that Cara wouldn't live a year. She was only 7. Yesterday was her 10th birthday. We went to see A Bug's Life. We all had a great time.

We have made a donation to the hospital in your honor. We'd give a whole wing if we could, and put your name on it. Thank you for taking care of our daughter.

Yours truly,

Cristina Capobianco
Mother of Cara Capobianco

TRAYNOR, HAND, WYZANSKI

222 CHURCH STREET
NEW SALEM, NARRAGANSETT 06555
(393) 876-5678

MEMORANDUM
Attorney Work Product

From:	David Greaves
To:	Sophie Diehl
RE:	Mrs. Maria Durkheim: Letter with New Information
Date:	April 6, 1999
Attachments:	

You said exactly the right things to Mrs. Durkheim. Custody turns on the best interests of the child, which has been interpreted by the Narragansett Supreme Court to mean that in a custody dispute, custody goes to the child's primary caretaker, absent a judicial finding of unfitness. It's an excellent rule; it not only insures continuity of care, it prevents one parent, typically the father, from threatening a custody fight as a means of applying leverage in the settlement negotiations. Most women are willing, as is Mrs. Durkheim, to give up "anything, everything" to secure custody.

There are no grounds for a finding of unfitness here. If weeping and late-night binging were considered adequate grounds for a finding of unfitness, the Primary Caretaker Rule would have no effect at all. Everyone getting a divorce feels sorry for himself, unless he feels self-righteous. I've come to believe that self-righteousness is simply a protective mechanism against self-pity (usually male) and the terrible sense of vulnerability that accompanies it. As for her omission, you shouldn't have been surprised. All clients, even well-dressed, well-spoken ones, lie to their lawyers. They want you to like them, to take their side. There may be more surprises, but if she's still holding anything back, it's more likely she's suffering from memory lapse or thinking the information unimportant rather than intentionally hiding something.

Dr. Durkheim probably believes what he said about his wife's "baleful influence," but I don't think he really wants physical custody, and he certainly doesn't want a long, drawn-out battle, which a formal custody hearing would entail. We could tie him up for at least two years. I know how to do that and I'll teach you if it becomes necessary. This being said, it doesn't mean that Dr. Durkheim won't sue for custody or, more likely, threaten to sue as a means of applying leverage, rule or no rule. He knows his wife is vulnerable on this point. This divorce could get very ugly. If anyone other than Ray Kahn were Dr. Durkheim's lawyer, I'd call him up and express our intentions to be reasonable. Kahn thinks if you make that kind of overture, you're weak.

You might follow up with a note to Mrs. Durkheim enclosing a copy of the Narragansett case *Paynter v. Paynter*, setting out the Primary Caretaker Rule. I don't have the cite, but it's about 10 years old. It should reassure her, as should the Narragansett child custody statute, which provides in relevant part: "The court shall not consider conduct of a proposed custodian that does not affect his relationship to the child." That goes for adultery and baleful behavior both.

An Apology and an Invitation

From: Sophie Diehl   4/6/99 10:14 AM
To: David Greaves <dagreaves@traynor.com>
Date: Tue, 6 Apr 1999 10:14:58
Subject: An Apology and an Invitation

Dear David:

Thanks for getting back to me on Mrs. D's letter. I'll write her a note and send her the *Paynter* case.

I am very sorry about my rambling memo; I've fallen into bad habits riding shotgun with the gang on the second floor. It won't happen again. I'll save memos like that for Joe.

I'd like to make it up to you. Would you like to have lunch on Friday with me and my mother, Elisabeth Dreyfus, a.k.a. Elisabeth Diehl? I'm betting you two would like each other. She's funny and smart and beautiful, too. She went to law school (after getting a Ph.D. in English) but never practiced. She's a mystery writer, pretty famous and admired. She wrote her first novel when she was pregnant with my brother Remy and put on bed rest. You may know it: *A Gun in the First Act*. After that, there was *The Scottish Play* (she—and I—wouldn't want you to think the Ph.D. didn't come in handy). I was thinking of going to Porter's. I have a friend who's a member, and he'll let me use his charge. I don't think she's ever been there—like me, she's unclubbable. There's no point taking her to one of the local chichi places. New Salem can't compete with the food she's used to eating in New York, so I say we go for the Dink Stover atmosphere. And those double lamb chops are pretty impressive.

I'm free-associating again. (It's a side effect of email correspondence, which unfortunately leaks into other modes of writing. Just wait.) Sorry.

Sophie

Re: An Apology and an Invitation

From: David Greaves

4/6/99 12:45 PM

To: Sophie Diehl <asdiehl@traynor.com>

Date: Tue, 6 Apr 1999 12:45:09

Subject: Re: An Apology and an Invitation

Dear Sophie—

Apology accepted.

Is your mother *the* Elisabeth Diehl; I never made the connection. But of course, it makes sense. I remember you saying you were raised up in the criminal courts. I assumed your father was the lawyer; a law professor lawyer. Serves me right. I'm a fan. I particularly liked *A Murder of Crows*, and of course, *A Gun in the First Act*.

I'd like very much to have lunch with you and your mother on Friday. You called her Elisabeth Dreyfus. What name does she go by?

I am a member of Porter's. If you'd allow me, I'd like you two to be my guests.

You should have a meeting with Mrs. D before she takes off for Hawaii. There's the addendum to the retainer to talk about, and you need to start thinking about an offer. You could also reassure her once again on custody.

David

TRAYNOR, HAND, WYZANSKI

222 CHURCH STREET
NEW SALEM, NARRAGANSETT 06555
(393) 876-5678

MEMORANDUM
Attorney Work Product

From: David Greaves
To: Fiona McGregor
RE: Matter of Durkheim
Date: April 6, 1999
Attachments:

Your letter to Maria Durkheim was out of line. It challenges my authority as Managing Partner, it undermines the values and the reputation of the firm, and it puts at risk important business relationships. Mrs. Durkheim sent a copy of your letter to me. I will keep this matter between us, and not bring it up at the Management Meeting next week, but I'd like assurances from you that this kind of behavior will not be repeated.

TRAYNOR, HAND, WYZANSKI

222 CHURCH STREET
NEW SALEM, NARRAGANSETT 06555
(393) 876-5678

MEMORANDUM
Attorney Work Product

From: Sophie Diehl
To: David Greaves
RE: Matter of Durkheim
Date: April 6, 1999
Attachments: Letter to Ray Kahn, Esq.

I've written a very rough draft of a letter to Ray Kahn in response to his letter of March 30, 1999, to Mrs. Durkheim. I've incorporated all of your suggestions, with two exceptions. (1) I said outright that Dr. Durkheim violated the Automatic Orders by closing the joint checking account and that we would not put up with that kind of behavior again. (2) Instead of asking Kahn to ask Dr. Durkheim how he intends to pay the bills, I would like to have Mrs. Durkheim transfer the $80,000 currently sitting in their joint savings account to an individual checking account in her name at a different bank. My letter would then inform Kahn, after the fact, that the transfer had been made and threaten a contempt motion if Dr. Durkheim took any further steps to "indicat[e] a separation of property." Anything less subtle is wasted on Kahn. Please let me know what you think of these modifications and also what other changes you would suggest. The letter should go out today. We are 30 days past the Return Date, and the financials are due tomorrow. We, of course, won't get ours in, and I don't think theirs will be ready either, but I'd like to get them something soon, so if we do have to go to court, Kahn can't claim they had no choice because we were carrying on a delaying action.

TRAYNOR, HAND, WYZANSKI

222 CHURCH STREET
NEW SALEM, NARRAGANSETT 06555
(393) 876-5678

MEMORANDUM
Attorney Work Product

From: David Greaves
To: Sophie Diehl
RE: Matter of Durkheim
Date: April 6, 1999
Attachments: Letter to Ray Kahn, Esq.

I agree that Mrs. Durkheim should remove the money from the savings account. They're playing hardball; we'll play too. You should call her immediately and have her do it today. I've never advised a client to do something like this so early in the game, but you're right to act decisively now. It will surprise them and also disconcert them. Good work.

Don't worry about all those deadlines Kahn has set. No one gets a divorce in this state that fast. We're moving at a fair clip; no judge will find us dilatory. The thing to remember is that they want to settle as soon as they can. If this case goes to court, Dr. Durkheim won't get his final decree (or his house) until August 2000 at the earliest.

TRAYNOR, HAND, WYZANSKI

222 CHURCH STREET
NEW SALEM, NARRAGANSETT 06555
(393) 876-5678

MEMORANDUM
Attorney Work Product

From: Sophie Diehl
To: David Greaves
RE: Matter of Durkheim
Date: April 6, 1999
Attachments: Letter to Ray Kahn, Esq.
               Draft Letter to Financial Institutions

Following up on your memo, I spoke with Mia Durkheim this afternoon and advised her to transfer the funds in the joint savings account to an individual checking account in her name at a different bank. I also advised her to put the treasury bills into a safe deposit account in her name. She agreed to do both. She called me back an hour later to say that she'd taken out $64,000 and put it in her new account. She decided to leave $16,000, the amount of Dr. Durkheim's legacy from his parents, in the account for him. She also stashed the treasury bills. She thanked me for recommending this step. She said it made her feel better, less helpless, to do something provocative. (She uses words very well, even in her 2 a.m. confessionals. My mother would like her style.)

I'm attaching here the letter to Kahn. If I do say so myself, it's very divorce-lawyerly. I could almost pass for the real thing, no? I have also drafted a letter to the various institutions holding the rest of their money (TIAA-CREF, Federated Central, etc.), letting them know that a divorce is under way and that none of the accounts should be modified, closed, or invaded. Let me know what you think of it.

222 CHURCH STREET
NEW SALEM, NARRAGANSETT 06555
(393) 876-5678
ATTORNEYS AT LAW

April 6, 1999

Ray Kahn
Kahn & Boyle
46 Broadway
New Salem, NA 06555

Dear Mr. Kahn:

I write on behalf of Mrs. Maria Meiklejohn Durkheim, who has retained
the services of Traynor, Hand, Wyzanski to represent her in the divorce
proceedings instituted by her husband, Dr. Daniel E. Durkheim. David
Greaves and I shall act for Mrs. Durkheim. In the future, please direct
all correspondence to one of us, not to our client. I enclose with this
letter copies of the Acceptance of Service, the Notice of Appearance, the
Answer to the Complaint, and the Certificate of Service, all of which
have been duly filed with the Court Clerk.

As you know, the Automatic Orders went into effect for Dr. Durkheim
on the day he filed his Complaint. By closing their joint checking account
on April 1, without his wife's consent, Dr. Durkheim violated those
Orders. Until the Durkheims have concluded their separation agreement,
we must insist that the financial arrangements they maintained during
their marriage continue in place. This includes all bank, charge, and
credit card accounts. If Dr. Durkheim takes another step to "indicat[e]
a separation of property," we will be compelled to file a motion for contempt. In the meantime, we have instructed Mrs. Durkheim to withdraw
$64,000 from their joint savings account at Federated Central Bank so
that she will have sufficient funds on hand to cover her customary and
usual household expenses during the period of negotiation. On our advice, Mrs. Durkheim has also placed $90,000 of treasury bills in a safe
deposit box to be redeemed only in the event negotiations break down

and the case goes to trial. I am sure you will understand that these steps were taken reluctantly, and only in response to Dr. Durkheim's act. We hope we will not have to resort to the courts to reestablish the *status quo ante*. Interim motions have the effect of delaying the proceedings.

The timetable you laid out for concluding the separation agreement seems overly optimistic. We will make every effort to cooperate with good-faith efforts to negotiate, and we will respond promptly to any reasonable offer that provides for adequate alimony, a fair and equitable division of marital property (including savings and pension funds), and a custody and visitation order acceptable to our client. In addition, such an offer should acknowledge the length of the marriage, the contributions Mrs. Durkheim made to her husband's career, and the income and employment opportunities Mrs. Durkheim lost when she moved with her husband to New Salem.

Mrs. Durkheim is in the process of preparing her financial statement. We shall forward it as soon as it is completed. We shall also forward the Certificate of Attendance for the Parent Education Class, which Mrs. Durkheim plans to take within the month. We would appreciate receiving both of these documents from Dr. Durkheim before beginning negotiations.

Sincerely,

Anne Sophie Diehl

Anne Sophie Diehl, Esq.

TRAYNOR, HAND, WYZANSKI

222 CHURCH STREET
NEW SALEM, NARRAGANSETT 06555
(393) 876-5678

MEMORANDUM
Attorney Work Product

From: David Greaves
To: Sophie Diehl
RE: Matter of Durkheim: Draft Letter to Financial Institutions
Date: April 6, 1999
Attachments:

Your draft letter to the various financial institutions is a good idea and a good letter. Send it out to the various institutions today, with cc's to Kahn.

As for your letter to Kahn, I liked the bit at the end about the Parent Education Class. Although it is legally mandated, the parties in negotiated cases usually sign a stipulation waiving the requirement. I've never before seen it used as a weapon this way, a nibbling-to-death-by-ducks type tactic. I imagine that your jaundiced criminal eye will spot many other opportunities to aggravate Kahn—and I must say I'm learning things from you about terrorist ways to negotiate a divorce—but don't get too carried away. Remember, in a divorce, it's the Big Picture that counts, and protracted negotiations are almost invariably less satisfactory in every way than expedited ones, especially in cases where there are children. The Durkheims must continue to have some kind of relationship after they're divorced, and to the extent we can keep to a minimum the opportunities for doing and saying things that can only increase the ill will between them, the better they will be able to function as Jane's parents.

TRAYNOR, HAND, WYZANSKI

222 CHURCH STREET
NEW SALEM, NARRAGANSETT 06555
(393) 876-5678

MEMORANDUM
Attorney Work Product

From: Sophie Diehl
To: Files
RE: Matter of Durkheim: Letter to Financial Institutions
Date: April 6, 1999
Attachments: Letter to Financial Institutions Re: Notice of Automatic
                Orders

Attached to this memo is a copy of a letter sent today to various financial institutions which hold accounts in the name of either or both of the Durkheims, giving notice to them of the Automatic Orders and informing them that Mrs. Durkheim will take prompt legal action in the event there is any violation. Letters, with cc's to Ray Kahn, were sent to the following institutions:

Alan M. Jaspers, Esq.
Senior Vice President for Legal Affairs
Federated Central Bank
110 Church Street
New Salem, NA 06555
RE: Maria M. and Daniel E. Durkheim
        Joint Checking Account: 444 976 8302
        Joint Savings Account: 444 976 8301
        Mortgage on house at 404 St. Cloud Street: M1997-00867-001

Deirdre Weiss, Esq.
Legal Department
TIAA-CREF
730 Third Avenue
New York, NY 10017

RE: Daniel E. Durkheim
          Retirement Accounts
          TIAA Contract Number: ZZ 88567342-3
          CREF Certificate Number: ZZ 88567342-8
          Premium Remitter: Mather University

Ira Lowenstein
Ira Lowenstein & Co.
21 Broadway
New Salem, NA 06555
RE: Maria M. and Daniel E. Durkheim
          Stock Market Investments Account Number: 04-0042-91
          Treasury Bills Account Number: 04-0042-93

          Daniel E. Durkheim
          401(k) Plan Account Number: 04-0043-92

TRAYNOR, HAND, WYZANSKI

222 CHURCH STREET
NEW SALEM, NARRAGANSETT 06555
(393) 876-5678
ATTORNEYS AT LAW

April 6, 1999

Alan M. Jaspers, Esq.
Senior Vice President for Legal Affairs
Federated Central Bank
110 Church Street
New Salem, NA 06555

RE: Maria M. and Daniel E. Durkheim
       Joint Checking Account: 444 976 8302
       Joint Savings Account: 444 976 8301
       Mortgage on house at 404 St. Cloud Street: M1997-00867-001

Dear Mr. Jaspers:

I write as attorney of record for Mrs. Maria Meiklejohn Durkheim, a.k.a. Maria Mather Meiklejohn, to inform you that Mrs. Durkheim and her husband, Dr. Daniel Edward Durkheim, are in the process of negotiating a legal separation, pursuant to a Complaint for Divorce filed by Dr. Durkheim against his wife on February 15, 1999. Under the laws of Narragansett, both parties are subject to Automatic Court Orders, effective the date of filing, forbidding them to "sell, transfer, encumber, conceal, assign, remove, or in any way dispose of any property individually or jointly held by the parties without the consent of the other party in writing or an order of the court, except in the usual course of business or for customary and usual household expenses or for reasonable attorney fees in connection with this action." I enclose a copy of the Notice of Automatic Court Orders.

Please be advised that Mrs. Durkheim will take prompt legal action in the event of any violation of this Court Order.

A copy of this letter has been sent to Ray Kahn, 46 Broadway, New Salem, NA 06555, the attorney of record for Dr. Durkheim.

Thank you for your cooperation.

Yours,

Anne Sophie Diehl

Anne Sophie Diehl, Esq.

cc: Ray Kahn

Re: Re: An Apology and an Invitation

From: Sophie Diehl   4/7/99 10:15 AM
To: David Greaves <dagreaves@traynor.com>
Date: Wed, 7 Apr 1999 10:15:06
Subject: Re: Re: An Apology and an Invitation

David—

My mother (Maman to us) now goes by Elisabeth Dreyfus, her maiden name. She and her parents were French Jews who came to America in 1947, after the war. She was a year old. (My grandparents' war stories are out of Kosinski. French friends hid them during the war, only steps away from Drancy; French neighbors rounded up their relations and sent them to the death camps.) My mother took my father's name when they were married, as was the custom of the day. (She's 53 now; she was married at 22, and had four children before she was 30. Somewhere in there, she got the Ph.D.; later, she went to law school. I don't know how she did it. Servants!) Although my parents have been divorced for years, she has kept his name professionally. She'd already written four books as a married woman under the name of Elisabeth Diehl, and her agent said she couldn't change it. She's never used my stepfather's name, which is Levi, and nobody except some of the more ancient members of New York Psychoanalytic ever call her Mrs. Levi. At one point, right after college, I thought of taking Dreyfus as my name; I thought it was more romantic—"J'accuse" and all that. My mother told me to stick with one name. So I did. In tricky situations, my friend Maggie and I will ask each other: WWFWD (What Would French Women Do)? The answer is almost always right though never obvious and rarely straightforward.

We are not descended from Captain Dreyfus (alas) or related to the Louis-Dreyfus family (alas, alas). It turns out Dreyfus is a common enough name for French Jews, so common, in fact (you won't believe this), the great French Jewish sociologist Emile Durkheim (*Suicide*) was married to a Louise Dreyfus, another person we're not related to. My sister and brothers and I all have French names (Jean

Luc, Remy, and Francoise) and speak serviceable French. (In Paris, I'm sometimes taken for a Belgian, which is their typically mean-spirited way of saying you speak tolerable French but your accent is not Parisian. At least they don't ask whether I'm Quebecois, the worst insult to a fluent speaker. For that I must thank my French grandmother, Grandmere, who only spoke French to us—dinner every Sunday, birthdays, holidays—and who always, in a kindly but firm way, corrected our betises.)

My father would have a stroke if he knew you—or anyone—thought he was a lawyer or a law professor. He's a Modern British historian at Columbia. He is left-wing, politically and historically. His name is John Diehl. He writes frequently for the *New York Review of Books*. (He's English, white, male—like everyone else who writes for them, but not Protestant. His family is Catholic.) The early Diehls owned a pottery, which was as famous in the 18th and 19th centuries as Wedgwood. They emigrated from Germany to England around 1730 (with, it is said, the secret recipe for soft-paste china, stolen from Meissen). They turned intellectual around 1870 and sold the company to Royal Crown Derby. My father has a complete set of Diehl Flora Munda porcelain dishes for 24 (over 300 pieces, each with a unique flower) from 1795 in mint condition. He says it's worth at least a hundred thousand pounds. They're the most beautiful plates I've ever seen, more beautiful than Flora Danica, but no one's ever eaten off any of them. What is the point? He says it's my dowry.

Thank you for the kind offer to take us to lunch at Porter's, but I cannot accept. I do not invite a gentleman to lunch and then fob off the bill on him.

I called Mrs. Durkheim. She's coming in tomorrow.

Don't forget, I'm leaving after lunch on Friday and won't be working all weekend. I'll have the memo on the proposed settlement to you before I take off.

Sophie

TRAYNOR, HAND, WYZANSKI

222 CHURCH STREET
NEW SALEM, NARRAGANSETT 06555
(393) 876-5678

MEMORANDUM
Attorney Work Product

From: Sophie Diehl
To: David Greaves
RE: Matter of Durkheim: Fee Agreement, Name Change,
                Settlement Discussion
Date: April 8, 1999
Attachments: Addendum to Fee Agreement
                MMM & DED: Income & Expenses 1998 by Year/Month/Week
                MMM & DED: Marital Assets & Liabilities April 1998

Maria Meiklejohn Durkheim came into the office today to read the
Addendum to the Fee Agreement and to discuss the terms of a settlement
agreement. I sent her home with the Addendum. I recommended she
consult independent counsel before signing it. She said that she would look
it over again but that she had no intention of getting an outside opinion on
the Addendum. She said I'd made the paper trail; she'd been duly warned,
forewarned, counseled, and cautioned, "everything but threatened," she
added with a laugh. She gave me a check for $12,000, twice the originally
agreed-upon retainer, "to show that I expect to pay twice as much for the
two lawyers I've hired for the price of two." She added that in the event her
husband gets stuck with her lawyers' fees, we should bill him only for my
services. The check was drawn on her new account.

Mrs. Durkheim has decided to resume her maiden name. I told her that
we would officially incorporate the name change into the agreement but
that in the meantime she could use it. As I understand the common-law
rule, a person can use any name she wants to so long as it isn't for purposes
of fraud. She will notify the banks, credit card companies, her employer,
her daughter's school, etc. The case will continue under the name of

Durkheim v. Durkheim; Mrs. Durkheim will henceforth be identified in all memoranda and correspondence as Maria Mather Meiklejohn.

Ms. Meiklejohn brought with her a statement on the family's income and expenses broken down by year, month, and week, and a list of assets and liabilities. They are not so detailed as our Divorce Work Sheets, but they give an adequate picture for purposes of negotiations. In 1998, their joint income, after taxes, was $300,000—$280,000 if you take away the $20,000 a year they get from Bruce Meiklejohn, which obviously should not be included in future projected income figures. They banked $75,000 ($20,000 of which is the Meiklejohn gift) and spent the rest. The net assets (their mortgage is their only liability) are almost $2 million.

Before crafting an offer to present to K&B, we will wait to see what Dr. Durkheim has to say. Our starting position will be 50% of the net family income after taxes (in a combination of spousal and child support), 50% of the joint assets, and physical custody of Jane. (I gave her a copy of the *Paynter* case; as you anticipated, she was reassured.) The financials are negotiable but not physical custody. Given that Ms. Meiklejohn's share will go for the support of two people, herself and her daughter, and Dr. Durkheim's will go for his support only, it's a tenable position. Ms. Meiklejohn and Jane are off to Hawaii for a week. It's his move.

No. 90-43

Paynter v. Paynter

Supreme Court of Narragansett
278 Nar. 487 (1991)

Cole, Ch.J., delivered the opinion of the Court.

On April 14, 1990, Judge Phillips Creighton of the Family Court of Tyler County issued a divorce decree, dissolving the marriage of Adam and Louisa Paynter, and awarded custody of their children, Michael, 11, and Jessica, 8, to their father. On an appeal by the mother, the Court of Appeals reversed, ruling that the trial judge had applied the wrong standard in making the custody award. We affirm.

The Paynters' divorce was in almost every way contentious and acrimonious. They could not reach agreement on spousal support, child support, ownership of the family residence, the distribution of personal property and effects, the education of their children, and, finally, the issue that brings us here today, child custody. Review of this voluminous record reveals that the only thing they could agree to, outside the walls of the Family Courthouse, was the custody of the family's 17-year-old diabetic cat. Mrs. Paynter agreed that her husband should have the cat as he had been the one giving it its insulin injections. Between 1985, when Mr. Paynter filed for divorce, and 1990, when Judge Creighton entered his decree, the Paynters were in court 11 times, not a record for Family Court, but an also-ran.

Mr. Paynter was the more aggressive, vindictive, and hostile; but Mrs. Paynter, with fewer resources, used stalling tactics in a kind of rearguard action that until the last stages was effective in its own way. Mr. Paynter's anger may be said to have understandable roots. In June 1985, Mr. Paynter discovered that Mrs. Paynter was having an affair with their neighbor Gregory Dexter, who was also his golfing buddy. Witnesses who came forward on both sides described a neighborhood straight out of John Updike's novel *Couples.* There was a lot of partying, drinking, flirting, naked swimming, and adultery. Mr. Paynter, a churchgoing banker, was disapproving of the louche atmosphere of the neighborhood, the most expensive in West Salem, but "for business reasons," he went to the parties. Mr. Paynter felt humiliated by the affair, thinking, not without reason, that everyone knew.

Mrs. Paynter immediately ended the affair and offered to move out of the neighborhood so as to spare her husband. They tried to make a go of the marriage, but his anger and her distress worked against it. Six months later, Mr. Paynter filed for divorce, citing his wife's adultery. In July 1986, Mrs. Paynter and the children moved into an apartment in New Salem; she went back to work at her former office, a large accounting firm. Mr. Paynter provided temporary support of $100 a week in alimony and $200 a week in child support. Mrs. Paynter, a CPA, who had not worked since Michael's birth, seven years earlier, held an entry-level accounting position, her skills and confidence having eroded over the years since she left the firm. Her salary was $28,000.

The children felt the effects of the divorce and its attendant hostilities. Michael's schoolwork suffered and Jessica became visibly withdrawn. Between work and the modest support she received, Mrs. Paynter was able to maintain herself and the children, but the circumstances of their new life may be described as straitened. The children's new school was not as good or as safe as the old one, and neither child was prepared for the grittiness of urban life. Both were bullied in school; they made few friends. They did not participate in sports or after-school activities as they had in West Salem, the opportunities being fewer and their sense of alienation isolating them. At the same time, Mrs. Paynter's original distress had turned to depression, and while she functioned at work and at home, the children could see the difference in her and were worried about her. They spent Saturdays with their father in their old home and neighborhood. It offered them a respite from the grimness of their daily life in New Salem.

In 1986, Mr. Paynter earned $84,000. The next year, he earned $88,000. Last year, he earned $98,000. His total payments to his wife over the course of this litigation have been $1,000 a month in child and spousal support, for an annual total of $12,000. He has occupied the family house and retained most of its possessions. Mr. Paynter's sense of being wronged manifested itself in his unwillingness to provide his wife with support. He believed he owed her nothing; she had betrayed the marriage. To support her in any way, he thought, was to reward her treacherous behavior, and he even resisted paying child support, lest she benefit from it. He agreed to alimony only because the tax consequences for him were more favorable than if all the money went for child support. His hostility toward his wife, which never abated and no doubt continues, did not extend to his feelings for his children, whom he loved and treated with affection and kindness. As the new school year was beginning in 1987, gauging the toll that their life with their mother in New Salem had taken, he sued for custody.

Judge Creighton appointed a lawyer to represent the children and a social worker to make a custody assessment. Both recommended that the children remain with their mother. Although their life in New Salem had its problems, by the spring of 1988, when the case was heard, they all were doing better. The children had made friends in the neighborhood; they were both playing soccer. Michael's schoolwork was improving, and he was taking drum lessons. Jessica had come out of her shell and was doing Suzuki violin at school. Mrs. Paynter was seeing a psychiatrist at the Clinic at Mather Hospital, and a combination of therapy and antidepressants had succeeded in lifting her depression. She had resumed her relationship with Gregory Dexter, who had been divorced in 1987. The children expressed love for their father and a continuing attachment to their former home, town, neighborhood, friends, and school, but wanted to remain with their mother. Michael was clear on this point. "Mom is doing a good job. We need her and she needs us." They were neutral about Mr. Dexter. Their mother saw him on Saturdays, when they were with their father.

Where parents can agree, the preference is to award joint custody, absent a finding of detriment to the child. 33 Nar. Stat.

§§812–13. In a disputed case, the Court looks first to the parents' fitness, §809, and then to the "best interests of the child." §810. Factors that lead to a finding of unfitness include: serious drug or alcohol problems; physical, sexual, or emotional abuse of the child, the other spouse, or a current partner; behavior indicating a *pattern* of neglect or danger; or an incapacitating mental or physical impairment. Here, the mother's adultery and depression are not disqualifying factors; nor is the father's unwillingness to pay spousal support. The parents are fit under the statutes. As §810 provides: "The Court shall not consider conduct of a proposed custodian that does not affect his relationship to the child." The Paynters may be commended for maintaining loving and supportive relationships with their children even as they went after each other tooth and claw.

There was a time, and not so long ago, when a mother's (though not a father's) infidelity would have justified a finding that she was unfit to have custody. This is no longer true. In 1978, Narragansett rewrote its divorce law, instituting "no fault" and narrowing the list of disqualifying factors in custody disputes to conduct that is essentially illegal as opposed to immoral. A wife's adultery remains grounds for divorce but not for a finding of parental unfitness. As for depression, it has never been an indicator of unfitness in divorce, only unhappiness.

The factors that determine the "best interests of the child" under the Narragansett statute are defined as: (a) the wishes of the child's parents as to his custody; (b) the reasonable preference of the child, if the Court deems the child old enough to express a preference; (c) the interaction and interrelationship of the child with his parents, his siblings, and any other person who may significantly affect the child's best interests; (d) the child's adjustment to his home, school, and community; (e) the length of time the child has lived in a stable, satisfactory environment and the desirability of maintaining continuity of care; (f) the permanence, as a family unit, of the existing or proposed custodial home; (g) the mental and physical health of all individuals involved; and (h) a parent's capacity to give the child love, affection, and guidance, and to support and facilitate the child's relationship with the other parent.

In applying these criteria to this case, the trial judge found that as to (a), (c), (f), and (h), both parents were equally, or unequally, suitable; as to (e), the mother better met the standard, and as to (d) and (g), the father. Judge Creighton discounted Michael's preference (b), finding he was too young. Weighing these factors, he concluded that custody should go to the father.

On review, our task is limited. We may disagree with the lower court's findings, but we will not overturn its decision unless it failed to apply the correct rule or made findings unsupported by the evidence. *Leithaus v. Leithaus*, 264 Nar. 377 (1983). In this case, the trial judge did not apply the correct rule.

Three years ago, in *O'Malley v. O'Malley*, 272 Nar. 391 (1987), we suggested that the "best interests" standard was in most cases best served by applying a Primary

Caretaker Rule, first espoused in *Garska v. McCoy*, 278 S.E.2d 357 (W.Va. 1981) by the West Virginia Supreme Court. Drawing on the soundest teachings of child psychology, the Primary Caretaker Rule recognizes that stability and continuity of care are the factors most crucial to a child's security, happiness, and growth. Disrupting the intimacy of a child's relationship with his primary caretaker by awarding custody to the non-primary caretaker is traumatic for a young child and jeopardizes his mental, emotional, and physical health. See, e.g., *Before the Best Interests of the Child* (1979).

The Primary Caretaker Rule serves a second purpose. It imposes an objective standard in cases that may be bitterly contested. The rule recognizes "the inherent difficulty of principled decision making" in custody cases, which too often reflect "ad hoc judgments by courts on the beliefs [and] lifestyles . . . of the proposed custodian." *Pikula v. Pikula*, 374 N.W.2d 705 (Minn. 1985).

A third factor is no less important: The rule discourages the strategic use of custody fights in negotiations over child support, spousal support, and property division. It has been widely recognized that "the primary caretaker parent . . . [is] willing to sacrifice everything in order to avoid the terrible prospect of losing the child in the unpredictable process of litigation." *Garska v. McCoy*, at 360. The Primary Caretaker Rule prevents the use of a threatened custody battle as an abusive litigation tactic, especially in cases where the parties have unequal resources and one of them is better able to financially pursue extended litigation. In this case, the father withheld resources, making life difficult for mother and children; he then argued that she was not providing the children with the education, housing, medical care, and other resources they should have. This is the catch-22 of divorce.

In determining the best interests of the child, we adopt *Garska*'s Primary Caretaker Rule. The case is remanded to the trial court (1) for a determination of which parent was the primary caretaker at the time Mr. Paynter sued for custody; and (2) for a reassessment of child and spousal support. After years of litigation, "to avoid the terrible prospect of losing the child[ren]," Mrs. Paynter accepted an exceptionally meager settlement. Until a final determination is made, the children will live with their mother as the parent with whom they were residing at the time the case was brought.

Fisher, J., Dunbar, J., Fimbel, J., Inui, J., and Solomon, J., join this opinion.

* * *

TRAYNOR, HAND, WYZANSKI

222 CHURCH STREET
NEW SALEM, NARRAGANSETT 06555
(393) 876-5678
ATTORNEYS AT LAW

ADDENDUM TO FEE AGREEMENT

I, **Maria Mather Meiklejohn, a.k.a. Maria M. Durkheim**, the "Client" of **404 St. Cloud Street, New Salem, NA,** having retained the firm of Traynor, Hand, Wyzanski, the "Attorneys," in connection with: **divorce proceedings** and such other work as may from time to time be performed by the Attorneys on the Client's behalf, hereby agree to the following terms and conditions as an Addendum to the Fee Agreement originally entered into on **17 March 1999**. In that I have asked **Anne Sophie Diehl**, a criminal lawyer with no prior experience in matrimonial law, to represent me, I agree to pay additional time charges at the hourly rate of: **$150.00** for experienced matrimonial lawyers to the extent the Attorneys determine that they are necessary to assist her. In recognition of this modification, I shall pay to the Attorneys **$12,000** as an initial retainer in this matter.

As an Addendum to the Fee Agreement of 17 March 1999, this agreement modifies it to the extent represented herein.

THIS IS A LEGALLY BINDING CONTRACT. OWING TO THE UNUSUAL TERMS AND CONDITIONS OF THIS CONTRACT, THE CLIENT IS URGED TO SEEK INDEPENDENT COUNSEL.

We, the Client and the Attorneys, have read the above Addendum to the Fee Agreement and understand and accept its terms. Both have signed it as their free act and deed, and the Client acknowledges receipt of a copy of the Addendum. Signed this **8th** day of **April 1999** .

Traynor, Hand, Wyzanski
By:

Maria Durkheim

Client   Maria M. Durkheim

Anne Sophie Diehl

Attorney   Anne Sophie Diehl

Maria Mather Meiklejohn and Daniel E. Durkheim
Income & Expenses 1998

Income	Yearly	Monthly	Weekly
Husband's Salary	370,000	30,833	7,115
Taxes, Soc Sec	100,000	8,333	1,923
NET	**270,000**	**22,500**	**5,192**
Wife's Salary	14,000	1,167	269
Taxes, Soc Sec	4,000	333	77
NET	**10,000**	**834**	**192**
NET Income	**$280,000[1]**	**$23,333**	**$5,384**

Expenses	Yearly	Monthly	Weekly
House (404 St. Cloud)			
Mortgage, Taxes	42,000	3,500	808
Utilities	4,800	400	92
Maintenance	3,600	300	69
Grounds	1,200	100	23
Housekeeper	26,000	2,167	500
Tuition (Jane)	13,000	1,083	250
Automobiles			
Audi	9,600	800	185
Saab	7,200	600	138

---

[1] Bruce Meiklejohn, Maria Meiklejohn's father, has given Dr. Durkheim and Ms. Meiklejohn each $10,000 a year as a tax-free gift for 16 years, since their marriage in 1982. That money has gone directly into savings. It does not figure in this accounting, since it will no longer be forthcoming. The total contribution not including compounded interest equals $320,000. We will hire a tax accountant to compute the current value of the amount at the generally acceptable rate of return.

Medical			
Insurance	1,800	150	35
Office visits	1,200	100	23
Prescriptions	800	66	15
Eyeglasses	1,800	150	35
Psychoanalysis (wife)	13,000	1,083	250
Food	15,600	1,300	300
Clothing	12,000	1,000	231
Debt			
Entertainment	12,000	1,000	231
Travel, Vacations	36,000	3,000	692
Pets	1,200	100	23
Spending Money	20,800	1,733	400
Savings			
Investments	25,000	2,083	480
401(k) DED	30,000	2,500	577
TOTAL Expenses	**$278,600**	**$23,217**	**$5,357**

Maria Mather Meiklejohn and Daniel E. Durkheim
Marital Assets & Liabilities
April 1999

Joint Assets & Liabilities

Joint Assets

Equity in Family Residence Jointly Owned	$240,000[1]
Daniel Durkheim's TIAA-CREF Retirement Accounts	600,000[2]
Daniel Durkheim's 401(k) Plan	300,000
Stock Market Investments Jointly Owned	700,000
Treasury Bills Jointly Owned	90,000
Joint Saving Accounts	80,000
Total Value of Assets Acquired After Marriage	**$2,010,000**

Jointly Owned Personal Property

Household Furnishings, Objects, Artwork	100,000

TOTAL VALUE OF ASSETS	**$2,110,000**

Joint Liabilities

30-Year Mortgage of Family Residence	$250,000

TOTAL VALUE OF LIABILITIES	**$250,000**

---

[1] The family residence at 404 St. Cloud cost, with the land, $375,000 to build. Dr. Durkheim and Ms. Meiklejohn put down $125,000 and took out a 30-year 8% mortgage for the remainder of $250,000. Virtually none of the principal has been paid yet. Since they built the house, land values in New Salem have increased greatly and the current value of the home is now $525,000. If the home were sold this year and the mortgage paid off, the Durkheim-Meiklejohns would recover their $125,000 down payment and realize a profit of $115,000 ($150,000 less the Realtor's fee of $31,500, calculated at 6% of the price, and closing costs of approximately $3,500), giving them $240,000 cash in hand.

[2] Dr. Durkheim joined TIAA-CREF on July 1, 1983, when he became a Resident at Presbyterian Hospital.

Separate Assets & Liabilities

Daniel Durkheim's Separate Assets
Inheritance from Parents, Distribution October 1998
    Cash $16,000
    1989 Honda

Maria Meiklejohn's Separate Assets
Martha's Vineyard Home, March 1979 $90,000[1]

---

[1] Ms. Meiklejohn and her father, Bruce Meiklejohn, inherited the house on Martha's Vineyard from Ms. Meiklejohn's mother on her death in 1979, before Ms. Meiklejohn and Dr. Durkheim married. They are tenants in the entirety under a trust, which means neither can sell his or her share and the survivor inherits all. At the time of *Mrs.* Meiklejohn's death, the property was valued at $90,000. The current rough estimated value of the house and land, the land being far more valuable than the house, which is a ramshackle place, is in the neighborhood of $3,000,000–$4,000,000. .

TRAYNOR, HAND, WYZANSKI

222 CHURCH STREET
NEW SALEM, NARRAGANSETT 06555
(393) 876-5678

MEMORANDUM
Attorney Work Product

From:	Fiona McGregor
To:	David Greaves
RE:	Matter of Durkheim: Representation
Date:	April 9, 1999
Attachments:	

I think your memo to me was unjust. I may not have followed the company line, but I did nothing that would injure the firm or its reputation and nothing contrary to the rules of governance. To the contrary, I maintain I acted properly and appropriately. Sophie Diehl is not fit to act in this case. I am, you are, Felix is. You will see that Mrs. Durkheim is not exposed, but the firm will wind up losing money. As Bruce Meiklejohn's lawyer, you of course make the final decision here, but as a member of the firm, I have a stake in the firm's reputation and the firm's profits. At the very least, I and the other lawyers in the practice should have been consulted.

I want to make clear that I am not operating with any personal animus against Sophie. My motivation was and remains purely professional.

Please take my letter to the Management Committee. The partners all know about our difference of opinion on this matter; they were cc'ed on the memos, and I'm cc'ing them on this. I don't think I did anything wrong. I felt a responsibility to Mrs. Durkheim and to the firm. And I still do.

cc:	Jason Bell	Frank O'Keefe
	William Frost	Joseph Salerno
	Proctor Hand	Katherine Sales
	Virginia Ladder	John Wynch
	Felix Landau	

TRAYNOR, HAND, WYZANSKI

222 CHURCH STREET
NEW SALEM, NARRAGANSETT 06555
(393) 876-5678

MEMORANDUM
Attorney Work Product

From:	David Greaves
To:	Fiona McGregor
RE:	Matter of Durkheim: Representation
Date:	April 9, 1999
Attachments:	

The letter will go before the Committee at next Thursday's meeting.
You're invited. Hannah will let you know the time.

TRAYNOR, HAND, WYZANSKI

· 222 CHURCH STREET
NEW SALEM, NARRAGANSETT 06555
(393) 876-5678

MEMORANDUM
Attorney Work Product

From: Fiona McGregor
To: David Greaves
RE: Matter of Durkheim: Representation
Date: April 9, 1999
Attachments:

I'm looking forward to the meeting, as I persist in thinking I'm right. I'll
see you next Thursday. Just let me know the time in the next day or two,
so I can work out next week's appointment calendar.

Thank You

From: David Greaves   4/9/99 4:55 PM
To: Sophie Diehl <asdiehl@traynor.com>
Date: Fri, 9 Apr 1999 16:55:12
Subject: Thank You

Dear Sophie:

Thank you for a wonderful lunch. I am now indebted to you on two counts. I haven't had such a good time at lunch since I argued the Loeb case. Your mother is terrific. But then you know that. I hope you had a good time. You were very quiet—or we were very talkative. Have a good weekend. And come in late Monday.

David

Weekend Wrap-Up

From: Sophie Diehl   4/11/99 3:44 PM
To: Maggie Pfeiffer <mcp15@mather.edu>
Date: Sun, 11 Apr 1999 15:44:19
Subject: Weekend Wrap-Up

Dearest Mags—

What a weekend. First things first: You were spectacular and so was the play. You are the Real Thing. You're doing what you were meant to do. I'm sure you'll hear directly from Maman, but she was astounded. She said to me, "You told me Maggie could act, but I didn't take it in properly. She's brilliant, like a young Vanessa Redgrave. When she's onstage, you can't take your eyes off her." Verbatim, that's what she said. Everyone was good—Harry was very happy—but you were sublime. We need a Kenneth Tynan to do your performance justice in print.

And now I backtrack. On Friday, I took Maman and DG to lunch at Porter's. He had Dover sole (typically chaste); Maman and I, needless to say, went for the double lamb chops. Do you think men like women who like to eat? I think the good ones do. Anyway, if the situation weren't so charged (as you said, the titans squaring off), I'd have to say that DG was smitten by the old girl. She wasn't being exactly flirtatious, but she was awfully charming. She even ran her fingers through her hair a couple of times. They hardly paid me any attention, so I watched them like an anthropologist studying middle-aged mating behavior. The thing about my mother is the quality of her attention; nothing in the world is like it. She makes you feel special simply because she is listening to you. I wish I could do that. It must be a French female thing. He had read a lot of her books; she knew my stories about him. They were so pleased with each other and themselves. He said nice things about me and my work, which is a sure way to win Maman over. She is still an exceptionally doting mother, though being French, her dotingness is never gushing; I don't know how she does it with all four of us, but she does.

She's probably ruined my brothers for other women—and yet they're both such good guys. By the way, Luc sends his love and congratulations. He called me this morning; Maman had already reported to him on the play.

I keep thinking about Jake and what he would think of their behavior. (Papa, of course, would have ignored it.) It's often hard to tell when he's angry or upset. I kept telling myself that they were just having a good time—and they're allowed to. I can imagine being married and loving my husband and still liking to flirt with attractive men. You're the expert on marriage. What do you think? DG's been married for ages, and his wife, Mary, is the nicest, easiest-going woman I've ever met. Some women wouldn't like their husband to be working so closely with a 30-year-old, but she doesn't seem to mind at all. In fact, he has had me over for dinner with them and their friends, and she always makes me feel wanted and liked when she drops by the office. I wonder if she'd feel that way about Maman. She may know her man and (rightly?) not see me as any threat. And the truth is, I can't see him messing around with someone young enough to be his daughter. Joe told me that Wynch, one of the real estate partners in the firm, left his wife for a woman 20 years younger than he (and a client no less; it was a major scandal but before my time); he said DG couldn't understand it. "What does he want with that kid?" he said. "Who wants someone who can't remember what she was doing when she heard that Kennedy had been shot?" I wonder if they realized what they were doing, how they were acting. Did they think my being there made it harmless? Did they go home and think about each other? This is making me uncomfortable. I will now try to stop thinking about it.

And that shouldn't be too hard because I've got other things to think about. All the signs indicate I'm falling for Harry (thinking about him too much and too often). Is that a terrible idea? I love that he's good at what he does, that he likes to make things happen, that he's articulate and funny and good-looking and sexy. On that last point, let's just say he is, as you first described him, very talented. He wants to do Pinter next; he loves those Brits. But not, thank God, *Betrayal*. I can't take any more adultery. I'm so glad I finished *Anna Karenina* and can now start *War and Peace*. Maman says there's a real, solid (though, alas, a second) marriage in *W&P*. Levin is too irritating for me to take his marriage to Kitty as any kind of model.

Anyway, Harry's been so wired the last two nights, nothing and I mean nothing could wind him down. And he was so happy. I like a man who can be happy. My father is capable of enthusiasm but not happiness. (I never seem to be able to get too far from my parents, the default templates of my life.) More to the point, Harry got up very early this morning and wrote me a poem, well, doggerel really. How can something be awful and heart-melting at the same time? Boy, does he have my number.

How are you doing? I know you've got six more performances in front of you. How are you holding up? Are you exhausted? I'm going to try to catch Tuesday's performance.

Work has been overwhelming. I'm getting the hang of divorce (law is law in a lot of ways), but it's so unnatural for me. I can't keep focused on the Big Picture, as DG calls it. If I find a statute or a rule that applies, I'm like a terrier with a bone; I want to run with it, even if dropping it would be to everyone's advantage, including mine. But I can't go against Joe's training. DG thinks this experience is good for me, opening me up to new ways of thinking. At least that's what he said to my mother. Maman defended me—or rather defended crime. Do you think they will have an affair? I couldn't bear it.

Next week the Management Committee is taking up the matter of Fiona McGregor's vendetta against me. (That's how I think of it, though as usual I exaggerate and put myself in the middle of a larger fight.) I can only lose. If she's vindicated, she'll rub my nose in it; if she's reprimanded, she'll rub my nose in it. I don't know what I did to rouse her enmity. I keep thinking she's jealous, but I can't think of what. She's great-looking, smart, successful (the youngest person ever made partner in the firm). She's not married—but then neither am I. There are various theories. Judge Howard says it's not so much Yale and the clerkship as the firm's patriarchy which sets the women against each other. Maman says it's not personal, Fiona's jealousy, but familial and free-floating, attaching to people who remind her of a young sibling. It doesn't matter who's right; neither makes it any easier. I'd prefer it to be personal. Enemies should be earned.

I need to go to bed. I just left Harry's. I've slept maybe 4 hours in the last two nights.

I feel like we haven't talked in ages.

Love,
Sophie

Sunday morning limerick

This morning while drinking my coffee,

I knew I'd been given a trophy,

For there, in my bed,

With gold eyes and gold head,

Was the girl nonpareil, lovely Sophie.

This is, I'm afraid, the best I can do.

I have no talent for poetry. But my heart is full.

Harry

222 CHURCH STREET
NEW SALEM, NARRAGANSETT 06555
(393) 876-5678

MEMORANDUM
Attorney Work Product

From:	Sophie Diehl
To:	David Greaves
RE:	Maria Meiklejohn
Date:	April 12, 1999
Attachments:	Letter from Helen Fincher to Maria Meiklejohn

On her way to the airport, Mia Meiklejohn dropped off a letter she'd received from Helen Fincher, Daniel Durkheim's first wife and the mother of Thomas (Tom) Maxwell Durkheim. She declared it "a complete surprise." They'd always gotten along, but 3M didn't know HF was paying any attention. "I always thought of her as belonging to the Mehitabel school of mothering," she said. "Perhaps I've been unfair." She wondered if she might call HF as a character witness should the case go to trial. "Can you imagine her credibility with the judge? I was, after all, the 'other woman.'"

Dear Mia,   April 7, 1999

I've been meaning to write now for weeks. Tom told me that you and Daniel are splitting. I'm so sorry. Tom is, as you may imagine, very upset about it. He doesn't remember life without you, and he's worried that you and Jane will disappear from his life, that he will lose not only his family life but his family. I'm certainly not giving him one thought this marriage might stick. (I may be spoiled and irresponsible, but I'm not self-deceiving.)

I want to thank you for all you've done for and been to Tom over all those, what is it, 18 years. I never worried when he was with you (meaning you, Mia, not you and Dan). Daniel's level of attentiveness diminishes geometrically as he travels from a hospital, and at the most basic level, I was always grateful to you for seeing that Tom ate breakfast, had clean clothes, crossed the street at the corner, wore his seat belt, had a babysitter. And then, you always made him feel a part of a family, and not like a stepchild. He thinks

of Jane as his sister, not his half sister. You
did that for him. I grew up with a mother,
a father, three stepmothers, two stepfathers,
four brothers, two half sisters, two half brothers,
and seven stepbrothers and sisters. This was
by the time I was 18; we don't even invite
each other to our weddings anymore, at
least not after the second.

I've told Tom that you won't give up on
him; nor will Jane. You've been great and
I'm sorry for the pain you're going through.
Things _will_ get better. I hope we'll always
stay in touch.

Who is Stephanie Roth? Tom had dinner
with her and Daniel last week. She asked him
if he'd been bar mitzvahed. When he said no,
she looked at Daniel reproachfully. Oy vey.
What are we all in for? I thought Daniel
reliably went for shiksas. Her voice, apparently,
is two octaves above middle C. Tom said she
(probably) wasn't stupid; she only sounded
stupid.

Again my thanks.

all the best,
Helen

TRAYNOR, HAND, WYZANSKI

222 CHURCH STREET
NEW SALEM, NARRAGANSETT 06555
(393) 876-5678

MINUTES OF THE MANAGEMENT COMMITTEE
Confidential

From:	Hannah Smith, Secretary, Management Committee
To:	Partnership Files
RE:	Hearing on Fiona McGregor
Date:	April 16, 1999
Attachments:	

The Management Committee of Traynor, Hand, Wyzanski convened at 11 a.m., Thursday, April 15, 1999, in Special Session with David Greaves, Chair, Proctor Hand, Virginia Ladder, and William Frost in attendance. Joseph Salerno was unable to attend. The Committee met to discuss the conduct of a partner, Fiona McGregor, in conjunction with the representation of Maria Meiklejohn in her divorce action. For the purposes of the Special Session, Proctor Hand acted as Chair.

David Greaves presented the grievance against Ms. McGregor. On learning that Anne Sophie Diehl had been assigned to represent Ms. Meiklejohn in her divorce proceedings, Ms. McGregor directly contacted Ms. Meiklejohn by letter, questioning Ms. Diehl's suitability as her lawyer and offering instead her services or those of the other divorce lawyers in the firm. Ms. Diehl and David Greaves had been assigned to the case at the express request of Ms. Meiklejohn. Ms. Diehl, a criminal lawyer with the firm, had been reluctant to represent Ms. Meiklejohn but had agreed after consultation with Mr. Greaves. On learning of Ms. McGregor's letter, Mr. Greaves told Ms. McGregor that she had not sufficiently recognized the professional considerations that had prompted the assignment and that, in writing her letter, she had challenged his authority and undermined the firm's values and reputation. He requested assurances from her that she would not repeat this kind of behavior. Ms. McGregor did not provide those assurances but requested a hearing before the Management Committee. Mr. Greaves stated that he believed personal animus against Ms. Diehl played a part in Ms. McGregor's conduct.

At 11:30, Ms. McGregor met with the Committee. She outlined the considerations that prompted her letter and that have continued to inform her judgment of what she characterized as an unfortunate and unprofessional decision. She expressed her belief that the use of Ms. Diehl compromised the professional standards and reputation of the firm, and she took the position that the double-billing arrangement that Ms. Diehl and Ms. Meiklejohn had agreed upon to assure the quality and professionalism of Ms. Diehl's representation would work to the economic disadvantage of the firm. She maintained there was no way the firm could recover the full cost of using a second lawyer and pointed to correspondence in the Durkheim file indicating that Mr. Greaves would write off some of his hours rather than bill Ms. Meiklejohn for the education of Ms. Diehl. After presenting her arguments, Ms. McGregor withdrew. Over the objections of the other members of the Committee, Mr. Greaves also withdrew in order to allow the other Committee members to discuss the matter fully and freely.

After reviewing the letters and other documents in the Durkheim file and the presentations of Mr. Greaves and Ms. McGregor, the Committee voted to approve Mr. Greaves's decision to assign Ms. Diehl and to reprimand Ms. McGregor for her conduct.

The Committee members instructed Mr. Hand to write a letter to Ms. McGregor explaining in detail the deliberations and conclusions of the Committee.

The Committee adjourned at 12:30 p.m.

TRAYNOR, HAND, WYZANSKI

222 CHURCH STREET
NEW SALEM, NARRAGANSETT 06555
(393) 876-5678
ATTORNEYS AT LAW

April 16, 1999

Fiona McGregor, Esq.
Traynor, Hand, Wyzanski
222 Church Street
New Salem, Narragansett 06555

PERSONAL AND CONFIDENTIAL

Dear Fiona:

I am writing in my official capacity as Acting Chair of the Management Committee to inform you of the Committee's findings and conclusions following the meeting convened on April 15, 1999, to review your conduct in relation to the firm's representation of Ms. Maria Meiklejohn. You should know that after making his presentation and hearing your response, David Greaves recused himself from the Committee. He was not a party to its deliberations or final disposition.

While recognizing the legitimacy of your concerns about the use of an associate attorney who had never before handled a divorce and the possible loss of income that would flow from the double-billing arrangement that had been entered into with Ms. Meiklejohn, the members of the Committee support Mr. Greaves's decision to assign Ms. Diehl to the case and to issue a private reprimand. Further, we find your conduct in this matter falling short of the standard we expect of our lawyers, to wit: (1) your letter to Ms. Meiklejohn, which publicly aired a private matter of firm management and which, if more widely circulated, could damage the standing and reputation of the firm, opening it to ridicule and gossip; (2) your shortsighted assessment of a situation that could put at risk the firm's important relationship with Ms. Meiklejohn's father, Bruce Meiklejohn; (3) your animus against a younger colleague in the firm who had done nothing in this matter to deserve the accusations leveled against her; (4) your disregard of the traditions, values, practices, and procedures of the firm; and (5) your lack of judgment in refusing to accept Mr. Greaves's private reprimand and in bringing the matter before the Management Committee. A lawyer's judgment is the most important tool in her professional arsenal.

I hope we will all be able to put it behind us.

Yours,

Proctor Hand

Proctor Hand, Esq.

cc: Files of the Management Committee

TRAYNOR, HAND, WYZANSKI

222 CHURCH STREET
NEW SALEM, NARRAGANSETT 06555
(393) 876-5678

MEMORANDUM
Attorney Work Product

From:	Joe Salerno
To:	Sophie Diehl
RE:	Fiona
Date:	April 16, 1999
Attachments:	Letter from Proctor Hand to Fiona

Sophie—

FYI. I thought you'd want to see the letter Hand wrote Fiona. Confidential, of course. Did David show it to you? I would guess not. I couldn't make the meeting. I don't agree with the Committee. Her behavior to you has been uncivil and unprofessional, but (no offense meant) she is right. You are not a divorce lawyer.

Stick with us cowfolks. We miss you upstairs. How in hell did you get caught in this anyway?

Love,

Joe

P.S. It was great to see your mom again. She dropped by when she was in town the other day to say hello to the gang—and to ask me about habeas corpus. Was that for a new book? Did you know she sent me a signed copy of her last one? She's a class act.

TRAYNOR, HAND, WYZANSKI

222 CHURCH STREET
NEW SALEM, NARRAGANSETT 06555
(393) 876-5678

MEMORANDUM
Attorney Work Product

From: Sophie Diehl
To: Joe Salerno
RE: Fiona McGregor
Date: April 16, 1999
Attachments:

Joe—

Do you really believe there are any confidential documents in this firm? I've already seen three copies—though you are the only *partner* to show it to me. My goose is cooked, stuffed, and dressed. Fiona won't forget. She's never liked me—which is okay; the feeling has become mutual—but I have never been able to figure out why. Up to now, she's pretty much ignored me unless she absolutely had to speak to me, at which point she would address me in the third person, calling me a "Yalie," as in "What would a Yalie do in this situation? Move to dismiss?" I have resisted sarcasm because Maman absolutely forbad it. She said it was worse than cursing.

I can understand that you wouldn't agree with Proctor's letter. He must have been very angry. "We find your conduct in this matter falling short of the standard we expect of our lawyers." There's a stomach churner for you. Do they want her to leave? I don't know that I could come to work the next day.

It's a short story how I got caught up in this. I miss you too. Everything's so much more straightforward upstairs—maybe because there's no property at stake, only life or liberty. There's endless to-ing and fro-ing with a civil suit. And not much fun.

Love,

Sophie

P.S. My mother said you called her "a real dame—and still a looker." She was thrilled.

You

From: Harry Mortensen   4/18/99 2:14 PM
To: Sophie Diehl <asdiehl@traynor.com>
Date: Sat, 18 Apr 1999 14:14:27
Subject: You

Sweet Sophie—

Do you remember the lines from *The Real Thing*, words of advice from father to daughter:

"Happiness is equilibrium. Shift your weight." I think of them when I think of you and practice shifting.

Harry

III. OFFER/COUNTEROFFER

KAHN & BOYLE
46 BROADWAY
NEW SALEM, NARRAGANSETT 06555
(393) 876-4343
ATTORNEYS AT LAW

April 19, 1999

David Greaves, Esq.
Traynor, Hand, Wyzanski
222 Church Street
New Salem, Narragansett 06555

Dear Dave:

As you know, I am representing Dr. Daniel Durkheim in his divorce against Mrs. Maria Durkheim. Dr. Durkheim would like to see the matter settled, and I'm sure we can agree that a long, drawn-out divorce is to no one's benefit. Your young associate Ms. Anne Sophie Diehl and I may have gotten off on the wrong foot, and I'm hoping you and I can put our heads together and resolve this matter expeditiously. Dr. Durkheim is prepared to be generous.

It is my understanding that during the marriage, Mrs. Durkheim handled the family finances. This should make massive orders of discovery superfluous. Dr. Durkheim says his wife knows what they have and where it is, and confirmation of this lies in Ms. Diehl's letters to the various financial institutions holding accounts in their joint and separate names. Your firm's knowledge of the Durkheims' income, assets, and liabilities appears comprehensive.

I have attached to this letter a formal offer from Dr. Durkheim. Before presenting our proposal, I shall put forth a brief overview of the financials and the general considerations behind it.

The most substantial family asset is Mrs. Durkheim's property on Martha's Vineyard, which is worth at least $6 million. The family residence, in contrast, was built for $375,000 and financed with a $250,000 mortgage, virtually none of which has been paid off. The equity in the house is the original deposit they made of $125,000. There are two automobiles, an Audi, which Dr. Durkheim drives, and a Saab hatchback, which Mrs. Durkheim drives.

Other assets include Dr. Durkheim's pension fund of approximately $600,000, Dr. Durkheim's 401(k) plan, which has $300,000 in it, stock market investments of $700,000, and a joint savings account originally holding $80,000 but now depleted by Mrs. Durkheim's recent withdrawal of $64,000. These accounts have been funded by savings from Dr. Durkheim's salary and gifts from Mrs. Durkheim's father, which total $320,000.

At this time, Dr. Durkheim is asking for joint legal and physical custody and will, of course, pay child support for Jane proportionate to the time she spends with her mother. He has expressed a desire for full physical custody, in light of Mrs. Durkheim's state of mind, but I have persuaded him for the moment not to press it. He is also willing to pay spousal support while Mrs. Durkheim finishes her Ph.D. at Mather.

With these factors in mind, I present on behalf of Dr. Durkheim a proposal that we believe fully and fairly accommodates the needs and contributions of the parties. I look forward to hearing from you. I believe that you and I can settle this matter promptly.

Yours,

Ray Kahn

Ray Kahn, Esq.

SETTLEMENT OFFER

From: Ray Kahn, Esq.
To: David Greaves, Esq.
RE: Durkheim v. Durkheim
Date: April 19, 1999

REAL PROPERTY:

Dr. Daniel Durkheim resigns any interest he may have, present and future, in the Martha's Vineyard house and property. This property is currently valued at $6 million. He will keep the St. Cloud Street house, which was purchased three (3) years ago for $375,000. He will assume the $250,000 mortgage and pay Mrs. Maria Durkheim $25,000 in recognition of her contribution to the down payment of $125,000. Dr. Durkheim will continue to pay the mortgage and maintenance costs of the house until the divorce is settled.

PERSONAL PROPERTY:

Dr. Durkheim will keep the Audi he has been using and assume the loan payments for it. Mrs. Durkheim will keep the Saab hatchback she has been using and assume the loan payments for it.

ASSETS:

Bank Accounts, Stocks, Bonds, Mutual Funds:

Stock market investments currently total approximately $700,000. Mrs. Durkheim will receive $320,000 of these funds, which totals the full amount of the annual gifts to both of them from her father over the 16 years of their marriage. Dr. Durkheim will receive the balance of $380,000.

On April 6, on instructions from her lawyer, Mrs. Durkheim withdrew $64,000 from the couple's joint savings account, leaving $16,000 in the account. If the amount Mrs. Durkheim withdrew from the savings account is added to her share of the proposed division of stock market investments, her total share of their assets comes to $384,000. If the remaining $16,000 in the savings account is added to Dr. Durkheim's share of the stocks, his total share of the assets comes to $396,000.

Retirement/Deferred Compensation Plans:

Dr. Durkheim will retain his retirement accounts with TIAA-CREF, which currently have a value of approximately $600,000. He will transfer the funds in his 401(k) plan, which currently holds $300,000, to Mrs. Durkheim.

CHILD CUSTODY:

Dr. Durkheim and Mrs. Durkheim will share legal and physical custody of their daughter, Jane.

CHILD SUPPORT:

Dr. Durkheim will pay child support to Mrs. Durkheim to the amount of $2,000 a month until Jane reaches the age of 18 or graduates from high school, whichever event occurs last. He will pay all her school fees and expenses, including all costs for college. He will pay her medical insurance and all medical fees.

SPOUSAL SUPPORT:

Dr. Durkheim will pay spousal support to Mrs. Durkheim to the amount of $3,000 a month for four (4) years to allow Mrs. Durkheim time to complete her degree at Mather and to secure employment.

TRAYNOR, HAND, WYZANSKI

222 CHURCH STREET
NEW SALEM, NARRAGANSETT 06555
(393) 876-5678

MEMORANDUM
Attorney Work Product

From: Joe Salerno
To: Sophie Diehl
RE: Fiona
Date: April 19,1999
Attachments: Letter from Fiona to Proctor

Sophie—

Act II. Confidential, of course. Fiona has a point. Wynch is still here, making money hand over fist. I am going to formally dissent in a minority absentee opinion. I wish I'd been at the meeting.

Love,

Joe

TRAYNOR, HAND, WYZANSKI

222 CHURCH STREET
NEW SALEM, NARRAGANSETT 06555
(393) 876-5678
ATTORNEYS AT LAW

April 19, 1999

Proctor Hand
Traynor, Hand, Wyzanski
222 Church Street
New Salem, NA 06555

Dear Proctor:

I write to protest the Committee's findings regarding my letter to Mrs. Durkheim. I persist in thinking that the decision to use Sophie Diehl was wrong and that I acted properly and professionally. If a client asked to hire Sophie to help them underwrite corporate bonds or arrange a construction loan for Mather University or advise the board of Octopus Enterprises, I cannot believe David would agree.

As for the Committee's report, I take serious exception to their finding that my conduct fell short of the standards expected of this firm's lawyers. You will recall that two years ago, a male partner had an affair with a female client that seriously compromised the case he was handling for her. Nothing was said to him; everyone just stepped in and mopped up—despite the fact that every lawyer in town knew about the matter. He is still here, doing real estate deals.

I think the firm is operating under a double standard.

Yours,

Fiona McGregor

Fiona McGregor

cc: Jason Bell   Frank O'Keefe
        William Frost   Joseph Salerno
        David Greaves   Katherine Sales
        Virginia Ladder   John Wynch
        Felix Landau

TRAYNOR, HAND, WYZANSKI

222 CHURCH STREET
NEW SALEM, NARRAGANSETT 06555
(393) 876-5678

MEMORANDUM
Attorney Work Product

From: Joe Salerno
To: Proctor Hand
RE: Fiona McGregor
Date: ·   April 19, 1999
Attachments:

I regret I was unable to attend the meeting of the Management Committee. I think my presence might have made a difference in the way the Committee responded to Fiona McGregor's letter. I do not think the Committee properly recognized the legitimacy of her complaints. She was not complaining only about the firm's profits but also its high-handed treatment of its divorce lawyers. As you all know, I am a great admirer of Sophie Diehl's, and I think she is a talented criminal lawyer. That being said, she is not a competent divorce lawyer. She is not even an incompetent divorce lawyer. It would have been much more proper for David to have served as the lead lawyer and to have used Sophie as his associate. The Meiklejohns, as I understand the matter, would have cheerfully paid full freight for both an experienced divorce lawyer and his raw associate.

I am now going to say two things that are unpleasant but that need to be said. First, the reprimand is sexist. There's no question about that. No male partner (or male associate for that matter) would be treated in this way. None has been treated this way. John Wynch was never disciplined by the Management Committee, and his behavior was far more compromising to the firm and its reputation. Second, the reprimand is racist, or whatever the term is that describes ethnic discrimination. I do not believe a WASP would have been treated in the same way. John Wynch does double duty here. Those of us who didn't attend Mather or Yale Law Schools, who don't come from one of the original New Salem families, who live by our wits, our brains, our talent, and our industry, seem to be held to a stricter standard than those from the WASP ascendency. If there is a difference between Fiona's behavior and Wynch's, virtue lies with Fiona. She issued a challenge to the firm's authority; so what? He undermined its standards of professional integrity.

cc: Jason Bell   Felix Landau
         William Frost   Frank O'Keefe
         David Greaves   Katherine Sales
         Virginia Ladder   John Wynch

Ineptitude

From: John Wynch   4/19/99 4:33 PM
To: David Greaves <dagreaves@traynor.com>
Date: Mon, 19 Apr 1999 16:33:14
Subject: Ineptitude

For fuck's sake, Greaves, what is going on here? Joe's absolutely right. I love Proctor, you know that, but he has a rod up his ass 50% of the time and shouldn't be allowed to run a meeting. And where the fuck were you? What do you mean getting your knickers in a twist because Fiona challenged your authority? That's what lawyers do every day. That's what we're paid to do.

I was a schmuck in love with a client (and also sleeping with her), but nobody went after me. I read Fiona's letter. She's absolutely right too. I bring in too much money to be disciplined. And I've got balls. But so does Fiona, for that matter.

Stop this shit now.

John

TRAYNOR, HAND, WYZANSKI

222 CHURCH STREET
NEW SALEM, NARRAGANSETT 06555
(393) 876-5678

MEMORANDUM
Attorney Work Product

From:	David Greaves
To:	Jason Bell
	William Frost
	Proctor Hand
	Virginia Ladder
	Felix Landau
	Fiona McGregor
	Frank O'Keefe
	Joseph Salerno
	Katherine Sales
	John Wynch
RE:	Partners' Meeting
Date:	April 20, 1999
Attachments:	

This memo confirms a meeting of the partners tomorrow, Wednesday, April 21, at 10 a.m., in the conference room.

Uproar at THW

From: Sophie Diehl   4/21/99 11:01 AM
To: Maggie Pfeiffer <mcp15@mather.edu>
Date: Wed, 21 Apr 1999 11:01:57
Subject: Uproar at THW

Dear Maggie—

The firm is in an absolute uproar. The management committee decided
to discipline Fiona for challenging my assignment to the Meiklejohn
case, and she protested. Then Joe stepped in and wrote a memo
supporting her and basically accusing the firm of being sexist and racist.
As I'm emailing you, a meeting of the partnership is going on. All we
mice are scurrying around, trying to pick up crumbs of information.
Joe has been really upset; I don't know that he's threatening to leave,
but I wouldn't be surprised. (He threatens to leave regularly for various
reasons, then some case pulls him back. But this is different.) I'm not
sure how the partners are going to be able to mend things. If Joe goes,
I'll have to go too. I love David (sometimes) but I'm not a civil lawyer.
And truth be told, I love Joe more. He's more fun. There's no fun on the
second floor.

Fiona's right. I just wish she didn't hate me.

xoxo,
Sophie

TRAYNOR, HAND, WYZANSKI

222 CHURCH STREET
NEW SALEM, NARRAGANSETT 06555
(393) 876-5678
ATTORNEYS AT LAW

April 22, 1999

Fiona McGregor, Esq.
Traynor, Hand, Wyzanski
222 Church Street
New Salem, Narragansett 06555

Dear Fiona:

I write on behalf of the partnership of the firm. The reprimand issued to you on April 16 has been withdrawn. The partners wish to apologize to you for issuing the reprimand and for criticizing your conduct in regard to your objection to the assignment of attorneys in the matter of Maria Meiklejohn. We recognize the sincerity and legitimacy of your concerns and deeply regret any offense that may have been given.

I hope you will accept this expression of regret. You have provided out-standing service to the firm, its clients, and the community in which we work and live.

Yours,

David Greaves

David Greaves

cc: Jason Bell
        William Frost
        Proctor Hand
        Virginia Ladder
        Felix Landau
        Frank O'Keefe
        Joseph Salerno
        Katherine Sales
        John Wynch

TRAYNOR, HAND, WYZANSKI

222 CHURCH STREET
NEW SALEM, NARRAGANSETT 06555
(393) 876-5678

MEMORANDUM
Attorney Work Product

From: David Greaves
To: Sophie Diehl
RE: Durkheim v. Durkheim: Settlement Offer
Date: April 22, 1999
Attachments: Letter from Ray Kahn
                Settlement Offer from Dr. Daniel E. Durkheim
                Letter from Bruce Meiklejohn

I am enclosing a letter I received from Ray Kahn with a settlement proposal from Dr. Durkheim. It's not so ridiculous that we can ignore it. They've shaped the proposal around Dr. Durkheim's willingness to relinquish any interest he might have in the Vineyard property. It sets a tone. No doubt they believe (not altogether unreasonably) that, should the case go to trial, the judge would take the value of that property into consideration even if he found that Dr. Durkheim had no rights to it. Ms. Meiklejohn is, after all, a putative heiress. There's also a veiled threat of a custody fight, but I don't take it seriously. Dr. Durkheim wants this settled, and a custody fight would drag things out. And we all know he doesn't want custody.

The letter and proposal are in their snakelike way artful. You will see that he'd like to keep you out of the loop. (He didn't actually say: "Let's keep the little lady out of this. We men can come to agreement better without her." But, of course, that's what he meant.) I shall respond by saying that I've asked you to look over the proposal and to draw up our counteroffer. That should make it clear he has to deal with you, which he won't like. (I may be having too much fun with this. Is this what you and Joe do all the time?) I will also draft a discovery request to send with the letter.

I have an idea for setting a tone of our own. I will say that we are exploring the possibility of including in our proposal the value, past, present, and future, of Dr. Durkheim's medical degree. Although there's no Narragansett case on point as far as I know, the revised divorce laws give a very expansive definition of property, and there are precedents, I believe, that have taken the value of an advanced degree into consideration, if not as property per se then as an element to be considered in awarding "reimbursement" alimony for the contributions one spouse made to the other's professional education and development. You need to do some research on this and get back to me ASAP. Look at N.Y., N.J., Conn., and Mass. law and the American Law Institute's proposed model law on Family Dissolution. Ah, the pleasures of saber rattling. They're right up there with early Robert De Niro movies. Kahn and his client will hate it. We could litigate the issue and make new law. That alone could take two years.

I am also enclosing a letter I received this week from Bruce Meiklejohn. He is taking the divorce very hard—not because of the hurt to his daughter and granddaughter but because of the wound to the family honor. I won't apologize for the anti-Semitism because I'm not responsible for it and because I believe anti-Semitism is offensive to everyone, not only Jews. But I want you to know I find it appalling. What does one do about clients with repellant beliefs and values? And yet, I like him too. Enormously. Human beings are a mystery. The short and long of the letter is that money is no object. Of course, we won't pile on the depositions or rack up the hours unless we need to and unless we have specific authorization from Ms. Meiklejohn. I'll answer Bruce Meiklejohn.

April 20, 1999

David Greaves
Traynor, Hand, Wyzanski
222 Church Street
New Salem, Narragansett 06555

Dear David:

Before she left on holiday in Hawaii, my daughter Maria told me she had made arrangements with your firm to use both you and a young associate in your firm, Ann Deal (or is it the Scotch version, Dalziel; I knew a James Dalziel at Mather, her father?), as her attorneys in her divorce. I was very pleased to hear of this arrangement. If you need a third or fourth attorney, do not hesitate to use one. I shall pay. I want her to have the best representation possible. To be frank, I want you to bury Durkheim.

I have never liked him. I tried my best but I couldn't. I invited him to my home and to the Vineyard place; I even spent a weekend with him (the longest of my life) playing golf at Augusta. After I put him up for the Cricket Club, he wanted me to put him up for the Plimouth Club. I tried to explain that the PC wasn't PC: no Jews except, of course, Jim Rosental, Mather's president. Can you believe he hired Ray Kahn to represent him?

I always thought Durkheim married Maria for her money and her connections. His first wife, Helen Fincher, was rich and well connected too. Can't be a co-incidence. I tried to warn Maria, but she was smitten. And now he walks out. He's gotten what he wanted from her. I can't help but feel that family honor is involved.

Maria won't talk to me about it, and you probably won't tell me anything either, all that attorney-client privilege blather. But I trust you and I know you'll do right by my family. I don't care what it costs, get the bastard. And if you need me to rattle chains at the hospital and the med school, let me know. It would be my pleasure.

Sincerely yours,

Bruce Meiklejohn

ELISABETH DREYFUS | 480 RIVERSIDE DRIVE, NEW YORK, NY 10027

April 10, 1999

Dear David:

Last night I went with Sophie to the Mather Rep to see the
Stoppard play, The Real Thing, starring her great friend,
Maggie Pfeiffer. Do you know the play? It's about marriage
and adultery and divorce and remarriage and adultery.
There was a speech in it that struck a chord, coming as
it did so soon after our lunch at Porter's. It's a husband's
explanation to his wife of the possibility of someone else.

> I don't want anyone else but sometimes, surprisingly,
> there's someone, not the prettiest or the most available,
> but you know that in another life it would be her.
> Or him, don't you find? A small quickening. The room
> responds slightly to being entered. Like a raised blind.
> Nothing intended, and a long way from doing anything,
> but you catch the glint of being someone else's possibility,
> and it's a sort of politeness to show you haven't
> missed it, so you push it a little, well within safety, but
> there's that sense of a promise almost being made in
> the touching and kissing without which no one can seem
> to say good morning in this poncy business and one
> more push would do it.
>
> The Real Thing (London 1982), p. 73

Today, I bought a copy of the play at the Co-op; I thought
I should send it to you—out of a sort of politeness.

Elisabeth

Terrible Discovery

From: Sophie Diehl   4/22/99 6:55 PM
To: Maggie Pfeiffer <mcp15@mather.edu>
Date: Thu, 22 Apr 1999 18:55:27
Subject: Terrible Discovery

Dear Maggie—

Where are you? I tried to call you but got no answer. I'm a wreck. I've just had an awful experience. I was in DG's office, looking through the Durkheim docket, the firm's collection of documents and correspondence relating to this damned divorce I've been hog-tied into doing, and came across a letter which didn't belong in the file and which I never, never should have seen. It was from my mother to DG. After we all had lunch and after she saw your play, she sent him a copy of *The Real Thing*. The letter quoted that bit from the play where your husband tells you about the "glint of someone else's possibility." I got light-headed reading it. Could Hannah have seen it and filed it? Did he misfile it himself? I didn't know what to do, so I took it. What do I do with it? What do I do about it? She signed off her letter, "out of a sort of politeness." How could she? And how could he be so indiscreet, leaving it there for anyone (Fiona even) to read? I can't believe they are behaving so badly. They should both be pilloried.

I should have cottoned earlier to all this. Earlier in the day, David had written me a memo uncharacteristically relaxed, almost playful (in spite of all post-Fiona fallout). He's always so matter-of-fact, precise, organized, in his writing. This one was rambling and filled with dangling pronouns. He said he was having fun with the case. He even talked about anti-Semitism in a way I'd never heard him talk before. He never liked it, of course, but he saw it as bad breeding. This time, he was indignant. I thought it was my good influence. I should have known better. It was my mother's bad influence.

Woe is me, Mags.

Sophie

From: Maggie Pfeiffer   4/22/99 7:10 PM

To: Sophie Diehl <asdiehl@traynor.com>

Date: Thu, 22 Apr 1999 19:10:19

Subject: Re: Terrible Discovery

Dear Sophie—

Don't assume the worst. I don't think anything has happened
between them—other than the lunch and the letter. Your mother
didn't proposition him, she only acknowledged an attraction. If she
wanted more, she would have done more. (Believe me, she knows
how.) And we don't even know if he responded—though only a
dope would have failed to respond in some way.

I'm guessing David wanted, still wants, to keep the letter, though
I'm sure he never intended to put it in the docket. Maybe in his
subconscious (WASPs have them too, you know), he wanted you to
know. It must have made him happy, getting it, and we always want
to share our happiness. Who but you is there to share it with? (You
know I'm right, crazy as it sounds. I even bet, in the lunatic part of
his brain that's spinning impossible fantasies of weekend trysts in
NY at the Carlyle, he hopes you're happy for him. It's *A Midsummer
Night's Dream*. And isn't it lovely to know that we still feel that way
in our 50s?) It's unlikely someone else would have gone through the
docket. But I don't think there's much point delving into that. The
real question is what to do with the letter now. DO NOT DESTROY IT.
Give it back. Slip it into one of his desk drawers. Now.

Don't say anything to your mother or David. You wouldn't mind if
it were my mother who was fooling around on her husband. (We'd
all be cheering her on.) And while you've got this proprietary sense
about David, you wouldn't be upset—only annoyed—if you found
out he was flirting with her. The fact that it's your mother who's
doing this is what's upsetting you.

You idolize her. You've always idolized her. You can still idolize her. (Or, you can finally stop now that you're almost 30.) Remember the whole point of that speech is that NOTHING real happens.

I don't mean to trivialize how you're feeling—I'm sure it was a blow, reading it—but it's not, as your mother would say, the end of the world. You've got your own real thing now. Let your mother and David have this small, safe, titillating fling or whatever it is. I don't think it's anything significant. Truly. My guess is that they don't want to "push it," as Stoppard says, but they don't want to give it up entirely either, whatever it is. It's too exciting. Who knows how we'll be misbehaving at 50? If that's the worst thing I do, I'll forgive myself—and hope my daughter, if she finds out, forgives me too.

Love,
Maggie

TRAYNOR, HAND, WYZANSKI

222 CHURCH STREET
NEW SALEM, NARRAGANSETT 06555
(393) 876-5678
ATTORNEYS AT LAW

April 23, 1999

Bruce Meiklejohn
50 Saint Cloud
New Salem, Narragansett 06555

Dear Bruce,

Don't worry. We shall do right by your daughter and granddaughter. The young lawyer's name is Anne Sophie Diehl, known as Sophie to her many friends, myself among them. You may know her dad, by reputation at least. He's John Diehl, University Professor at Columbia and one of the last great Marxist historians. She's smart as a whip and on top of the case. Most important, your daughter has great confidence in her.

The best thing you can do at the moment is not rattle chains at the hospital or blackball Daniel Durkheim's membership in the Plimouth Club but support your daughter and granddaughter. We're in a strong negotiating position. If we need to call out the cavalry, I'll let you know.

Yours truly,

David Greaves

David Greaves

TRAYNOR, HAND, WYZANSKI

222 CHURCH STREET
NEW SALEM, NARRAGANSETT 06555
(393) 876-5678

MEMORANDUM
Attorney Work Product

From:	Sophie Diehl
To:	David Greaves
RE:	Matter of Durkheim: Rehabilitation Alimony
	for Ms. Meiklejohn
Date:	April 23, 1999
Attachments:	

I spoke briefly on the phone this morning with Maria Meiklejohn, who is back from Hawaii. (Her husband did not change the locks while she was away—or close any more accounts.) I gave her a rundown on the settlement offer, and I'll forward a copy of it to her with a letter later today.

While she was away, Ms. Meiklejohn thought about her future, specifically her work and career; she came to the conclusion that she ought to go to law school rather than complete the Ph.D. Her thinking went like this: after the divorce, she'll have to make money (she won't get alimony forever, and she doesn't want to live off her father), and the J.D. is the more useful, more remunerative degree. As she put it, "Who's going to hire a 46-year-old newly minted American studies Ph.D.?" She also thought she'd like practicing law and would be good at it. "I find my divorce mentally stimulating—when it's not emotionally shattering." She'd like to go to Mather Law School (and her chances of getting in are very good), but she'd be willing to go to the University of Narragansett. If she gets into Mather, she should go there. Mather is probably the second-best law school in the country (ha!), and the better the school, the greater the job opportunities, particularly for someone her age.

The projected annual tuition for Mather Law (averaged over three years for the academic years 2001–02 through 2003–04) is $30,000; for Narragansett, it's $14,000. Ms. Meiklejohn thinks Dr. Durkheim should pay the tuition. We could frame the offer to provide both traditional alimony or spousal support for living expenses and rehabilitation alimony or support for tuition at law school. Traditional support would cease with employment at $48,000 a year; rehabilitative support would cease after three (3) years.

I suggested to Ms. Meiklejohn that she might also think about business school and an M.B.A. in public or private management. (The last client of mine who wanted my non-legal advice wanted to know if I could set him up with a drug connection while he was in prison.)

I am finishing up the memo on the value of Dr. Durkheim's medical degree and the possibility of "reimbursement alimony." I'll get it to you before the end of the day. I've prepared two versions, excessive and redacted. I'll send you the redacted and put the longer version in the files.

TRAYNOR, HAND, WYZANSKI

222 CHURCH STREET
NEW SALEM, NARRAGANSETT 06555
(393) 876-5678

MEMORANDUM OF LAW AND FACT
Attorney Work Product

From: Anne Sophie Diehl
To: David Greaves
RE: Matter of Durkheim: The Value of a Medical Degree
Date: April 23, 1999
Attachments:

Memorandum of Law

The issue here is whether a Narragansett court might consider the value of a medical degree in fashioning a divorce settlement under the Equitable Distribution Statute (EDS), Section 830, Title 33, Narragansett Code.

Prior to the divorce revolution of the 1980s, a medical degree was not treated anywhere as an asset or other property interest to be divided or distributed in a divorce, not having any of the usual attributes of property; i.e., it could not be bought, sold, transferred, conveyed, pledged, attached, assigned, or inherited. Further, it had no exchange value on an open market. A court might award the family home to one of the spouses; alternatively, it could order it sold and distribute the proceeds between the parties according to their financial needs and earning abilities. With a medical degree, a court had no such options. Only the degree's recipient could practice medicine. See *In re Marriage of Graham*, 194 Colo. 429, 574 P.2d 75 (1978).

Despite this refusal to consider a medical degree as property, traditional courts nonetheless recognized the value of a medical or other professional degree and took it into account in reaching an equitable divorce settlement, most often as a factor in calculating current and future child support and alimony. They also found that a spouse may be entitled to compensation for her contributions to the acquisition of the other's degree. *In re Marriage of Horstmann*, 263 N.W.2d 885 (Iowa 1978); *Hubbard v. Hubbard*, 603 P.2d 747 (Okl. 1979).

In 1982 the New Jersey Supreme Court explicitly introduced the concept of "reimbursement" alimony, to be awarded in those instances when the contributions by one spouse to the education and training of the other were "made with the mutual and shared expectation that both parties to the marriage [would] derive increased income and material benefits" from the educated spouse's professional practice. *Mahoney v. Mahoney*, 91 N.J. 488 (1982). Two years later, a lower New Jersey court expanded the concept of "reimbursement alimony" to distinguish it from ordinary alimony, which usually carries an automatic cutoff event, typically death, remarriage, or a designated term of years. In *Reiss v. Reiss*, a wife who had put her husband through medical school was awarded reimbursement alimony in a sum of $46,706.70, to be paid in monthly installments of $1,500. When, after receiving the first two monthly payments, the wife remarried, the husband sued to terminate the reimbursement alimony. The court denied his claim, pointing out that, unlike true alimony, which is based on the future needs of the recipient and the anticipated ability of the payer to pay, "reimbursement" alimony recognized a past obligation and called for payment in full. 478 A.2d 441 (Ch. 1984).

For the last 14 years, New York has treated a medical degree as a form of garden-variety marital property, no different from a house or Persian rug or '89 Honda. In 1985 the New York Court of Appeals ruled that the wife was entitled to a 40 percent interest in her husband's medical license. She had contributed more than 75 percent of the couple's total income while the husband completed his education and training, and his medical license was the only tangible asset of their nine-year marriage. *O'Brien v. O'Brien*, 66 N.Y.2d 576 (1985).

Current Narragansett divorce law plainly allows for these new forms of alimony, if not specifically for "reimbursement" alimony with its debt-like features. The Narragansett Supreme Court has consistently given a liberal interpretation to the EDS principle of "equitable distribution." Most recently, in the *Matter of Lemon*, the court awarded a lump sum of "compensatory" alimony to a wife "who had relinquished employment opportunities to accommodate the marital relationship, and was in consequence less able than her husband to support herself." 293 Nar. 966 (1998). Reimbursing a wife for her financial contributions to his education seems a natural next step. As the court wrote in *Lemon*:

> The legislature clearly intended the [EDS] to protect the spouse with less wealth and lower earning capacity and to insure against

a patent disparity between the spouses' standards of living after divorce. Whether we characterize an award as "compensatory" or "rehabilitation" alimony, or as "a distribution of marital property," the fundamental principle is the same. The division of assets and the distribution of income must recognize the parties' relative financial needs and earning abilities as well as their contributions to the wealth of the marriage.

Memorandum of Fact

Dr. Daniel Durkheim, the husband of our client Ms. Maria Meiklejohn, had finished his medical education (both the M.D. and the Ph.D.) before he met Ms. Meiklejohn. Because he took the joint M.D./Ph.D. degree, his education was completely paid for. In 1980, when he and Ms. Meiklejohn began living together, Dr. Durkheim was finishing his training, working as a postdoctoral fellow earning $18,000. All of his salary (after taxes) and then some (from Ms. Meiklejohn) went to pay his child support obligation of $15,000 for his son, Tom, from his first marriage. In 1980, Ms. Meiklejohn earned $19,000 and received from her father a gift of $10,000. After their marriage, he gave each of them $10,000 a year.

Dr. Durkheim's post-degree training (postdoc, internship, and residency) lasted eight years, and until he was appointed an assistant professor in 1987 with a salary of $80,000, he never earned more than $30,000 a year; most if not all went, after taxes, to child support. As an example, in 1987, when he was earning $30,000, Ms. Meiklejohn earned $42,000; in addition, she may be credited with the $20,000 annual gift to the couple from her father. It's plain that, saddled with child support obligations, Dr. Durkheim could not have pursued the kind of elite, ill-paying postdoctoral training he did without his wife's financial contributions, but would have had to either go deeply into debt or pursue a different kind of medical practice, one more immediately remunerative but unlikely to lead to the outstanding academic career he has had.

Given (i) the financial support Ms. Meiklejohn provided to her husband during the crucial later years of his training; (ii) her "relinquish[ment] of employment opportunities [in NY] to accommodate the marital relationship," by moving to New Salem, *Matter of Lemon*; and (iii) the Narragansett Court's expansive reading of the EDS, it is worth including "reimbursement" alimony in our counteroffer, both as a legitimate demand and a negotiating tactic.

Narragansett Statutes
Title 33 of the Narragansett Code, Sections 801ff.
Dissolution of Marriage, Annulment, and Legal Separation

Sec. 830. Equitable distribution.

In the division of assets, the distribution of income, the assignment of property, the award of child support, the award of alimony, and all other allocations of resources, the court must recognize the parties' relative financial needs and earning abilities as well as their contributions to the wealth of the marriage.

Evil Thoughts

From: Sophie Diehl   4/23/99 11:54 PM
To: Maggie Pfeiffer <mcp15@mather.edu>
Date: Fri, 23 Apr 1999 23:54:42
Subject: Evil Thoughts

Dear Maggie—

I am having evil thoughts. It's almost midnight and I'm still at work; I just finished up a memo for THE DIVORCE. Never get divorced. The things you fight about are so demeaning. Everything comes down to money. I keep thinking of Oscar Wilde's definition of a cynic as someone who knows the price of everything and the value of nothing. He was talking about a divorce lawyer.

I've been drafting an email to DG in my head; it oozes artless innocence:

> *Dear David—*
>
> *Have you heard anything from my mom? She told me she so enjoyed meeting you. We could do it again sometime when she's in town.*
>
> *Yours,*
> *Sophie*

I can't stop myself from thinking about it when it's late and I'm tired. I find my thoughts turning dark and mean. They are not behaving well. And of course, neither am I.

I haven't seen or heard from Harry in days. He sent me an email the epitome of short and sweet, with a quote from *The Real Thing* (Henry on happiness) last Saturday, but since then nothing. No answer at his place. Is he alive?

Love,
Sophie

Re: Evil Thoughts

From: Maggie Pfeiffer

To: Sophie Diehl <asdiehl@traynor.com>

Date: Sat, 24 Apr 1999 10:33:09

Subject: Re: Evil Thoughts

4/24/99 10:33 AM

Dear Sophie—

DO NOT, repeat, DO NOT send an email like that to David. You will regret it. I know you're hurt and maybe a little jealous too, but you'll wreck your relationship with him if you go through with it. DO NOT DO IT.

If you need to hash it out with one of the miscreants, hash it out with your mother. (I'm not recommending this; I'm only saying that talking to her is better than going after him.) Of course, if you talk to your mother, you won't do the damage you'd do if you sent that email to David. She won't be in the least embarrassed, only annoyed. And she'll let you have it, with both barrels. (Here I go, channeling Elisabeth Diehl.) She'll tell you to grow up, mind your own business, and get on with your own life. She'll say you're not the only one who's allowed to behave badly now and again. And she's right.

Harry left New Salem after closing night on the 19th. He said he had an emergency in NYC and took off at 4 am right after the set was struck. He looked tired and worn and worried and sad. Something was wrong. I thought you knew.

I am too tired to write another word. I need to go to bed. Matt and I went to a party in NY last night and didn't get home until 3. Don't do anything stupid or rash. I'm sorry if I've been rough here and hurt your feelings; I haven't the energy to be more tactful. You've got to finish up this divorce. Can't you read them the riot act and tell them to shape up and get this thing over? It's not good for you. (It must be truly terrible for them.)

Love,
Maggie

TRAYNOR, HAND, WYZANSKI

222 CHURCH STREET
NEW SALEM, NARRAGANSETT 06555
(393) 876-5678
ATTORNEYS AT LAW

april 26, 1999

Dear Joe,

I am writing to you personally because I want to clear the air. You were right about Fiona's reprimand. I was wrong. Proctor was wrong. I don't know that I'd have dug in the way I did if she were a man. We didn't do anything with Wynch; she was right about that. You saw the letter I wrote. I also spoke to her privately and expressed my personal apologies and regret.

As for your second accusation, I think, as my Welsh granny used to say, you're over-egging the pudding. This firm is not racist or ethnically discriminatory. As someone who belongs to what you refer to as the WASP ascendency, I don't know how it feels to be excluded from it, but I'm having serious trouble (and I mean real serious trouble) seeing you as an outsider. You went to Harvard and Harvard Law School; your dad was a federal judge; you made partner here at 33; Harvard Law woos you every other year, and we have to up your share to keep you. Which we do.

Fiona's got a thing against Sophie, which I don't understand—but that's beside the point. I don't know if she will stay. She's very angry—and not only at Sophie.

Yours,
David

Valuing a Medical Degree

From: Fiona McGregor   4/26/99 12:32 PM
To: David Greaves <dagreaves@traynor.com>
cc: Sophie Diehl <asdiehl@traynor.com>
Date: Mon, 26 Apr 1999 12:32:07
Subject: Valuing a Medical Degree

David,

I just saw Sophie's memo on valuing a medical degree. There's a case
now on appeal to the Narragansett Appellate Court, 2nd Division, *Petrus
v. Petrus,* No 1998-456. I hope she didn't spend too much time on the
memo or charge the clients too much for the work. The briefs pretty
much lay out both sides. I'm not sure how she missed it. Could she have
forgotten to look at Narragansett cases? I've cc'ed her.

Fiona

TRAYNOR, HAND, WYZANSKI

222 CHURCH STREET
NEW SALEM, NARRAGANSETT 06555
(393) 876-5678
ATTORNEYS AT LAW

April 27, 1999

Ray Kahn, Esq.
Kahn & Boyle
46 Broadway
New Salem, NA 06555

Dear Ray:

I have given copies of your letter of April 19 and Dr. Durkheim's settlement offer to my associate, Anne Sophie Diehl, who will respond to the offer in detail after she has discussed it with our client, Maria Meiklejohn, and reviewed all the relevant documentary evidence. Ms. Diehl is the person best acquainted with the case and is accordingly the best person to answer you. You can expect her letter and Ms. Meiklejohn's counteroffer as soon as we are confident that we have a full and accurate picture of the family's financials. We will move as quickly as we can—we too would like to see the matter settled expeditiously—but we want to give Dr. Durkheim's offer the attention it deserves and craft a counteroffer that represents the best interests of our client and their daughter, Jane.

While we agree that Ms. Meiklejohn's knowledge of the couple's financial situation is fairly complete, we do not believe we can in good faith dispense with discovery. It would be irresponsible of us to proceed without knowing that we have the best information available to us. Following usual firm policy in cases of this sort, we have asked Patrick O'Dell, a private investigator the firm has on retainer, to conduct a complete investigation of the couple's assets and property. We have also lined up John Katz, a forensic accountant with Addison & Co., to review all the materials and information produced through the discovery process and Mr. O'Dell's inquiries. Mr. Katz will also be able to provide an actuarial assessment of the annual gifts Bruce Meikle-john has made to the couple over the 16 years of their marriage and a statement on the present and future value of Dr. Durkheim's medical degree. On this latter point, we believe Ms. Meiklejohn has a right to some form of reimbursement alimony for the contributions she made to her husband's career. As you know, she supported him for eight years while he was doing his postdoc, internships, and residency; she also gave up her career in New York to move with him to New Salem.

There are other steps we need to take as well. We will want a current assessment of the St. Cloud Street house. We have asked Laura Buch-oltz of RealProperties Inc. to conduct it. I don't think there's anyone in New Salem who knows the high-end market better than she does. Last year she sold nine homes in the St. Cloud Street area, and she currently is acting as broker for three others.

I am enclosing our discovery requests with this letter. I don't imagine that Dr. Durkheim has any secret Swiss bank accounts, but if he does, you will of course let us know. We will respond promptly to any discovery requests you make of Ms. Meiklejohn.

Yours truly,

David Greaves

David Greaves

Commonwealth of Narragansett
Family Court

County: Tyler   **Docket No:** 99-27

Notice of Request
Mandatory Disclosure & Production

Daniel E. Durkheim   **Plaintiff**

v.

Maria M. Durkheim   **Defendant**

Now comes the defendant **Maria M. Durkheim** by her attorneys, and serves a Notice of Request for Mandatory Disclosure and Production on the plaintiff **Daniel E. Durkheim** for the following records and documents:

1. Three (3) years tax returns, including corporate and partnership, April 1996 to April 1999
2. Three (3) years IRS 1099s and K-1s, April 1996 to April 1999
3. Three (3) years pay stubs (or other evidence of income), April 1996 to April 1999
4. Three (3) years records of NIH and all other grants and awards, public and private, April 1996 to April 1999
5. Three (3) years records of all income from self-employment, honorariums, bonuses, residuals, royalties, advances against royalties, and other similar forms of remuneration, April 1996 to April 1999
6. Three (3) years records, certificates, and statements of all accounts in financial institutions or with brokers and/or financial managers, domestic and foreign, including but not limited to all holdings and shares in stocks, bonds, mutual funds, real estate cooperatives, and other financial packages, April 1996 to April 1999
7. Three (3) years records and statements of all pension, retirement, profit-sharing, and deferred compensation plans, including but not limited to all Keogh, IRA, 401(k), and TIAA-CREF accounts, April 1996 to April 1999

8. Three (3) years records and statements of all other financial holdings and accounts, April 1996 to April 1999

9. Current written appraisals of all interests in real property owned or held by plaintiff in whole or part as of March 1999

10. Current written appraisals of any asset and or item of personal property valued at $4,999 or more owned or held by plaintiff in whole or part as of March 1999

11. Three (3) years records of all transactions relating to the sale or other transfer or conveyance of real and/or personal property owned or held by the plaintiff in whole or part, April 1996 to April 1999

12. Current written appraisals of all motor vehicles owned or leased by plaintiff as of March 1999

13. Three (3) years statements of all life and disability insurance policies on plaintiff, April 1996 to April 1999

14. All other records and statements of property, assets, holdings, or interests held by or on behalf of the plaintiff relevant to an equitable distribution of such property, assets, holdings, and interests pursuant to the dissolution of the marriage of **Daniel E. Durkheim** and **Maria M. Durkheim**.

Plaintiff's duty to disclose is ongoing. The requests made here do not preclude other discovery requests or motions.

Certificate of Service

I, **David Greaves**, Esquire, hereby certify that on the **27th** day of **April 1999**, I caused a copy of the foregoing Notice of Request for Mandatory Disclosure and Production to be served on plaintiff's attorney by mailing a copy, first-class, postage prepaid, to:

Ray Kahn, 46 Broadway, New Salem, NA 06555.

Signature of Attorney: **David Greaves, Traynor, Hand, Wyzanski**

Re: Valuing a Medical Degree

From: Sophie Diehl   4/28/99 9:04 AM

To: David Greaves <dagreaves@traynor.com>

Date: Wed, 28 Apr 1999 9:04:32

Subject: Re: Valuing a Medical Degree

Dear David,

I'm following up on Fiona's email on valuing a medical degree. I'm so sorry—and so embarrassed. I missed *Petrus*. I read the briefs last night. I say pretty much the same things, but their fact situation is much stronger. Wife has no family money, no job, no education, and she worked solidly to put her husband through college, medical school, and internship. So maybe, given Ms. Meiklejohn's situation, it's different??? I'm feeling stupid.

Sophie

TRAYNOR, HAND, WYZANSKI

222 CHURCH STREET
NEW SALEM, NARRAGANSETT 06555
(393) 876-5678
ATTORNEYS AT LAW

April 27, 1999

Maria Mather Meiklejohn
404 St. Cloud Street
New Salem, NA 06556

Dear Mia:

I am forwarding to you a letter from Ray Kahn together with a settlement offer from your husband. The offer is unreasonable but not so unreasonable that we can ignore it. Look it over, then call the office for an appointment. We'll thrash out a response, equally unreasonable but not so unreasonable *they* can ignore it.

I am also forwarding a letter David Greaves sent Kahn this morning, responding to his smarmy suggestion that the two men put their heads together and come up with an agreement. David is not defending me or my role in the negotiations ("As if you need defending," he said); he's defending you the best way he knows how. If he thought for a minute that the two of them could hammer out a satisfactory agreement quickly and privately, he'd do it. Instead, he has written a letter that is at once disingenuous and bullying, and sent with it a fairly harassing set of discovery requests. My bet is they will annoy your husband. Be prepared (#4 especially is a zinger).

Don't panic at the request for joint custody or the veiled threat of sole custody. Kahn can't expect his client to win on that point; he is negotiating. (Kahn's a bit like a pit bull piddling his way down a lane to mark his territory, completely oblivious to the fact that the dog next door is a very large, ill-tempered rottweiler.) He is likely to give it up when we give up our request for the house. To be truthful, I've never understood—or appreciated—the so-called art of negotiation whereby each side stakes out an extreme position and then sits down at the table and begins horse trading, the cat for the dog, the Jenny Holzer for the Persian rug, the pension for the 401(k) plan, the child for the house. But men believe in it (it must make losing easier), so we shall have to play along.

Your father wrote to David to let him know he approves of the two-lawyer arrangement. He also said that if we find we need to bring in a third or fourth, he would pay. We don't think it will ever come to that, but it's nice to know we can call out the troops if we need them and if *you* find it acceptable. We will do nothing of the kind without your explicit and informed consent. We may want to employ a private investigator and a forensic accountant—or at least threaten to employ them, if, as David says, it becomes necessary in "a case of this sort."

I've got some ideas about a counteroffer; I look forward to hearing what you think.

Yours,

Anne Sophie Diehl

Anne Sophie Diehl

April 29, 1999

Anne Sophie Diehl
Traynor, Hand, Wyzanski
222 Church Street
New Salem, NA 06555

Dear Sophie:

Your letter with the enclosures brought on an attack of nausea. I'm
not kidding. I felt a rise in my gorge when I saw the fat envelope with
your firm's name on the flap. I took a Xanax before I opened it. I would
never have guessed getting divorced was so mentally disorganizing.
I was ready for depression, but this is something else. I feel I've lost
my underpinnings, literally, like a desk chair that's thrown a pin and
wobbles precariously on its shaft. And yet, I don't feel as miserable as
I thought I would. After that breakdown in your office three weeks
ago, I'm more anxious and worried than depressed—and intermittently
more optimistic too. Do you know the Emily Dickinson line "Hope
is a thing with feathers"? Every so I often I feel a fluttering of hope,
hovering nearby, like a hummingbird at my shoulder. I'm also really
pissed at Daniel.

I know I shouldn't go on like this, and I'm truly ashamed of myself,
but I don't know who else to talk to. I'm the first in my crowd to go
through a divorce. Cortez upon a peak in Darien. It's funny, a couple
of acquaintances—not real friends, but parents at Jane's school—have
asked me out to lunch, ostensibly to offer support but really, I think,
to see what it's like, being dumped and having to rethink your whole

future. I let them know it isn't pretty. Whatever thoughts they had of getting out of their marriage, they sober up quickly. Then they start worrying that I might be after their husbands. As if.

I know you said Danny's offer was unreasonable, but did you do the math? He's offered to pay $24,000 in child support, $14,000 for Jane's tuition, and $36,000 in alimony, for a total annual outlay of $74,000. If you take away $12,000 for the taxes I'll have to pay on the alimony and the tuition, which I'll never see but will go directly to the school, Jane and I would have $48,000 a year. Rent will take at least half that and my car another sixth. Meanwhile, Danny gets to keep $200,000 a year after taxes, probably more, since the alimony is tax-deductible.

Then there's his request for joint physical custody and the threat perhaps of asking for sole custody. How can he be so cynical about his own child? He hasn't spent a whole day with Jane since we moved to New Salem—not even when I've been in Philadelphia visiting my sister. And don't say it's his lawyer telling him what to do. He hired that lawyer. He wanted that kind of advice. What a shithead. If he keeps up that crap, I swear I'll sic my father on him. I know you think (not without cause) that my father is an anti-Semitic asshole. Well, he is, in his class-bound, hidebound way (though with Daniel, his hatred is personal and aboriginal, going back to their first meeting, for reasons I've never fathomed), but he's more than that. When he's not being a jerk, he can concentrate wonderfully—and he has a genius for revenge. You wait. If David Greaves gives my father the go-ahead, he'll dismember him, limb by limb, and Danny won't know what happened to him until he looks down and sees he's been cut off at the knees or, better yet, the balls. (I somehow feel uninhibited writing to you. I figure you have to have heard worse.)

I called this morning to see about coming in tomorrow, but they said you had a criminal court date. On Monday, the 3rd, I'm going down to

Philadelphia to see my sister. I'll be back on Tuesday night. I've made an appointment to see you on Wednesday morning, the 5th. Unless, it's an emergency, I'd rather not put off my visit to Cordelia. We always plan our visits ahead of time, and she counts on my coming.

Your discovery order was very thorough. Danny's going to have a fit over your request for all the records of his NIH grants. There's always money in a grant for the chief investigator, though I've never been quite sure how it was handled. I've always assumed it was included in his salary and W-2 forms, but it may not be. Of course, you should hire an accountant and a detective if you think they would be useful. You can hire an enforcer and a voodoo priest if you think *they* would be useful. I'll pay. I trust you and David.

Yours,

Mia Meiklejohn

P.S. April 23 was Jane's 11th birthday. She was wretched and I was wretched, but her father was as jolly as a Macy's Santa. He wanted to have a celebratory dinner with her and couldn't understand why she didn't want to go. He told her to buck up. I thought she'd burst into tears. As a present, he got her Rollerblades but no helmet, no knee pads, no wrist guards. Let's hear it for pediatricians.

P.P.S. Where in God's name did they get the $6 million valuation of my mother's house? We haven't had it appraised since she died. It's worth real money, or at least the land is, but not that much. They are so full of shit. Excuse me.

MRS. DANIEL E. DURKHEIM
245 CLAREMONT AVENUE
NEW YORK, NY 10027

May Day

Sophie,

I've made a major sociological breakthrough. I've discovered the seven stages of divorce, a kind of parallel to the twelve stages of grief. (Have you noticed how many things come in twelves and sevens? With twelves, there are AA's Steps, the Tribes of Israel, the months of the year. With sevens, there are the Pillars of Wisdom, Snow White's dwarves, the deadly sins.) Right now, I'm smack in the middle of Fury, No. 4. First, there was Shock, No. 1, which lasted about a week, followed by a month of Despair, No. 2, and two months of Numbness, No. 3. I'm waiting for the last three, or what I imagine them to be: Vengeance, No. 5, Relief, No. 6, and Bliss, No. 7. (I played with the idea of adding an eighth,

Self-Pity, but that is so pervasive, I think of it as the Muse of divorce rather than a stage.) I`m expecting Vengeance to kick in shortly and stick around at least until the settlement signing, which will herald Relief. Bliss is a new house with a brand-new king-sized bed—and the news that Danny`s dick has fallen off. (I`m counting on that voodoo priest for that.)

As always,

Mia

P.S. Don`t you love the monogram? A first-anniversary wedding present. I found it as I was going through some old papers.

Sanity

From: Sophie Diehl   5/2/99 1:23 PM
To: Maggie Pfeiffer <mcp15@mather.edu>
Date: Sun, 2 May 1999 13:23:16
Subject: Sanity

Dear Maggie—

Thanks for talking me down last weekend. I was a mess. I went home and slept for the next 11 hours. When I woke up, I had a message on my answering machine from Harry. He said he had been called away on an emergency and would be back in New Salem the end of this week, Friday at the latest. I spent all of last weekend reading *What Maisie Knew*. Have you read it? I thought it was going to be cool and ironic (I don't know why). Not a bit. It is so cruel, at times I couldn't go on reading. Maisie's parents are so awful, so mean, the absolute worst, not counting those who lock their children in closets or put their cigarettes out on their legs. (And I can't seem to get away from divorce.) But slowly, sanity returned, as it must with James. You have to pay attention to those goddamn sentences.

I won't do anything about my mother's letter. I reread my deranged email. You were right. I was jealous. And infantile. Our parents don't want us to have sex until we're grown. And we never want them to have it.

Let's have dinner Tuesday night. I'll take you and Matt to Racquets. You take such good care of me. What would I do without you? Well, we know the answer to that. I'd ruin everything and make an ass of myself to boot.

Love,
Sophie

TRAYNOR, HAND, WYZANSKI

222 CHURCH STREET
NEW SALEM, NARRAGANSETT 06555
(393) 876-5678

MEMORANDUM
Attorney Work Product

From: Sophie Diehl
To: David Greaves
RE: Letter from Mia Meiklejohn on Settlement Offer
Date: May 3, 1999
Attachments: Letter from MMM

Mia Meiklejohn wrote me a letter responding to the Settlement Offer from her husband. It's a doozy. Is that the way divorce clients usually respond? She seems to think so. If Jerry Springer ever decides to do a talk show with Mensa members, she'd be a natural. Among my clients, those who show an epistolary bent tend to ramble incoherently, suggesting improbable alibis or character witnesses (I've been asked to depose the pope and Hillary Clinton) or attacking the prosecution (one client said the assistant district attorney was prejudiced against him because he had killed two children and she was a mother).

Ms. Meiklejohn's decision to go to law school strikes me as very sensible. She's logical and sharp. She did the math, adding up the proposed child support and alimony offers. There can't be many clients who are able to focus so clearly and so effectively at this stage of a divorce, if ever. (Do you remember she got a valuation on the St. Cloud Street house even before she met with me?) It's a bit daunting. I don't think I've ever had a client who wasn't a psychopath who was smarter than I. Or better read. I had to call my mother to find out what she meant by "Cortez upon a peak in Darien." (Keats, "On First Looking into Chapman's Homer." You knew that, didn't you? Your generation is so much better educated than mine.) It threw me for a loop. I kept thinking of Darien, CT, which made no sense.

Ms. Meiklejohn is coming in Wednesday morning at 10. We'll hammer out a bottom-line proposal as well as an extravagant counteroffer to send Ray Kahn. She suggested (humorously?) we hire an enforcer. Did she realize that I actually know enforcers, the whole range of hired goons, from stalkers to bone breakers to hit men? With most clients, I'd say no; with Ms. Meiklejohn, who's to say. She's one tough cookie.

Did you notice the letterhead? On April 8 (I was so curious that I went back through the docket to find my memo), Ms. Meiklejohn told me she was going to resume her maiden name. In three weeks, she has had new stationery printed up—even though she's probably going to move out of the St. Cloud house within the next six months. (The envelope only has the address, so she can keep using the old ones. A savings!) Once again, I am reduced to saying admiringly, the rich are different. (Fitzgerald 2; Hemingway 0.)

Bliss is a new king-sized bed. Is that true for men too?

THE UNIVERSITY OF NARRAGANSETT
SCHOOL OF LAW

The Dean of the
University of Narragansett School of Law
and Mrs. Seamus FitzGerald
request the pleasure of the company of

Ms. Anne Sophie Diehl

at a dinner in honor of

Fiona McGregor, '85
PARTNER, TRAYNOR, HAND, WYZANSKI

James R. Donaldson, '70
PARTNER, MARTIN, MILLER & DONALDSON

and

Robert Fenstermacher, '55
PARTNER, FARROW ALLERTON

SATURDAY, JUNE 5, 1999
AT 7 O'CLOCK IN THE EVENING

HOTEL NARRAGANSETT
74 WHALLEY AVENUE
NEW SALEM, NARRAGANSETT

Black Tie RSVP 393-875-8777

TRAYNOR, HAND, WYZANSKI

222 CHURCH STREET
NEW SALEM, NARRAGANSETT 06555
(393) 876-5678

MEMORANDUM
Attorney Work Product

From: David Greaves
To: Sophie Diehl
RE: Letter from Mia Meiklejohn on Settlement Offer
Date: May 3, 1999
Attachments:

Mia Meiklejohn's short math exercise hits the nail on the head. It should go in your letter, right at the top. She'll make an excellent lawyer. She's a natural—and she wants to win.

Her letter is more literate and much more literary than most, but substantively, it's pretty much what you'd expect. Most divorcing clients say terrible things to their lawyers about their spouses. And they say even worse things to each other, often in front of their lawyers. Body parts figure prominently.

She's right about her father. If we let him loose, he will take Durkheim apart, and as she says, Durkheim won't know it until it's over and Bruce Meiklejohn has handed him his head on a tray. (Different body parts, same modus operandi.) He didn't get to be so successful by ranting against Jews, though early in his career, it may have served him. People underestimate him. Never do that, Sophie. You've never met him. Under the right circumstances, he can be highly engaging. Maybe I'll set up a lunch. It might do you good. It might do him good.

I do know the Keats poem; I read it in English 101 my freshman year at Mather. Maybe we old guys were better educated back then, but that's no excuse for not having read Keats. And you can't blame Columbia for not knowing that poem. (Doesn't Columbia still have a Great Books curriculum?) People over 21 are allowed to read Keats. Your education doesn't stop when you graduate.

I'm sure she knows you know enforcers. I bet her father knows them too.

I've gotten used to the rich; they rarely surprise me anymore. I knew a woman who had monogrammed paper tissues, white with three blue initials. That did surprise me.

Recently divorced women buy new beds; recently divorced men buy big-screen TVs. You tell me what it means.

TRAYNOR, HAND, WYZANSKI

NEW SALEM, NARRAGANSETT 06555
(393) 876-5678

MEMORANDUM
Attorney Work Product

From:	Sophie Diehl
To:	David Greaves
RE:	Matter of Durkheim: Draft Bottom-Line Settlement Counteroffer
Date:	May 7, 1999
Attachments:	*Settlement Breakdowns:*
	Summary, Income & Expenses, Assets & Liabilities

Ms. Meiklejohn and I came up with the following bottom-line settlement proposal. At the end, I've attached a series of charts summarizing the proposal. Their purpose is to provide snapshot views of the various allocations and distributions. Their redundancy is offset, I hope, by their usefulness. (I'm being maniacally zealous, aren't I?) Our counteroffer will be larger, not outrageous but excessive. Ray Kahn needs to win some, so we'll need room to retreat. I'll draft it after you've reviewed this.

CUSTODY
Ms. Meiklejohn will ask for joint legal custody and sole physical custody of their daughter, Jane, with generous visitation for Dr. Durkheim, including weekends and holidays. Given the demanding schedule he follows at work, joint physical custody would not be in Jane's best interests.

INCOME & EXPENSES ALLOCATION
Child Support
Ms. Meiklejohn will ask for $72,000 in child support for the first year, the amount to increase (or decrease) after that, proportionate to the increases (or decreases) in Dr. Durkheim's income. As an example, if Dr. Durkheim's salary increases by 8% next year, child support will increase by 8%. Out of this allotment, Ms. Meiklejohn will pay for Jane's school fees,

THE DIVORCE PAPERS (Page 209)

clothes, food, vacations, and other ordinary expenses. Child support will continue until April 23, 2011, Jane Durkheim's 23rd birthday, or the last day of the month of her graduation from college, whichever event comes first. These alternative termination dates allow Jane to go through college on the five-year plan.

The child support figure represents just under 20% of Dr. Durkheim's gross income. Narragansett has Child Support Guidelines, but they do not apply if the family income is above $40,000 a year. At $40,000, the amount payable for four or more children under the guidelines is 30% of the *family's* gross income, with each parent paying a part of the total, proportionate to his or her income. The figure for one child is 20%.

College Costs

Dr. Durkheim will pay the cost of tuition for the college of Jane's choice; Ms. Meiklejohn will pay the cost of room, board, and expenses. Any contribution from one of the party's employers will be credited to the obligation of that party, reducing his or her payment accordingly. For example, if Dr. Durkheim's employer contributes $10,000 toward tuition totaling $35,000 (estimated tuition for Mather University in 2006, Jane's projected freshman year), Dr. Durkheim will be required to pay only $25,000. If Ms. Meiklejohn's future employer contributes $10,000 toward tuition, that amount will be deducted from her obligation for room and board (estimated at $20,000), reducing her payment to $10,000. If both parties, as now, are employed by a single employer who gives only one scholarship per child annually, each party will be credited with one-half the total, regardless of who made the formal application; in our example, each will be credited with $5,000.

Each year on her birthday, Jane has received a gift of $10,000 from her grandfather, Bruce Meiklejohn. By the time she is 18 and ready for college, that fund, if he continues to make the annual gift, should be worth $350,000 or so. Dr. Durkheim may insist that this money be used for college, reducing both his and his former wife's obligation.

Traditional Alimony or Spousal Support

Ms. Meiklejohn will ask for $48,000 in alimony for seven (7) years, to compensate her for the lost income and employment opportunities of the last seven (7) years. The seven-year cutoff also coincides with Jane's graduation from high school. Alimony will automatically cease upon her death, remarriage, or employment at an annual salary of $48,000 or more. (This dollar figure was pegged to her highest salary, $47,000, which she earned in 1991.)

Rehabilitation Alimony
Ms. Meiklejohn will ask for rehabilitation alimony of a maximum of $30,000/year for three (3) years ($90,000 total) to pay law school tuition at Mather (less at Narragansett). There will be no automatic cessation event such as marriage, except not attending law school or dropping out.

Compensatory or Reimbursement Alimony
Ms. Meiklejohn is willing to relinquish all claims to compensatory or reimbursement alimony, including any claim for compensation for Dr. Durkheim's medical degree, in the final settlement if the other terms are satisfactory.

Summary on Impact of Spousal and Child Support Offers
Under this proposal, Ms. Meiklejohn would receive a total of $150,000 a year from Dr. Durkheim in alimony (including law school tuition in the form of rehabilitation alimony) and child support, of which the $78,000 in spousal support and rehabilitation alimony would be taxable to her. After taxes of approximately $20,000, her net income would be $130,000. Ms. Meiklejohn's expenses post-divorce are estimated at $173,300, $42,300 more than her net income. The difference will be made up by the interest income on her investments, reductions in expenses for travel and clothes, and summer employment during law school.

Having paid his wife $150,000, Dr. Durkheim would have $220,000 left. He would have to pay taxes on the $72,000 child support, but not on the $78,000 in alimony, which would be taxable to Ms. Meiklejohn. His total tax bill would probably be $60,000 (assuming deductions for property taxes, mortgage, and alimony), giving him an after-tax income of approximately $160,000. With his living expenses estimated at $162,500, he has a shortfall of only $2,500. I spoke with Ms. Meiklejohn about hiring a forensic accountant to do precise tax and interest analyses, but these rough figures show that Dr. Durkheim would not have to curtail his standard of living or give up the house. Ms. Meiklejohn would take over many of the expenditures that formerly came out of the pooled family income.

Medical Insurance
Ms. Meiklejohn will pay $3,200 for a COBRA account to continue her coverage under Dr. Durkheim's plan. Jane will continue on Dr. Durkheim's policy.

Automobiles
Ms. Meiklejohn will take the 1997 Saab, the car she normally drives. It is two years old and has two years left on its loan. Its original cost was $32,000. Its current value is $22,000. Dr. Durkheim can keep the 1999 Audi, which is under a four-year lease. The car cost $68,000. It is worth now more than $60,000.

SEPARATE ASSETS

Property acquired by inheritance and/or before marriage is the parties' separate property and shall remain so. It is not subject to equitable distribution.

Ms. Meiklejohn's Separate Assets
Before her marriage, Ms. Meiklejohn inherited a house on Martha's Vineyard from her mother. She owns this house as a tenant in the entirety under a trust with her father. Her interest is not transferable, nor is it vested; it depends on her outliving her father, a statistical likelihood undercut by the fact that her mother died in 1979, at age 46, of breast cancer.

Dr. Durkheim's Separate Assets
In October 1998, Dr. Durkheim inherited from his mother $16,000 in cash and a 1989 Honda, which he donated to a charity. The money was deposited in a joint savings account. It will be subtracted from the total amount in the joint savings account prior to division and given to Dr. Durkheim.

JOINT ASSETS

The governing principle in the division of joint assets and liabilities is equitable distribution. Title does not determine ownership. All the assets to be divided were acquired during the marriage. In making the division, we recognize the parties' intentions and expectations during the marriage, Ms. Meiklejohn's lost income and employment opportunities, her financial contributions in the early years of their marriage, and Bruce Meiklejohn's annual $20,000 gifts to the couple for 16 years.

Family Residence: $240,000

The family residence at 404 St. Cloud cost, with the land, $375,000 to build. Dr. Durkheim and Ms. Meiklejohn put down $125,000 and took out a 30-year 8% mortgage for the remainder of $250,000. To date, virtually none of the principal has been paid off. Since they built the house, land values in New Salem have increased greatly, and the current value of the home, according to Laura Bucholtz of RealProperties Inc., is now $525,000. If the home were sold this year and the mortgage paid off, the Durkheim-Meiklejohns would recover their $125,000 down payment and realize a clean profit of $115,000 (the difference of $150,000, less the Realtor's fee of $31,500, calculated at 6% of the sale price, and closing costs of approximately $3,500), giving them $240,000 cash in hand. Ms. Meiklejohn is willing for Dr. Durkheim to keep the house, but she would like to recoup some of the down payment of $125,000 and realize some of the profit of $115,000. She will ask for $120,000, half the current equity. In lieu of forcing a sale, she suggests receiving this amount from stock market investments. Under this arrangement, Dr. Durkheim assumes the mortgage.

Stock Market Investments: $700,000

These investments should be divided equally, each receiving $350,000. If Dr. Durkheim wishes to keep the house, Ms. Meiklejohn suggests recouping her proposed $120,000 share of the equity in the St. Cloud Street house from these investments. This amount should be subtracted from Dr. Durkheim's share of $350,000 and added to her share of $350,000, leaving him with $230,000 and her with $470,000.

Dr. Durkheim's 401(k) Plan: $300,000

This account should be divided equally, each party receiving $150,000.

Dr. Durkheim's TIAA-CREF Retirement Accounts: $600,000

This account should be divided equally between the parties, given the assumption during the marriage that Dr. Durkheim would accumulate a retirement fund for both himself and his wife. Each party receives $300,000.

Treasury Bills: $90,000

These investments should be divided equally, each party receiving $45,000.

Joint Savings Accounts: $80,000

In principle, these accounts should be divided equally after subtracting $16,000, which represents Dr. Durkheim's inheritance from his mother, giving Dr. Durkheim $48,000 and Ms. Meiklejohn $32,000. In fact, this account holds only $16,000, the remaining $64,000 having been withdrawn by Ms. Meiklejohn to cover her expenses during the negotiation period in response to Dr. Durkheim's decision to close their joint checking account. The $16,000 goes to Dr. Durkheim.

Household Furnishings, Objects & Artworks: $100,000

The value of the household furnishings is skewed by the value of three items that Ms. Meiklejohn thinks she and her husband will both want: a Persian rug ($45,000), a Jenny Holzer piece, and a Cindy Sherman photograph. They also own some very good paintings by other artists (a Wolf Kahn, an Ephraim Rubenstein, a Robert Sweeney, a Boris Chaliapin) and some '50s modern furniture (a particularly nice Eames shelf), but Ms. Meiklejohn expects they will be able to divide them without too much acrimony. Ms. Meiklejohn would give up the Persian rug (which was a wedding gift from her grandparents) for the other stuff. She doesn't think Dr. Durkheim likes either the Holzer or Sherman (she bought them in the late '80s), but he knows their value. Bruce Meiklejohn will want his daughter to keep the rug and will, she believes, be annoyed (and incredulous) at her choice.

EQUITABLE DISTRIBUTION WITH SALE OF FAMILY RESIDENCE

Item	Marital Assets	Husband	Wife
Family Residence Sold	$ 240,000	120,000	120,000
TIAA-CREF	600,000	300,000	300,000
401(k) Plan	300,000	150,000	150,000
Stock Market Investments	700,000	350,000	350,000
Treasury Bills	90,000	45,000	45,000
Savings Accounts	16,000	16,000	0
TOTAL	**$1,946,000**	**$981,000**	**$965,000**

Maria Mather Meiklejohn and Daniel E. Durkheim
Settlement Breakdown: Income & Expenses 1998

INCOME	Family 1998 Pre-Divorce	Husband Post-Divorce	Wife Post-Divorce
Husband's Salary	370,000	370,000	
Taxes, Soc Sec	(100,000)	(60,000)	
Wife's Salary	14,000		
Taxes, Soc Sec	(4,000)		
Child Support		(72,000)	72,000
Alimony			
Spousal support		(48,000)	48,000
Rehabilitation Alimony		(30,000)	30,000
Taxes			(20,000)
NET Income	**280,000**	**160,000**	**130,000**

EXPENSES	Family 1998 Pre-Divorce	Husband Post-Divorce	Wife Post-Divorce
House (404 St. Cloud)	51,600	51,600	
House for Ms. Meiklejohn			24,000
Housekeeper	26,000	13,000	13,000
Tuition (Jane)	13,000		13,000
Tuition (MMM)			30,000
Automobiles			
Audi	9,600	9,600	
Saab	7,200		7,200
Medical			
Insurance	1,800	1,800	3,200
Office Visits	1,200	600	600
Prescriptions	800	200	600
Eyeglasses	1,800	900	900
Psychoanalysis MMM	13,000		13,000

Food	15,600	7,600	8,000
Clothing	12,000	7,500	4,500
Debt			
Entertainment	12,000	7,500	4,500
Travel, Vacations	36,000	16,000	20,000
Pets	1,200	800	400
Spending Money	20,800	10,400	10,400
Savings			
Investments	35,000	20,000	10,000
401(k) DED	20,000	15,000	10,000
TOTAL Expenses	**$278,600**	**$162,500**	**$173,300**
Expenses & Income	**$2,000**	**($2,500)**	**($42,300)**

Dissed by Fiona

From: Sophie Diehl   5/7/99 10:17 AM
To: Maggie Pfeiffer <mcp15@mather.edu>
Date: Fri, 7 May 1999 10:17:11
Subject: Dissed by Fiona

Dear Maggie,

I just had a very unsettling conversation with Fiona. Well, not exactly
a conversation; I was too dumbfounded to say anything. She's being
honored by the University of Narragansett Law School on June 5, at its
annual alumni dinner. The dean (who clerked for Judge Howard) invited
all the partners and associates at Traynor, Hand, and the firm purchased
four tables. We all regarded it as a command performance. She poked
her head into my office (a first!) and said, "Look, I don't expect you want
to attend the dinner on the 5th. I told the dean it was unlikely you could
make it." Poof. She was gone.

David and Proctor were awful, not consulting her on the divorce case,
reprimanding her the way they did, but instead of going after them, she
seems to have decided it's my fault. Or maybe she can't uninvite them?

WWFWD? I'm working on that.

xoxoxo,
Sophie

Harry

From: Sophie Diehl   5/8/99 4:23 PM
To: Maggie Pfeiffer <mcp15@mather.edu>
Date: Sat, 8 May 1999 16:23:09
Subject: Harry

Dear Mags—

I don't know where to begin. I finally saw Harry today. He called last night, after three weeks of silence (not counting that single phone message). He said he couldn't talk then—he was too tired—but asked me to meet him tomorrow (today now) at Golightly's at noon. He sounded awful. I got a dreaded sense of deja vu. "Shit," I thought, "he's going to break up with me there, in public, in front of everyone." What next for Golightly's? Someone getting fired?

Harry's married; he's separated—not legally but "geographically, physically, and emotionally," was the way he put it—but nonetheless married. Her name is Tessa Gregg; she's an actress/waitress in New York. They were married in 1994 and separated in July 1997, at her instigation. She decided she didn't want to go to New Salem with him and didn't want to commute. It was a precipitous break. Two days after she told him she wasn't moving with him, she moved out—and moved in with someone else, an actor/bartender named Sly Slammer (or Spanner or Scanner—I didn't catch the name and didn't think I needed to). Harry was devastated. He went off to the drama school and proceeded then to sleep with every actress in the first- and second-year programs except you. The famous fuck-cure.

Harry and Tessa met in 1992 at an acting class in the city. After a few months of dating, she got pregnant. She had an abortion. They kept going out. After two years she told him she wanted to get married or break up. He was crazy about her. They got married. He had felt terrible about the abortion, but I don't think that's why he married her. I think he married her because she was beautiful, unreliable, careless, and sexually imaginative. (This is my summary of a much longer narrative.) He said he married her because she made him feel more alive than he'd ever felt. My heart sank. His description reminded me of Monkey in *Portnoy's Complaint*. We bill payers don't stand a chance against those girls.

About a year ago Tessa called him to say that she was going to speak with a lawyer about getting a divorce. Harry said okay. He didn't hear from her—or about her—again until midnight on the 18th, when you were all striking the set. He got a call from a resident at New York Hospital telling him that his wife had attempted suicide and was in the intensive care unit. She had taken 60 Tylenol with a pint of gin, apparently a lethal combo. Your liver shuts down. It was touch and go for three days, but she pulled through. For the last three weeks he's been mostly in New York. He's been trying to sort out Tessa's affairs and get her settled. She took the pills because she and Sly broke up and she felt lost; he left her for a model. (Apparently, no one has ever walked out on Tessa before; she's the bolter.) She has no money, no health insurance, no job. Her parents flew in from Minnesota, but they are straight out of Lake Wobegon and didn't have a clue about their daughter or her life. They've been helping out with money, thank God, but leaning on Harry to make all the arrangements. (They are grateful for his help; they knew that Tessa and Harry had separated for now.) Harry got her into Austen Riggs. She says she wants to go to California. She said it wasn't a serious attempt, only a "gesture." Sly never called or showed up.

Harry apologized for not getting in touch with me sooner, but said he was too distracted by everything and wasn't ready to talk about Tessa. I asked him if he was over her. He said he didn't know how he felt about her, but he knew he needed to get away from her permanently. He asked me to find him a divorce lawyer. "Not Fiona," he said, smiling wanly, the only smile I got from him at lunch.

I wanted to ask how he felt about me, about us, but it didn't seem the moment. I told him I was sorry for all his unhappiness and said I'd find him a lawyer, cheaper than someone in my firm. He said he'd call me in a week or two. He had to clear his head. WWFWD? She used to say: If you can't do what makes you feel good, do what makes you feel least bad.

I told Harry not to call me. I said I'd get him the name of a lawyer and email it to him. I told him his life was too messy at the moment and I didn't want to get involved, or more involved. "I didn't know you had a wife," I said. "Why didn't you tell me?" I couldn't help myself. He was too tired to answer.

And then I left. I decided the best, or least bad, thing to do was break it off, right then. I didn't want to sit around waiting for him to call. I didn't want to hope and then have my hopes smashed. I didn't want to be around during the next fuck-cure.

I'm unhappy right now, but I couldn't sit home and wait for him to call. I'm no Griselda.

Did I do the right thing? I have a terrible track record with men. Could he be bad boyfriend No. 6?

Love,
Sophie

Re: Harry   5/9/99 5:18 PM
From: Maggie Pfeiffer
To: Sophie Diehl <asdiehl@traynor.com>
Date: Sun, 9 May 1999 17:18:24
Subject: Re: Harry

> Dear Sophie,
>
> I feel so badly for you. I had no idea Harry was married; I don't think
> anyone at the drama school did—or does. He had a reputation as a
> rake, a heartbreaker, a swordsman, but I always thought that was a
> cover. He wasn't completely honest with you, with anyone, but the
> story he told you says he's a good guy. He feels he has an obligation
> to his wife—and she is still his wife, which can mean that Harry's good
> husband material but maybe lousy boyfriend material.
>
> Sometimes men make loving them so hard.
>
> I'm sorry too that Fiona's giving you grief. If things with Harry were
> better, you could put up with her and her nonsense. But you know
> that. Why don't you come to dinner tonight?
>
> Love,
> Maggie

Divorce Announcement

Dear Maggie:

I probably should have accepted your dinner invitation, but misery didn't want company tonight and I had the evening's meal already carefully planned (representing the 5 basic food groups: fat, salt, sugar, alcohol, tobacco): frozen chocolate chip cookie dough, prefab margaritas, and a pack of Marlboros. I ate standing up, listening to *All Things Considered*. It was a very slow news day (nothing on Clinton or Monica), and at the top of the hour, they featured an interview with a Florida newspaper editor whose title was Editor of New Initiatives. He had introduced a new feature, Pet Obituaries. They weren't real obits; pet owners wrote them themselves and paid to have them published in a special section of the classifieds. The editor had written the first one, to introduce the concept. It went something like this:

> A year ago today, the Newton family's beloved cocker spaniel, Jock, died. He was 13 years old. The Newtons had raised him since he was 8 weeks old and considered him a member of the family. He couldn't do any tricks, but he was sweet-natured and obedient, mostly, once he'd grown out of eating shoes. He loved to play fetch, and he never begged for table scraps unless there were guests. When a family member was sick, he'd spend the day in the sickroom, keeping the invalid company. He liked to sleep on the living room couch, and as he got older, he was allowed to. He is deeply missed.
> —Jim, Angela, Billy, and Bobby Newton

The margaritas were very stimulating, and I got to thinking about other possible New Initiatives. My best idea, brilliant really, is for separation and divorce announcements, to go on the society pages, alongside (as a bracing, cautionary note) the engagement and wedding announcements. A separation announcement would be a real public service, for the couple and the larger community. It would not only formally give notice that the marriage was ending (getting the news out there once and for all and avoiding the endless retelling of your pathetic story), it would operate as a combo stealth dating service and real estate classified section. And there could be pictures—wedding photos torn in half. People love this kind of thing. (Did you know that the issue of the *New Salem Courier* that publishes the annual property assessments of private residences in the city is the biggest seller every year?)

I've drafted an example, to introduce the concept. What do you think? Has it a future? They used to say a lady's name only appeared in the newspaper when she was hatched, matched, and dispatched. This would add a fourth: detached. Don't you think it's a winning idea? I spent a lot of time (fonts, margins) making it look just like the wedding announcements. I'm planning to write Harry's next.

Love,
Sophie

The New Salami Courier

SUNDAY
MAY 9, 1999

NEW SALAMI, NARRAGANSETT

MARIA MEIKLEJOHN, DANIEL DURKHEIM TO SPLIT AFTER 17 YEARS; HIS REMARRIAGE TO PARK AVENUE DERMATOLOGIST TO FOLLOW

Ms. Maria Mather Meiklejohn Durkheim, 41, and Dr. Daniel E. Durkheim, 52, both of New Salami, NA, announced today that they are unable to reconcile their unhappy differences and have decided to separate pursuant to divorce. They have been married 17 years. Ms. Meiklejohn, who has resumed her maiden name, has retained the firm of Traynor, Hand, Wyzanski to represent her in the divorce. Dr. Durkheim has retained Ray Kahn of Kahn & Boyle as his attorney.

The couple currently reside at 404 St. Cloud Street, New Salami, with their daughter, Jane, age 11, a fifth-grade student at the Peabody School. Dr. Durkheim has a son, Thomas Maxwell Durkheim, 22, from an earlier marriage.

Ms. Meiklejohn is the daughter of Bruce Meiklejohn, Chairman of Octopus Enterprises and President Emeritus of the Plimouth Club, and the late Maria Maple Mather Meiklejohn, who was a trustee of the Peabody School. Ms. Meiklejohn is a descendant of Increase Mather, father of Cotton Mather, the founder of Mather University. Male members of her family have attended Mather in every generation since its founding. She is also a descendant of Isaiah Maple, who came over on the *Dolphin*, in 1631; he and his fellow emigrants spent eight years starving in Boston before seeking out sunnier climes and founding the New Salami colony. The Maples founded the first press in Narragansett in 1725, and the family has continued in the publishing business down to the present day. Ms. Meiklejohn's cousin, Peter Maple, is Executive Editor of the *Courier*. Dr. Durkheim is the son of the late Leah and Herbert Durkheim, who owned a printing business, Durk & Co., in Queens, New York. The family's original name was Durkheimer. It was cropped when Dr. Durkheim's grandfather arrived in 1892 at Ellis Island. He is no relation to Emile Durkheim, the eminent late 19th–early 20th-century sociologist.

Ms. Meiklejohn, a magna cum laude graduate of the University of Chicago, is a Ph.D. student in American studies at Mather University and a writing tutor at Mather College. She is planning to start at Mather Law in the fall of 2001, the first woman in the Mather family to attend the university. Dr. Durkheim is Chief of Pediatric Oncology and Dowling Professor of Pediatrics at Mather Medical School, where he directs the Children's Cancer Center. He graduated from Columbia summa cum laude and went on to do a joint M.D./Ph.D. there at Columbia's College of Physicians & Surgeons.

Last year he was awarded the *Freeman Prize* for Pediatric Research. He was also shortlisted for the Lasker.

Under the terms of their agreement, Dr. Durkheim will retain the St. Cloud Street residence. Ms. Meiklejohn has physical custody of their daughter; the couple share legal custody. Dr. Durkheim will get the Audi and the family dog, Fido, Ms. Mather the Saab and the cat, Tito. Some items of personal property have not yet been distributed, notably a Cindy Sherman photograph and a Jenny Holzer electric sign.

The financial terms of the settlement include alimony and child support to be paid by Dr. Durkheim to Ms. Meiklejohn for a limited period of years and an equitable distribution of their savings accounts, investments, and pension plans. Ms. Meiklejohn, with her father, retains ownership of the Mather Estate on Martha's Vineyard.

Dr. Durkheim was previously married to Helen Maxwell Fincher of New York; they divorced in 1982. Their son, Thomas, a graduate of Amherst College, is currently employed at Fincher & Co., in New York. Upon the entry of the final decree in the divorce, Dr. Durkheim is expected to marry Dr. Stephanie Roth, 47, a New York dermatologist specializing in Botox. ∎

Trash my last email

From: Sophie Diehl   5/10/99 2:41 AM
To: Maggie Pfeiffer <mcp15@mather.edu>
Date: Mon, 10 May 1999 02:41:55
Subject: Trash my last email

Mags—

Please, please delete the Durkheim Divorce Announcement. And don't tell anyone. It's privileged information, what isn't made up. I got a bit carried away. Oh, God, what a mess. Trash it and then empty the trash.

I am utterly degraded. Drunk, too. And I've done exactly what DG worried most about with email. If Fiona found out. I can't even think about that.

Sophie

TRAYNOR, HAND, WYZANSKI

222 CHURCH STREET
NEW SALEM, NARRAGANSETT 06555
(393) 876-5678

MEMORANDUM
Attorney Work Product

From:	David Greaves
To:	Sophie Diehl
RE:	Maria Meiklejohn: Bottom-Line Offer and Counteroffer
Date:	May 10, 1999
Attachments:	

I like the bottom-line proposal and I like your brass. I hope you get it, but don't count on it. Some people might consider that a top-of-the-line offer. Remember, she is Bruce Meiklejohn's daughter, and every judge in this town, hell, in this state, knows it. There's no way she'll end up on the street. If she can't sell the Martha's Vineyard house, she can borrow against it.

Let me see your counteroffer and a draft of the cover letter by the end of the week. Make sure you tell Kahn the offer is subject to our discovery notice and the reports from O'Dell and Katz. I've made the point in my letter, but it's worth repeating.

The Canon of Ethics says a lawyer should defend her client "zealously within the bounds of the law." You were far more thorough than I would have been, but your approach may well be the right one; sometimes an experienced practitioner coasts, doing the same things over and over. It's good for me to see how a skilled practitioner with no matrimonial experience goes about the job. Old dogs can learn new tricks. (Your presentation was exhaustive; that is what my mother would have called a suspenders-belt job. I suspect that's your style and not simply your response to a new kind of case, no?)

Good work, Sophie.

TRAYNOR, HAND, WYZANSKI

222 CHURCH STREET
NEW SALEM, NARRAGANSETT 06555
(393) 876-5678

MEMORANDUM
Attorney Work Product

From: Sophie Diehl
To: David Greaves
RE: Maria Meiklejohn: Bottom-Line Offer and Counteroffer
Date: May 10, 1999
Attachments:

Thanks for the kind words. I'll have the draft and counteroffer to you on Friday. (You're right, I am a suspenders-belt kinda girl; I'm always afraid I'll leave something out. My mother says I *start* with the kitchen sink.)

I need some advice. A friend of mine needs a local divorce lawyer. He can't afford us. (I'm not sure he can afford anyone; he's a student.) Can you recommend someone? I don't know the divorce bar in New Salem. Thanks.

TRAYNOR, HAND, WYZANSKI

222 CHURCH STREET
NEW SALEM, NARRAGANSETT 06555
(393) 876-5678

MEMORANDUM
Attorney Work Product

From: David Greaves
To: Sophie Diehl
RE: Finding a Divorce Lawyer
Date: May 10, 1999
Attachments:

Funny you should ask. About two years ago I wrote a column on finding a divorce lawyer for the Consumer column in the *Courier*. It pretty much says everything I have to say about the subject. I've attached a copy. You can send it to your friend. Since he's a student, I can't imagine he has much money—or income. He might try to do it *pro se*, or through Legal Aid. He'll have trouble finding someone for less than $80 an hour, and the hours can add up. (By the way, how many hours have you accrued in the Durkheim case? I'd like to have an idea; we probably should send Ms. Meiklejohn a billing statement.)

As for concrete recommendations, I offer the following three: Victoria Beaumont, Esq.; Megan Benett of Benett & Ratzan; and Max Rivington at Miller, Pierce and Maleri. They're all good lawyers. They're younger—and correspondingly cheaper—than older lawyers, but they're all experienced in matrimonial law. Your friend can choose from among a solo practitioner, a member of a small firm, and an associate at a large one. You might also ask Felix for his recommendations; he knows everyone in the matrimonial bar.

The New Salem Courier

SUNDAY
JAN 19, 1997

NEW SALEM, NARRAGANSETT

THE COURIER CONSUMER: FINDING A DIVORCE LAWYER

This month, the Courier Consumer asked David Greaves, Esq., a partner in the New Salem law firm of Traynor, Hand, Wyzanski, to tell our readers how to find a divorce lawyer. We've had many requests for a column on this topic. And we know why. In 1996, in Tyler County, 1,519 couples got married; 687 got divorced. That's a 45% divorce rate. Here's what Mr. Greaves has to say.

The first question I'd put to someone looking for a divorce lawyer is this: How complicated will your divorce be? Is it a contested divorce? Does your wife want support? Do you want support? Are you still living together? Have you been separated for a while, living independently and each supporting yourself? Do you both live in-state? If not, will your husband submit to jurisdiction in Narragansett? Do you have children? Is custody in dispute?

It's possible in Narragansett for people to do their own divorces. These are called *pro se* divorces. While I don't recommend a *pro se* divorce for people with young children, substantial assets, or emotional baggage, it might do in a case where the marriage has been one of short duration between people of similar resources and the divorce is uncontested.* Mediation is also a possibility in an uncontested divorce.**

If the case is more complicated but your resources are minimal, you might call Legal Services and see whether you are eligible for free representation.*** If you're ineligible for Legal Services, then you'll need to hire a private lawyer. It will be difficult to find one who'll work for less than $75 an hour, and the hours add up. Even an uncontested divorce will probably cost each party at least $1,000. The fact is, there are no really cheap divorces and no really cheap good divorce lawyers. Be wary of the lawyer who says he can do it all for a set price of, say, $499. If the case turns out to be more complicated than anticipated, the fee will rise. And the case is almost always more complicated than anticipated. In my experience, it pays to hire a lawyer who bills by the hour.

Hiring the right lawyer takes time. Most people never think about hiring a lawyer until they need one urgently, and the result can be disastrous (losing custody, the family home, alimony) or expensive (hiring a second lawyer to undo the mess made by the first), as with any decision made precipitously, without research, in times of trouble. People ask a friend or, if they don't have a friend who knows a lawyer, they look in the Yellow Pages or take a telephone number off a bus advertisement, e.g.,

1-700-DIVORCES. They then call up, make an appointment, and sign on the dotted line, right there. They never think of interviewing the lawyer to see if she's the right one; and they never think of interviewing more than one. The truth is, they don't really want a divorce lawyer, not at that moment; they want a fairy godmother, someone to rescue them. Even professionals can become helpless and feckless in the face of divorce.

Asking friends, acquaintances, and colleagues for a recommendation is a good place to start, but don't ask just anyone. Pick your sources carefully: a friend who has survived a divorce with his dignity intact or a colleague whose judgment is sound.****

You'll want a consultation before you hire anyone. Prepare a brief summary of your situation in advance; time is money to a lawyer, and you don't want to waste her time or your money. After you've laid out the matter, ask the lawyer how she will proceed, how long she expects the divorce to take, and how much she thinks it will cost. Most divorces are based on separation agreements, but approximately 10% end up in the courts. If the case goes to court, the cost will mount dramatically. Do not sign right there. Thank the lawyer and say you'll be in touch. You'll want to talk to the other lawyers on your list and then review the consultations in order to figure out which one is likely to give you the best representation.

I don't know that other lawyers would agree with me, but I think it's important to like and respect your lawyer. You don't have to want to have dinner with her, but you should feel comfortable in her company and trust her judgment. In my experience in civil litigation generally and in divorce especially, people who hire a lawyer they don't particularly like but think they need (a shark, a pit bull, a well-connected politico) are making a mistake. There's a quid pro quo to the lawyer-client relationship, as there is in most relationships. If a client doesn't like his lawyer, chances are the lawyer doesn't like the client. Divorce is difficult enough without having your advocate despise you too. This being said, a client should never hire a friend as his divorce lawyer. (It goes without saying, of course, that a person should never hire a lawyer who's a friend of both him and his wife, and no lawyer should take on that case. It's instant death to the friendship and often to the lawyer's reputation, especially in a small city.) People do and say terrible things in front of their lawyers during a divorce; after it's all over, most people don't want to have anything more to do with their lawyer. They don't want a reminder of that time in their life—or of their own awful behavior during it.

Clients also need to keep in mind that their interests and their lawyers' don't perfectly coincide. Lawyers work for their clients, but also for themselves. A lawyer has a reputation to maintain, other clients to service, an office to run, bills to pay, a practice to cultivate, and a private life to live, factors all of which influence her actions on the client's behalf. No client ever feels his lawyer gives his case the attention it deserves, and no lawyer can give it that kind of attention. There's too much going on in the lawyer's life, too little time, and, more often than not, too little money (even at $75 an hour). In divorce, there are very few satisfied customers. As in book publishing or home renovation, people enter the lawyer-client relationship with unreasonable expectations. (The publisher will run a nationwide ad campaign; the builder will give me my dream kitchen and still come in under budget; the lawyer will get me everything I want and deserve.) The first task of a good divorce lawyer is to educate the client, to get him to understand that negotiation is a two-way street and that the best agreement is one that allows each side to claim victory on some grounds. The most satisfactory divorces I've handled have ended up with both the husband and wife feeling slightly but tolerably aggrieved. There are no winners in divorce, but there don't have to be any losers.

*You can pick up a copy of the Narragansett Do It Yourself Divorce Guide, published by the Narragansett Judicial Branch, from the Tyler County Clerk or the New Salem Law Society Library. This booklet outlines all the steps in a pro se divorce and includes copies of all the forms; it is intended only for "uncomplicated cases," where the spouses "agree on the basic issues." There are also books, published by commercial publishers, that outline the steps in a pro se divorce and provide sample agreements as well as the official forms. An example is The Uncontested Divorce in Narragansett: A How-To Manual, published by Self-Help Press.

**A final note about mediation. A trained mediator who is a member of the New Salem Mediation Bureau can handle a divorce if—and here comes a series of big ifs—the parties both think mediation is the way to go; they have comparable resources; they are prepared to be not merely reasonable but generous; they love their children and have their best interests at heart; and they are not at daggers with each other. After coming to an agreement, each of them needs to hire a lawyer to look over the agreement and make sure it's fair. (Narragansett law requires that.)

***The income cutoff is $17,000 a year. As of December 20, Legal Services was doing divorces, but with all the cutbacks that they've been facing, they may decide that their resources are better spent on more urgent cases. Call before turning up on their doorstep (393-555-0101).

****You can also consult the Law Society (393-555-6789), which will provide you with the names of divorce specialists along with their professional biographies. Once you've collected a number of names, call three of them and make appointments, asking first what it will cost, if anything, to have a consultation about representation. ∎

TRAYNOR, HAND, WYZANSKI

222 CHURCH STREET
NEW SALEM, NARRAGANSETT 06555
(393) 876-5678

MEMORANDUM
Attorney Work Product

From:	Sophie Diehl
To:	David Greaves
RE:	Your Treatise on Finding a Lawyer
Date:	May 10, 1999
Attachments:	

The bit about liking your lawyer. I never thought about that or most of the other things you said. My cases are all assigned by a court or a senior partner, and criminal clients are notoriously ungrateful. Last year I spent 7 months negotiating with the DA on an armed robbery case (serious stuff, armed robbery), and when I got the perp a 48-month sentence (including time served), 18 months off the oxymoronic mandatory minimum for a repeat offender, he said: "Why did I need a lawyer for that?" I wanted to say, "Don't take the deal. Go to trial," but I didn't. Joe's first rule of client representation is: "Roll with the insults. These are people who aren't allowed to have shoelaces."

I need more advice. I'd like to find a way of burying the hatchet with Fiona, other than in my back. If I say hello to her, she says, "Oh, . . . Sophie . . . you," and turns away. If I run into her in the kitchen, she'll leave directly, saying something like, "I'll get out of your way." The other day I asked her for advice on the Durkheim case, a real question on rehabilitation alimony; you weren't here, nor was Felix, and I didn't want to screw up the way I did with the medical degree. We were in the hallway outside her office. I had gone there to talk to her. She said, "Just read the cases, read the statutes, read the *New Salem Law Journal*. It's not rocket science." Then she turned her back to me, went into her office, and closed the door. Have you heard the joke about Irish Alzheimer's? They forget everything but the grievances.

Does this go on with other lawyers in the firm? What do I do?

TRAYNOR, HAND, WYZANSKI

222 CHURCH STREET
NEW SALEM, NARRAGANSETT 06555
(393) 876-5678

MEMORANDUM
Attorney Work Product

From:	Sophie Diehl
To:	David Greaves
RE:	Maria Meiklejohn
Date:	May 11, 1999
Attachments:	May 6 Letter from MMM

This morning's mail brought a letter from Mia Meiklejohn, an account of a fight with her husband, precipitated by our letter and discovery request to Ray Kahn. She certainly held her own.

I love that Meiklejohn's company is called Octopus Enterprises, but what does that stand for? Why not Orca? Or King Kong?

May 6, 1999

Anne Sophie Diehl
Traynor, Hand, Wyzanski
222 Church Street
New Salem, NA 06555

Dear Sophie:

David's letter to Ray Kahn and discovery request set off a bomb. Danny was furious. He came up to my room last night and ranted at me. How could I think he had hidden assets? What right did my lawyers have to see his research grants? And what in hell gave my lawyers the balls (his word) to tell him to attend Parent Education Classes? He said I had been a "fucking albatross" hanging around his neck for years. He asked me to move out of the house—with Jane; he said he had found an apartment for us at the Albany (three bedrooms, big living room, nice kitchen, good views, parking place) and would pay the rent, $1,600 a month, until we signed a settlement. He'd pay for the move too. There were more personal attacks too. He called me a parasite, sucking the life out of everyone around me, and a dilettante, who wouldn't grow up. "Get on with your life," he bellowed, "and get out of mine."

I used to fold when he yelled at me like that, but I didn't this time. I yelled back. I told him if he fought me on custody for Jane, I'd fight him all the way to the Supreme Court, adding as a coda, "You'll be 60 before we're divorced." I told him I wouldn't move out until we had a signed agreement, so he had better get serious and come up with a reasonable offer. And I said if Dr. Stephanie kept calling the house, I'd start calling her house and her office. That last remark really set him off. He said I was sick and a madwoman. "If you ever call or threaten her, I'll grind you to dust." That really got me going. "That's great, that's terrific," I said. "You think I'm crazy to call her, but it's okay for her to call your house, where your child lives. It's okay if Jane finds out her father is screwing another woman." That stopped him cold. He looked stunned and then walked out without another word.

I'm right, aren't I, not to move out until we've got a settlement? It's the only real leverage I have on him. It's not just that he wants the house, he wants me out of it. If I leave without an agreement, he'll then take his time and try to starve me into submission.

I'm beginning to feel sorry for you, sorry I asked you to take on my case. When I'm a lawyer, I won't do divorces. (But you said that, too.) This has become so awful, so ugly. If you had met Danny and me socially, you'd have liked us. I used to like us. He used to call me Mia Bella.

Thanks for your help and support.

Yours,

Mia

TRAYNOR, HAND, WYZANSKI

222 CHURCH STREET
NEW SALEM, NARRAGANSETT 06555
(393) 876-5678

MEMORANDUM
Attorney Work Product

From: David Greaves
To: Sophie Diehl
RE: Maria Meiklejohn's Letter; Finding a Lawyer;
                    Business in New York
Date: May 11, 1999
Attachments:

What were you doing in college? Didn't you ever read Frank Norris's *The Octopus*? It is Bruce Meiklejohn's favorite book. The company is named for the book itself, not the Southern Pacific Railroad. Or maybe it is.

I didn't realize that you and Fiona were still at odds, but of course, it happens with others in the firm. What should you do? You've no choice, you have to suck it up, as your generation so vividly puts it. It happens all the time. We make enemies, sometimes through no fault of our own, and sometimes our enemies become badges of honor. I don't know if you know, but my father was on Nixon's Enemy's List. He was very proud to have made it and counted it among his lifetime achievements. When he was interviewed by the *Courier* for his obituary, he asked them to include it. They did. My mother was very proud too. This may not be any consolation to you. There may be no consolation. Just keep doing your work. And don't respond in kind to Fiona. Joe's rule is a good one across the board.

I'll be out of town, in New York on business, for the next two days. There's a meeting of the board of Octopus Enterprises. I don't expect to be back until Friday afternoon at the earliest, so you don't need to have the draft of the Durkheim letter and counteroffer to me until Monday afternoon.

THE DIVORCE PAPERS (Page 236)

Adults May Be Misbehaving

From: Sophie Diehl   5/11/99 10:18 PM
To: Maggie Pfeiffer <mcp15@mather.edu>
Date: Tue, 11 May 1999 22:18:29
Subject: Adults May Be Misbehaving

Dear Maggie—

It never seems to end. This morning I got a memo from DG saying he
was going to be in New York City for the rest of the week. Meanwhile,
my stepfather is off in Colorado hiking with his sons. What do you bet
that DG and Maman are having a rendezvous? DG hardly ever goes to
NY on business.

These are the scenarios I've imagined late at night. (1) Maman and DG
have an affair, which goes badly. DG is hurt and full of resentment. He
decides that I'm too painful a reminder. I am fired. (2) Maman and DG
have an affair, and Fiona finds out and makes trouble for DG and me.
I am fired. (3) Maman and DG fall madly in love and decide to divorce
their current spouses and get married, which succeeds in ruining both
my professional and personal lives. I quit. (4) Maman and DG have
a fling; DG breaks it off, having vowed never to do this kind of thing.
Maman is *philosophique*. (5) The Nelson Rockefeller scenario: DG has a
heart attack in a hotel room while Maman is with him. (This one is so
awful, I never go any further.)

There was a time in my life, barely two months ago, when I never
thought about divorce or adultery—I thought I was doing a halfway
decent job putting my parents' messes behind me. Since I was hog-tied
into doing this divorce: I'm practicing a kind of law I don't like; Fiona has
me in her sights; my mother and my boss are playing with fire; and the
man I was falling in love with turns out to have a crazy wife with whom
he's still in love. Is this chaos theory? (I wrote a memo to DG about Fiona
this week. I shouldn't have done it. I sounded childish, pathetic; he was
not at all sympathetic.)

I don't know what to do about Harry. I hate having this feeling of being stuck and unhappy. Which reminds me: I think Papa and Sally may be having tough times. He's being very difficult. (Nothing new there, but there's a sharper edge to his unhappiness. Luc noticed it, too.) He's staying by himself up at the country house most of the week. And this summer he's planning to be in England, to do research on his book on the Boer War, and I don't think Sally's going with him.

I don't think humans, as a species, are very highly evolved. (And we're not evolving anymore, apparently. I read it in the *Times*. Because everyone now reaches reproductive age, we're no longer weeding out the weak stock.) Look at all these people: they're all smart, well educated, meaningfully employed, living in the richest country in the world, surrounded by people who care for them. Still, they're unhappy and misbehaving. What more do they need? What more do *I* need?

I'm obsessing and free-associating, aren't I? Off to bed then.

Love,
Sophie

Lawyers' Names

From: Sophie Diehl   5/12/99 8:49 PM
To: Harry Mortensen <hlm11@mather.edu>
Date: Wed, 12 May 1999 20:49:58
Subject: Lawyers' Names

Dear Harry—

I asked my boss for some lawyers' names. It turns out he's written an
article on finding a divorce lawyer for the local paper. I've put a copy of
the article in the mail. It gives very good advice on choosing a private
lawyer as well as some cheaper ideas for representation (Legal Aid, do-
it-yourself kits). He also gave me the names of three local lawyers. I
called and left their names on your answering machine. He says they're
all good lawyers. They're younger—and correspondingly cheaper—than
older lawyers, but they're experienced in matrimonial law. The first is a
solo practitioner, the second a member of a small firm, and the last a
senior associate at a large one.

I hope this is helpful. If you need anything else, let me know.

Take care of yourself.

Yours,
Sophie

TRAYNOR, HAND, WYZANSKI

222 CHURCH STREET
NEW SALEM, NARRAGANSETT 06555
(393) 876-5678
ATTORNEYS AT LAW

May 12, 1999

Maria Mather Meiklejohn
404 St. Cloud Street
New Salem, NA 06556

Dear Mia:

Please don't worry about saddling me with your troubles. We lawyers traffic in human misery; we make our money off of it. I only wish I could be more helpful to you during these difficult times.

You are right to stay put now, and both David and I would advise you strongly against moving out before you've reached and signed a settlement. While you have the money from the savings account available to you for your current expenses and the treasury bills in reserve, if you moved out without a settlement, you would not be able to make any concrete plans for your future (where you'll live, if you can afford Mather Law School, whether you can buy Prada). You would also have effectively ceded the house to him, before the negotiations had begun. And then there is the matter of the furnishings, including the rug and the Jenny Holzer. Hold your ground. Stay put.

I say this knowing that his offer of putting you and Jane up in the Albany is especially tempting because he would be in effect relinquishing his claim to physical custody. But in fact, he is giving up nothing. You will not lose Jane; you are and have always been her primary caretaker, and there's no way he can show that you are unfit. Reread *Paynter* if you're feeling scared.

I am drafting our counteroffer. As soon as I have finished, I'll be in touch to run it by you.

Yours,

Anne Sophie Diehl

Anne Sophie Diehl

Sophie, Sophie, Sophie,

What am I to do with you? Forget about your mother and DG. Misbehaving is one of the prerogatives of adulthood. If it's anyone's problem, it's Jake's, not yours. And nothing is going on.

All this fuss you're making, it's about you and Harry, not your mother and DG. Coming from those soigne European parents, how did you get to be such a thoroughgoing buttoned-down American? You look like them, so I know you're theirs. What is it Jake always says? Being grown-up means tolerating ambiguity.

When we were little, I wanted your parents to adopt me. They were so sophisticated, so charming, so romantic, so intellectual, so glamorous, and so, so generous. They took me in, they talked to me, they listened to me and encouraged me. They took me along to Wellfleet every summer; they paid for my college applications and textbooks; they threw birthday parties for me. Your dad was the one who made me apply to Harvard. Your mother came to every play I was ever in and told me I could be an actress. I would have walked on coals for them. (They walked on water to me.) And you won't cut them any slack. You've got to let go, Sophie; you've got to let them be. They shouldn't matter that much, not anymore.

If in fact your mom's having a fling with DG, you don't have to worry. She's not going to leave Jake. And she'll make sure that she and DG part on good terms. She knows how to do that. And Jake will never find out unless she wants him to.

Stop thinking about what your parents are up to, and start thinking about Harry. Do you really want to walk away?

Love,
Maggie

I'm Hopeless

From: Sophie Diehl   5/13/99 1:32 AM
To: Maggie Pfeiffer <mcp15@mather.edu>
Date: Thu, 13 May 1999 1:32:47
Subject: I'm Hopeless

Dear Maggie,

The truth is, I haven't in some ways gotten over my parents' divorce.
It's been, what, 13 years? At the end, they were so awful, we couldn't
wait until they split, but until then they were, as you say, wonderful.
I had the best childhood ever. I even liked junior high school. I know
they're happier now. I know they'll never get back together. But the
divorce broke my heart. If they had been normal-sized, maybe I could
have gotten over it. (If they were normal-sized, maybe they would have
stayed married.) Maman called the divorce Waterloo: "The English
vanquished the French," she said, shrugging. "They always do. We've
got no principles, no convictions. We'd rather eat than fight." (Papa used
to quote Churchill on the French to us: "They were rotten on the inside
before they crumbled from without.") You're right. I'm not French, and
I'm not English. I'm a petite bourgeoise, of a distinctly American stripe.
To top it off, I've got an unforgiving heart. Maman once said I was more
lovable than loving—after I broke up with Jack. She didn't say it unkindly,
only matter-of-factly, the way she might have said I have yellow eyes,
not brown. I was mortified. But I didn't change; I couldn't. I never spoke
to Jack again. And that's how I feel now, with Harry. I remember history
and I repeat it. Stuff it, Santayana.

Maybe I should have a fling. Why wait for Harry to come round, or not
come round? Jake always says self-knowledge only takes you so far. What
is it Catholics call it? A firm purpose of amendment. I'll work on it.

Love,
Sophie

P.S. But I do feel badly, very badly, about Harry.

Hello

From: Sophie Diehl   5/19/99 11:33 PM
To: Harry Mortensen <hlm11@mather.edu>
Date: Wed, 19 May 1999 23:33:13
Subject: Hello

Dear Harry,

I've not been a good friend. I'm sorry. If there's some way I can help, something I can do, please call me.

Sophie

TRAYNOR, HAND, WYZANSKI

222 CHURCH STREET
NEW SALEM, NARRAGANSETT 06555
(393) 876-5678

MEMORANDUM
Attorney Work Product

From: Sophie Diehl
To: David Greaves
RE: DED v. MMM: Counteroffer; Billable Hours
Date: May 20, 1999
Attachments: Letter to RK with Counteroffer
             DED v. MMM: Summary Statement on Counteroffer
             ASD Time Sheet

Here is the counteroffer to Dr. Durkheim's offer. I gave it one more go-round.

I've interpreted "equitable distribution" to mean "equal distribution." I've split everything down the middle, including his annual income. The saving clause is that two people will live on one half and only one on the other. How can Dr. Durkheim complain? In working this distribution, I've upped the ordinary alimony to $60,000 a year. We can go down to $48,000, as I outlined in the bottom-line offer, during negotiations, and perhaps give him a larger share of the assets. We can also give up the reimbursement alimony, or a part of it, but not the rehabilitation alimony for law school.

I didn't say, though I'm tempted, that the valuation on the Martha's Vineyard property was pure fantasy. Kahn's too cheap to have an appraisal done; as Ms. Meiklejohn said aptly, if rudely, he pulled the figure out of his butt.

Ms. Meiklejohn will be coming in on Monday afternoon to review the letter and offer. I expect them to go out to Kahn on the 25th.

I've included here my Time Sheet on the Meiklejohn case. Let me know if it's okay, and I'll prepare her bill. I've racked up 31 hours and change. Is it too large? I included the time I spent researching and writing the memo on Valuing a Medical Degree. Should we eat those ten hours? As we know, a real divorce lawyer (Fiona!) would have known about that. Our fact situation is very different, so the argument is somewhat different, but it makes me a bit uneasy (and of course, I still feel stupid). Will you be billing for your time too? Do you want me to prepare a combined bill? And will you be charging only $150 an hour, as the agreement provides? Isn't your regular fee at least twice that? If you get your hours to me by noon on Monday, I can include them in the bill for Ms. Meiklejohn. I'm nervous about this. (Can you tell?) I've never before handed a bill to a client. My stepfather, Jake, does it all the time. One of his patients would regularly pay him in cash, counting out the twenties, licking his thumb as he did it. Like paying a whore, Jake said. (This is a betrayal of the physician-patient privilege, once removed. Don't tell anyone I told you.)

TRAYNOR, HAND, WYZANSKI

222 CHURCH STREET
NEW SALEM, NARRAGANSETT 06555
(393) 876-5678
ATTORNEYS AT LAW

May 25, 1999

Ray Kahn, Esq.
Kahn & Boyle
46 Broadway
New Salem, NA 06555

Dear Mr. Kahn:

I am responding on behalf of Ms. Maria Meiklejohn to your settlement offer of April 19. I will be direct. Dr. Durkheim's proposal is unacceptable in every respect. I will start with custody. While Ms. Meiklejohn expects to share legal custody of their daughter, Jane, with Dr. Durkheim, she will be asking for and has every reason to believe she will be awarded physical custody. I refer you to the Narragansett's Supreme Court opinion in *Paynter v. Paynter*, 278 Nar. 487 (1991), and the Primary Caretaker Rule. Second, Dr. Durkheim's offers of spousal and child support are patently inadequate and inequitable. He has offered to pay $24,000 in child support, $36,000 in alimony, and $14,000 in tuition fees, for a total payout of $78,000. The following chart shows the grossly unequal net financial consequences of this offer for the two parties.

Income	Dr. Durkheim	Ms. Meiklejohn
Husband's Salary	$370,000	
Taxes, Soc Sec	(80,000)	
Child Support	(24,000)	24,000
Spousal Support	(36,000)	36,000
Taxes		(12,000)
School Fees	(14,000)	
Net Income	**$216,000**	**$48,000**

Under his offer, Dr. Durkheim winds up with 450% more money than his wife and daughter. Our counteroffer works an equitable distribution. It includes: child support, ordinary alimony, reimbursement alimony, and rehabilitation alimony. Ms. Meiklejohn will be asking for reimbursement alimony of $100,000, representing the support she provided Dr. Durkheim for the years 1982 to 1987 while he was pursuing his postgraduate training. His salary went entirely for child support to his son from his first marriage. The expectation is that the reimbursement alimony will be paid out over 10 years, at $10,000 a year. The request for reimbursement alimony is made in lieu of a request for a share of the value of Dr. Durkheim's medical degree. Ms. Meiklejohn is asking for rehabilitation alimony so that she might attend law school, at Mather if possible. The expectation is that remarriage or death will terminate ordinary alimony but not rehabilitation or reimbursement alimony.

Laura Bucholtz of RealProperties Inc. has appraised the family residence at 404 St. Cloud at a current market value of $525,000. Upon sale, broker's fees and closing costs will come to approximately $35,000, leaving $240,000 in net equity. Ms. Meiklejohn is asking for one-half.

Ms. Meiklejohn will ask for one half of the couple's investments and retirement funds. She will relinquish the $16,000 remaining in the joint savings account to Dr. Durkheim in recognition of his inheritance from his parents. All of these funds and investments were accumulated during the couple's 17-year marriage.

Ms. Meiklejohn's proposal is premised on the principle of equitable distribution as formulated last year by the Supreme Court of Narragansett in *Lemon v. Lemon*, 293 Nar. 966, 973 (1998), and shaped by the tax consequences of child support and alimony. The proposal recognizes Ms. Meiklejohn's contributions to Dr. Durkheim's outstanding medical career, the annual gifts from Ms. Meiklejohn's father over the last 16 years, and Ms. Meiklejohn's loss of employment opportunities occasioned by the relocation to New Salem.

All of the terms of this proposal are subject to the discovery request filed on April 27 and assume that Ms. Meiklejohn is in possession of a complete and accurate statement of Dr. Durkheim's assets and income.

No mention is made in this proposal of Ms. Meiklejohn's interest in the Mather Estate in Aquinnah, formerly Gay Head, on Martha's Vineyard. Dr. Durkheim has no right to or claim on the Estate.

The following chart indicates the effect of the proposed agreement during its first year.

Income	Dr. Durkheim	Ms. Meiklejohn
Salary	$370,000	
Taxes, Soc Sec	(60,000)	
Child Support	(72,000)	72,000
Ordinary Alimony	(60,000)	60,000
Rehabilitative Alimony	(30,000)	30,000
Reimbursement Alimony	(10,000)	10,000
Tax on Alimony		(35,000)
Net Income	**$138,000**	**$137,000**

After three (3) years, Dr. Durkheim would no longer have to pay rehabilitation alimony and his ordinary alimony would likely be substantially reduced if not eliminated. We look forward to hearing from you.

Yours,

Anne Sophie Diehl

Anne Sophie Diehl

Maria Mather Meiklejohn and Daniel E. Durkheim
Proposed Settlement: Summary Statement

Custody
Physical Custody: sole to Maria Meiklejohn
Legal Custody: joint to Maria Meiklejohn and Daniel Durkheim

Child Support
Daniel Durkheim to pay $72,000/year for seven (7) years (through high school); Maria Meiklejohn to pay school fees
Daniel Durkheim to pay $24,000/year until Jane's graduation from college or 23rd birthday (whichever is earlier)
Escalator clause tied to Daniel Durkheim's salary

College Costs
Daniel Durkheim to pay all college costs (tuition, room, board, books, miscellaneous expenses)

Ordinary Alimony or Spousal Support
Daniel Durkheim to pay $60,000/year to Maria Meiklejohn for seven (7) years from signing or terminating event
Qualification: Daniel Durkheim to pay up to $60,000/year, reduced dollar for dollar by Maria Meiklejohn's salary
Terminating event: remarriage
Escalator clause tied to Daniel Durkheim's salary

Rehabilitation Alimony
Daniel Durkheim to pay $30,000/year to Maria Meiklejohn for three (3) years for law school tuition
Terminating event: nonattendance at law school

Reimbursement Alimony
Daniel Durkheim to pay $100,000 over 10 years at $10,000/year
No terminating event

Medical Insurance
Maria Meiklejohn to pay $3,200 for COBRA account on Daniel Durkheim's policy

Family Residence: Current Value: $525,000; Net Equity: $240,000
Daniel Durkheim to receive $120,000; Maria Meiklejohn to
receive $120,000
Maria Meiklejohn to receive her share from stock market investments
if house kept by Daniel Durkheim

Daniel Durkheim's TIAA-CREF Retirement Accounts: $600,000
Daniel Durkheim to receive $300,000; Maria Meiklejohn to receive
$300,000

Daniel Durkheim's 401(k) Plan: $300,000
Daniel Durkheim to receive $150,000; Maria Meiklejohn to receive
$150,000

Stock Market Investments: $700,000
Daniel Durkheim to receive $350,000; Maria Meiklejohn to receive
$350,000

Treasury Bills: $90,000
Maria Meiklejohn to receive $45,000; Daniel Durkheim to receive
$45,000

Joint Savings Account: $16,000
Daniel Durkheim to receive $16,000
Given in recognition of Daniel Durkheim's $16,000 inheritance

TRAYNOR, HAND, WYZANSKI

222 CHURCH STREET
NEW SALEM, NARRAGANSETT 06555
(393) 876-5678

TIME SHEET
Attorney Work Product

Client: Maria Mather Meiklejohn
Attorney: Anne Sophie Diehl
Date: May 21, 1999
Rate: $150/hour

Date	Item	Hour(s)
3/17/99	Interview with MMM	1
	Write-Up of Interview	1½
3/29/99	Meeting ASD & DG	½
	Write-Up of Memo on Meeting	1
	Drafting Recusal Letter to MMM	n.c. (½)
4/5/99	Drafting Memo to DG on Next Steps	1
	Drafting Acceptance of Summons, Etc.	¼
	Meeting with MMM	½
4/6/99	Drafting Letter to RK Re: Automatic Orders	1
	Phone Conversation with MMM	
	Re: Withdrawing Money	¼
	Drafting Letters to Financial Institutions	1
4/7/99	Drafting Addendum to Fee Agreement	½
4/8/99	Meeting with MMM	
	Re: Addendum to Fee Agreement	1½
	Preparing Statements: Income/Expenses, Assets/Liabilities	1½
4/23/99	Phone Conversation with MMM	
	Re: Settlement Offer	¼
	Preparing Memo on Conversation	1
	Research on Value of Medical Degree	3 (?)
	Drafting Memo on Value of Medical Degree	3 (?)

4/27/99	Drafting Letter to MMM on DED	
	Settlement Offer	1
	Letter to RK Re: DED Settlement Offer	1
	Preparation of Discovery Request	1
5/5/99	Meeting with MMM on DED Settlement Offer	1½
5/7/99	Drafting Bottom-Line Settlement Offer	3
5/10/99	Review of Bottom-Line Settlement Offer	¾
5/12/99	Drafting Letter to MMM	
	Re: Bottom-Line Settlement Offer	1
5/20/99	Drafting Letter to RK with Counteroffer	2
5/21/99	Review of Counteroffer	1

Total Hours 31½

Bill $4,725

TRAYNOR, HAND, WYZANSKI

222 CHURCH STREET
NEW SALEM, NARRAGANSETT 06555
(393) 876-5678

MEMORANDUM
Attorney Work Product

From:	David Greaves
To:	Sophie Diehl
RE:	Maria Meiklejohn
Date:	May 21, 1999
Attachments:	

I approve your letter and settlement offer. Send it to Kahn if Ms. Meiklejohn approves, but be prepared for fireworks. Dr. Durkheim will be seriously displeased. I begin to think Ms. Meiklejohn is very canny. She sized you up at a glance and decided that you would be the perfect foil to someone like Kahn. You're not a member of the club; you're young; you're inexperienced; you don't know the rules or won't play by them. There's a kind of formal minuet divorce lawyers dance. You're doing the tango, and Kahn & Co. don't know the steps. You come at them with a nothing-to-lose-I-don't-give-a-damn attitude.

Your hours look fine, including the adjusted time put in on the M.D. memo. The issue still hasn't been decided by an appellate court in Narragansett, *Petrus* is still pending, and your memo speaks to the Meiklejohn's particular fact situation, which is unusual. It's a win-win situation for us. If they go along, Ms. Meiklejohn will get $100,000 for $900 worth of work, an excellent return on the time spent. And if they balk, it gives us something to give up in the negotiations. I've given your Time Sheet to Hannah; she already has mine. I'll be billing at $150, and I've made adjustments so that Ms. Meiklejohn won't be double-charged. Hannah will prepare the bill for you to give Ms. Meiklejohn at your meeting Monday. And we don't accept cash, ever, to avoid even the appearance of money laundering. Still, our clients find ways to insult us. One of these days, the honeymoon with Ms. Meiklejohn will come to an end

THE DIVORCE PAPERS (Page 253)

and she'll turn on you, if only briefly. They always do, or almost always. As I said in my article, in divorce, there are very few satisfied customers.

Which brings me to your May 12 letter to Ms. Meiklejohn. "We lawyers traffic in human misery; we make our money off of it." In the future, save that kind of observation for Joe or one of the other cowboys upstairs, over a beer. A remark like that invites contempt for the profession and displays a corrosive cynicism about lawyers, which in the long run can only damage the lawyer-client relationship. If you don't respect what you do, neither will she. Remember, she's not a friend or a colleague but a paying client who wants to think she's hired a competent professional to protect her interests.

Maybe you should take a week off and go somewhere tropical. You don't seem quite yourself. What is it about this divorce that's getting to you? As I recall, you defended a child murderer without blinking.

TRAYNOR, HAND, WYZANSKI

222 CHURCH STREET
NEW SALEM, NARRAGANSETT 06555
(393) 876-5678

TIME SHEET
Attorney Work Product

Client:	Maria Mather Meiklejohn
Attorney:	David Greaves
Date:	May 21, 1999
Rate:	$150/hour

Date	Item	Hour(s)
3/16/99	Preparing Memo to ASD on Divorce Interview	n.c. (1)
3/23/99	Review of Interview Documents	n.c. (1)
	Preparing Memo to ASD on Representation	n.c. (¼)
3/29/99	Meeting ASD & DG	½
	Review of ASD Recusal Letter	n.c. (¼)
	Memo to ASD on Recusal Letter to MMM	n.c. (¼)
4/5/99	Review of Official Documents	¼
	Memo to ASD on Proposed Next Steps	1¼
4/6/99	Review of MMM Letter & Memo	¼
	Review of Draft Letter to RK	¼
	Review of Draft Letters to Financial Institutions	¼
4/22/99	Review of DED Settlement Offer & Letter from RK	½
	Memo to ASD on DED Settlement Offer	½
4/27/99	Drafting Response to RK on DED Settlement Offer	½
	Preparing Discovery Requests	½
5/3/99	Review of MMM Letter on DED Settlement Offer	¼
	Preparing Memo to ASD on MMM Letter	¼

5/10/99	Review of Draft MMM Counteroffer	½
	Preparing Memo to ASD on MMM Counteroffer	¼
5/21/99	Review of Letter to RK and Final MMM Counteroffer	½

Total Hours 6½

Bill $975

TRAYNOR, HAND, WYZANSKI

222 CHURCH STREET
NEW SALEM, NARRAGANSETT 06555
(393) 876-5678

BILL FOR SERVICES
Attorney Work Product

Client: Maria Mather Meiklejohn
Rate: $150/hour
Period: 3/16/99 to 5/21/99
Date: May 21, 1999

Attorney: David Greaves
             6½ Hours $975

Attorney: Anne Sophie Diehl
             31½ Hours $4,725
                                                      ───────

Total: $5,700

TRAYNOR, HAND, WYZANSKI

222 CHURCH STREET
NEW SALEM, NARRAGANSETT 06555
(393) 876-5678

MEMORANDUM
Attorney Work Product

From:	Sophie Diehl
To:	David Greaves
RE:	Ms. Maria Meiklejohn: Settlement Offer Approved
Date:	May 24, 1999
Attachments:	

Ms. Meiklejohn waltzed into my office today, all smiles and complaisance, nothing like her recent correspondence. She approved the letter and settlement offer I drafted for Kahn, the bottom-line offer, and the bill. They made her practically giddy with pleasure—she positively hooted several times as she read over the papers—and she was surprised the bill was so low. "I thought I'd used up the retainer. Are you sure you're not undercharging me?" She liked the request for reimbursement alimony and thought the time I spent on the memo well worth it. She said her husband was going to go berserk when he read the offer. "I'm feeling like Napoleon at Trafalgar. I'm not going to win, but I'll do serious damage to the other side." (My mother once said something very much to the same effect, though tailored more to my parents' particularly apt nationalities. I thought it was a French/British thing; apparently not. Do all divorcing women feel like Napoleon, grandiose and fatalistic? What do all divorcing men feel like?) She smiled at me. "It's better to die on one's feet than to live on one's knees, no?" I asked if she was worried about her husband's response. "Oh, I'm ready for him," she said. "There's really nothing he can do to me. Jane is the only thing that really matters, and if he challenges me on custody, I'll sic my father on him. Just let me know if you need more money." And then she was gone. She must have upped her meds.

The offer will go out tomorrow.

P.S. I shouldn't have been disrespectful about lawyers in my letter to Ms. Meiklejohn. I'll do my best to see it doesn't happen again.

P.P.S. You must agree that having to behave oneself all the time is a downside of civil practice. Don't you find it at least a bit constricting? Don't you ever want to say what you're really thinking?

IV. NEGOTIATIONS

BRUCE MEIKLEJOHN
50 SAINT CLOUD
NEW SALEM, NARRAGANSETT 06555

May 25, 1999

David Greaves
Traynor, Hand, Wyzanski
222 Church Street
New Salem, NA 06555

Dear David:

Maria showed me the settlement offer. That little Sophie Diehl is dynamite. I'd like her to work for me. Just kidding. Where did she go to law school?

The bill was a surprise. You charge me that much for a tenth of the time. You don't have to eat the bill. I'll pay. It's worth it. I'd give anything to be in the room when Durkheim reads that letter.

I'd like to take you and Ms. Diehl to lunch at the Plimouth Club. What do you say to next Thursday, June 3?

Thanks for coming to the New York meeting. I know you don't like being window dressing (not for three days), but having you there was very useful. For the first time since negotiations started, they looked worried. As they should. I'm going to take them over, one way or the other. You made them see that. How many shares will I have to sell to pay that bill? Just kidding.

Let me know about the 3rd.

Sincerely,

Bruce

Harry Redux

From: Sophie Diehl   5/26/99 11:28 PM
To: Maggie Pfeiffer <mcp15@mather.edu>
Date: Wed, 26 May 1999 23:28:54
Subject: Harry Redux

Dear Maggie:

Harry showed up tonight around 9, drunk as a skunk. I don't think I've seen anyone that drunk since high school. He couldn't stand up and was sloppily affectionate. (Memories of Jack.) At least he didn't puke all over everything. In high school the boys always puked everywhere, on the car seat, on themselves, on you. Did they drink to puke? Anyway, Harry kept on saying how sorry he was. God, I hate drunks. I put him in the shower, made him drink a quart of water, then put him to bed. He's there now. He hasn't shaved in days, and he's got huge, dark shadows under his eyes, like Nehru. He looks awful and yet he's still so beautiful. I don't know what he's been up to—other than his cups in Jack Daniel's. I couldn't get a coherent word out of him, except, of course, "Sorry." Do I sleep on the couch, or do I get into bed with him?

I don't know what I'm doing.

Love,
Sophie

TRAYNOR, HAND, WYZANSKI

222 CHURCH STREET
NEW SALEM, NARRAGANSETT 06555
(393) 876-5678

MEMORANDUM
Attorney Work Product

From:	David Greaves
To:	Sophie Diehl
RE:	Bruce Meiklejohn's Letter on MMM's Settlement Offer
Date:	May 27, 1999
Attachments:	Bruce Meiklejohn's Letter of May 25, 1999

Bruce Meiklejohn has invited you and me to lunch at the Plimouth Club on June 3. Can you make it? I think you'd enjoy yourself. Let me know. We can go somewhere else. Porter's would work for you, wouldn't it? He was very impressed with your work on the settlement offer. He said he wanted you to work for him. I've attached his letter.

That quote from Ms. Meiklejohn about dying on your feet. Where's that from? Hemingway? No Frenchman said that, nor any Englishman. Men think they're Sherman marching on Atlanta or Grant taking Richmond. Again, divorce as war, but a civil war, and victory is not in doubt.

P.S. I'm sorry I roped you into this divorce. But, come clean, aren't you having a little fun with it? Truce?

TRAYNOR, HAND, WYZANSKI

222 CHURCH STREET
NEW SALEM, NARRAGANSETT 06555
(393) 876-5678

MEMORANDUM
Attorney Work Product

From: Sophie Diehl
To: David Greaves
RE: Bruce Meiklejohn's Invitation
Date: May 27, 1999
Attachments:

I'd like to have lunch with Bruce Meiklejohn—at Porter's, not at the Plimouth Club, but we'll have to change the date. I've got an evidentiary hearing on the 3rd. How about next Tuesday, the 8th? I promise to behave myself, but of course I can't work for him. I'd be disowned. If you think I'm cranky now, just put me in the library with the Uniform Commercial Code. The only thing I remember from my course on commercial transactions (viz., the only thing I *had* to remember, according to my professor) was that the bank never loses.

The quote about dying on one's feet is attributed to La Pasionaria, during the Spanish Civil War. Hemingway wasn't a bad guess (he may even have used it in *For Whom the Bell Tolls*), though you clearly didn't grow up under the tutelage of a Marxist father. (See supra, on being disowned.) That was my father's favorite war. (Mine is WWI, the most heartbreaking slaughter.) He even wrote a book on England's tacit support of Franco and the Nationalists (Papa's interpretation), *The Sixth Column*.

I was planning to take off tomorrow for the Memorial Day weekend. I hope that's okay. I'm going to Wellfleet, to my mother's and Jake's. My sibs are all coming. Is there anything else I need to do before I go? I'm up on all my other cases.

My parents' divorce was a guerrilla war. The collateral damage was extensive and the pacification program unsuccessful.

TRAYNOR, HAND, WYZANSKI

222 CHURCH STREET
NEW SALEM, NARRAGANSETT 06555
(393) 876-5678
ATTORNEYS AT LAW

May 27, 1999

Bruce Meiklejohn
50 Saint Cloud Street
New Salem, NA 06555

Dear Bruce:

I am glad you approve of the legal work the firm is doing for your daughter. Sophie Diehl is first-rate, smart as they come. She graduated from Yale, where she spent most of her time working on capital cases with Stephen Bright and his Southern Center for Human Rights. She then clerked for Anne Howard on the 13th Circuit. She's not for you; she doesn't know a tort from a breach of contract. That being said, she and I would like very much to have lunch, though she can't make the 3rd. She's got a very busy criminal calendar. Could you do the 8th? And would you be our guest at Porter's? Sophie has a weakness for their double lamb chops.

Yours,

David Greaves

David Greaves

I did it again

From: Sophie Diehl   5/27/99 7:18 PM
To: Maggie Pfeiffer <mcp15@mather.edu>
Date: Thu, 27 May 1999 19:18:03
Subject: I did it again

Dear Maggie—

You were right. Again. DG showed me a letter from the Big Client
that made it clear he was in New York on firm business, advising on a
takeover. If he saw my mother (and he *still* may have), she wasn't the
object of the trip. Just a fringe benefit.

I don't know what to say about last night. I haven't been able to wrap
my mind around it. Harry slept for about six hours. When he woke
up at about 4 a.m., he hadn't a clue how or why he came over. He
was very apologetic (replaying the earlier part of the evening) about
barging in. I don't think the original apologies had to do with his turning
up; I don't know what they had to do with. Thank God, I slept on the
sofa. As he got dressed to leave, I told him that he'd shown up about
9:30, completely slammered, sentimental, and apologetic. (I intended
"completely" to modify all three adjectives.) He was embarrassed, but
not as embarrassed as he might have been, or should have been. "I'm
a wreck," he said, smiling wanly and shrugging. Papa would have done
the same thing. The gorge rose in my American throat. I wanted to say
something mean like "I'm not charmed," but I held my tongue. (Am I
showing progress?) He apologized once more and left.

I'm off to Wellfleet for the weekend. The sibs are all coming. Perhaps I'll
ask my mother point-blank if she's messing around with my boss. What's
the worst she can do? Perhaps I won't ask her.

I feel better, though I'm not sure why. Because Harry showed up?
Because I wasn't charmed? I often wish I could be like my father and
Harry, self-dramatizing and self-forgiving. Buttoned-up is what you said I
was, no? You were right. But those drama queens need sane people like

me. No wonder my mother married Jake after all those years with Papa. I don't know how he does it, but he never behaves badly. Jake says it's because he was overanalyzed.

What time tomorrow are you leaving for Williamstown? How will you celebrate your anniversary?

Love to you and Matt,

Sophie

P.S. I'm so happy you and Matt like the print. My divorce client told me that paper was the proper gift for the first anniversary, so I thought, what better than an Ed Ruscha. But there's paper and then there's paper. "In my mother's family," my client told me, "the standard gift was engraved monogrammed note cards. Cream vellum, charcoal or navy lettering. I got seven sets on our first anniversary, from various great-aunts, two in the name of Mrs. Daniel E. Durkheim, one spelled 'Durkhiem.' " What was it like to open that seventh box? Do you laugh, or do you cry? No returns possible, or regifting.

TRAYNOR, HAND, WYZANSKI

222 CHURCH STREET
NEW SALEM, NARRAGANSETT 06555
(393) 876-5678

MEMORANDUM
Attorney Work Product

From:	David Greaves
To:	Sophie Diehl
RE:	Meiklejohn at Porter's Next Week
Date:	June 2, 1999
Attachments:	Letter from Bruce Meiklejohn
	Letter to Bruce Meiklejohn from Mia Meiklejohn

I received a very interesting letter this morning from Bruce Meiklejohn, with an enclosure, another very interesting letter, from his daughter to him.

Lunch is on with him on the 8th at 12:30 at Porter's.

BRUCE MEIKLEJOHN
50 SAINT CLOUD
NEW SALEM, NARRAGANSETT 06555

May 29, 1999

David Greaves
Traynor, Hand, Wyzanski
222 Church Street
New Salem, NA 06555

Dear David:

When I got your note about lunch, I called my daughter and asked her what was going on. I told her I'd invited her lawyers out to lunch at the Plimouth but they'd turned the tables on me and asked me to Porter's. Mia said I was a dinosaur and hung up on me. Then she sent me the enclosed letter.

Is Mia right? She's never said anything to me like that before. I wonder. Is this a new Mia? Or is she regularly like that with others?

I'll go to Porter's with you, of course, but please, I'd like you to be my guests. And the 8th is fine. Is Elisabeth Diehl Sophie Diehl's mother? I like her books, especially *Death Duties*.

Mia's really mad at me. I couldn't bear it if she didn't let me see Jane. I love that little girl more than anyone else in the world.

You're not Jewish, are you? It's fine, of course, if you are. I was just wondering.

Yours truly,

Bruce

MARIA MATHER MEIKLEJOHN
404 ST. CLOUD STREET
NEW SALEM, NA 06556

May 29, 1999

Father—

Sophie Diehl kyboshed the Plimouth Club because she doesn't eat at restricted clubs. She's not only the daughter of an English Catholic Marxist, she's the daughter of a French Jew. You may have heard of her mother; she's the mystery writer Elisabeth Diehl. (You did your research; I did mine.)

It's time you got over your knee-jerk anti-Semitism, if for no other reason than it makes you look stupid and benighted. Everyone marries Jews these days, not only Helen Fincher and I. And they're everywhere. Your beloved law firm has Jews, including some of the senior partners. Daniel Durkheim may have behaved badly, but let me assure you, WASPs behave just as badly, often worse. And I don't think he married me for my connections. I like to think I have—or had—other things going for me. And he was on the fast track to success, whomever he married. Then there's the obvious. Your granddaughter is Jewish, or half-Jewish, which, I need not tell you, was Jewish enough for Hitler. I want you to keep one thing in mind. He's her father, and he'll always be in her life. If you don't shape up, I'm not going to see you anymore.

Nor will Jane.

I'm going to outlive you, you know, and inherit mother's house on the Vineyard, free and clear. And when I die, I'm going to leave it to the United Jewish Appeal.

And by the way, mother was called Maria; I'm,

As always,

Mia

TRAYNOR, HAND, WYZANSKI

222 CHURCH STREET
NEW SALEM, NARRAGANSETT 06555
(393) 876-5678

MEMORANDUM
Attorney Work Product

From: Sophie Diehl
To: David Greaves
RE: Daniel Durkheim's Response to the Offer
Date: June 2, 1999
Attachments: Letter from Mia Meiklejohn

It seems to have been a memorable Memorial Day weekend at the Meiklejohn/Durkheims. I also received a letter this morning, from Mia Meiklejohn. Dr. Durkheim hit the roof after he read the counteroffer. What happens next? Do I tell her to sit tight? Do we sit tight? I hate the way children get caught up in divorce.

Bruce Meiklejohn's letter was moving in its perplexity. Mia's to him was a doozer. She must have been working on it secretly for 15 years. It is the Mia I know. Wait till the UJA hears about the legacy.

I didn't know Proctor Hand was Jewish.

May 29, 1999

Anne Sophie Diehl
Traynor, Hand, Wyzanski
222 Church Street
New Salem, NA 06555

Dear Sophie:

Things took a bad turn last night. As I predicted, Daniel went berserk when he read the counteroffer. He came home last night at about 10 and roared into my bedroom, yelling his head off. "Where do you get off asking for my medical degree? And law school? I should pay for you to go to law school? This is highway robbery." (This is an expurgated version of the conversations. I left out the endearments. "Goddamned fucking cunt" was the most memorable, probably because it was repeated so often.) His face was red and sweat was pouring off him. I told him to get out of my room. "You won't get away with this," he said.

Just as he was turning to leave, I looked toward the doorway and saw Jane standing there sobbing. It was so awful. Danny reached out to comfort her, but she threw off his arm and ran to her room. I ran after her. I found her lying on her bed, crying so uncontrollably she couldn't catch her breath. I don't know how much she heard. She couldn't talk. She cried for at least half an hour. It was so heartbreaking. After she finally calmed down, I made her some hot chocolate and then sat holding her in her bed until she fell asleep.

The next morning Danny came down to breakfast while Jane and I were eating. He looked whipped and haggard. He apologized profusely to her, saying how sorry he was that she had heard all he had said. She wouldn't look at him, but stirred her cereal. "You're not sorry you said it, are you?" she asked. "Only that I heard it?" He said he was sorry for everything. She shrugged, and kept stirring her cereal.

I don't know if I can take any more. I can face down Danny, but I can't stand what this is doing to Jane. I keep thinking we should move out. I'm sure my father would support us if I asked him, for no other reason than he could tell everyone what a dick Danny was for tossing us out without a cent.

I won't do anything without talking to you, but the situation is approaching the intolerable.

If he does anything like that again, can I get an eviction order against him?

Yours,

Mia

P.S. For 18 years, I was caught between my husband and my father, who couldn't stand each other. I spent hours and hours negotiating awful social occasions with them both, pouring oil on the troubled waters, trying to achieve a shaky truce. Now I find I'm at war with both of them. And I say to hell with both of them.

TRAYNOR, HAND, WYZANSKI

222 CHURCH STREET
NEW SALEM, NARRAGANSETT 06555
(393) 876-5678

MEMORANDUM
Attorney Work Product

From:	David Greaves
To:	Sophie Diehl
RE:	Ms. Maria Meiklejohn's Letter
Date:	June 2, 1999
Attachments:	*Peele v. Peele* Application for a TRO

Talk to Ms. Meiklejohn. I don't know that an exclusion order will fly, but you can certainly look into it. You may remember the Peele case had one; Kahn's client, Jason Peele, filed one against his wife, our client, and then locked her out. It didn't fly—the judge was plainly annoyed and gave it very short shrift—and ultimately, it backfired. It put Mrs. Peele's back up; she made it clear to her husband she was willing to have the judge, the same judge, decide everything. I have attached Peele's affidavit here. Amazing chutzpah he had. It's what made him the success he was in business. You should draft a letter to Kahn, talking about the incident, and threatening to have Dr. Durkheim excluded from the family residence if there's a repeat. Then tell him to come up with a serious offer. Enough of this prancing about. Let's get this thing over and get Ms. Meiklejohn and Jane out of there.

Ms. Meiklejohn will make an excellent lawyer. Her first impulse was to flee. She was thinking like a mother. Seconds later, she's rallied and asks you about an eviction order. She doesn't scare—or she doesn't stay scared—and she's always thinking. Play to that part of her personality. Make her feel strong, competent. Give her something to do. She and Jane may have to move out, but I don't think that time has come; if she moves out now, she'll lose her leverage. I wouldn't mince words with her. Lay it out, coldly, matter-of-factly. She'll get it.

Commonwealth of Narragansett
Family Court

County: Tyler   **Docket No:** 96-82

Witness Protection Application for a
Temporary Restraining Order

Witness's Affidavit

My name is Jason Peele. I live at 620 St. Cloud Street in New Salem, NA. On October 2, 1996, I sued my wife, Rebecca Peele, for divorce on grounds of irreconcilable differences. The marriage had been dead for years; my wife refused to perform the ordinary duties a man rightfully expects from his partner and helpmate. The divorce has stalled. My wife has been using devious, dishonest, underhanded, and dilatory tactics in order to bully me into settling. She has made blatantly unreasonable and exorbitant demands for alimony, child support, and property.

I am the Chairman of Narragansett Industries (NI), a major multi-national corporation and one of the Fortune 500. The job is an enormously demanding and responsible one, and I have been a very successful steward, widely and publicly recognized for my business acumen and leadership. I've been profiled in *Time*, *Barron's*, and *Forbes*, and *Forbes* put me on the cover. I frequently work at home evenings and weekends. I also entertain at home, at least twice a week. Because the house is also a workspace, NI pays many of its expenses, including the services of a secretary, a cook, a butler, two maids, a driver, and a gardener. Additional staff are hired as needed, e.g., for large parties. The house is 20,000 square feet, of which 10,000 feet are public spaces, set aside for business and entertaining. These include three large reception rooms; two dining rooms, one large enough for a sit-down dinner for 48, the other more intimate, seating 16; a home theater; a gymnasium; a home office for me; a separate office for my secretary; a swimming pool; a greenhouse; and a professional kitchen. Norman Foster designed the house.

I am petitioning the Court for a temporary restraining order excluding my wife and children from the house until the divorce goes through. Her continued presence has created a poisonous environment. She drops into my home office when I am working there. She does this unexpectedly with the calculated purpose of upsetting me. I have asked her to communicate with me only through our attorneys, but she persists in speaking to me directly. At professional parties in the house, she makes appearances, walking through the rooms among the guests, drinking cocktails with them and having conversations. I do not know what she says about me, but I have every reason to believe that her comments are denigrating and insulting, putting me in a compromising position with my company and jeopardizing my business relationships. She is also turning the children against me. One of them called me a "deadbeat dad."

My wife's continued presence in the house is causing me serious emotional anguish and distress. I am having trouble sleeping and eating. I fear that unless my wife and I live separately, I will not be able to do my job. I have leased an apartment for my wife and our two children at 72 Randall Road, two blocks from where we are now all living. I have generously offered to pay the rent, all educational costs for the children, and her car payments, and to provide my wife with a monthly stipend of $2,000. Her removal with the children to this apartment will be in everyone's best interest. The children will not have to witness their parents' fights, and I will be able to continue to do the work that makes it possible for me to provide for their support.

Name of Witness	Address of Witness	
Jason Peele	620 St. Cloud Street, New Salem, NA 06556	

Signed (APPLICANT)	Subscribed and sworn to before me	Date Signed
X *Jason Peele*	Signed (CLERK, NOTARY) *Mary Murphy*	16 January 1997

Discretion

From: Sophie Diehl   6/2/99 9:03 PM
To: Maggie Pfeiffer <mcp15@mather.edu>
Date: Wed, 2 June 1999 21:03:58
Subject: Discretion

Dearest Mags,

You can relax. I'm sane again. I didn't say anything to my mother.
(I'm still sort of scared of her.) I don't think she's messing around with
DG; it's not her way. She might have slept with the chairman of my
father's department—and let word get around—but she had serious
grievances against Papa. She loves me too much; and, more to the
point, she loves Jake. I see that now. They were terrific together this
weekend—playful, affectionate, combative (a sure sign my mother
is happy). They had a huge argument about Clinton. Maman said the
whole thing was ridiculous. "Americans are so afraid of sex. They think
it matters too much." Jake would have none of that. "Sex is the means
of reproduction. Of course, it matters too much. And, don't say," he
said, looking hard at Maman, "that the connection is incidental." Maman
accused him of being a Darwinian, not a Freudian. And they were off. All
weekend, they kept coming back to Clinton. They argued about Hillary,
why she didn't leave him. Maman said a discreet affair was one thing,
but no woman should put up with that kind of public humiliation. Jake
disagreed. "We don't know what goes on with the Clintons. They may
have other, more important needs that are being met." He then said
that in many marriages, infidelity was not necessarily a death blow.
After all that divorce stuff, it was so nice to see a married couple who
liked each other, who interested each other, who took pleasure in each
other's company. Maman wouldn't risk her marriage for a fling. As for
Jake, whatever he said about other people's marriages, I'm pretty sure
he would find infidelity a serious threat to *theirs*.

When I got home, I had a message from Harry. He called to invite me to
dinner this Friday. It was as though he were asking me out for the first

time. He sounded unsure, diffident. Well, he should be. I don't know if I want to start up again. Suppose I really fall in love with him? Do I want to marry someone who's already been married? Don't I want to be my first husband's first wife, the standard against which all subsequent wives are measured—and fall short? I'm a firstborn, remember. I have this theory: firstborns don't marry divorced people, or if they do, they don't marry divorced people with children. They don't compete. But then there's my client, who's a firstborn; she married a formerly married man who had a child. I may have to refine the theory.

How is Williamstown? What plays will you be doing? It must be beautiful up there, if you like nature. Not my cup of tea. What is it Woody Allen said? I am at two with Nature. What I can't figure out is why I stayed in New Salem after clerking. Why aren't I in New York? My life has been ad-libbed. I need to make plans. I feel sometimes like one of those exasperating Austen heroines, Marianne or Emma, ardent and self-centered. But they turn out all right, so maybe . . .

I miss you. Much love,
Sophie

TRAYNOR, HAND, WYZANSKI

222 CHURCH STREET
NEW SALEM, NARRAGANSETT 06555
(393) 876-5678

MEMORANDUM
Attorney Work Product

From: Sophie Diehl
To: David Greaves
RE: TRO
Date: June 3, 1999
Attachments:

I've drafted a letter to Ray Kahn threatening to file a temporary restraining order against Dr. Durkheim. I said we weren't planning to file the TRO unless there was another incident but warned him that we would go forward if Dr. Durkheim went on the rampage again.

Ms. Meiklejohn is on board. She's very worried about Jane, who has become, in her mother's words, "a very sad little girl."

Jason Peele is a pig.

TRAYNOR, HAND, WYZANSKI

222 CHURCH STREET
NEW SALEM, NARRAGANSETT 06555
(393) 876-5678
ATTORNEYS AT LAW

June 3, 1999

Ray Kahn, Esq.
Kahn & Boyle
46 Broadway
New Salem, NA 06555

RE: Dr. Daniel Durkheim

Dear Mr. Kahn:

On May 28, 1999, your client, Dr. Daniel Durkheim, had a bitter and vituperative argument with his wife, Ms. Maria Meiklejohn, which was witnessed by their daughter, Jane, age 11. The experience was deeply upsetting to Jane, and even now, a week later, she continues to show signs of extreme emotional distress. Ms. Meiklejohn is worried for her psychological well-being. While ugly arguments between divorcing couples are not unusual, when they reach a level of aggression that threatens to endanger a child's welfare, steps need to be taken to protect the child and isolate her from their destructive effects. These steps may include a Temporary Restraining Order.

On advice of counsel, Ms. Meiklejohn has submitted a draft statement in support of a TRO excluding Dr. Durkheim from the family residence. We will not file it now, but in the event there is a second incident of the kind she describes in the affidavit, we shall recommend that she go forward with an application.

Concluding the separation agreement seems a far better solution than a TRO, an action that can only exacerbate the ill will between the parties and delay a final resolution. To that end, I urge you and your client to review our offer of May 25 and send a timely response.

We expect there will be no further incidents that endanger Jane's safety and welfare. Moving out of the family residence is not an option Ms. Meiklejohn will entertain without a separation agreement or, in the event the parties cannot reach an accord, a divorce decree.

Yours,

Anne Sophie Diehl

Anne Sophie Diehl

cc: Maria Mather Meiklejohn

Re: Discretion

From: Maggie Pfeiffer   6/3/99 11:11PM

To: Sophie Diehl <asdiehl@traynor.com>

Date: Thu, 3 June 1999 23:11:33

Subject: Re: Discretion

Dear Sophie—

I am so glad you've come to your senses. I had this sinking deja vu feeling of you at 16, furious at your parents for getting divorced. Who would be 16 again?

I'm having a wonderful time. Williamstown is Shangri-la, gorgeous and unreal, like a stage set. I could be superior to it all if it weren't so fabulous and so easy to take. No visible suffering. Matt is working away in the library, when he's not working out at the college's gym, which is state-of-the-art. Boys and their equipment.

I've been cast in three plays, wonderful roles all. Julia, the cardinal's mistress, in *The Duchess of Malfi*, Cecily in Stoppard's *Travesties*, and, joy of joys, Hypatia in *Misalliance*. Rehearsing for three plays is exhausting and confusing. I'm having trouble learning my lines. Both Stoppard and Shaw are so witty and wordy, I can't keep them straight. (Matt says I'm always like this learning lines, but I think he's just being kind.) I die in *The Duchess* but no real lines.

The *Travesties* role is nothing to sneer at, but Hypatia is divine, Lizzie Bennet as Darcy; i.e., she's got the wit and the money. At the end of the play, she asks her rich and doting father to give up his objections to her penniless suitor and let her marry him. "Papa," she says cajolingly, wooing him with the confident charm of a beloved, indulged child, "buy the brute for me." Sometimes, the line makes me want to cry—for myself, course. (And who else do we ever cry for?) My father wouldn't buy me goldfish.

And speaking of papas, I had a John Diehl sighting. I was so surprised. We ran into him and Sally at MASS MoCA in North Adams. He didn't look well (wrecked but still so handsome), but he was his old sweet self—funny, warm, interested in finding out everything we were doing. They were taking a long weekend in the country. Sally is always very quiet with me, but not unfriendly. They're off to England the end of the month, or at least your dad is. It wasn't clear that Sally was going. She seemed worried about him; she kept her hand on his arm the whole time. (I've become a kind of voyeur, taking in people's movements and gestures, thinking about the ways I can use them.) When was the last time you were in touch with him? You've got to see him, sweetie. He misses you. He was very sorry to hear about your divorce detail. "God," he said, "that must be torture for her. She can't stand divorcing parents." He's crazy about you, in his own peculiar, Diehlian, English way. Cut him some slack, please, Sophie. He didn't mean to hurt you. He couldn't help himself; he's got those demons. I know I shouldn't lecture you. After all, who am I to talk? I haven't spoken to my father in ten years (not that he's noticed). But let's be fair, there's a huge difference between our fathers. Your father isn't drunk all the time; your father hasn't scrounged off your mother for the last 20 years; your father paid for your education, your braces, your bikes, your prom dresses (and some of my mine too).

I'd love you to come up for a weekend; and we've got room for you (and guest). Please, think about it. I want you to see me in *Misalliance*, but I'll settle for *Travesties*. *Duchess* isn't worth the detour, not if you're coming to see me. Of course, I want your mom to come to a performance. She's seen everything I've ever been in since I made my debut in 5th grade, in *Iphigenia at Aulis*. My first death scene. Ah, progressive education. You know, I wouldn't have gone to Bank Street—or Brearley or Harvard, for that matter—if it weren't for your parents. When I was little, I thought they were paying for my education. My *Great Expectations* fantasy. I didn't know about scholarships. The truth is, Sophie, my love, if it weren't for your parents, I'd probably be a drunk like the old man, living off my mother in that wretched basement apartment, sleeping with skinheads, waiting for death. They saved my life. And gave me you.

Let me know how the big date goes tomorrow.

Love,
Maggie

Papa

From: Sophie Diehl   6/4/99 2:51 PM
To: Maggie Pfeiffer <mcp15@mather.edu>
Date: Fri, 4 June 1999 14:51:16
Subject: Papa

Dear Mags,

What a hat trick. You must have wowed them. I don't know *Misalliance*, but I take your word on Hypatia's divinity. You seem to be developing a specialty in Stoppard. Of course, I'll come see you. And Maman said she'd come, too.

I am planning to see my father before he goes off to England, but I'm dreading it. He's been so critical of me lately, so unkind. I come away from our visits utterly demoralized. He's interested in hearing about what you're doing because he thinks it's terrific you're an actor. He's not interested in what I do. I start telling him about a case and his eyes glaze over. He says lawyers are jackals. He'd have preferred if I had become a cop, and I really thought about it too, to please him. But I don't like guns or blood and it's too hard a life. I love working with cops, but most of them are alienated, secretive, withholding, distrustful. And their most important relationships are with other cops.

I keep telling myself Papa's disappointment with me is a proxy for his disappointment with himself. He will never be, he thinks, in the ranks of his idols, E. P. Thompson, Eric Hobsbawm, Christopher Hill. When he won the Wolfson History Prize, the fact Hobsbawm had won it meant nothing to him; he called it a "prize for popularizers."

I want things to be the way they used to be, when I was Best Girl and you were Best Girl's Best Girl. He used to be so great, mostly. Reading me all of Laura Ingalls Wilder and *Anne of Green Gables*. Teaching me to sail the *Swallow* (which Luc and I took out last weekend) and to play cricket. Taking me to jazz concerts and insisting I listen to his old Coltrane recordings. And then we all got divorced. He became distant, irascible. He thought we all sided with Maman—which we did, of course, because she was the one who paid attention to us. I thought when he married Sally he'd warm toward us, toward me—she's a very nice woman, kind, thoughtful, a good mother to her own kids—but I think she's afraid of him, or afraid of criticizing or correcting him. And then Jake has been so terrific to all of us.

Jake always says a child only needs one good parent to come out all right—so long as the good parent, besides doing the good things, protects the children from the bad parent. During that terrible summer they were separating, Papa said I wasn't worth talking to, I'd become so stupid. Maman overheard him. She said if he ever said anything like that again to one of the children, she'd hire someone to break both his legs. (In case anyone asks WWFWD, ha!) He laughed, but he knew she meant it. She of course knew people who did that for a living, as I do. I met my first with her at the West End. I was maybe 14. He didn't look like a gangster; he looked like a dentist. He used a tire iron, Maman said. I've got to run. I have an evidentiary hearing in criminal court and then home to shave my legs for my big night.

Love,
Sophie

Pettigrew Flowers
350 TEMPLE AVENUE
NEW SALEM, NA 06555
(393) 876-2363

June 5

Dear Fiona,

Congratulations.
Wishing you all the best,

Sophie

The Morning After

From: Sophie Diehl   6/5/99 11:19 AM
To: Maggie Pfeiffer <mcp15@mather.edu>
Date: Sat, 5 June 1999 11:19:08
Subject: The Morning After

Dearest Mags,

Where to begin? The beginning, I guess. (Maman always says that
the virtues of chronological storytelling cannot be overstated.) Harry
showed up at 8 sharp, clutching tulips. He remembered they were my
second-favorite flowers. He offered them apologetically, saying he had
really wanted to bring peonies but couldn't find any. It was so awkward;
I felt 14 and clammy. The reservation he'd made at Printemps wasn't
until 9, so I decided we should get drunk. I made us martinis, without
vermouth. And we smoked. It's good we were in easy walking distance.
We each had at least three. I just looked at the gin bottle. It's half gone.

We talked about our work. He's running the Cabaret at Mather this
summer and is doing three different evenings of three one-act plays.
He calls it Three by Three. He was doing a couple of Ives, including *The
Universal Language*, and a couple of Alan Bennett's *Talking Heads*. I told
him about my divorce case and its catastrophic effect on my personality.
He said, "I guess my saga with Tessa didn't help." That opened the door
to a very serious conversation. He said Tessa had been discharged from
Austen Riggs and was back in Manhattan. He hired a lawyer, who drew
up a separation agreement. Tessa has it; he thinks she'll balk at signing.
She doesn't like the idea of not being attached to someone. The lawyer
says that if she refuses to sign, he can sue for divorce on grounds of
desertion. He hates the thought but said he'll do it if that's the only way
of extricating himself. I think it's really over. She was impossible to deal
with, refusing to admit she had tried to kill herself and acting as though
he'd engineered everything to get her back. The night he drove her back
to the city, she took off all her clothes while he was in the bathroom
and asked if he wanted to fuck. He was surprised to realize he didn't.
"I never thought I would turn her down," he said.

I didn't sleep with him. If I liked him less, I might have. But you know me, when I really like someone, sex can make me think I'm in love. I'm not taking that chance with him, not now. And anyway, we were so drunk at the end of the evening, neither of us could muster any enthusiasm, let alone libido. He walked me home, kissed me on the nose, and said he'd call me. I stumbled into bed and fell asleep in seconds, only to wake up three hours later, my mouth caked, my throat parched, my head pounding. I'm a lousy drinker, like all the women in my family. BUT Harry's not the only man in my life making a comeback. My father called last night. He wants to see me. He reminded me it's been eight months since we saw each other. I'm amazed he was keeping track. He invited me down the weekend after next but said if that wasn't good for me, he'd come up. He made me very nervous. They say that suicides often get in touch with everyone, to say goodbye before they act. I'm going to call Sally and find out what's up. He's not the kind to take drugs. A shooter or a jumper is my guess. I'll kill him if he does it.

Love,
Sophie

P.S. I may be hungover and half heartbroken, but I remembered to call the florist and ordered two dozen yellow roses for Fiona. Let's see what that does.

Party for Fiona

From: David Greaves   6/7/99 8:36 AM
To: Sophie Diehl <asdiehl@traynor.com>
Date: Mon, 7 June 1999 8:36:58
Subject: Party for Fiona

Sophie—

Where were you Saturday night? We missed you at the party for Fiona
that Seamus FitzGerald threw. It was an important event for her, to be
honored as one of the year's outstanding alumni of Narragansett Law
School. Every other lawyer in the firm was there. And everyone noticed
your absence. I don't think of you as being vindictive or mean-spirited.
Were you ill? Was it some other occasion, a wedding?

David

Re: Party for Fiona
From: Sophie Diehl   6/7/99 9:03 AM
To: David Greaves <dagreaves@traynor.com>
Date: Mon, 7 June 1999 9:03:19
Subject: Re: Party for Fiona

> Dear David,
>
> Fiona made it clear that she didn't want me there. I didn't tell you.
> (It's the new Sophie.) I was sucking it up. I took counsel with Joe. He
> said he'd tell Proctor's secretary, who was handling the tables, that
> I couldn't make it. And I wrote to Seamus, sending my regrets. After
> all the fuss, I couldn't go around telling everyone in the firm I'd been
> dissed. Instead, I get to look rude, churlish, and mean-spirited. But
> I'm taking it on the chin.
>
> Sophie
>
> P.S. I'm taking a new tack with Fiona. Killing with kindness.

Lunch in the Enemy Camp

From: Sophie Diehl   6/8/99 11:14 PM
To: Maggie Pfeiffer <mcp15@mather.edu>
Date: Tue, 8 Jun 1999 23:14:56
Subject: Lunch in the Enemy Camp

Dear Mags,

I had a lunch today that blew my socks off. Implosively, not explosively.
I shouldn't be writing this to you (lawyer-client confidentiality blah
blah blah), but I need to tell someone. The aftershocks persist.
Bruce Meiklejohn, CEO of Octopus Enterprises, Corporate Raider
Extraordinaire, and father of my divorce client, Mia Meiklejohn, took
DG and me to lunch at Porter's. He originally invited us to the Plimouth,
but I held true to my French Jewish English Marxist 14th Amendment
American heritage and refused to go there. Actually DG did the refusing.
But that is a sidebar. Everyone has always said Meiklejohn is an anti-
Semitic troglodyte. Not true. Or, at least, not the whole truth. He's a
great charmer and very astute. While we were eating (I had the double
lamp chops), the husband of my client, Meiklejohn's son-in-law, Daniel
E. Durkheim, M.D., came into the dining room. From everything I'd
heard about him, I thought he would be a rude, arrogant son of a
bitch, thin-lipped and too well dressed. George Sanders in *All About
Eve*. But he wasn't. He was hamish, like Elliott Gould in *MASH*. A really
nice-looking, rumpled, comfortable Jewish man who is 15 pounds
overweight and fine about it and fine about your extra 15 pounds too.
(You know, my father always reminded me of Donald Sutherland. Also
MASH. Not a comfortable Jewish man. Not comfortable at all. And not
comforting.) Bruce Meiklejohn, who, my sources (impeccable) tell me,
hates his son-in-law, got up from the table, went over to Dr. Durkheim,
shook his hand, and patted him on the back in the friendliest way. He
then brought him over to our table and introduced him to DG and me,
identifying us, not exactly apologetically, more regretfully, as his lawyers
and also his daughter's. "You're John Diehl's daughter, aren't you,"
Dr. D said as we shook hands. "I took his course on England at war at

Columbia. He was a great teacher. I'm very happy to meet you." He had a good voice, low and gravelly. I felt suddenly very stupid; I'd committed the great sin of lawyers. I had demonized the other side. I should have known Ms. Meiklejohn wouldn't have married a complete loser. It made me sad. I'll bet, in their day, they were an adorable couple.

After Durkheim went back to his table, DG asked Meiklejohn what that was all about. Meiklejohn reached into his pocket and took out a letter he had received the day before from his granddaughter, Jane, the Durkheims' 11-year-old. In the letter, she asked him to tell her dad not to go through with the divorce. It was a heartbreaker. As I read, my eyes welled with tears. Meiklejohn thought I was crying for Jane. He squeezed my arm gently. I almost lost it. There I was, back in that wretched summer of my parents' divorce. (As you said, we cry for ourselves.) It was so awful for all of us but worst for Francoise, who was only 11. She stopped washing her hair. I never told you this. I was too ashamed. We all forgot about her. After a few weeks, I finally noticed and asked her what was going on. She said she wasn't going to wash it until Maman said something. She went three months. My mother wept when she found out. Of course, Papa didn't notice; how could he? He spent the summer in Amagansett, and the fall too. Did you know he was sent to boarding school on his 7th birthday? How could they do that? Granny used to say how much Remy reminded her of Papa when he was small, so exuberant, so affectionate, so naughty. We thought she was bonkers.

I just reread this email. I've been casting my very own family movie. Raul Julia would have been perfect for Jake; second choice, Harvey Keitel. It's the way they're both sexy. (Did I really say that? Oy.) For Maman, I'm thinking Anouk Aimee; 15 years ago, she'd have been perfect. Those great bones. Is she still alive? Do you remember *A Man and a Woman*? Wasn't that that the best cry ever? After *Beaches*, and *Two for the Road*, of course. I'm off to bed. Miss you.

xoxoxoxox.

Sophie

TRAYNOR, HAND, WYZANSKI

222 CHURCH STREET
NEW SALEM, NARRAGANSETT 06555
(393) 876-5678

MEMORANDUM
Attorney Work Product

From: David Greaves
To: Sophie Diehl
RE: Durkheim/Meiklejohn
Date: June 9, 1999
Attachments: Jane Durkheim's Letter

That was some lunch—and some letter. I don't know that anyone has ever addressed Bruce Meiklejohn with that sweetness and confidence. That little girl knows he loves her, and she loves him back and trusts him. I'm betting that's a first for him. He may tell his daughter he'll underwrite the divorce and her post-divorce life, though I can't see her going along unless he stops rewriting his will and creates an irrevocable living trust that she can control and/or invade. That would be my advice. What's yours?

Bruce Meiklejohn never ceases to surprise me. I've been his lawyer for 22 years, and I've never been able to second-guess him.

JANE DURKHEIM

Dear Poppa,

Thank you for the new computer. I love it! It's absolutely
beautiful. I never saw a purple one before. All my friends are
jealus. I'm glad its a powerbook. I can use it everyweher. My
typing is getting better. Mommy says she is going to show me
how to use the Internet but I know how. We use computers at
school all the time. I don't have spelchekker on this computer
so my spelling is sometimes odd. I do it foneticaly. I hope you
don't mind. I can read much better than I can spell. I can see
where it's wrong. I just don't know how to make it right.

I need to talk to you about Daddy. I don't understand why he
stopped loving Mommy and me. Do you? Mommy is sad and I'm sad
too. I cry sometimes but I try not to let Mommy see. I know it
makes her feel sadder. Tito is very sad too. I can tell. He's very
mopey. Fido hasn't changed. He's always cheerful. Lucky dog.

I have a very big favor to ask you. Would you ask Daddy not
to do this divorce. I bet he would listen to you. He says your
very very smart. You just fake being stupid. Tell him I promise to be good and I'll behave myself.

You never got divorced. You got married again because Granny
died. I think that's the way to do it. Mommy isn't going to die
at 46 is she? She promises she wont but she still could. Who
will take care of me then? I cant live with Daddy. Could I live
with you? Cindy might not like it. I have a lot of things to
worry about.

Your loving granddaughter,
Jane

MEMORANDUM
Attorney Work Product

From:	Sophie Diehl
To:	David Greaves
RE:	Ms. Maria Meiklejohn
Date:	June 9, 1999
Attachments:	

What does Jane mean when she says she couldn't live with her father if something happened to her mother? You don't think he's hurting her in some way, do you?

My advice to Ms. Meiklejohn has been to stay the course. The house is the key to the settlement. Bruce Meiklejohn may love Jane more than anyone else, but I don't think he'll ever relinquish control of his money. Have you read his latest will? I did. I wanted the full measure of the man. The Law Against Perpetuities has met its match. He's got everything tied up for decades. He'll be pulling the strings long after he's dead. Ms. M may finally get her hands on some dough when she's 70. (Of course, in next month's will, he may decide to put all the money in a charitable foundation.) I did learn something interesting. Her mother left an estate of about $900,000, in addition to the Martha's Vineyard house, which she put in trusts for her children. She left $400,000 to Cordelia, and $400,000 to Ms. M. She also made a direct bequest of $100,000 to a scholarship fund at the Peabody School in memory of James Meiklejohn. Who is he? The money to Ms. M vests in 2007, when Ms. M is 50. Cordelia's remains in a trust. Ms. M never mentioned her trust. Does she know about it? It's got to be at least $2 million now, unless of course a bank was doing the investing. It must be 20 years since her mother died. Proctor is a trustee of both trusts, and he has the power to invade in the event of "necessity." He said he'd give me the numbers after the June 30 statements arrive; he reviews the accounts semiannually. He seems to think the money was invested in blue chips.

Bruce Meiklejohn currently pays all of Cordelia's expenses, and he has made arrangements in his will for her to be taken care of for the rest of her life. Do we have to let Kahn and Dr. D know about this money? I suppose so.

How did Meiklejohn find a purple computer? That was genius. He qualifies for the *Guinness Book of Granddads* with that one.

Casting Your Life

From: Maggie Pfeiffer   6/9/99 7:33 PM
To: Sophie Diehl <asdiehl@traynor.com>
Date: Wed, 9 June 1999 19:33:24
Subject: Casting Your Life

Dearest Sophie—

I know your dad was hard on you during the bad years. I saw it even
though you tried to protect me (or was it him you were protecting, from
my bad opinion?). But it wasn't only you. He was hard on Luc, too. And
he barely paid Francoise any attention at all. (I used to wonder if he
thought she was David Cummings's daughter. Where did that unwashed
bronze hair come from?) Remy somehow avoided his wrath. Think of
your parents' divorce as war. Now it's over, time to draw up a peace
treaty. Keep it simple. I think he behaves badly because he feels guilty.
Does that make sense?

Sometimes, Sophie, it's hard to hear your complaints against your
parents. It's not only that I love them and that they saved my life; they
are by any standard you can think of so much better than my parents.
I had this fantasy when I was 10 or 11 that my parents had kidnapped
me, that I was really the daughter of cultured and distinguished people
(your parents!?). Classic family romance, but what did I know then?
Your mother somehow got wind of this, probably something I said,
and decided to do an intervention. I can picture it to this day; it's like a
scene in play. We were in the kitchen, just the two of us. I don't know
where you and your siblings were. I was sitting at the table, drinking
chocolate milk; she was cooking. "Magpie," she said, "you belong to
a very lucky tribe, did you know that?" I must have looked startled, if
not incredulous. "Yes," she went on, "the self-made. Against the odds,
despite your tough upbringing, you will be brilliantly successful. You
don't need rich or royal parents or even me and John. You'll do it by
dint of brains, beauty, talent, drive, guts, and, most important, hard,
hard work. I know it." I would have died for her, right there, on the
spot. And I believed her.

Interestingly, she never ever criticized my parents, only my "upbringing." Once when I was older, maybe 15, I was complaining to her about my dad's drinking, and she said, with no hint of criticism (of me or him), but with that simple, direct style of hers that could turn someone else's rhetorical questions into legitimate ones: "Do you think he decided to be an alcoholic? Do you think that's what he wants to be?" That stopped me in my tracks. I had never given him a point of view. I had only asked: Why doesn't he stop it and behave responsibly?

Your dad's depressed and has been, I'm guessing, most of his life (probably since Granny Diehl packed him off to boarding school), and being English public school, he regards therapy and drugs as crutches. I can still hear him saying to one of you (and sometimes to me, too), "Pull up your socks, old man." You're never going to change him; he's never going to change. You might be able to change. That's your best hope. I am now going to pull up my socks and learn some lines till bedtime. (It worked for me; I am a perfect monument to sock-up-pulling.)

Love you,
Maggie

TRAYNOR, HAND, WYZANSKI

222 CHURCH STREET
NEW SALEM, NARRAGANSETT 06555
(393) 876-5678

MEMORANDUM
Attorney Work Product

From: Sophie Diehl
To: David Greaves
RE: A Letter from Bruce Meiklejohn
Date: June 11, 1999
Attachments: Bruce Meiklejohn's Letter

Mia Meiklejohn sent me a copy of a letter her father sent Jane in response to her letter to him. I can't imagine a letter that could make Jane feel better, safer, or more loved. I'll bet it made her feel smart, too. It's perfection. How did he know how to do that? No question: he is really and truly very smart.

June 8

Dear Pumpkin,

You can live with me anytime you want to, always and forever. You can live with me for a day, a week, a year, a decade, a century, or a millennium. I won't die until you're all grown up. But your mommy is not going to die either, so you can stop worrying about that. (And, just in case you're worrying about your own health, you are not going to die until you are very, very old, at least 99.)

You are my number 1 person and all-around champ.

Here's my direct telephone number: 393-875-7575. Isn't that a good number? Only three people in the world have this number: my secretary, Dulcie, Cordelia's houseparents, and YOU. You can leave a message if I don't answer. I check the messages every day, usually once an hour. If you need me, I can get wherever you are in a trice.

I love you,

Poppa

P.S. I don't know how to use a computer. If I buy one, will you teach me? Do you have email? We should get it, you and I, so we can always be in touch.

Grandparents

From: Sophie Diehl   6/11/99 4:56 PM
To: David Greaves <dagreaves@traynor.com>
Date: Fri, 11 June 1999 16:56:22
Subject: Grandparents

Dear David—

I'm sorry I broke down in your office the other day. It was the correspondence between Bruce Meiklejohn and Jane that undid me. This divorce has revived all kinds of terrible memories. You were very kind to listen. And you were right about my parents. They were so much better than their own parents. My grandmothers, who were doting and adoring of my sibs and me, were basically incapable of saying a single nice thing to or about their own children. (These are vocabulary words I learned from hearing my parents talk about their mothers: *harridan*, *virago*, *termagant*, *shrew*.) It was a bond between my parents, a shared source of grief and outrage. They had both been raised under harsh and rigid disciplinary regimes, and they reeled with shock and amazement at the love, generosity, kindness, and praise their martinet mothers heaped on us. We—the children—didn't know what to do. We could see the difference, and it shamed and embarrassed us (and of course also pleased us).

The weekend I turned 10 we were visiting Grandmere at her house on the Cape. In the course of doing a handstand in her living room, I knocked over and broke an antique Lalique candy dish. "Oh, that old thing," she said, taking me in her arms, "Ne t'inquiete pas, cherie. As long as *you* don't break." Next day, at breakfast, with all of us sitting at table, Maman knocked over a juice glass as she was lifting Francoise onto her lap. Grandmere made a big fuss about cleaning it up, pushing Maman away and saying: "You were always so clumsy." We all looked down at our eggs. When I was 15, I asked Grandmere whether she loved my mother. "Of course. A mother always loves her children even if they're not lovable." And she went on her way, lavishing kisses on the grandchildren and abusing her daughter.

Granny Diehl's style was equally cruel, but less direct, passive-aggressive, county Tory style. She was always saying things like "Your father could have done anything—he's got an excellent brain—I'll never understand why he teaches at an American university. Has anyone heard of Columbia? None of my friends have, except the vicar of course. Harvard, now there's a university we all know about, like Oxford or Cambridge. Why doesn't he teach at Harvard?" This is a woman whose husband was the English publisher of Margaret Mead and Moses Hadas. When Papa won the Wolfson Prize in History, Granny asked him if it was as important as the Booker. There was no point explaining. My theory is Papa became a communist (at 12) in the hope that come the revolution, she would be rounded up, jailed, tortured, and hanged. When I finally asked her why she was so tough on Papa, she denied it. "Oh, no, sweetheart, he's a fine man. Look at all you darling children."

And here is the question we've been waiting for: What effect did their mothers' meanness have on my parents? Maman made a determined, and successful, effort to be different from her mother; if she didn't like something we'd done, she'd simply say: "I don't like that." Papa did not escape unscathed. He'd lavish us with praise and affection when we pleased him, and when we didn't, he made us feel terrible: stupid, incompetent, beneath notice. Sometimes mid-screed, he'd suddenly realize what he was doing and apologize, but not often enough. If he comes to New Salem to visit me as he is threatening, I probably won't bring him to the office. I keep him out of my life; I keep the people I care for away from him. It's safer. I know it isn't at all what Keats meant, but I call what I do Negative Capability: since I can't make him be nice to me, I'm not nice to him. I come away from a meeting with my father feeling hateful, toward him, toward myself. It's hard enough to love someone who's mean to you; it's almost impossible to love someone who brings out the worst in you.

It's plain I shouldn't do divorces anymore. Thanks for listening to me; thanks for being interested and kind.

Sophie

TRAYNOR, HAND, WYZANSKI

222 CHURCH STREET
NEW SALEM, NARRAGANSETT 06555
(393) 876-5678

MEMORANDUM
Attorney Work Product

From: Sophie Diehl
To: David Greaves
RE: Another Letter from Jane Durkheim
Date: June 15, 1999
Attachments:

I just got off the phone with Mia Meiklejohn. Dr. Durkheim struck again while she was in Philadelphia visiting her sister. Jane had written him a letter—the computer as muse—and he decided to talk to her about it over dinner last night. Jane was worried about where she and her mom would live after the divorce. Dr. D said they would find a nice house in town or, if she wanted, she could stay in their house and live with him. He said that's what he'd like best. Jane's response to this was to burst into tears. Dr. D asked her what was wrong; she shook her head and said she couldn't live with him. He asked her why. She wouldn't answer but said, through sobs, she had to live with Mommy. "But why," he asked, "can't you live with me? I love you; I'll always take care of you." As he spoke, trying to reassure her, she became inconsolable, almost hysterical. He took her into his arms and held her close, but he couldn't soothe her. She was crying so hard, she couldn't catch her breath. He called his wife in Philadelphia. She immediately got on the road. By the time she got back three hours later, Jane had fallen asleep, exhausted from weeping. Luz, their housekeeper, was sitting on Jane's bed, watching over her. Dr. D had called her and sent a cab to fetch her when he couldn't get Jane to stop crying.

Dr. D and MMM got into a huge fight. He accused her of poisoning their child against him. She said he was full of crap. "Would I leave her with you for two days if I thought you were a monster?" she asked. She told him she didn't know why Jane had written the letter or why she had said she couldn't live with him. They went seven rounds. At the end, 3M said, her husband was no longer angry, only worried and anguished. They decided Jane should see a therapist. Good thinking. Question: Should we (they) ask for an evaluation or recommendation from the therapist in case there's a custody fight or a dispute over visitation, or should they go for treatment only?

TRAYNOR, HAND, WYZANSKI

222 CHURCH STREET
NEW SALEM, NARRAGANSETT 06555
(393) 876-5678

MEMORANDUM
Attorney Work Product

From: David Greaves
To: Sophie Diehl
RE: A Therapist for Jane Durkheim
Date: June 16, 1999
Attachments:

Jane should see someone. I'm glad her parents see that. Something's going on here, and we need to get to the bottom of it. Children often blame themselves for their parents' divorce; they think it's their fault. The downside of their artless egotism. But you know that.

Here are the general ground rules on divorce therapy for children. Ms. Meiklejohn and Dr. Durkheim need to agree on the therapist, and they need to meet with her first, explaining to her together what the problem is. They should let her know that she might be called to testify or provide a custody and/or visitation report. If she isn't comfortable with that, they will want to look for someone else. In the event they can't agree on custody and/or visitation, the judge will very likely order a home visit and psych evaluation. And then everything is up for grabs. You never know whom a judge will pick to do an evaluation. Good judges pick good therapists, bad, bad. There's no test or license to become a court-appointed psych evaluator (called a "forensic"), and some of them are snake-oil salesmen. Judges don't have to follow an evaluator's recommendation, but they often do. Better the parents should make the decision on the therapist and not leave it to chance.

Make it very clear to Ms. Meiklejohn, and to Dr. Durkheim as well (via Kahn if necessary), that Jane is the client, and tell them to split the fees. I've seen too many cases where the parent paying the bills starts putting pressure on the therapist. "Just remember, Doc, I'm the one paying you." They should probably not use anyone with an appointment at Mather Medical School, though in this town, that may be difficult. As I recall, in the honeymoon period of their divorce, the Durkheim-Meiklejohns paid a visit to Rachel Fischer at the Mather Child Study Center, to get some pointers about talking to Jane. As I also recall, Dr. Durkheim ignored her advice. But she would be a good choice—if Dr. Durkheim is willing to face her again. (That's probably not a problem. Didn't his wife say he had a Jesus complex? Despite his rumpled suits and warm smile, he's a pretty typical Big Star Doctor, one of those never-apologize-never-explain types.) I've known Rachel for years. She's not only a first-rate psychiatrist, she's an experienced professional witness. Lawyers for Children, the Tyler County child advocacy group, use her regularly when they need to bring in a heavy hitter. The judges, the good judges, respect her. There are others I'd recommend if she doesn't work out.

We need to let the other side know about Mrs. Meiklejohn's trust. When you've got the details, you should send a letter to Kahn.

Artless Egotism

Dear David—

This is my last confession, but I feel your last memo should not go
unanswered.

Artless egotism, is it? I've never thought I had anything to do with my
parents' divorce, nor did my siblings. They spared us that. We felt like
its casualties. We had cast our lot with them, and they betrayed us.
My parents were the stars of all our lives, and we, the children, were
the supporting players. We had speaking parts but no big scenes. My
mother's chief reaction to us was a combination of affection, interest,
and amusement; she loved us but she was curiously (literally "curiously")
detached in her assessments of us. She looked at us with a naturalist's
eye, like Jacques Cousteau or the Leakeys. She found us endlessly
diverting, only occasionally annoying. Papa, on the other hand, was
more dramatic. It's funny; we always think of the English as cool and the
French, and other Latins, as fiery (though *sangfroid* is a French word).
But it was the opposite in our family. Maman was calm, steady, Papa,
emotional, volcanic, especially in the later years. He could be wildly
funny, passionately engaged, ferociously angry, worryingly depressed.
(Papa gets adjectives *and* adverbs.) His mood didn't seem to have
anything to do with us. He had his own weather system. If we could make
him laugh, we felt like heroes. They both thought children should be
children, and not little adults. They made the decisions and in their own
way protected us, if not from themselves, then from the monsters under
the bed. I loved them both so fiercely; I still do. The divorce broke my
heart.

Sophie

Re: Artless Egotism

From: David Greaves   6/17/99 10:57 AM

To: Sophie Diehl <asdiehl@traynor.com>

Date: Thu, 17 June 1999 10:57:44

Subject: Re: Artless Egotism

Sophie—

You make your father sound like Zeus, with all those Jovian adverbs and adjectives. You were what, 16 when your parents divorced? And now you're almost 30, no? Do you still see him that way? Is he still that way?

Somewhere in my late 20s, I realized that I had the upper hand with my parents. (I think this is pretty standard.) They wanted my company more than I wanted theirs. They missed me; I didn't miss them. I was totally absorbed in my new grown-up life, and in the limited free time I had, I wanted to be with my wife, children, and friends. That's perhaps an oversimplification but not so broad it misstates the case. (Let me say that I loved and respected both of them; they were good parents and very nice to their children.) It might have been easier for you to grow up and away from them at 16, seizing an independent life, knowing that they were together, but I get the sense that their marriage was volatile and tumultuous, and you and your siblings are probably better off with them apart than together. Just think, if you'd missed having Jake in your life, you might be attracted to "volcanic" personalities, men who are admittedly compellingly attractive but not the sort who make good husbands and fathers. Jake has given you a different model.

I may have crossed a line here, but your email called for a serious response. What is it Dickens wrote about becoming the hero of one's own life? You're a terrific person, Sophie. To borrow your "star" analogy, it's time you took center stage.

David

From: Sophie Diehl   6/17/99 11:20 AM
To: David Greaves <dagreaves@traynor.com>
Date: Thu, 17 June 1999 11:20:09
Subject: Re: Re: Artless Egotism

Dear David—

Thank you for your note. In some way, I know, I'm resisting growing up.
My parents still feel bigger than life. You know what my mother can
do; you saw it at Porter's. Well, my father can do it too, and with an
English accent. (I'm making excuses. Whenever I talk like this in front
of Jake, he asks me simply: "What's in it for you, Sophie? What are you
getting out of this?") Then there's the generational shift. I know a lot
of other immature people my age; 30 is the new 21. (Economically, I've
been self-sufficient since college; my parents are helping me pay off
my law school loans, but I am the debtor of record and have paid my
way these last eight years. They were in agreement on this. If my sibs
and I wanted to drink, smoke dope, and have sex, we had to do it in
our own homes, not theirs, and we had to pay for them. They took the
holistic approach to being a grown-up. Of course, every so often—or
oftener—my mother buys me a wonderful dress or takes me to a play
or sends me books; and my father gives me big cash gifts for birthdays
and Christmas. Both take me on vacations, with sibs and stepsibs.)

Jake is a great guy, but he may have come into my life too late to make
a difference in my choice of husband. I've always thought I should get
married in the Church of England so that the banns could be published
weeks in advance and the vicar could ask the congregation at the start
of the ceremony if there was any reason why this couple shouldn't
be joined together in holy matrimony. Then my best friend, Maggie
Pfeiffer, would stand up and say, "Sophie, you can't marry this man;
he's all wrong for you. Don't you see!" Jane saved from Mr. Rochester.

I'm a work in progress.

Sophie

TRAYNOR, HAND, WYZANSKI

222 CHURCH STREET
NEW SALEM, NARRAGANSETT 06555
(393) 876-5678

MEMORANDUM
Attorney Work Product

From:	Sophie Diehl
To:	David Greaves
RE:	Therapy for Jane Durkheim
Date:	June 18, 1999
Attachments:	Jane Durkheim's Letter

Mia Meiklejohn dropped off Jane's letter to her dad this afternoon. A heartbreaker. My mother says that the pathos of children is the beginning of tragedy. I can't figure out what's going on with that little girl. I don't think it's the usual horrors we think of—dads abusing their little girls, moms turning them against their dads. And I don't think she's blaming herself. It's very peculiar.

Ms. Meiklejohn and I had a long talk. She and her husband are moving ahead with Dr. Fischer. They met with her together this morning to set things up, and according to Ms. M, they behaved themselves. The plan is for Jane to see her once a week for several weeks. Dr. Fischer will also meet with the parents separately for a few sessions and then with each of them with Jane. She'll write up an evaluation, which she will provide to the parents. They have all agreed that her evaluation will be submitted to the judge in the event there's a dispute over custody or visitation. (Is it wise to reduce their agreement to writing?) At this point they don't anticipate a custody fight. They both agree (for the moment) that Jane should live with her mother. Dr. Durkheim told his wife he's working with his lawyers on a response to our counteroffer. She says he appears subdued and chastened. She doesn't expect the mood to last, but she's feeling more optimistic about reaching an agreement. I showed her Jane's letter to her grandfather and made her a copy to show her husband and the therapist.

I raised the matter of her mother's trust. She had forgotten entirely about it and had no idea how much money was in it. The statements have always gone to her father. She said she would talk to Proctor about the account and arrange for the statements to come to her. "My father is going to be very unhappy. He hates losing control."

As she was leaving, I asked her who James Meiklejohn was. She looked startled, then sad. I thought she might cry. I quickly explained that I had seen his name in her mother's will. She told me he was her older brother. He died of leukemia when he was 11, and she was 10. "My childhood ended when he died," she said. Her mother never recovered from his death. Cordelia was the "replacement" baby, and Mrs. Meiklejohn was devoted to her, almost to the exclusion of everything and everyone else. When she was dying (breast cancer), she was frantically worried about what would happen to Cordelia. She made Ms. M promise she'd always look after her. Jane was named for Ms. M's brother.

Narragansett Statutes
Title 33 of the Narragansett Code, Sections 801ff.
Dissolution of Marriage, Annulment, and Legal Separation

Sec. 811. Psychiatric or psychological evaluation of the child.
In proceedings on custody or visitation, the court may order a
psychiatric or psychological evaluation of the child if such an
evaluation would, in the court's opinion, assist its determination
of the best interests of the child.

JANE DURKHEIM

Dear Daddy:

I don't understand why you don't love mommy and me anymore.
What did we do to make you mad at us? I know I sometimes don't
listen to you. I know mommy sometimes doesn't listen. Is that
the reason? It won't happen again.

Mommy is sad. I'm sure you can see it. I think she still loves
you. You should give her a second chance. She makes you laugh.
Isn't that a good thing?

I'll be good if you will love us again. I promise. I won't sulk
and I won't whine, ever. Cross my heart and hope to die. I love
you Daddy.

Your loving daughter,
Jane

ps If you and Mommy get divorced, where will Mommy and me
live? Will we live in the house in Marthas Vinyard? It has
no toilet inside. That's all right in the summer but not in
January.

ps2 Where will Tito and Fido live? If they could talk, they'd
say they're very sad about the divorce.

ps3 What happens if Mommy dies? I can live with Poppa. He
says I can live with him always and forever. But I want us all
together, you, Mommy, and me. We are the 3 Musketeers. 1 for
all and all for 1.

Harry

From: Sophie Diehl   6/19/99 4:18 PM
To: Maggie Pfeiffer <mcp15@mather.edu>
Date: Sat, 19 June 1999 16:18:51
Subject: Harry

Dear Maggie,

I had brunch this morning with Harry. We're back to the early days of dating (though not *our* early days, more like Gidget's. He picks me up, he drops me off, he kisses me chastely on the cheek and leaves). It is almost too weird (that sounds as if regular weird were okay). Truth is, I don't much feel like having sex with him, and I don't know if I can take much more of this. We talk easily enough, sometimes even about Monkey, but there's no heat. He doesn't want to see me anymore (it's oddly not personal, and I take it that way, oddly for me), but he wants to be a decent person and he can't see a way out without being a dog. I shall have to break it off, another bye-Jacking. I've been breaking up with boys for over a decade, ever since Jack. What is the matter with men? Just once I'd like a boy to break up with me, to do the manly thing, face-to-face, and not in public. Jack said it was always easier if the girl did the breaking up, and I guess it's a fraternity policy. It worked for him. He was such a master; he even cried when I told him I was breaking up with him for being so drunk and so mean. Ah, Jack, sexy, drunk, mean Jack—the platonic bad boyfriend, a bad boyfriend for the *Guinness Book of Bad Boyfriends,* high school division. Harry isn't so much a bad boyfriend these days as a non-boyfriend. And it's not his fault and it's not mine. Maman's advice was to marry American Jewish, and not fancy American Jewish (no *Mayflower* Sephardim, no Temple Emanu-El Jews, no displaced Czech match kings, no French Jews—which goes without saying), just your standard-issue, wild, funny, ambitious Russian Jew.

I'll be up to see you in the Shaw the weekend of the 10th. Maman's coming with me. She got us a room at the Williamstown Inn, so I won't be camping on your couch. You're not to think about us—it's a working weekend for you—except that we'll be in the audience Saturday night, center row, center seats, cheering for you. And, of course, we'll come backstage after.

Love,
Sophie

My Father

From: Sophie Diehl   6/20/99 10:29 PM
To: Maggie Pfeiffer <mcp15@mather.edu>
Date: Sun, 20 June 1999 22:29:49
Subject: My Father

Maggie—

Terrible news. My father has prostate cancer. He says it's not life-threatening and he's not doing anything about it—just watching and waiting. (Waiting for what? Stage 4?) English medicine. I didn't get to see him. He called. He got the diagnosis about a month ago. He was waiting for the right time to tell me and then realized there is no right time. (I tried to call you, but there was no answer and I couldn't leave this message on a phone machine.)

I am so upset. I was all ready to blast him for horribleness to us all, and he gets a fatal disease. Just like him. How long do you have to wait before you can get angry at someone with cancer? Does it make a difference if it's your father? I'm thinking 3 weeks.

And don't tell me this anger is just a mask for my terror at the thought he is dying. It's typical of him. He's untouchable. I don't think any of us ever got to tell him what a wretch of a father he was. He had that English way of making it impermissible. (Not that Maman took personal criticism well. When we'd start in, she'd say, "I'm not interested in that. Talk to me about something interesting.") The closest was Francoise, who refused to kiss him for years. (I'm not sure she's started up again.) It started when she was about 13, after he began to notice her. In the beginning, he'd ask her why, laughing as though it was a secret they were sharing. "Just don't feel like it," she'd say, or "Not in the mood." As time wore on, he made a joke of it, sort of, leaning down to kiss her, then drawing back, saying, "Ah, I forgot, no kisses." But she would just look at him, unsmiling. God, she had perseverance. So admirable. If grudge holding were a sport, she'd have medaled in it. Reminds me of the joke about Irish Alzheimer's. Maybe she *is* Cummings's daughter.

I don't want him to die, Mags. Tomorrow I have to call Sally to find out the real story. Of course, I called Maman straightaway. It made her sad, I could tell. She doesn't want him to die either, not yet; she wants him to apologize to her first. And she wants him to live for our sakes.

Maybe I'll write him a letter.

I'm being awful. I know you love him too. I told him I'd tell you. He said that was okay. I know he'd like to hear from you. Now I'm going on Yahoo to look up prostate cancer.

Love,
Sophie

The New Salem Courier

NEW SALEM, NARRAGANSETT

POLICE BLOTTER

New Salem Police report that the first day of summer has brought its usual round of hooliganism and mayhem.

VANDALISM TO SAINT CLOUD LAWN, GARDEN. 404 Saint Cloud Street: At 4 p.m., Sunday, June 20, police were called to the residence of Dr. Daniel E. Durkheim, in response to reported acts of vandalism to the house and grounds. Sometime in the early morning on Sunday, an individual in a Hummer or other large 4X4 vehicle with super-sized, all-terrain tires drove across the lawn and gardens of the property, tearing up the sod and driving over the beds. A large copper beech was deeply gouged, and a 40-foot hedgerow was badly damaged. The copper beech may have to come down, a great loss to Saint Cloud Street. Dating back to the beginning of the 19th century, it is one of 20 copper beeches that stand over 50 feet tall and line the street. The house on the property was also subject to vandalism; graffiti was sprayed across the front walls and windows, with the words: "$AVE US FROM DOCTOR$." Damages are likely to exceed $20,000. Several other properties on nearby streets were vandalized (see items 3 and 7 below), but the damage to those properties was far less extensive, involving mostly broken windows and demolished mailboxes, the likely victims of mailbox baseball. The police have concluded that different parties were involved in the other reported incidents. ∎

June 22, 1999

Dear Papa,

I've been wretched—and afraid—since you called. I called Maman straightaway. She said Jake knows all the plumbers at P&S and Sloan-Kettering and would be happy to talk doctors with you. We're all very conventional. We think you should do something. You said you were going to watch it, but nobody trusts you; you're a horrible patient. And you have no use for doctors. Will you get it checked regularly? "Regularly" for prostate cancer (according to Yahoo) is every year. You're more likely to follow the Russian plan, five years. That won't do, Papa. You're not allowed to die. I am not ready for it, even if you are. When I think that you had three children by the time you were my age, I am embarrassed on my own behalf; I am so monumentally immature. Maggie says I'm not attentive enough to have goldfish. Which I got from you and which is why I worry so much now that you won't try to live longer. You're just 55; the earlier you get prostate cancer, the deadlier the disease (Yahoo again). (I know, I know, generally speaking; you may be the statistical anomaly that skews all the data.) (It's so annoying having to qualify every sentence I write you to make sure I've not carelessly, sourcelessly generalized.) Luc said you weren't going to die; he said I was drama-queening it up. That's one way of dealing with it, taking the completely optimistic position. He's got his exams in two weeks; he can't be derailed by grief.

This letter is going nowhere. How do you write to your father when he's just been diagnosed with cancer? You must know. The English have pro-tocols for every occasion. Speaking of which, have you told the Ancient Ps? Isn't there a rule against predeceasing your parents in peacetime? I can't imagine the disease that would take down Gran.

Please, please do something, for me.

Sophie

TRAYNOR, HAND, WYZANSKI

222 CHURCH STREET

NEW SALEM, NARRAGANSETT 06555

(393) 876-5678

MEMORANDUM
Attorney Work Product

From:	Sophie Diehl
To:	David Greaves
RE:	Criminal Mischief at the Meiklejohn/Durkheims'
Date:	June 22, 1999
Attachments:	Newspaper Clipping

I am assuming you read yesterday's police blotter in the *Courier*. Vandalism at the Durkheim manse. It's sad, actually (and funny, of course, too—and please don't give me a lecture; divorce lawyer humor is much more tasteful than criminal lawyer humor). They have a great copper beech that may need to be taken down. The hedge and lawn were torn up, and someone spray-painted anti-doctor graffiti on the house. I just got off the phone with Ms. Meiklejohn. Dr. Durkheim accused her of being behind it. She laughed at him and told him not to make himself ridiculous; "You know damn well that Consigliere Kahn arranged it," she said, "to make you out the victim. It's a barefaced Tawana Brawley maneuver." I don't think she believes that for one minute, but of course that's not her point.

I told her that as the owner of the house, she couldn't be charged with vandalism. I also told her that if she talks to the police, she should tell the truth or not say anything at all. She laughed when I said that. "You think I may have done it, don't you." I said, no, I didn't, but that I thought she was capable of doing it. "Right you are," she said. We agreed to talk again if the police wanted to interview her.

Vandalism

From: Mia Meiklejohn   6/22/99   3:17 PM
To: Sophie Diehl <asdiehl@traynor.com>
Date: Tue, 22 June 1999 15:17:22
Subject: Vandalism

Dear Sophie—

I hope I have the right email address for you. I finally got myself a
Durkheim-less email address. It took ages. Some authoritarian techie
said I couldn't do it without a court-ordered name change. I tried,
successively, reason, charm, pathos, insults, and threats, but he didn't
budge. (He had the soul of an immigration officer.) I should have
known he wouldn't respond to threats. No one threatens more than
a disgruntled faculty member. His boss finally made the change. And
so, eccomi. I had to change my name officially. It made me feel like an
imposter, an American ship sailing under Liberian registry.

I didn't want to bother you on the phone again, but I thought you'd want
to know about my follow-up conversation with my asshole husband, the
eminent oncologist. He accused me for a second time of orchestrating
the vandalism. I couldn't believe it. I told him that if I'd wanted to wreck
the house, I wouldn't have yielded that pleasure to a third party but
would have rented an earth mover and driven the mother through the
plate glass window in the library and then taken it for a spin through
all the downstairs rooms. Anyway, the asshole called the police and
said they should interview me. What was he thinking? Everyone on
the force not only knows my father, they live on land he owns. (Do you
want to talk patrimony? Here's the embarrassing bottom line: my father
owns 10% + of the real estate in Tyler County—not including churches
and church property or Mather U holdings, but including the land
beneath Police Headquarters and two miles of shoreline. My father's
approach to land is English; he retains ownership of the land and lets his
leaseholders put up the buildings, subject to his approval. His taste is
retro conventional. He loves Mather's Gothic and the colonial churches
on the green.) The chief got on the phone and assured him that they

would do a complete and thorough investigation; he then asked to speak to me. He was very nice. He said he wanted to speak with both Daniel and me, separately given our domestic rift, to find out if we knew of anyone who might have had a grudge against us or otherwise might have reason to vandalize our property. I said I'd be happy to speak to him or another officer, either at home or at headquarters, but I'd like my lawyer to attend, "given our domestic rift." He couldn't have been more agreeable and said I should speak with my lawyer and then call back to schedule a time. He said he'd also schedule a meeting with Daniel and his lawyer, if he wished. I told him Kahn was Daniel's lawyer. (I don't know what you know about the mob scene in this part of the world, but Kahn represents Vinnie "the Cod" Massaccio, the capo of eastern Narragansett, in his "business interests," some of which, I believe, are legal. My father's done business with Vinnie—which doesn't prove anything.) "Really," he responded. "And who's yours?" When I told him, he laughed. "Sophie Diehl is a pistol," he said. "I'll look forward to meeting with the two of you."

Is there a time you can make it? (See? I was right to hire a criminal lawyer to defend me against Daniel.) I'm flexible these next few days. The only thing I have to do is study for the LSAT. I'm taking a prep course and relearning algebra.

Best,
Mia

June 22, 1999

Dear Daniel—

I'm planning to meet with Chief Pogodinski later in the week. I understand he'll be talking to you too. He wants to know if we have any enemies, people who might bear us grudges—other than each other, of course. You see, we don't count. We can't commit vandalism to our own property. If either of us had done the deed, it would not be considered vandalism but extreme landscaping and renovation. Vandalism is a crime against the property <u>of others</u>.

What I resent most about your accusation against me is the low opinion you have of my character and capabilities. As if I would do so cowardly, paltry, and ham-fisted a deed. If I was feeling destructive, I'd simply have turned on all the faucets, closed the drains, and drowned the fucking house.

There's no damage like water damage. It's so easy, so economical, so reliably devastating. And I'd have left a note on the fridge. "I did it. xoxo, M."

But I didn't do it, asshole. Someone else doesn't like you. Better lock your bedroom door and windows.

M.

P.S. Instead of hurling absurd and irresponsible accusations at your wife, you might talk to the neighbors. Someone might have seen something. A truck raging across our front lawn isn't, after all, a normal St. Cloud Street event; it might have attracted notice.

TRAYNOR, HAND, WYZANSKI

222 CHURCH STREET
NEW SALEM, NARRAGANSETT 06555
(393) 876-5678

MEMORANDUM
Attorney Work Product

From: Sophie Diehl
To: David Greaves
RE: Destruction at the Durkheim Residence
Date: June 23, 1999
Attachments:

I got a call this afternoon from Jim Pogodinski. He has a lead on the vandalism at the Durkheims'. He sent one of his officers around to interview their neighbors this morning; one of them noticed a man on Saturday, first sitting in a pickup across the street and then nosing around the property. He took down the license number. The police are running the plate. They'll keep us posted.

THE DIVORCE PAPERS (Page 325)

TRAYNOR, HAND, WYZANSKI

222 CHURCH STREET
NEW SALEM, NARRAGANSETT 06555
(393) 876-5678

MEMORANDUM
Attorney Work Product

From: Sophie Diehl
To: David Greaves
RE: Destruction at the Durkheim Residence: Culprit ID'ed
Date: June 24, 1999
Attachments:

The police have gotten to the bottom of the vandalism at the Durkheims'. It's a sad, sad story, and (needless to say?) our client had nothing to do with it. The culprit is Louis Falk, a fireman in the NSFD and a resident of Emsworth, NA. His daughter, Candace, was a patient of Daniel Durkheim's. She died four weeks ago, on Memorial Day, at age 6. She had been Durkheim's patient since she was 2 and first diagnosed with a terrible brain cancer, an atypical teratoid rhabdoid tumor (AT/RT). Her prognosis had always been grim, but Durkheim had managed to keep her alive much longer than anyone expected, almost four years. For the last two years, she was undergoing a highly experimental protocol, which Falk's insurance wouldn't cover. To pay for the drugs and chemo, he mortgaged his house and maxed out seven credit cards. When she died, he had accumulated debts of over $300,000. He had said nothing about this to Durkheim, only that he could cover the costs and that everything possible should be done for his daughter. Two weeks ago the bank foreclosed on his house. When the police came to question him, he met them on the porch and said, "I did it." He hasn't said anything since. His wife is beside herself. They have two other children and nowhere to live. Durkheim feels dreadful, not having known anything about the Falks' finances. He's hired a lawyer (not from K&B, but a proper bankruptcy attorney, someone from the Booker firm) to help the Falks sort out their finances and prevent foreclosure. He's asked the police not to file charges against Falk, on the grounds of Falk's severe mental distress.

Pogodinski said he couldn't let Falk go scot-free but would work it out so that he'd only be charged with misdemeanor vandalism. (He told Durkheim that because he—Durkheim—had made such a huge fuss, thinking it was his wife, "the whole damn police force knew about it and expected something to be done.") Pogo's also offered to work with Durkheim to see that Falk doesn't lose his job. (He's already been in touch with the fire chief and the head of the firefighters' union; they're working on a medical leave.) They're both trying to keep the story out of the *Courier*. Durkheim may have to ask his wife to talk to the editor about it. (Peter Maple is her cousin.) Pogo said he suggested to Durkheim that he apologize to her. I haven't said anything to 3M about this; I'm waiting to see if D2 does it.

Falk used his own pickup to tear up the Durkheims' grounds; the Hummer was pure fantasy by the reporter writing for the Police Blotter.

THE WHITE HART
Shipton-under-Wychwood

28 June 1999

My darling Sophie,

I got your loving, deranged letter and felt it called for
a letter in return, loving but not deranged, more fact-
based, less volatile. I have no desire, no interest at all, in
dying before my biblical allotment, and with luck and,
no doubt, overzealous medical intervention, I shall live as
long as the Ancient Ps, who now drink gin at breakfast
as well as lunch and dinner and swear it is the elixir of
life. It's easier all around, I must say. No chance of either of them remembering anything said.

I am not simply watching and waiting. The proper term
is "active surveillance"; I will have annual checkups and
PSA tests and, if necessary, biopsies. I consulted a very
smart diagnosing urologist, my man Maturin, who then
sent me to a barbershop quartet of specialists, all eminent but with the personality disorders we would expect
to find in what Maman calls dick doctors. They were
in order of descending pathology: Sweeney Todd (bass/
classic butchery), Dr. Who (baritone/robotic laparoscopy),
Johnny Appleseed (countertenor/radiation pellets), and

Jack Frost (tenor/cryosurgery). Except for the urologist, they all hawked their own procedures, warning me as violently against their colleagues' quackery as against W&W. One of them actually said to me when I refused to sign up right then and there, "Well, it's your funeral." Next up: Dr. Hugo Z. Hackenbush. In fact, by every indicator—PSA, stage, Gleason score—I am an excellent candidate for waiting. Now, please calm down.

If you'll have me, I'd like to come up to New Salem in the fall for a visit. I'd like to meet your gang and watch you at work. Hearsay, Your Honor. What do you say? I'm working well. Nothing like a bit o' cancer to set right one's priorities (at least briefly; no doubt, I'll backslide—and downslide—as soon as I get comfortable with encroaching mortality).

It will be all right, Sophie girl. All my love,

Papa

P.S. I found this old stationery in my desk. Do you remember the White Hart? We stayed there in 1978, I think it was, when Christopher and Bridget Hill retired from Balliol. You and Luc spoke French the whole time and pretended not to understand English. You insisted that Maman translate, so of course she mistranslated wildly, enraging you and cracking you up. It was one of the too-good times, do you remember?

TRAYNOR, HAND, WYZANSKI

222 CHURCH STREET
NEW SALEM, NARRAGANSETT 06555
(393) 876-5678

MEMORANDUM
Attorney Work Product

From:	Sophie Diehl
To:	David Greaves
RE:	Meiklejohn/Durkheim Settlement Conference
Date:	July 1, 1999
Attachments:	

A meeting has been scheduled with Ms. Meiklejohn, Dr. Durkheim, Kahn, and me to talk settlement. There's been a slight rapprochement over the Falk crisis. Last Friday, unsolicited, 3M did an intervention with her cousin at the *Courier* and managed to keep the paper from publishing anything about Falk. Dr. Durkheim did not apologize to his wife for his accusation or thank her for making the call. Instead, he called Maple to express admiration for his "editorial judgment and leadership." Maple, who reported all to 3M, would have none of it. He told him he had no interest in writing an article which would expose Mather Med to "general obloquy" (his words) and there was no way of writing the article without discussing the cost of the child's treatment and the Children's Cancer Center's complete indifference to the family's financial plight. "We all know that medical expenses are the second-most common grounds for bankruptcy in this state," he said. "I didn't expect that kind of ruthless insensitivity on the part of this community's hospital. Down the line, we may look at the larger issue and then write a story about the very sick children whose health insurance doesn't cover their diseases, but we will not write about Falk's vandalism, now or later. That's not the crime here." Durkheim sputtered out a thank-you and hung up. Later that evening, he suggested the four-way meeting to his wife as a way to get things moving.

Setting up a time was almost impossible. Kahn doesn't keep his own calendar, but he doesn't allow his secretary to book anything without first consulting him. After two days of back-and-forth, I threw up my hands and told 3M that she'd have to arrange things. I gave her the times I had available. I said we would meet in their offices. (Joe taught me always to offer to go to them. It makes us look obliging, even deferential. But that is not the case. Having it in his office allows us to break it off and walk out. Which I suspect will be the outcome. The Durkheims are not yet ready to deal; they still want to fight.)

More to the point, 3M called her husband last night on his inside line at home and told him if he wanted the meeting, he'd have to set it up, since Kahn was being a first-class asshole (her word). This morning at 9:06, Kahn's secretary called to say we could meet July 7, 4 p.m., in their offices. 3M says her husband gets up at 5:45 and makes his business calls at 7, leaving terse, acerbic messages when the sluggards aren't there to answer. Do you want to attend? I assume not, but then you might not trust me to behave myself in the same room with Kahn. Do I have to shake his hand? My plan is to reiterate the offer I sent them. It's their turn for the counter-counter. Do you agree?

Drama

From: Mia Meiklejohn   7/7/99 6:02 PM
To: Sophie Diehl <asdiehl@traynor.com>
Date: Wed, 7 July 1999 18:02:47
Subject: Drama

Dear Sophie—

I want to apologize to you for making a scene in Kahn's office. (I don't
want to apologize to anyone else; I needed to get a few things off my
chest, and I find I love embarrassing Daniel. The end of the white-
glove wife.) I also want to thank you for standing up for me. Kahn is
a swine, there's no other word for him. Do you know Becky Danton,
formerly Becky Peele? Felix Someone in your firm represented her, and
Kahn represented her husband, Jason Peele, ex-chair of Narragansett
Industries, in their divorce. How's that for fearful symmetry. Maybe
you read the file? I recommend it. It is unbelievable, except, of course,
it isn't, because there it all is, in black and white, in our very own Tyler
County Court House. In Becky's case, Kahn ordered DNA tests for their
three children, ages 11, 6, and 2, to make sure they were her husband's.
She told me all about Kahn over dinner last Friday. Our daughters are
in the same class at Peabody. We'd talked a few times in the parking
lot, she was very kind when she heard that D and I had separated, but
she called me up last week and said we should get together; she might
be able to provide useful information. She'd heard from a friend at the
hospital that Daniel had hired Kahn. She's filed charges against him,
against Kahn, with the state bar, and they're doing an investigation.
(There's an NA law about the assumption of paternity within marriage
that he apparently violated by ordering DNA tests for the children when
Jason Peele hadn't claimed adultery.) I don't know if you caught that
reference in my tirade, but Kahn plainly did. I don't know that Daniel
knows he is up on ethics charges. (My father did a hostile takeover of NI
two years ago and ousted Peele. Peele had a golden parachute, which
my father refused to pay. They're still in litigation; if my father has his
way, which I expect will happen, Peele will die in chancery. Becky said to
kiss my father on both cheeks for her.)

My analyst is always telling me to be "awake at the moment." Well, I was awake this afternoon. I said everything I wanted to say, everything I needed to say, even everything I could have hoped to say. Even now, in repose, I can't think of anything I'd want to have done or said differently, though if I had had a fork at hand, I might have plunged it into Daniel's thigh or Kahn's throat. But that would have been a mistake; that would have been going too far.

Now I suppose we must get down to business, get "serious," as you said to them.

My cousin wants to do the story on the sick children; he just doesn't have the staff now to do it. I like knowing that; it's like money in the bank.

Best,
Mia

TRAYNOR, HAND, WYZANSKI

222 CHURCH STREET
NEW SALEM, NARRAGANSETT 06555
(393) 876-5678

MEMORANDUM
Attorney Work Product

From: Sophie Diehl
To: David Greaves
RE: Meiklejohn/Durkheim Conference, July 7, 1999
Date: July 8, 1999
Attachments: Email from Mia Meiklejohn, July 7, 1999, "Drama"

So, we met yesterday afternoon, Durkheim, Kahn, 3M, and I, to talk about a settlement. Only, we didn't do it. Kahn's gambit, something about sending an adjuster to assess the Martha's Vineyard property, set her off, and I mean "off." She looked at him straight on and said, "After the assessment, are you planning on ordering any DNA tests for Jane? I hope you'll let me know if you are, because I'm prepared to go to the state bar if you do." She then turned to Daniel. "You know, don't you, that Kahn is very thorough and he doesn't think a husband should pay child support for a child who may not be his. Has he said he's planning to test Jane?" I thought Durkheim would pop a blood vessel. She then went on, turning to Kahn, who was gulping for air. "I believe that all your other clients work in the carting business, isn't that so?" Then she turned to her husband: "I'm assuming you gave him his retainer in cash, tens and twenties, right?" Kahn looked daggers at her, his face blotchy with anger. Before she could regroup, Durkheim stepped in. "Let's get down to business. Let's talk about alimony. Where do you get off thinking you should get $72,000 a year?" 3M turned her gimlet eye to her husband. "Getting you off, asshole, for 17 years." She then gave a brief disquisition on their sex life, which ended with the line "I always thought you could f*** a corpse, that you'd prefer it, actually." I turned to look at Durkheim as she was speaking. His face was at war, equal parts anger and embarrassment. For a nice-looking, rumpled man, his mouth had taken an ugly turn. He looked at me, then Kahn. I did a facial shrug (mouth down, eyebrows up). Kahn, his manhood unimpeached, leapt in, waxing indignant and pomp-ass. "Miss Diehl, I've never heard anything like that in my life. Really, you need to keep your client in check." I threw him a sitcom double take, the way Elaine might do it. "Give me a break, Mr. Kahn," I said. "This is nursery school stuff, and you know it. Tell your client to stop acting aggrieved and behaving as though he doesn't have an obligation to support his wife and child at a level they are entitled to be supported at, and we'll come up with a workable agreement." I then turned to 3M and said, "I don't think they're serious. Let's go." And out we walked.

I haven't given you the full report; I can't bring myself to do it. I hope you understand. There were words I never heard anyone but Richard Pryor say. She was firing away, rat-a-tat, rat-a-tat, so fast and furiously I couldn't keep up with her. I had to take a few deep breaths to keep my countenance, as Papa used to say. When we got out onto the street, I asked, "Spontaneous or rehearsed?" She smiled slyly. "Just great good luck," she said. The DNA testing was a reference to the Peele divorce. Flush with victory, 3M sent me the attached email last night. It provides color.

Narragansett Statutes
Title 33 of the Narragansett Code, Sections 801ff.
Dissolution of Marriage, Annulment, and Legal Separation

Sec. 806. Paternity establishment.
There is a presumption that a child born during a marriage is the issue of the marriage, and no person may challenge this presumption save the parties to the marriage.

TRAYNOR, HAND, WYZANSKI

222 CHURCH STREET
NEW SALEM, NARRAGANSETT 06555
(393) 876-5678

MEMORANDUM
Attorney Work Product

From:	Proctor Hand
To:	Sophie Diehl
RE:	The Maria Maple Mather Meiklejohn Trusts
Date:	July 9, 1999
Attachments:	

Mrs. Meiklejohn's will, probated in 1982, set up two trusts, one for Mia Meiklejohn and one for Cordelia Meiklejohn. Each trust had an original principal of $400,000. Mia's vests on her 50th birthday. I am her sole trustee. Cordelia's money will remain in trust, with Bruce Meiklejohn and me acting as trustees, until Cordelia's death, at which time the remaining funds, if any, will be settled on Mia or, if she has died, her children. Cordelia's trusts may be invaded for purposes of "necessity," Mia's for "emergency" purposes only. To date, there have been no invasions. The money has been invested in blue chip stocks averaging approximately 8% a year. Each currently stands at $1.47 million. Under the rule of 72, I would expect Ms. Meiklejohn's to double by the time it vests.

I can, if you think it useful, provide a trustee's letter to Dr. Durkheim, outlining the terms of his wife's trust and its current balance. I submit a letter annually to Probate Court; I can send him a copy. I can also include in the covering letter, if you like, a paragraph on the Vineyard property. I understand the other side keeps raising the matter of the Vineyard property. It might be helpful if they knew the terms limiting its use.

Let me know if you need anything else. It is my position that the terms of Bruce Meiklejohn's will are irrelevant to any settlement talks.

TRAYNOR, HAND, WYZANSKI

222 CHURCH STREET
NEW SALEM, NARRAGANSETT 06555
(393) 876-5678

MEMORANDUM
Attorney Work Product

From:	Sophie Diehl
To:	David Greaves
RE:	The Maria Maple Mather Meiklejohn Trust
Date:	July 9, 1999
Attachments:	Meiklejohn Trust Memo

I've spoken to Proctor and examined Mrs. Meiklejohn's trust. Proctor also wrote a brief memo, which I attach here. Some interesting additional facts: Mrs. Meiklejohn (4M) died in 1979; it took three years to settle her estate. There must have been a lot of other money and property. 3M's "issue" is the residual beneficiaries of both trusts. If there are no children surviving, the money goes to Planned Parenthood of New Salem. (Proctor says 4M was on their board and helped underwrite the first abortion-rights case in Narragansett, *McMillan v. Bishop*, which pre-*Roe* upheld the right to abortion in Narragansett in the first 16 weeks.)

In the last 17 years, both trusts have grown considerably, the beneficiaries of early investment and a rising market. (Go Suze Orman; oh, for the courage to be rich.) By the time 3M's vests, it may have reached $3 million. The annual statements have been sent to Bruce Meiklejohn, which probably explains 3M's ignorance. In the event of Proctor's death or retirement from the firm, William Frost is Proctor's successor trustee. Frost's successor trustee, should it come to that, is the then-managing partner of Traynor, Hand. If you live a very long time . . .

In light of this trust and the Vineyard house tenancy, we can be more flexible on the 401(k), etc., but not on the matter of alimony. 3M doesn't need a retirement fund, but she does need money for the next seven years. No doubt Dr. D and Kahn will argue in favor of invading the trust now. I'll do a quick survey of the law and find out what the standard for an "emergency" is. Proctor has offered to write a letter to Kahn. Kahn's going to go ape with this. I can hear him now, accusing us of withholding important information that affects every part of the agreement.

Trust

From: Sophie Diehl   7/9/99 4:02 PM
To: Mia Meiklejohn <mia.meiklejohn@mather.edu>
Date: Fri, 9 July 1999 16:02:19
Subject: Trust

Mia—

I'm following up on our conversation regarding your mother's trust.
I will be sending you overland a formal letter, giving the terms of the
trust and also the restrictions on the Aquinnah property. You can
show the letter to Daniel and see what he has to say. I think he was
truly shocked by the DNA testing. (Caveat: he may not remember his
horror, however, given the meeting's second act.) If we can't count
on Daniel's better nature in the negotiations, we can count on his
political instincts. He has a reputation to maintain in this community,
and roughing up Bruce Meiklejohn's daughter and granddaughter will
do him no good if it gets about, especially after he bankrupted the
fireman. And on that score, word about that has got around. Peter
Maple? Nothing Jason Peele did ever surprised anyone. That was
the source of his great success. He'd do whatever was necessary to
succeed, though I'm guessing he drew the line at violent felonies. I
can't imagine the person who would have married him, and yet you
say she's lovely. But I digress. Let me know how the conversation goes.
You're a brave woman.

Yours,
Sophie

TRAYNOR, HAND, WYZANSKI

222 CHURCH STREET
NEW SALEM, NARRAGANSETT 06555
(393) 876-5678
ATTORNEYS AT LAW

July 9, 1999

Mia Meiklejohn
404 St. Cloud Street
New Salem, NA 06556

Dear Mia:

I have two items for you to think about as we work on coming up with a settlement. The first regards the trust set up under your mother's will. The second involves the property on Martha's Vineyard.

As to the first item, I have spoken with Proctor Hand, who serves as Trustee of the Maria Maple Mather Meiklejohn Trust. He has provided the following report as of June 30, 1999. The trust in your name was set up in 1982 with $400,000. It will vest on your 50th birthday. It currently has approximately $1,470,000. At 8% interest (which it is averaging), it is likely to double by 2007. It can be invaded prior to vesting for "emergencies" but not for ordinary support (i.e., food, clothing, shelter, or education).

As to the second item, prior to her death, your mother donated 8 acres of the 13 she owned in Gay Head (now Aquinnah) to the Martha's Vineyard Land Bank. These acres cannot be developed; they can be used for agricultural cultivation or pasture. The other 5 acres cannot be subdivided; there is a 3-acre lot minimum for houses in the area. While the 5 acres, with their views and protected farmlands, are valuable, they are not as valuable as your husband and his lawyer believe. The house, as I understand, is in serious disrepair and has no particular architectural value, being an ordinary, run-down 1840 Greek Revival farmhouse with less than 3,000 square feet, a damp 4-foot cellar, blocked chimneys, a kitchen last updated in the Depression, and no inside commodes. (Proctor said he spent the most uncomfortable weekend of his life at that house. "As much as I loved Maria," he said, "she could never get me up again. The outhouse was a completely uncharming feature.")

As the benefits of both the trust and the house do not accrue to you in the near future, they should not figure in the settlement negotiations for child care and alimony.

You may wish to discuss this with your husband. I will also send a letter to Mr. Kahn.

Yours,

Anne Sophie Diehl

Anne Sophie Diehl

Stupendous

From: Sophie Diehl   7/12/99 8:41 AM
To: Maggie Pfeiffer <mcp15@mather.edu>
Date: Mon, 12 July 1999 8:41:07
Subject: Stupendous

Dear Maggie—

What a wonderful weekend. You were fabulous. I didn't know the
play; I haven't seen much Shaw (I saw the movie *My Fair Lady* on TV;
not as good as *Seven Brides for Seven Brothers*, but then what is?), and
I'm always confusing him with Wilde. But what a fabulous lark. I don't
think there's anything you can't do.

You won't believe this: Maman and I ran into Papa yesterday at lunch
on our way out of town. We were eating at the diner on the Pittsfield
Road, and in he walked. He'd been to the play last night. Did he go
backstage to see you? Did you hear from him? No, of course not.
Stealth Diehl. He came right over to the table. "You saw her, didn't
you," he said, without so much as a hug or even a hello. He was so
pleased with you, so proud. He kept saying, "Isn't she wonderful? Isn't
she brilliant?" We agreed. He was very charming to Maman. "How are
you, Elisabeth?" he asked. "Still beautiful, I see." She wasn't having
any of it. "And you, how are you, John, still . . . still . . . ?" He laughed.
"Yes, I'm afraid so." And what I want to know, Maggie, is this: Can't
he see me, or does he simply find me uninteresting? He paid me no
mind. Maman could have been sitting in the booth alone. I hadn't seen
him for months. It was enraging. "How are you, Papa?" I asked, too
loudly. "I'm not dying," he said, "if that's the drift of your question."
He then smiled. "Well, of course, I'm going to die. It's in my DNA, but
not this year or next or even the one after that. I'm thinking 82. What
do you say, Sophie girl?" He then sat down at the booth and talked
about his cancer and his decision to watch and wait. Maman thought
it a reasonable plan but added, nodding toward me, "I'm not sure our
daughter agrees. We haven't got that American need to do something.

I've never known an American man with your prognosis who hasn't immediately signed up for surgery. Americans have no patience." She stopped then, to make an editorial adjustment. "But with you," she continued, looking at Papa, "with you, it's not patience but some sort of balkiness . . ." She trailed off momentarily. "It's the Hamlet part of your personality. Not to be confused with the Lear part." He laughed. "Never waste an opportunity, Elisabeth, that's what I say." He then turned (finally!) to me and said he was going to come visit me in September. He asked if I would let him sit in on a motion or a trial I was doing. (He actually used the word *motion*—who thought he knew it? Could it be now and again he paid attention?) And then he patted my hand, got up, and went to sit at the counter. I know my father is a far better father than yours, but you must admit he has some pretty severe deficits. Maman, as if reading my mind, gave me a sharp look and said, "Sophie, he's not going to change. He can't. It all works too well for him. If you don't let go, you'll make yourself miserable."

But wasn't it just like him to go to see you and never say anything? I think I'm a little jealous. Maybe a lot. He's so unabashedly proud of you. If you'd been sitting in the diner, he'd have noticed you.

All the men in my life are crapping out on me. Harry and I are kaput, well and truly. I didn't want to say anything to you this weekend, but you must have seen it coming. We had dinner on Friday night, and I said I thought we'd reached the end of the line. He tried to look surprised and sad, but undiluted relief shone through. I'm not the right one for him. Monkey may not be the right person for him, but he wants someone more like her than like me, someone who takes him by the throat, someone like Melanie Griffith in *Something Wild*, or Zero Mostel in *The Producers*. It's all right. He left his underpants on the floor.

You were great. You are great. I'll try to get up for *Travesties*.

Love,
Sophie

The UnTrust

From: Mia Meiklejohn   7/13/99 11:05 AM
To: Sophie Diehl <asdiehl@traynor.com>
Date: Tue, 13 July 1999 11:05:22
Subject: The UnTrust

Dear Sophie—

I've been trying to figure out why my mother would not have the trust
vest until I was 50 and only allow invasion in the case of an emergency.
I've come up with two possible explanations, both revelatory of an
untrusting nature: (1) She knew how controlling my father was and
how tightfisted he could be (a Scottish stereotype, which is proved in
his case). She didn't want him to abdicate responsibility for his older
daughter because she had a large trust. She wanted him to step up and
pay for college, the debutante ball (alas, yes), a dowry (ha!), a wedding
or two, etc. The trust money was to be there in case I really, really, really
needed it. (2) She didn't want me to be loved for my money. She had
been an heiress of sorts, or at least the beneficiary of a rich man's will
and famous name, and always thought the swarms of swains lounging
on the doorstep were after, if not the money, then the prestige. She
married my father, she used to say, because he thought it a hoot that
there actually was someone alive in 1955 who was a descendant of
Cotton Mather. He didn't expect her to be rich. One of his gnomic (and
no doubt keen) observations was to the effect that "old families who
stay in one place run out of money by the third generation. They've no
enterprise, no ambition, and within a century, the money is drunk or
gambled away."

I suppose we have to moderate our demands now. That makes me a
little sad, not that I want the money, only that Danny will be so pleased.
He really doesn't want to give me anything. I suppose we can't now up
the alimony and child support requests, can we . . .

I do not have a good character.

Yours,
Mia

P.S. Regarding the Aquinnah house, you wouldn't know from my mother's will, being a Cape Codder, but its site is spectacular, with near views of Squibnocket Pond and more distant views of the Atlantic. Every room, except the water closets, has a water view. Further, the Land Bank land basically surrounds our land, keeping our views in every direction forever pristine. We haven't had it appraised since my mother's estate was settled, but I would guess it's worth a lot. The land, not the house. (The house is a mess, hardly more comfortable than the one in that law case you sent me about that old couple.) One of the conditions of my mother's will was that my father and I had to agree on any changes, and we can't. (I want inside toilets and a stove with at least three burners; he wants the Breakers.) And did I mention that the Onassis estate is close by and we run into Caroline Kennedy and her kids all the time? And the house has a key to Black Point Beach, which I think we can sell separately but I'm not sure. (Someday I'll explain the MV private beach system, which I disapprove of and benefit from. The rich liberal's perpetual dilemma.)

M.

Huge Fight

From: Mia Meiklejohn   7/15/99 3:44 AM
To: Sophie Diehl <asdiehl@traynor.com>
Date: Thu, 15 July 1999 3:44:33
Subject: Huge Fight

Dear Sophie—

I can't believe how tough I've become. I'm channeling Richard Holbrooke. Bring on Slobodan Milosevic. I keep saying to myself when I get scared, which I do every night at bedtime: What is the worst he can do to me? And the answer is (in my saner moments): nothing. He can yell at me, of course, and he can make me cry (I cry at Kodak commercials, so that's not a test), but he can't really do anything else. I'm lucky. I don't have money, but I have access to money. I won't end up sleeping under Narragansett Bridge. Women should never give up their jobs when they get married (or their names); they've got to have money. If you have money, you can get through it. That's the bottom line. Tell all your friends, all your clients. Put it in the newspapers, print it in circulars and stick them under doors. DON'T GIVE UP YOUR JOB.

I left your letter for Daniel on Monday, with, I'll admit, a poisonous Post-it. (I told him to stop scratching his hairy ass and get down to business.) He didn't say anything to me. I didn't even see him for two days. Finally today, or rather yesterday, Wednesday, I bearded him as he was coming home in the evening. "When are we going to get this settled?" I asked him. "Let's get it done." He said he couldn't stand to be in the same room with me and would only deal through his lawyer. Have your lawyer send Kahn a letter. I said okay, but if that was the case, we'd probably still be married when my trust vested. "What do you mean?" he said. I told him, "You know he's a shit; you wanted a shit. Well, guess what, he's not a particularly effective shit. And I'm perfectly willing to go to court." He walked out of the room, closed the door, and got on the phone with his dermatologist. Did I mention she's had work? I don't think she can blink her eyes. Her skin is blemish-free, and her mind is idea-free.

I'm reaching the end of my rope. I've really come to detest Daniel for what he's done to Jane, to me, to all of us. Lately I've taken to planning his funeral. A moving and beautiful event at Mather Chapel, with live music, and not only the great organ, but singers, an alto and cantor. I'm thinking the "Erbarme dich" aria (which he loves) from the St. Matthew Passion and the Kaddish.

I'm going to bed now. It's very late. I'm weepingly tired. I'd like a boys' chorus to sing "Jerusalem" at my funeral.

What changes do you recommend making to our settlement offer?

Best,
Mia

July 16, 1999

Maria Mather Meiklejohn
404 St. Cloud Street
New Salem, NA 06556

Dear Mia:

I've reworked the savings and retirement terms of our offer under the separation agreement in recognition of your mother's trust, giving you all the stock money and giving Daniel the rest. They will have trouble refuting it, as you are only receiving the funds (with interest) which your father gave you and Daniel as gifts over the last 16 years. I'm of two minds whether (a) I should simply give Kahn notice of the trust and its terms and see how he responds, or (b) I should put forward the offer. I'm not, as you know, a huge fan of conventional negotiations (taking two extreme positions and lurching toward rationality), and the approach I've used so far has been to say: "This is what we're offering, and we mean it. If you don't like it, we'll let the judge settle it." There will likely be resistance to the new offer, but I recommend brazening it out. I know you want the matter settled, but time is a tool and the longer we put off the settlement, the more likely we are to get the terms we want. Also, we need the psychiatrist's report on Jane. Hang in there.

Yours,

Anne Sophie Diehl

Anne Sophie Diehl

You GO Girl

From: Mia Meiklejohn   7/20/99 8:11 PM
To: Sophie Diehl <asdiehl@traynor.com>
Date: Tue, 20 July 1999 20:11:49
Subject: You GO Girl

Dear Sophie—

You're right, they're not going to like it, but I like it and I'm the client.

Jane has been to see Dr. Fischer five times now. She's doing better. She's crying less and talking back some. Last night at dinner, she said, "Daddy thinks he's the center of the universe, and you think I am. You're both wrong." Ah, the dueling Durkheim solar systems. She's right. I've got two appointments with Dr. Fischer set up, and next week Jane and I go to see her together. I'm assuming Daniel will see her also, and if he doesn't, res ipsa loquitur, as you lawyers say. (I've not only been studying for the LSATs, I've been browsing in various law books. Why is a tort called a tort?)

Did I ever tell you that one of the reasons I was attracted initially to Daniel was his last name? I somehow thought he was related to the *Suicide* sociologist Durkheim, but as you know, the family name had originally been Durkheimer. I'm glad I didn't know that when we met. It would have spoiled the romance in my head. I was working at Monk's House, which somehow made me related to Virginia Woolf. It turns out suicide has absolutely no charm for me; murder's more up my alley. I knew you were the right lawyer for me.

Best,
Mia

Maman Explains

From: Sophie Diehl   7/20/99 10:48 PM
To: Maggie Pfeiffer <mcp15@mather.edu>
Date: Tue, 20 July 1999 22:48:29
Subject: Maman Explains

Dear Maggie,

I just got off the phone with Maman. I called her to talk about our
run-in with Papa at the diner. I couldn't get it out of my mind; I
don't understand why he does those things. Maman was most
uncharacteristically forthcoming. She never talks about Papa to me
or the sibs, though in his presence she can be mean as a ferret, which
says a lot in its own way. She said she guessed she knew how I felt
because, especially in the late years of their marriage, he didn't pay
her any mind either. He liked the way she looked; he liked the money
she made (though *he* was mean as a ferret about the books she
wrote); he liked the family life, the four attractive French-speaking
children, the dinner parties, the summers in Wellfleet. But he didn't
listen to her. What most infuriated her, she said, were the times he'd
tell her something X had said when it was something she had said to
him only a few days earlier. The final blow was the time he said, "I
was talking to Michael Wood about *The Big Chill* and he said that the
most interesting thing about the Kevin Kline character was not all the
money he made in his post-hippie years or impregnating the friend
but the insider trading." She was making dinner and almost hit him
with a skillet. Two days earlier, as they were walking out of the movie,
she had said, almost verbatim, what Wood had said. "That's the last
time I cooked him dinner when I didn't have to feed you children as
well." She went on, "Our marriage ended because I couldn't make him
see me or hear me or do anything I wanted or needed. I could only
be as selfish and mean as he was to get his attention. And that was
ruinous." Maman said she thought it was a generational thing, the
inability of men born before 1955 to listen to their wives. "They could
listen to other women if they had to (a boss, a professor, a judge, even
a professional colleague) but not to their wives. I used to think it was

the timbre of the voice, the higher pitch of women's voices, but I had a low voice, and it didn't dent your father's consciousness. I keep hoping men of your generation are better. I think your brothers are better, but I'm not their girlfriends. But look," she said, "he's your father, not your husband. You can't divorce him, and you can't abandon him, not on grounds of inattention. You've got to find a way to make him see you and hear you. I couldn't do it, but I wasn't his daughter. He loves you, in his own troubled and tortured way."

I wondered, as Maman was speaking, if she was crying. Probably not, she never does, but, boy, she sounded so sad. It's true: you never get over that first big love when it goes wrong. It breaks your heart or hardens it. I think it did both to Maman.

Love,
Sophie

TRAYNOR, HAND, WYZANSKI

222 CHURCH STREET
NEW SALEM, NARRAGANSETT 06555
(393) 876-5678
ATTORNEYS AT LAW

July 21, 1999

Ray Kahn
Kahn & Boyle
46 Broadway
New Salem, Narragansett 06555

Dear Mr. Kahn:

It has come to our attention recently that our client, Maria Meiklejohn, is the beneficiary of a testamentary trust, created under her late mother's will. The trust vests in 2007, on Ms. Meiklejohn's 50th birthday. The trust held $400,000 at the time of probate in 1982. It will no doubt yield a considerable sum at the time of vesting, but it provides no mechanism for invasion prior to vesting in the absence of an emergency. Proctor Hand is the trustee.

We expect that the existence of the trust will affect the allocation of investments and retirement funds under the Durkheim/Meiklejohn separation agreement, but we do not expect it to affect child support, maintenance, or other property divisions. I have attached a revised settlement offer affecting savings and retirement investments.

Clapper's Narragansett Legal Dictionary defines an *emergency* as "an unforeseen occurrence or event, an accident; an unexpected, undesirable event, often resulting in harm or damage or the threat of harm or damage." *Webster's Third New International Dictionary* defines *emergency* as "an unforeseen combination of circumstances or the resulting state that calls for immediate action; a pressing need [or] exigency . . ."

The Narragansett courts have uniformly applied a restrictive reading of an "emergency." In *Baxter v. Baxter*, 283 Nar. 443 (1995), the Narragansett Supreme Court, quoting both *Clapper's* and *Webster's*, characterized an emergency as a "limiting term" that "allows the invasion of a trust only under extraordinary circumstances." It specifically rejected the argument that an emergency could encompass "a beneficiary's expenses for health, education, support, or maintenance," contrasting it with the "far looser standard of necessity," which would cover "the essentials reasonably needed to maintain a beneficiary's station in life." It is clear that the trust cannot be invaded on behalf of Ms. Meiklejohn for her maintenance or support.

Yours,

Anne Sophie Diehl

Anne Sophie Diehl

Maria Mather Meiklejohn and Daniel E. Durkheim
Settlement Breakdown: Summary

Revised Offer

Daniel Durkheim's TIAA-CREF Retirement Accounts: $600,000
Counteroffer: Daniel Durkheim to receive $300,000; Maria Meiklejohn
to receive $300,000
Revised Counteroffer: Daniel Durkheim to keep $600,000

Daniel Durkheim's 401(k) Plan: $300,000
Counteroffer: Daniel Durkheim to receive $150,000; Maria Meiklejohn
to receive $150,000
Revised Counteroffer: Daniel Durkheim to keep $300,000

Stock Market Investments: $700,000
Counteroffer: Daniel Durkheim to receive $350,000; Maria Meiklejohn
to receive $350,000
Revised Counteroffer: Maria Meiklejohn to receive $700,000

Treasury Bills: $90,000
Counteroffer: Maria Meiklejohn to receive $45,000; Daniel Durkheim to
receive $45,000
Revised Counteroffer: Daniel Durkheim to receive $90,000

Joint Savings Account: Originally $80,000; Now $16,000
Counteroffer: Daniel Durkheim to receive $16,000
Revised Counteroffer: Maria Meiklejohn to receive $16,000

Revised Counteroffer: Comparison with Original Counteroffer

Account	DD Revised	MMM Revised	DD Original	MMM Original
TIAA-CREF	$600,000	0	300,000	300,000
401(k) Plan	300,000	0	150,000	150,000
Stocks	0	700,000	350,000	350,000
T Bills	90,000	0	45,000	45,000
Savings	0	16,000	16,000	0
TOTAL	**$990,000**	**$716,000***	**$861,000**	**$845,000**

The total amount in retirement funds and savings is $1,706,000. Under the revised offer, Dr. Durkheim receives $274,000 more than Ms. Meiklejohn, and $131,000 more than he would have received under the original offer. Previously, he would have received only $16,000 more than Ms. Meiklejohn.

July 21, 1999

---

* Bruce Meiklejohn has given the couple $20,000 a year as gifts ($10,000 each) for the last 16 years. At 8% compounded annually, those funds (totaling $320,000) would have grown to approximately $650,000, an amount roughly equivalent to the stock fund. The $16,000 in savings acknowledges Ms. Meiklejohn's contribution to the down payment of the St. Cloud Street house. The operating principle here is that each party keeps roughly the monies he/she contributed to his/her separate and joint accounts.

Re: Maman Explains

From: Maggie Pfeiffer   7/21/99 11:23 PM

To: Sophie Diehl <asdiehl@traynor.com>

Date: Wed, 21 July 1999 23:23:14

Subject: Re: Maman Explains

Dearest Sophie—

I'm sorry I've been so slow getting back to you. It's exhausting doing these plays, exhilarating but exhausting.

I never heard from your dad. He never told me he saw me in the play; he never dropped a line about my performance. I wouldn't have known he had seen it, or seen me, if you hadn't run into him at the diner. He may not be completely human; or is it just his Englishness? I find it moving, his inability to tell me I was good, but as your mother said, I'm not his daughter. I can see how painful it was for you.

Take heart. There are young men out there who do listen, who are supportive, who see you and hear you. Keep your eyes open; you'll find someone who's worth talking to. But I should probably check him out first.

Love,
Maggie

July 27, 1999

Ms. Anne Sophie Diehl
Traynor, Hand, Wyzanski
222 Church Street
New Salem, Narragansett 06555

Dear Ms. Diehl:

I am in receipt of your letter of July 21. I was surprised on two grounds: first, that we hadn't previously been informed of the trust; and second, that you have made adjustments only in your demands for Ms. Meiklejohn's share of the investment funds and are continuing to make exorbitant child support and alimony claims. Dr. Durkheim entered into negotiations entirely in good faith and made an offer he thought was generous. In light of the trust, he thinks that his original offer is exceedingly generous and sees no basis to make any changes to the child and spousal support offers. As for the various investment accounts, he finds untenable your assumption that Ms. Meiklejohn should recover all the gift money provided by her father to the couple. Half the money was gifted to Dr. Durkheim, and he has every reason to believe it was sincerely gifted. It would be cynical to think differently. A fairer distribution of investment funds would recognize his share of the gift money as well as Ms. Meiklejohn's expectations under the trust, which in seven years is likely to reach $4 million. We propose the following:

Account	Dr. Durkheim	Ms. Meiklejohn
TIAA-CREF	600,000	0
401(k) Plan	300,000	0
Stocks	350,000	350,000
T Bills	45,000	45,000
Savings	40,000	40,000
TOTAL	1,335,000	435,000

I look forward to hearing from you. I have every confidence that we shall be able to conclude this agreement promptly. The terms Dr. Durkheim offers are fair and balanced.

Sincerely yours,

Ray Kahn

Ray Kahn

MARIA MATHER MEIKLEJOHN
404 ST. CLOUD STREET
NEW SALEM, NA 06556

August 3, 1999

Daniel—

Your lawyer is giving you bad advice. I could well be dead before either the MV house or my mother's trust vests. As you know, my mother had a virulent form of breast cancer, dead in under 2 years. Her mother also died in her 40s of breast cancer. I'm careful; I get checked; treatment's better, but that could very well happen to me. So stop being such a shit. And stop feeling sorry for yourself (as you tell Jane all the time because she doesn't have leukemia). I don't have any money now. I want to go to law school. I supported you for years. I came to New Salem with you. I'm so tired of you. Piranha as victim. I'm not beggaring you, and I'd be using a lot of the money to make sure Jane's life doesn't change more than it has to. How much more unhappy does she have to get before you stop dicking around? Get yourself a lawyer who can make a deal. We'll never get anywhere with that piece of lowlife scum you hired. What made you hire him? He's under investigation by the state bar, for God's sakes. Do you know who else hired him? Jason Peele.

If you don't stop dicking around, here's how it's going to play out. (1) I am not only NOT going to move out of the house, I'm going to ask for the house. It's the house Jane grew up in; she should stay there. And if you come back asking for custody, (2) I'm going to depose Dr. Stephanie to find out how she'll help raise Jane, and then I'll depose all your research and departmental staff on the number of hours you work each week. Then we'll have all of Jane's teachers deposed on how she's doing in school. And her doctor, her soccer coach, her piano teacher, and Luz. (3) Are you still smoking the odd joint for medicinal purposes? (4) I'm going to ask the judge to appraise your medical degrees (as the most valuable asset of the marriage) and ask for future earnings separate from alimony. (If my mother's house is on the block, so are your M.D. and Ph.D.) (5) I'm going to ask for the Audi instead of the Saab. I drive more than you; I should have the better car. (6) I'm going to ask for Fido. He's devoted to Jane and Jane is devoted to him. And there's Tito to consider; he would be very lonely without Fido. (7) I'm going to sic Traynor, Hand's PI and forensic accountant on you, and they're going to find out every dime not to say every fart you ever made. (Of course, we'll want to know every grant application you have pending, so you might provide that information. Otherwise we'll go to the NIH and NSF.) (8) I'm going to make sure all this takes at least five years, and if you continue to act like an asshole, (9) I'm going to bring an eviction proceeding against you; and (10) I'm going to turn my cousin loose; he intervened to stop publication of the Falk story for my sake and Jane's. Not the hospital's; not yours. He thinks you're an asshole, too, an arrogant asshole.

If you do stop dicking around, you'll also need to: (1) Sign up for the Parent Education Class. You can't get a court date unless you've taken the class or we've agreed to forgo. And why would I agree to that? (2) Make appointments to see Dr. Fischer. We each agreed to meet with her.

As the old joke goes, you are such a schmuck, you are the world's second-biggest schmuck.

Mia

P.S. Jane and I are off to Martha's Vineyard on Saturday for three weeks. Let's finish this.

JANE DURKHEIM

August 10

Dear Poppa,

I'm going to ask you a very very very big favor. You and Mom
have to stop fewding about the house and get some inside toilets. I hate the outhouses even with the new Sweedish compost-
ing toilets. If I have to go to the bathroom at night, I wake
Mom up. I don't want to go out there in the dark by myself.
It's too too scary. And I hate the chamber pots. You have to
admit they are soooo gross. I agree with Mom. I don't want a
fancy house, just one with white inside flush toilets. If you
would do that for me, I'd be very greatful to you. Mom says we
could put one toilet in the linen closet upstairs and one in
the dish cabinet next to the kitchen. We could also put one
in the upstairs bathroom.

Mom said your house on Grove Street had inside toilets when
you were growing up. Inside toilets aren't a luxery anymore.

This is not a put-up job, Poppa. Mom didn't tell me to write
to you. She's so used to the outhouses, she doesn't mind using
them even though she thinks it's nuts in 1999 not to have inside toilets. But I think they are truly disgusting. Mom and
I thought we should write a book about Martha's Vineyard and
call it "Big House on the Little Island," by Jane Ingalls Durkheim. We'd call you GrandPaw. I'm practicing calling Mom Ma.

I know I am asking a very big favor of you, but I would love
a real toilet.

I'm going to sailing camp every morning. I'm getting pretty
good with the sunfish. Yesterday, we took Fido to Black Point
and he ran up and down the shore and fetched balls from the
ocean. We had to clean up his poop. Mom did that. :) Mom and
I play tennis in the afternoon. She's not as good as Dad but
she's still better than me. I'm not a game person; I'm a runner. I've been practicing on the high school track here. I'm
faster than most of the men who run and boy O boy do they hate
to be passed by me. They try to catch up but I leave them in
the dust. :):) Mom says I'm nothing but lungs and legs.
I wish you would come up too.

I love you,
Jane

P.S. Toilets!

TRAYNOR, HAND, WYZANSKI

222 CHURCH STREET
NEW SALEM, NARRAGANSETT 06555
(393) 876-5678

MEMORANDUM
Attorney Work Product

From: David Greaves
To: Sophie Diehl
RE: Ray Kahn
Date: August 10, 1999
Attachments: Narragansett State Bar Disciplinary Actions, August 9, 1999

I don't know if you saw this. I'm guessing it's the Peele case. You might want to send it to Ms. Meiklejohn, who in turn might want to show it to her husband, as a spur to action.

NARRAGANSETT STATE BAR
Disciplinary Actions
August 9, 1999

REPRIMANDS

ELWOOD CARSTON JR of New Salem was reprimanded by the Grievance Committee for assisting a disbarred lawyer in the unauthorized practice of law.

GEORGE M. HUBBELL of New Salem was reprimanded by the Grievance Committee for failing to supervise his paralegal. Hubbell allowed his paralegal to substitute her professional judgment for those of associate lawyers in his office and allowed her to modify those lawyers' work product.

RAY KAHN of New Salem was reprimanded by the Grievance Committee for challenging the presumption of paternity in a divorce case.

RITA J. MARTINELLI of Compton was reprimanded by the Grievance Committee for assisting a disbarred lawyer in the unauthorized practice of law.

SUSPENSIONS

PRUDENCE D. CAULDER of New Salem commingled funds, did not maintain proper trust account records, and did not reconcile her trust account. She was suspended from the practice of law for four years by the Grievance Committee.

GARRETT MCCORMICK of Springfield made sexual comments to and inappropriately touched two clients. He was suspended from the practice of law for three years by the Grievance Committee.

DISBARMENTS

PATRICK GRANTHAM of Compton was disbarred by the Narragansett District Court from the practice of law for embezzling client funds and funds withheld for the benefit of the Internal Revenue Service from employees' paychecks.

The Last of Harry

From: Sophie Diehl   8/12/99 5:06 PM
To: Maggie Pfeiffer <mcp15@mather.edu>
Date: Thu, 12 Aug 1999 17:06:15
Subject: The Last of Harry

Dear Maggie,

You won't believe what took place this afternoon in the august corridors of Traynor, Hand. Tessa Gregg, Harry's semi-ex, showed up at reception at about 3:15, saying she urgently needed to see me. The receptionist asked for a name and said she'd check if I were in. Tessa announced herself as "Harry's Wife. She'll know." I told the receptionist I'd come down to reception.

She's a real looker, more than that, drop-dead gorgeous, long dancer's legs, a tiny waist, and a neck out of Modigliani, with a small, elegant head perched on top. Dark hair, thick, wavy, and short, eyelashes like a four-year-old's, light blue-gray wolf's eyes, red mouth, dressed in a silky purple dress that clung to her. Catching sight of me, she started yelling, "You tramp, you, you slut. What are you doing with my husband? Can't you get one of your own? God, and you dress like a dog, no makeup. What is it, blow jobs?" And so it went for about two minutes. The offices started to empty out, and soon the reception area was ringed with lawyers watching her yell at me, transfixed. She was so beautiful and so crazy. I was stunned, too embarrassed to know what to do. And no one seemed to want to stop the show. Rescue finally came. Joe, who knows crazy when he sees it and doesn't care for it, no matter the packaging, took charge. He stepped between us, facing her. "I've just asked the receptionist to call the police. If you are not gone in two minutes, they'll be here, and I will swear a warrant against you for disturbing the peace, trespass, stalking, and assault." He didn't touch her; he just stood there. She was knocked off her game. She's crazy but not stupid. "Well, fuck you, horn nose," she said to him, and walked out. "Get back to work," Joe said to everyone, and they did. He walked me back to my office. "Don't explain, to me or anyone. We criminal lawyers have crazy clients with crazy wives." He left, returning shortly with a small glass of scotch. "Drink this. You'll feel better." I did and I did.

As I thought about the scene, I got furious with Harry. Why had he told her about me? I phoned him up and told him what happened. "Keep her away from me," I said. "And if you can't, I will swear out a warrant for stalking. What were you thinking, talking to her about me? Showing off?" He mumbled an apology cum explanation. "I mentioned your name once or twice; she couldn't understand that I didn't want her. In her mind, there had to be another woman." How's that for manly behavior? "Don't make me think you're a complete jerk," I said, and hung up. I have to say I do think he's a jerk. And I am glad it's over. He didn't protect me. Good men protect their women. And vice versa, of course.

I think I'm all right. A bit shaky though, too ragged to work. No one has ever been jealous of me before. I've always been the best friend, not the competition. Of course, she's crazy. I'm going home now—or maybe I'll have another scotch with Joe. Wasn't he great? That's what I need, someone like Joe but 25 years younger.

Love,
Sophie

V. SETTLEMENT

FIONA McGREGOR

Formerly of Traynor, Hand, Wyzanski

Has Become a Member

of

Farrow Allerton

280 Church Street
New Salem, Narragansett 06555

SEPTEMBER 1, 1999

TRAYNOR, HAND, WYZANSKI

222 CHURCH STREET
NEW SALEM, NARRAGANSETT 06555
(393) 876-5678

MEMORANDUM
Attorney Work Product

From: David Greaves, Managing Partner
To: Members and Associates
RE: Fiona McGregor
Date: September 1, 1999
Attachments: Farrow Allerton Announcement

On August 31, 1999, Fiona McGregor, a partner at Traynor, Hand, Wyzanski since 1992, resigned from the firm. She will be joining Farrow Allerton. She has been a valued colleague, a first-rate litigator, and an astute counselor. We wish her all the best.

Fiona McGregor

From: Sophie Diehl   9/1/99 8:34 AM
To: David Greaves <dagreaves@traynor.com>
Date: Wed, 1 Sep 1999 8:34:07
Subject: Fiona McGregor

Dear David,

I was blown away by the news of Fiona's departure. Farrow Allerton?
I didn't think there were any members who hadn't come over in the
Mayflower or sunk on the *Titanic*. Good for them. Good for her. Good
for us? We're down to two women partners, out of ten. Mather won't
like that; they look for firms with at least 30%.

I can't help feeling somehow responsible for this (the way a child feels
responsible for a parent's divorce, a kind of grandiosity?). And even if
it isn't my fault, I think people somehow will think it is.

I am very sorry it came to this.

Sophie

Office Politics

From: Sophie Diehl   9/1/99 9:02 AM
To: Maggie Pfeiffer <mcp15@mather.edu>
Date: Wed, 1 Sep 1999 9:02:36
Subject: Office Politics

Dear Maggie,

My life is a Russian soap opera. The latest: Fiona has decamped for
Farrow Allerton, the old-line white-shoe law firm that only represents
Plimouth Club life members. They used to do a lot of work for the
University, but with the recent Jewish ascendency, they've been
pushed aside. I'm not sure they even have a Jewish partner. I think
Fiona will be only their second woman partner, out of 20+. But then,
we're down to only two too with Fiona's departure.

I keep thinking that everyone is looking at me funny, as though it was
my doing that she left. With all the fuss over the Meiklejohn divorce,
most of the lawyers (and the staff too) probably breathed a sigh of
relief; still I get the feeling some of them wouldn't mind if I left too.
The old gang hasn't abandoned me, but the rest are suspicious and
cranky, as if I were going to filch their clients too. David supports
me and the Meiklejohns protect me, but their protection doesn't
make me any more popular. Joe has been great. And his advice about
Tessa was spot-on. Anytime someone mentioned the incident to
me, I just shook my head and mumbled: "I should have been a trusts
and estates lawyer." I wish I had been able to respond to her; I was
so aghast I couldn't move. Joe said next time I'll do better. "You're
too polite, sweetheart," he always says to me. "We've got to knock
the Brearley out of you." I bet Mia Meiklejohn wouldn't have stood
there dumbfounded, though of course, she might not have resolved
the situation with Joe's finesse. They probably would have ended
up duking it out. Both she and Tessa rely on the good manners or
inhibitions of others. And then they're both so very beautiful. Beautiful
women are bolder. Comme Maman. Comme toi. I'm not complaining

about my looks—I've had my admirers, I know that—but would anyone love me for myself alone, and not my yellow hair? At least I've been spared the problem of beautiful women. Did you know there was a problem? They—you—attract too many men; there's no built-in screening device, separating the pearls from the swine. I've always felt I had to talk my way into someone's heart.

I'm so glad it's a holiday weekend. I can't wait to get to Wellfleet. I'm cutting out at 2 today, if not earlier. When do you think you'll get there? The key's under the back steps if you get there first. Luc is coming too. What larks.

xoxoxo

Sophie

Re: Fiona McGregor

From: David Greaves   9/1/99 11:46 AM

To: Sophie Diehl <asdiehl@traynor.com>

Date: Wed, 1 Sep 1999 11:46:22

Subject: Re: Fiona McGregor

Sophie,

You're not completely wrong. The people you speak of know rationally it's not your fault (and it's not, see next paragraph), but we're not a particularly rational species. We are, however, a reliably venal one, and everyone at the firm recognizes the service you're doing. That may be the real problem: your relationship with the Meiklejohns. There are men, I'm told, who don't much like other people's success, especially when they know they could do it a thousand times better than a girl, given the chance.

The problem here, as you point out, is that we've lost one of our three women partners. That's not good. And she left I believe because of the letter of reprimand, even though it was withdrawn and many sincere apologies made. She accused us, and rightly so, of operating under a double standard. I know you know about this. Everyone hears everything. It's my understanding the night porter gave his opinion on it.

Chin up, Sophie. You'll get through this and soon and be back with the boys in the back room.

David

From: Maggie Pfeiffer   9/1/99 3:40 PM
To: Sophie Diehl <asdiehl@traynor.com>
Date: Wed, 1 Sep 1999 15:40:21
Subject: Re: Office Politics

Dear Sophie—

I hate to be yelled at. I've never been able to yell back, except, of
course, onstage, where I've played several harridans, my favorite
being Martha in *Who's Afraid of Virginia Woolf?* A liberating part.
I can't lay it at Brearley's feet, this lack of combativeness. I can be
very ambitious, outspoken, aggressive even, when it comes to my
career. I just hate yelling. It's no doubt a vestige of early home life
when my father wasn't so defeated but still blamed my mother
for everything. I used to burn for my mother to fight back, but she
couldn't. And now I can't. BUT, I didn't marry my father—or my
mother. Matt never yells at me. He knows I can't take it. When he's
truly exasperated with me (maybe once a month), he says, "You've
got to shape up, girl." And I don't yell at him, either. I just nag or sulk.

Don't worry about Fiona. In two months, no one will remember she even
worked at the firm. And between David and Joe, you're in like Flynn.

I'm so looking forward to Wellfleet this weekend. I haven't seen Luc in ages.
And, of course, your mother and Jake spoil us so. Matt's making a chocolate
cake to bring along. I'm bringing a script for *The Rivals*. The rep is putting
it on this spring. I'm going to try out for Lydia Languish. Isn't that the best
name for a heroine? I'm counting on you all to help me with the part.

Love,
Maggie

P.S. What's this nonsense about talking your way into someone's heart?
Talking may clinch the deal, but it doesn't open the negotiations. Harry
took one look at you and swooned. You look just like your mother, only
blond. Sock-pulling time.

xoxo

Apologies

From: Sophie Diehl   9/3/99 9:26 AM
To: David Greaves <dagreaves@traynor.com>
Date: Fri, 3 Sep 1999 09:26:57
Subject: Apologies

Dear David,

I'm keeping my chin up as we speak, but it's a mystery why you put up with me so patiently. Why do you?

Sophie

Re: Apologies

From: David Greaves   9/3/99 11:32 AM
To: Sophie Diehl <asdiehl@traynor.com>
Date: Fri, 3 Sep 1999 11:32:19
Subject: Re: Apologies

> Dear Sophie,
>
> I think of it as deep mentoring. You're a very talented lawyer. You're worth the investment.
>
> David

TRAYNOR, HAND, WYZANSKI

222 CHURCH STREET
NEW SALEM, NARRAGANSETT 06555
(393) 876-5678

MEMORANDUM
Attorney Work Product

From: Sophie Diehl
To: David Greaves
RE: Maria Meiklejohn: Dr. Rachel Fischer's Report on
             Jane Durkheim
Date: September 7, 1999
Attachments: Letter and Report

Mia Meiklejohn dropped off Dr. Fischer's report on Jane Durkheim. It's long and interesting. I'm not going to do anything about it right now but wait to see if Durkheim or Kahn react. Mia said she and her husband each received their copy yesterday, and he took his up to his room to read. Afterward, she thought he looked unwell, almost remorseful. "I say 'almost,'" she explained, "because his emotions are never unmixed. He was, yes, remorseful, but also angry and injured." She thanked me for sending her the Kahn notice of reprimand by the Bar Association. She left it for her husband but hasn't heard anything. "He couldn't have missed it," she said. "I taped it to the inside windshield of his car and drew arrows all around Kahn's name." This from someone who wrote her master's essay on Henry James.

September 3, 1999

Maria M. Meiklejohn
Daniel Durkheim, M.D.
404 St. Cloud Street
New Salem, NA 06556

Dear Ms. Meiklejohn and Dr. Durkheim:

I am enclosing with this letter a copy of my forensic psychiatric evaluation of your daughter, Jane Mather Durkheim. It was done at your request to facilitate the negotiation of a marital separation agreement under Narragansett law; it was also done with the understanding that in the event of a dispute over custody and/or visitation, it would be submitted to the court for its consideration along with a copy of this letter.[1]

The report was based on interviews with Jane, interviews with each of you and Jane together, interviews with each of you alone, and an interview with Jane's grandfather, Bruce Meiklejohn. I also consulted with Jane's classroom teacher in 1998–99 and the headmistress of her school.

In my interviews with you, I stressed that the conversations we had would not be confidential and that I would include in my evaluation everything I thought pertinent to the resolution of unresolved custody issues. I told

---

[1] It needs to be said that the court would be acting within its authority if it chose to disregard the report. It could also order *sua sponte* a new and independent evaluation by another evaluator, one not agreed upon by the parents.

Jane the same thing but with the proviso that if there was something very important she felt I needed to know but that she wished me not to say to her parents or include in the report, I would respect her wishes unless I believed either (1) that her parents and/or the judge needed the information to make the best decision; or (2) that failing to disclose the information might be harmful to her well-being, now or in the future. In either event, I told her, I would let her know in advance and explain my reasoning. I told her she was my client, the one whose welfare and well-being I was charged to protect and advance. I also told her I would write up what I found and what I thought as simply, as clearly, and as accurately as I could; I would not sugarcoat or vilify. It is my sense Jane understood the purpose of our meetings and the report I would write.

Yours,

Rachel Fischer, MD
Professor of Practice

CHILD EVALUATION FORM

Child:	Jane Mather Durkheim
Evaluator:	Rachel Fischer, M.D., Professor of Practice
Date:	September 3, 1999

INTRODUCTION

At the request of Maria Meiklejohn and Daniel Durkheim, a married couple seeking dissolution of their marriage, I was asked to evaluate their daughter and only child, Jane Mather Durkheim, a preadolescent, and to recommend custody arrangements in the event Ms. Meiklejohn should die before Jane reaches her majority. Jane's parents have agreed that they will share custody and Jane will live with her mother. The circumstances behind the decision to seek a psychiatric evaluation were Jane's highly emotional response to any suggestion that she might live with her father and not her mother and her acute anxiety over the possibility of her mother dying in the next few years and her living arrangements in the event of her mother's death.

In the preparation of this report, I conducted eight (8) 45-minute interviews with Jane; two (2) with Ms. Meiklejohn; and one (1) with Dr. Durkheim. In addition, I met twice with Ms. Meiklejohn and Jane together, and once with Dr. Durkheim and Jane. Dr. Durkheim was unable to schedule a second individual interview or a second joint interview with Jane. I also consulted by phone Eliza Wolfe, headmistress of Peabody, Jane's school, and Victoria Crane, Jane's 5th-grade teacher. Last, I met with Bruce Meiklejohn, Jane's maternal grandfather. With permission, all the interviews and phone conversations were recorded.

INTERVIEWS WITH JANE (June 25, 30, July 8, 14, 20, 27, Aug 2, 9)

Jane is 11 years old. She was born on April 23, 1988, Shakespeare's 424th (1564) birthday, she told me, and the 372nd (1616) anniversary of his death. "He died on his birthday. My father says that's more common than you'd think." She is entering 6th grade at the Peabody School. She is an attractive child, on the cusp of puberty, well built and athletic, with the lanky frame of a runner. She is both confident and self-questioning, common indicators of intelligence and self-consciousness. Thoughtful and articulate, she works to express herself accurately. She struggles to be fair to her parents and fair to herself, not an easy task for anyone, let alone an 11-year-old. She loves both her parents very much and believes she is well loved by them, but since talk of divorce began, she has found them to be self-regarding and neglectful. "They want me to be more grown-up than I am. And they both want me on their side. I can't do that. Who do they think I am, King Solomon?" To a significant extent, her parents' self-involvement and anger has relieved her of feeling responsible for the separation, though she retains the sense that if she "bucks up," her father might change his mind.

Both parents are demanding in their expectations of her. Her father sometimes compares her with the very sick children he works with, telling her not to complain or feel sorry for herself. Her mother, the product of a strict upbringing, finds herself passing on some of the rigorous lessons of her own childhood. "In *Eloise*," Jane told me, "Eloise is always being told 'being bored is not allowed.' That's House Rule No. 2 according to my mother. House Rule No. 1: no whining. Rule No. 3: no duffers." She explained. "That's from *Swallows and Amazons*. There are four children, the youngest is 5, the oldest is my age. They have a sailboat, the *Swallow*, and they want to sail it to a nearby island. Their dad's away in the army doing army things. Their mother sends him a telegram asking him if she should let them go. He sends a reply telegram: 'Better drowned than duffers. If not duffers, won't drown.' I love that line. My mother does too. We use it about people we know, are they or aren't they?" Jane looked at me to see if I understood. She went on. "There's a lot of quoting that goes on in our house. Books are very important to all of us, especially me and my mother."

I asked her if there were any more house rules. She thought for a bit. "It's not exactly a rule, more of a reminder. Both my parents tell me to 'know my luck.' I do know I'm lucky, but it's hard to know it all the time." She looked as if she might cry but didn't. Comparing her parents with other children's parents, Jane thinks they are "more difficult and more interesting." Comparing them with each other, she said: "My mother is who she is. My father is what he does." Although in our sessions with her parents she called them Mommy and Daddy, or Mom and Dad, when speaking of them, in their absence, she always used Mother and Father. It is an oddly and noticeably mature locution; in my experience, a preadolescent would use Mommy and Daddy in both situations.

At our first meeting, all Jane wanted to talk about was an act of recent vandalism at her house by a fireman whose child, a patient of her father's, had died of cancer. She said the fireman must have been "heartbroken" and "crazy with grief," locutions I suspect she picked up from her mother. "If I died," she said, "my mother would never recover. My father would be okay after a while. He sees children die all the time." I asked her if she thought he might feel differently about his own child. "He'd feel very sad," she said, "but he'd get over it. He's used to dying. And anyway, his work is more important on a daily basis to him than I am." I asked her why she thought that. "He spends all his time with the sick children, and he talks about them all the time. I understand," she continued. "I'm lucky; I'm healthy. He doesn't need to fix me. They're sick. They need him more. He felt terrible about the fireman's daughter. I remember him talking about her, even before the fireman went crazy. She had a very rare brain cancer. He kept her alive much longer than any other person with that disease." The last sentence she said with evident pride.

At almost every session I had with Jane alone, she spoke about death or dying. It took a number of forms. She was very worried that her mother would die. Her maternal grandmother and great-grandmother had both died of breast cancer in their 40s. She knew about the breast cancer gene and wondered if her mother or she had it. "My mother says she's not going to die until she's old, but she can't see the future. I don't like to talk about it though. It makes me scared. I don't think I could live without my mother." When I said she'd still have her father, she shook her head. "That's different." She spoke often about the sick children her father took care of. "He really loves them, I can tell," she said. "They're always on his mind. It's a very hard job, taking care of sick children. I'm so lucky I don't have cancer." With some regularity, she mentioned her mother's older brother, James, who died of leukemia when he was 11, "the age I am now," she said sadly. She told me a number of times that she had been named for James. "I'll be glad when I've turned 12," she said, as if by passing her 12th birthday, she would have survived the deadly parallels that seem to spook her, dying at 11 and dying on her birthday.

The only person she spoke of often whom she didn't link to death was, interestingly, the oldest, her grandfather, Bruce Meiklejohn. Although she didn't say this explicitly, it became plain that he makes her feel safe, and for some reason, she thinks he'll live as long as she needs him to live, "90 at least," she said. "Poppa is indestructible." She also said quietly and confidingly that she thought she was "his favorite person in the whole world." "He'd do anything for me," she said; "he'd even put toilets in the Martha's Vineyard house." After she said that, she hooted with mirth, realizing how funny that sounded. "Our summer house only has outhouses. Really," she said, nodding her head, as if I wouldn't believe her, "and my mother and Poppa can't agree about fixing it. My father says they are at war over the house. But I think I could bring Poppa 'round." She always called her grandfather Poppa, not "my grandfather." She felt a little guilty about her preferred status with her grandfather but understood she couldn't do anything about it. "I wish Poppa loved my mother more," she said. "We don't talk about how much he loves me, but she understands. She often says we can't choose who we love. It's outside our control." She sighed after saying this. "It's a bad system, don't you think?"

She has apparently negotiated with her grandfather to live with him if her mother dies. She has told her mother this but not her father, though she has told him she couldn't live with him; she could only visit him. She is actively and more or less efficiently negotiating on her own behalf, not trusting her parents to get it right for her, only for themselves. She tends to see herself as one of the principals of the divorce, as being or getting divorced, not uncommon with an only child.

In our second session, I told her specifically that one of the reasons she was talking to me was to talk about custody, after the separation and/or in the event of the death of one of her parents. She grilled me on this. "What are you going to say?" she asked. I told her I didn't know yet; she and I would have to talk more about it and I'd have to talk about it with her parents. I asked her if she'd like me to talk about it when I talked with her together with each of her parents. She said I could talk about it with her mother; she wasn't sure about her father. "I don't worry about my father dying even though he's older than my mother. I feel he's been vaccinated against death, by all those medicines he gives the children." She looked at me closely, expecting me to laugh or tell her she was being silly. I told her that just as we love whom we love, we feel what we feel. She sighed. "That can be a bad system too," she said. We agreed.

She is reading *Jane Eyre* and loving it. "I read a lot," she said. "I always have. It's like company." Most of her favorite books are about children living on their own, situational orphans if not actual ones, proper heroines, in short. When she was younger, she loved *The Boxcar Children*; now her favorites are *Swallows and Amazons*, *Understood Betsy*, and *Anne of Green Gables*. She has copies of her mother's books as a girl. She always brought one with her to our sessions in her book bag. Whenever I went to the waiting room to get her, she'd be reading.

Her half brother, Tom, is 22. She loves him and feels sorry for him. "He must feel no one loves anyone very long. Helen, his mother, has been married three times. And now his father is getting married for the third time." She looked at me knowingly. "He's got a girlfriend in New York. Grass doesn't grow under his feet." I asked her where she had heard that saying. "Poppa. He said it about my father, but then he said it was true for him too because he married his wife Cindy only 11 months after my granny died. I didn't know my granny." She is worried about Tom. She thought no one was thinking about him. "He's close to my mother; she's looked after him. They have a good relationship. But my father acts as though the divorce won't bother him at all. Like changing teachers." She looked at me coolly. "I'll tell you something about my father. If you're a child and you don't have cancer, he thinks you have nothing to worry about, nothing to complain about. It's only life or death with him."

She made a point of her own excellent health. "I almost never get sick. I've never had strep or flu or an ear infection," she said, ticking off the common primary-schoolers' ailments. She realized early on that getting ill but not getting fatally ill would cut no ice with her father. Her brother is less healthy, and as she sees it, less lucky, in the family parlance. Premature at birth, he has had chronic lung problems all his life. He has serious asthma, which has required hospitalization on several occasions, and he gets bronchitis and pneumonia regularly, at least once a winter. When he was 16, his junior year at the Cabot School, he spent a month in the infirmary. He almost lost the term. "Tom isn't healthy. I think my father thinks he's a hypochondriac. He's not. He had to stop playing soccer because of his asthma, and he cried." She looked as though she would cry.

In our fifth session, I asked Jane if she could tell me why she had gotten so upset the night her father said she could live with him. She looked very sad. "Once, when I was 7, I remember exactly, I had a doctor's appointment. I told him I didn't want to go. I hated going to the doctor. It was scary. He said that was ridiculous. There was no reason to be scared. Dr. Foreman was a very good doctor and also a very nice person." She looked at me to see if I got it. I nodded. "That's a big difference between my father and my grandfather. If I told Poppa I was scared, he'd ask me if I wanted him to come along as my protector." She laughed. "I'll bet, when my mother was little and she said she was scared about going to the doctor, Poppa said to her, 'Oh, don't be a ninny. The doctor is a very nice man.'"

I asked Jane if she was afraid of dying. Her eyes filled with tears. She nodded. I asked if that was why she didn't want to live with her father. She looked puzzled. I asked if she thought she would die if she lived with him, like the children he took care of. Her face crumpled. "Maybe," she said. I then asked her if she thought she might get sick if she had to live with him. "Maybe," this in a whisper. She started crying. "I always worry about dying or getting brain cancer, that's the worst, I've worried about that for years." Suddenly she looked so much older than 11. "But that's not why I got upset."

She got upset that night not because she was afraid of living with her father— "I wouldn't stay; I'd run away," she said—but because she was afraid of telling him. He'd deny it. Her big fear was that if she *wasn't* sick, he wouldn't pay attention to her, and even if she got sick, he wouldn't pay attention unless she was so sick she'd probably die. And if he didn't pay her any attention, who would? "It's hard to get my father's attention. He has so many things on his mind." She understands that telling me is a way of telling him, and she plainly wants me or her mother to run interference, to make him understand she can't and won't live with him. She felt bad saying this, and it all came out with tears and pauses, but she was very clear about her course of action: she wasn't going to live with him, and no judge could make her. "We can have a lot of fun together, my father and me. We play games, soccer and squash. I like them okay and I'm getting pretty good. But he just doesn't see how a healthy child can have any problems."

I asked her if she would mind staying with her father overnight, on weekends and holidays, or going on vacation with him. She said that was okay, "so long as it wasn't permanent." I asked her if Tom had ever lived with her and her parents. She shook her head. He'd come for vacations; and once he stayed a whole month, but then he got an asthma attack and went home.

INTERVIEWS WITH JANE AND HER MOTHER (July 14, July 21)
In my two sessions with Jane and her mother, we talked frankly about Jane's fears and her insistence on not living with her father. We also talked about her fear that her mother might die. Ms. Meiklejohn turned to her and said with absolute conviction, "I am not going to die until you're all grown up, with children of your own." Jane, her courage screwed up, persisted. "But what if you do?" Ms. Meiklejohn smiled at her daughter. "You mean, what if I went to the end of town, like James James Morrison Morrison's mother?" They laughed but Jane had the bit between her teeth now. "You could get run over or die in a plane crash or," she added, suddenly looking stricken, in a very small voice, "you could get leukemia or"—she paused and spoke in a whisper, as if the words themselves might bring on the illness—"breast cancer." Ms. Meiklejohn pulled Jane onto her lap. "I'll make sure you live with the person you want to live with. That's Poppa, isn't it? And I'll make sure that Daddy knows and agrees." Jane shook her head. "How can you make that happen?" Ms. Meiklejohn was very clear in her answer. "Your daddy loves you, Jane. He'll do the right thing. We'll write it down in the separation agreement. It will be there in print, signed by the judge. It will be official. It will be the law. I will show it to you." Jane buried her head in her mother's neck and wept softly. When we said goodbye that afternoon, Jane shook my hand and said thank you.

INTERVIEWS WITH MS. MEIKLEJOHN (June 30, July 7)
In my two sessions with Ms. Meiklejohn alone, we talked about her brother's death and its effect on her, her younger sister, Cordelia, with Down's, the marriage, and Jane. She thought that Dr. Durkheim had been drawn to her in part because she had had a brother who died young of cancer. "He thought I'd understand how important his work was. I did, I do, but what he never saw, what he never understood was that James's death ruined my childhood. It took years for me to understand that I was furious at him for dying, for leaving me alone with a grieving mother, and for occupying so much emotional space in our lives even though he was dead." She smiled a small smile. "Six years of analysis went into that statement." She added, "My father didn't and doesn't much care for Daniel, but he thought the marriage was good, evolutionarily speaking. We were different ethnicities; our children would likely be spared the afflictions of

the inbred. I think he believes James's leukemia and Cordelia's Down's were the product of inbreeding. He once said with grim humor, 'We Mathers and Meiklejohns, we're the swank Jukes and the Kallikaks.'"

I asked her how she thought her husband would deal with Jane's fears and her emphatic refusal to live with him in the event of her mother's death. "Jane's got him right. He's Mrs. Jellyby all over." She said it would be helpful if I brought up the matter and discussed it with him, but that if I didn't, she knew it would be part of this report. "I'll make it clear, after he's read it, that she has to go live with my father in the event I die in the next few years. He'll of course have generous visitation, but Jane will officially 'live' with my father. But I don't think it will be a problem, once she's outlived James." She added, smiling thinly, "And if she lives with my father, Daniel won't have to pay support. My father wouldn't take money from him, or from anyone, to support Jane. She's the love of his life." She paused. "I won't make a big point of that, the money, that is; it's one of those things better left unsaid, by me at least, and Daniel's no deadbeat. He's just a rotter. Still, there would be pecuniary benefits for him to the arrangement." I reminded her that I could include her statement in my report. She gave a little laugh. "Well, of course you will. Why else are we talking together?"

I asked her how she felt, knowing Jane was so beloved by her grandfather, in her words, "the love of his life." She sighed. "It is so complicated. I've spent years sorting out my feelings toward my parents. The short answer is that James's death left my parents bereft, and they pulled back from me, I believe, to spare the pain another death might cause them. I don't know that I could survive Jane's death. And loving her as I do, I have been able to understand my parents' terrible grief." She continued, "So my father's love for Jane is the happiest outcome now imaginable. I think it wonderful that he loves someone as much as he loves Jane and wonderful that he could give himself over at last to the love of a child. He didn't miss that. Of course, I think it wonderful too that she's half-Jewish. He's got a streak of anti-Semitism, and Jane turns it all on its head."

I asked her about Dr. Durkheim's visitation rights. "I leave Jane with him now regularly when I visit my sister. I have no trouble with her staying with him when she wants to. I can't see making her visit him, nor would he, but she would want to. He loves her in his way, and she loves him in hers."

INTERVIEW WITH JANE AND HER FATHER (August 19)

I met with Jane and Dr. Durkheim once; it wasn't possible to schedule a second, owing to Dr. Durkheim's schedule. In my interview with them, they started the session by speaking about the things they did together. He is a huge sports fan and has always played recreational sports, first soccer and now squash. "I'm too big and too slow-moving to play either well, but I'm wily," he said. Jane plays both games—her father taught her squash, and she belongs to the New Salem children's soccer league—but her favorite athletic activity, she said, was running. He looked surprised, preferring, as he told her, the "head-to-head competition" of the other games. She shot me a quick glance, then looked at him, "The fun of squash and soccer is in winning, but the fun of running is just the running." He started to interrupt, then stopped himself. She continued, looking at me, not him, "No one's there to trip you up, or bong you with their racquet or kick you with their cleats. I like to win at running, I want to be the best, but I like that no one gets in my way." He shook his head and talked about the challenge of competitive games; then seeing she was looking out the window, stopped. "Maybe you'll change your mind," he said, "when you're older and the competition is better." He turned to me. "She's a natural athlete, much better than almost anyone else I've seen her age." She answered, "Maybe I won't play then. Maybe I'll just run, like Atalanta." She then let out a loud hoot. "You don't like to run because you're so slow and I can beat you." She looked at me. "The first time I beat him in a running race I was 7." He laughed. "Well, you were almost 8."

The other thing Jane and Dr. Durkheim do together regularly is watch movies. "We're both movie nuts," he said. On most Sunday nights, at 7, they have Sunday Night at the Movies. They watch a video. They go to the video store and pick a film together. "Daddy has pretty good taste in movies, and since he's seen so many more than me, I usually go with his picks." The two of them have been doing this for about three years now. Ms. Meiklejohn rarely attends. "She likes movies; she doesn't love them," Jane explained. "But she was the one who picked my favorite movie for us to watch. *Dirty Dancing*." Her father groaned. "I thought our favorite was *The Dirty Dozen*," he said. She said to him, "No, not that, and not *Cheaper by the Dozen*." He didn't say anything for several seconds, then said, "I'm out." "How about *Twelve Angry Men*?" she asked. He shook his head. They have this game they play with movie titles, playing off the words in a title. "You can use the same word a third time—I could have said

Dirty Harry—but it hurts your reputation as a player," Jane said. "*Cheaper by the Dozen*," Dr. Durkheim said, "is a killer. It doesn't go anywhere."

Dr. Durkheim was not physically affectionate with Jane. He might tug at her braid or poke her, but otherwise he didn't touch her. This may be the way the two of them have always been together, or it may be his response to her changing body as adolescence looms. At our joint session, neither of them raised the matter of her living arrangements in the event her mother died and neither mentioned the night she collapsed in hysterics when he suggested she might live with him.

INTERVIEW WITH DR. DURKHEIM (August 10)
I had only a single session with Dr. Durkheim alone. He was not able to schedule a second. I used it to discuss custody. I began the discussion with the obvious question: Why did he think Jane had broken down so completely when he spoke to her about living with him? He looked at me straight on, blank-faced, revealing nothing. "Isn't that the shrink's job?" he said. "You tell me." I told him what I knew: that in the event of her mother's death or inability to care for her, Jane didn't want to live with him but with her grandfather; that she had said she'd run away if she was made to live with him; that she'd made arrangements with her mother and grandfather and they both would back her up. He started to protest, to argue with me, then stopped himself. "I've not been around much. Her mother has done 90% of the child raising. And she spends more time with Meiklejohn than she does with me. It's my job. It can't be helped."

I asked him if he performed or had in the past performed any of the functions of a caretaking parent, such as bathing and putting her to bed at night, making doctors' appointments for her and taking her there, arranging playdates and parties for her, attending school conferences, coaching her at sports, providing her with religious education, making her meals, buying her clothes, and the like. He responded by saying: "I've just told you her mother has done 90% of the child raising."

I asked him if he would challenge a custody order that gave Jane's grandfather in effect physical custody—not legal—in the event her mother died in the next seven years. He asked what that would mean. I said that he would, of course, see her regularly, as much as he wanted or was able, and would participate in all important decisions affecting Jane, but that she would live with her grandfather.

"This is so much fuss over an unlikely hypothetical," he said. I asked him if he would challenge his wife on custody. He shook his head. I asked him why not. "I thought I explained that," he said. I then asked him what would prompt him to challenge his father-in-law on custody. His schedule wouldn't change. He accused me of laying a trap for him. I asked him if he wanted custody. "I love my daughter," he said. I repeated that Jane had said she would run away if he was given custody. "She would run to her grandfather, you know," I said, "and at that point, Mr. Meiklejohn would likely sue you for custody." Dr. Durkheim shook his head slightly, as if batting away a mosquito. I asked him what he would do if his wife refused to sign a separation agreement unless physical custody on her death was given to her father. He sighed with irritation. "If we can't resolve things, the judge will have to do it." I asked him if he understood that the judge might take it on himself then to review the entire agreement. It would become in effect a contested divorce. He took that in. "I will talk to my lawyer." He then added, "This is psychological blackmail."

Assuming Jane would live with his wife, I asked him whether it would be important or necessary to him to include in the settlement a formal visiting schedule for him. He said no. "That's not necessary. She'll let me see Jane whenever I want to, whenever I can. We've never fought about Jane. Let's not get mired in alternate Simchas Torahs and that crap." I then asked whether, in the event his father-in-law had custody, he would want a formal visiting schedule. "This is ridiculous. I'm not making plans about a hypothetical future." He then added, "I will say this. My father-in-law doesn't care for me one whit, but he loves Jane; he'd never do anything to harm her."

I asked him about his son, Tom, and the effect he thought the divorce would have on him. He responded as Jane had earlier said. "Why should it affect him? She's not his mother." In our conversation, Dr. Durkheim never referred to his wife by name but only as Jane's mother or, more generally, "her." I asked if he was planning to remarry in the near future. He said no. I then asked if the prospect of remarriage would have any effect on his thinking about custody. He said no again.

We had been speaking for 25 minutes. I told him that I had no more questions but I'd like to hear anything he had to say about Jane and the question of custody. "I deeply resent this intrusion into my life. I resent the suppositions behind your questions and the power you wield in resolving this dispute.

I realize there's nothing else to be done, but I object hugely, hugely, to this process." He got up and walked out.

INTERVIEW WITH BRUCE MEIKLEJOHN (August 24)

I scheduled a meeting with Bruce Meiklejohn, Jane's grandfather, in late August, after I had finished all the other interviews and consultations, thinking it essential before coming to any conclusions to find out what he knew about Jane's custody preferences and what he was prepared to do on her behalf in the event of his daughter's death. On first meeting, Mr. Meiklejohn thanked me for inviting him. "I will do anything and everything that needs to be done for my granddaughter, Jane." He knew that Jane was worried about her mother's death and her living arrangements in the event her mother died in the next few years. He showed me a letter she had written him in June and his reply. "I meant what I wrote. And when I told you I'd do anything and everything, I wasn't expressing myself fully. What I should have said, what I meant to have said, was that there's nothing, nothing I wouldn't do for Jane."

I told him that Jane wanted to live with him, her grandfather, if her mother died, that she had said she would run away if she had to live with her father. Mr. Meiklejohn nodded. "I know. Mia has talked to me." I asked him if he would be willing to have Jane live with him and share custody with Dr. Durkheim. He nodded again. "I'm not saying it would be easy to share custody with Durkheim; he would, not unreasonably, resent me. I imagine he would feel humiliated publicly that I had custody, but he knows it makes no sense, absolutely no sense, for reasons completely unrelated to Jane's fears, for him to have her live with him. He can't do his job and be a single parent. I can. I can make myself available to Jane whenever I want to, whenever she needs me." He stopped. "Look, I'm a businessman, I know how to get along when I want to. We'd get along. I'd make it easy for him to cooperate with me." I asked him how he would do that. "I would not keep Jane from him; I'd give him access to my house at all times, his own key. He could come whenever he liked. I'd make sure he knew about every important event in her life; I'd include him in all celebrations. I'd put in toilets and invite him to stay at the guesthouse on Martha's Vineyard." He smiled. "That's a point of contention between my daughter and me—we have a huge house with outhouses, no inside toilets. I want to fix the whole place up; she doesn't. So we do nothing. But I'm weakening. Jane wants inside toilets."

I asked Mr. Meiklejohn about his wife, Cindy. Would she want Jane living with them? Would it be agreeable to her? Would she find a child at this point in her life, living in her house, a nuisance? "Cindy has always been pleasant to Jane, but she has no children of her own, never wanted them, and she thinks of them generally as Martians. But she has never been and never would be unkind to Jane; that's not in her nature. And Jane's a very attractive and agreeable child, and Cindy likes her. But as I would make it easy for Durkheim to have Jane living in my house, I'd make it easy for Cindy too. She would not be asked to do any of the tending, no carpooling, no Saturdays at the races, no homework duty. I'd hire a wonderful nanny, wonderful tutors if needed. And I'm pretty good at homework, and I'd be the one to go to her races, meet with her teachers, set her curfew, teach her to drive stick. I'm in." He went on. "Cindy and I now have been married almost 20 years. She understands me. She's a good wife. She'd go along."

I asked how he'd feel in his later years, giving up so much of his time to a young child, if it came to that. "After my son, James, died, I more or less shut down. Then Cordelia was born so seriously afflicted. Then Maria, Mia's mother, got cancer. Dead two years later. It was a terrible decade. I remarried very soon after. I needed someone alive and healthy and not needy. Mia got the short end of the stick. I know that, but I was too sore myself to take care of her. Jane gives me a second shot. She's very like Mia too, or the way Mia was before James died. So direct, so slyly humorous, so thoughtful and sensitive, yet resilient. I see James in her too. She is a wonderful athlete, a great runner. And she's smart as a whip, smarter than all of us. I love that girl with all my heart." He stopped for a second, then continued. "Look, I don't think Mia's going to die before Jane grows up. This is all highly speculative. We're doing this to make sure Jane feels safe now. But if that terrible event happened, I would be there. And in some way, I could make amends to Mia, doing for her daughter what I couldn't do, what I didn't do for her."

I asked him about his age and his health. He laughed. "I wondered if you'd go there, but then I said to myself, oh, yes, she'll ask. She's a pro. I am 68. I am in excellent health, and I will let you speak to my physician if you want. I exercise regularly, I don't take any medicines, other than the odd Advil for my stiff right knee. My memory is pretty good. I forget names now and then without even intending to. That's about it. My mother lived to 96, my father to 90. Both kept their health and wits. I am the youngest of six children, all still living. My oldest sibling, Jonathan, is 87 and a senior judge on the 13th Circuit. My next oldest sibling, Rebecca, is 82. She plays competitive bridge. We're all cut from the same cloth, strong as horses, stubborn as mules. And I think Mia is cut from that cloth too. She's really all Meiklejohn, very little Mather, except of course for the bookishness."

I asked him how he'd work out the financial arrangements with Dr. Durkheim. "There's nothing you won't ask, is there? Good for you. I am a rich man. I'm not Bill Gates or Warren Buffett rich, but I've got more than any person needs. I can easily support Jane and would, but I would work it out with her father. I had offered years ago to pay for her schooling, college, graduate school, psychoanalysis, and I stand ready to do that wherever she lives. In the event of my death, I've made arrangements for Cordelia's permanent support, given a life interest in one-half of my estate to my wife, Cindy, and set up a foundation with $25 million outright, and after Cindy's death, that half of my estate. The rest goes to Mia and Jane. Jane will be an heiress. Mia too. I've structured it so that Jane will have a regular income until she's 35. After that, it's all hers. Mia inherits immediately, and she can dispose of her estate as she wishes; I haven't made her give it over to Jane. I did all this recently. I think it's my eighth will in six years. It was hard for me, to give up that power, but I did it. Cindy told me I had to. She said I was becoming unattractively controlling." He laughed. "Did you ever read *Portrait of a Lady?*" I nodded. "Mia gave it to me. Wonderful book. Ralph ruined Isabel, giving her all that money. It was a cruel experiment. I'm susceptible to literature; I believe in it, especially when it supports my prejudices. I want Jane to have my money, but I don't want her to be a victim of a fortune hunter. I know Durkheim didn't marry Mia for her money—he left Helen Fincher for Mia, and the Finchers have more money than the sultan of Dubai—but real money is a huge magnet. I've made Jane and Mia trustees of the foundation so they'll get to give away money, something I have trouble doing, and they can give away their own too. Do you need to know how much money I have?" I told him I did not.

My final question had to do with his response in the event his daughter died and Dr. Durkheim wanted Jane to stay with him. "It would depend on Jane. If she wanted to live with me, I would sue for custody. If not, not. This is not a pissing contest. This is not about me or Durkheim. This is about Jane."

TELEPHONE CONSULTATIONS WITH PEABODY SCHOOL STAFF (June 29)
At the end of June, during the last week of classes at the Peabody School, I

spoke on the phone with the headmistress, Eliza Wolfe, and Jane's 5th-grade teacher, Victoria Crane. Both had met Ms. Meiklejohn on several occasions; Ms. Wolfe had also met Dr. Durkheim during an initial interview, when Jane was applying to the kindergarten class at Peabody in 1993. Ms. Crane described Jane as an excellent student and good citizen. She is organized, disciplined, hardworking, and bright. She is popular with her classmates, both boys and girls, and an outstanding athlete. Before her parents decided to separate, Ms. Crane would have described Jane as outgoing and outspoken, but since her parents' decision to split, she has receded. "She's sad, not so sad that she can't forget her grief," Ms. Crane said, "but sad enough that we all can see it. She speaks less in class, argues less with the boys. She's doing well in her classes, but she's less a presence in the classroom. I could always count on her to say something interesting. She was eager to participate. She's quieter, more remote. She'll be all right. She's intellectually gifted and self-confident. It's just been a huge blow. We had a long talk about it one day. She had been on the brink of tears all morning. I took her to the cafeteria for a cup of cocoa. She kept saying to me, 'I didn't see it coming. Why didn't I see it coming?' As if she might have forestalled it by foreseeing it."

Ms. Crane described Ms. Meiklejohn as a "semi-active parent." She explained. "There are several parents, mothers really, who are hyperactive. It's almost as if they see it as a job. Ms. Meiklejohn is not in that group. She comes to sing most Friday afternoons, she attends all of Jane's class performances and athletic events, but she doesn't hang around the school. She did go on the class trip to the Southport Aquarium this past fall, but confided afterward that she wasn't cut out for trips that involved bus rides with 80 children, and in the future would instead bring the cupcakes for the Sports Day." Ms. Crane laughed. "I like Ms. Meiklejohn. She can be very funny, and she always treats the teachers with respect. There are some parents who think of us as their employees. I saw her once intercede on behalf of a teacher, Liz Sugarman, Jane's 3rd-grade teacher, though *intercede* is not exactly the right word. It was just about two years ago. A child in Jane's class had been sent to the headmistress's office for swearing at Liz. The parents were called in and the father made a scene. He started yelling, in the hallway, at Liz for making a fuss about nothing. Ms. Meiklejohn, who was fetching Jane, saw what was happening. She went up to the father and said, 'Excuse me, but you're a fucking asshole.' The father swung around and yelled at her, 'Who the hell are you, and where do you get off calling me a name like that?' Ms. Meiklejohn said, 'Well, that's what my daughter told me your son said to Ms. Sugarman, though he didn't say "Excuse me." I thought it was rude, but I wanted to test it on someone. I see it is rude, and upsetting.' The father turned bright red. His wife started to cry, a good move, I thought." Ms. Crane had never met Dr. Durkheim, though she had seen him at Sports Day in October.

Ms. Wolfe said she'd like to tell a story about Ms. Meiklejohn as a parent. "It's not a story about seeing her interact with Jane," she said. "Rather, it's a story that told me how thoughtful she was as a mother." Two years ago, she had sounded Ms. Meiklejohn out about joining the school's Board of Trustees; Ms. Meiklejohn turned her down, saying she would not serve while Jane was still a student there. "'It's been my experience,' Ms. Meiklejohn explained, 'that trustees who are parents of current students almost invariably take their child's point of view when they find themselves in situations where their allegiances are divided. Suppose you caught Jane smoking in the bathroom, or setting fire to the bathroom,' she said. 'Would you kick her out? I think it's a serious conflict of interest. I have to be on Jane's side. Ask me again when Jane has finished up.'" Ms. Wolfe said that no parent, to her knowledge, had ever before acknowledged a conflict; nor had she faced up to it. She said that at a subsequent retreat of the board, she arranged for an outside facilitator to address the question of parent-trustees and their role in situations that might compromise their fiduciary responsibilities. "Half my board are current parents. But that's down from 75%, and that's because of Mia Meiklejohn."

Ms. Wolfe had spoken with Dr. Durkheim only once, at the parent interview when Jane was applying to kindergarten; he was interested in the science curriculum. Ms. Wolfe asked if I wanted her opinion on custody. I asked her what it was. "There's no question but that Jane should live with her mother. Victoria would say the same thing. In fact, all of Jane's teachers would. He simply isn't around. More than that, he isn't available."

CONCLUSION

The question I have specifically been asked to address is Jane's custody in the event her mother dies in the next few years. For Jane this is not a hypothetical question but a real fear. Ms. Meiklejohn is 42. Both her mother and grandmother died at 46 of breast cancer. Ms. Meiklejohn has been the primary caretaker since Jane's birth, and Jane's parents have agreed that under their separation agreement, Jane will live with her mother. Dr. Durkheim will have generous visiting and overnight rights. He does not think it necessary to spell out the terms of his rights (e.g., alternate weekends, Jewish holidays), but trusts he and his wife will be able to work it out. Ms. Meiklejohn concurs. Since they do not disagree on this point and since Jane is reaching an age where her wishes and preferences will count as much as if not more than theirs, I do not think it necessary or useful to specify terms but recommend leaving them open.

On the subject of custody in the event Ms. Meiklejohn dies before Jane is 18, I support Jane's position and recommend that joint custody be granted her father and grandfather and that she live with her grandfather on the same terms as she lived with her mother. There is no question that Dr. Durkheim loves his daughter and is legally fit to be her custodian and caretaker, but he has made no effort to take on any of the caretaking responsibilities that a custodial parent regularly assumes; neither has he given any indication, in sharp contrast to his father-in-law, Bruce Meiklejohn, that he could easily, selflessly take on those responsibilities in the event Jane's mother died. It is my sense that he knows he is not the right person to take on the task of the caretaking parent but feels chagrined by this failing and Jane's perception of it and, in consequence, has assumed a self-protective mask of stony recalcitrance. Affronted by a process of evaluation that showed him to disadvantage, Dr. Durkheim refused to argue on his own behalf or to step aside in favor of his father-in-law, preferring to appear arrogant rather than to admit deficiency. It is a self-protective act but also one protective of Jane. He is caught in a dilemma. If he fights for custody, he knows, as she knows, that he is not acting in her best interests. At the same time, if he doesn't fight for custody, he fears, I believe, that she may feel abandoned by him.

FINDINGS

I make this recommendation based on the following findings: (1) that Jane's best interests *now* are served by a custody agreement that has her living with her grandfather in the event of her mother's death; (2) that Dr. Durkheim is not unfit to act as Jane's primary caretaker and custodian but that, owing to the demands of his job, he could not take on that role in the event of his wife's death and maintain the same level of commitment to his work; (3) that Dr. Durkheim has acknowledged his limited role in Jane's care and upbringing to date and cannot foresee curtailing professional commitments and responsibilities in a way that would allow him to take a more active and involved role now or in the future; (4) that Mr. Meiklejohn has asserted his willingness to act as Jane's caretaker and has undertaken to work closely with Dr. Durkheim to make the arrangement work; (5) that Jane has made clear not only her preferences but also her intentions and that her grandfather would likely sue for custody if Jane were made to live with Dr. Durkheim against her wishes; (6) that both of Jane's parents understood prior to consulting me that a recommendation in favor of Bruce Meiklejohn was a possible outcome of this evaluation; and (7) that changed circumstances might overtake this arrangement and that its purpose is to secure Jane's peace of mind now and in the near future.

Narragansett Statutes
Title 33 of the Narragansett Code, Sections 801ff.
Dissolution of Marriage, Annulment, and Legal Separation

Sec. 807. Orders regarding custody and support of minor children.
In any controversy before the Narragansett Family Court as to the custody or care of minor children, the court may at any time make or modify any order regarding the education and support of the children and of care, custody, and visitation. The court may assign the custody of any child to the parents jointly, to either parent, or to a third party, according to its best judgment upon the facts of the case. The court may also make any order granting the right of visitation of any child to a third party, including stepparents, grandparents, and other family members.

Sec. 813. Presumption regarding best interest of child to be in custody of parent.
In any dispute as to the custody of a minor child involving a parent and a nonparent, there shall be a presumption that it is in the best interest of the child to be in the custody of the parent, which presumption may be rebutted by showing that it would be detrimental to the child's best interest to permit the parent to have custody.

MARIA MATHER MEIKLEJOHN
404 ST. CLOUD STREET
NEW SALEM, NA 06556

September 14

Dear Sophie,

A quick note to keep you up to date on the domestic
front at the Meiklejohn—Durkheims. I saw my old friend
Jacques Valery last week in Philadelphia, when I was
visiting Cordelia. We went for a long walk and caught up
with each other. He followed up with a note to the house,
which I've attached. It was very good for my morale,
being with him. I recommend a Frenchman, if not as the
entrée, then the cheese course.

I'm writing because I think Daniel may have opened
the letter. I'm not sure. The flap was all bunched up,
as though it had been resealed. He didn't say anything.
He may simply think I've resumed an old relationship.
He knew about Jacques, Part 1, and he might not have
realized that Jacques was writing about Part 2. Then

again, he may not give a tinker's damn; he may be relieved that I'm moving on. He seems less angry at me since we got Dr. Fischer's report. I don't want to feel any sympathy for him, and yet when he's not being a perfect swine, I find my throat catching. Enough of this twaddle. Oh, where did my stiff upper lip go?

All the best,

Mia

10 September

Chère Mia,

I was so happy to see you again. I'm so glad you called. It is an awful experience getting divorced, though I've heard friends say the second one, c'est du gateau. You're doing very well. And you're looking very well, but thinner. Don't get too thin. Men—real men, French men—like something to hold on to.

I was not surprised by the news, but surprised you were. I saw it coming, like a train in the night. Let lawyers do the fighting for you. That is my only advice.

Will I get to see you again? Don't you think we should go to Gabriella's, for old time's sake? The maître d' always asks after you. "What happened to la bella bionda?" he asks. I give him my best Gallic shrug, and he nods sagely, the discreet repository of old love affairs.

Another inducement: tickets for the 76ers. Or the Barnes Collection.

Avec amour, comme toujours.

Jacques

SANGER & BOOTH
300 CHURCH STREET
NEW SALEM, NARRAGANSETT 06555
(393) 876-6767
ATTORNEYS AT LAW

September 17, 1999

Anne Sophie Diehl
Traynor, Hand, Wyzanski
222 Church Street
New Salem, Narragansett 06555

Dear Sophie,

This letter serves as notice of new representation. I am writing on behalf of
our client, Dr. Daniel Durkheim, who has retained Sanger & Booth, as of
September 20, to represent him in his separation negotiations and dissolution proceedings with his wife, Maria Meiklejohn. Kahn & Boyle will no
longer be representing him.

We will contact you again shortly with a new offer from Dr. Durkheim. He
believes that a prompt resolution of all issues is in everyone's best interest,
and he has instructed us to put forward an offer that promotes agreement.

Yours,

Mary Booth

Mary Booth
Attorney at Law

Happy Birthday

From: Maggie Pfeiffer   9/21/99 8:07 AM
To: Sophie Diehl <asdiehl@traynor.com>
Date: Tue, 21 Sep 1999 8:07:02
Subject: Happy Birthday

Happy Birthday, darling Sophie. I know I'll see you tonight, but I wanted you to start the day with my best, best wishes on your 30th birthday.

Don't bring anything, just your sweet self.

All my love,
Maggie

P.S. Time to start cramming for the judging exams now that you're 30. No more "dicking around," as your divorce client likes to say.

Happy Birthday

From: Harry Mortensen   9/21/99 11:54 AM
To: Sophie Diehl <asdiehl@traynor.com>
Date: Tue, 21 Sep 1999 11:54:29
Subject: Happy Birthday

I remembered this morning that today was your birthday. You had described yourself as an equinocturnal girl. Happy Birthday, Sweet Sophie.

I want to apologize for the way things wound up, for the way I behaved. I was—still am—really crazy about you, but with Tessa acting out, I couldn't—and still can't—have any kind of real relationship. She hasn't gone away. She's ill, seriously ill. I'm sure that's why Scammer left. I've hired a lawyer, but it's been very hard going. She doesn't have, as they say, a known fixed address. I don't know where or how she's living. She calls regularly, sometimes 15 or 16 times a night, to harangue me. I turn the ringer off. I turn the phone off. She leaves rambling messages. Her phone number changes all the time, and when I call back, no one answers. I don't know how or when I'll find myself clear of her.

I say this only by way of explanation. It was the wrong time for us. You were, are wonderful. The time we were together, during the rehearsal and run of *The Real Thing*, was for me the happiest in years. I wanted to tell you that.

Harry

P.S. I'm sorry I told Tessa about you. I'm sorry she made a scene in your office. But I couldn't help it.

It just came out, like a breath.

My Birthday

From: Sophie Diehl   9/21/99 11:07 PM
To: Maggie Pfeiffer <mcp15@mather.edu>
Date: Tue, 21 Sep 1999 23:07:25
Subject: My Birthday

Dear Maggie,

You and Matt were great. Not the birthday party I expected. I wish, or almost wish, Harry hadn't written to me. I'm okay. I'll be okay. For him, it's awful. You said you weren't surprised. I know you kept telling me not to give up on him. But it wouldn't have worked out; he says that, he knows that.

Thanks for everything. The food was delicious. How many bottles of wine did we drink? I saw at least three dead bottles on the table. Almost enough to drown one's sorrows.

Love,
Sophie

TRAYNOR, HAND, WYZANSKI

222 CHURCH STREET
NEW SALEM, NARRAGANSETT 06555
(393) 876-5678
ATTORNEYS AT LAW

September 23, 1999

Maria Mather Meiklejohn
404 St. Cloud Street
New Salem, NA 06556

Dear Mia,

Unexpected good news. Daniel has gotten himself new lawyers, Sanger & Booth, a small, good firm, two women partners, two women associates. They specialize in family law and often do cases for the state, representing children in termination of parental rights proceedings. I know the principals, Sarah (Sadie) Sanger and Mary (Mamie) Booth. They're first-rate in every respect: professional, competent, ethical, honorable. Dr. Fischer's report may be responsible for this. Or Kahn's reprimand. Or your 10-point letter? Or all of the above. I think we'll be able to make a deal. Hold steady.

I am attaching their letter giving notice of new representation. Isn't there a Star Trek movie, *The End of Kahn*?

Yours,

Anne Sophie Diehl

Anne Sophie Diehl

cc: David Greaves

SUSANNA GIOVANNITTI
Formerly of Middleton, Murray

&

CAROLINE LEWISOHN
Formerly of Seward, Matland & Janney

Have Become Members

of

Farrow Allerton
280 Church Street
New Salem, Narragansett 06555

OCTOBER 1, 1999

SANGER & BOOTH
300 CHURCH STREET
NEW SALEM, NARRAGANSETT 06555
(393) 876-6767
ATTORNEYS AT LAW

October 1, 1999

Anne Sophie Diehl
Traynor, Hand, Wyzanski
222 Church Street
New Salem, Narragansett 06555

Dear Sophie,

I am sending you Dr. Daniel Durkheim's new offer. I have appropriated your form to allow clear and easy comparisons.

The offer is based on Dr. Durkheim's current salary of $370,000. As you will see, he has accepted most of the terms your client, Maria Meiklejohn, offered, including rehabilitation alimony in the form of law school tuition. After taxes (estimated at $100,000/year), this offer allocates $150,000, 55% of his net income, in a combination of alimony and child support, to Ms. Meiklejohn and Jane. In light of these substantial payments, the offer does not include any escalator clauses or cost-of-living adjustments.

In distributing retirement funds, investments, and property, this offer recognizes, as is only fair, Ms. Meiklejohn's inheritance from her mother, not the house, but the trust, which will vest when she's 50. At the same time, the rehabilitation alimony recognizes that the trust will not vest until she's 50. Dr. Durkheim will retain his retirement funds and in addition $206,000 in more liquid assets. Ms. Meiklejohn will receive 6/7th of the stock investment. Dr. Durkheim will retain the house for seven years, in line with the alimony and child support arrangement. At the end of seven years, he will pay Ms. Meiklejohn $120,000, one-half of the current net equity as calculated in your offer.

Dr. Durkheim would like the Persian rug; in exchange, he offers to relinquish his interest in all art owned by the couple.

I look forward to hearing from you.

Yours,

Mary Booth
Mary Booth

SANGER & BOOTH
Maria Mather Meiklejohn and Daniel E. Durkheim
New Settlement Offer: Custody & Support

Custody
Physical Custody: sole to Maria Meiklejohn
Legal Custody: joint to Maria Meiklejohn & Daniel Durkheim

Child Support
Daniel Durkheim to pay $60,000/year for seven (7) years (through high school); Maria Meiklejohn to pay school tuition and fees
Daniel Durkheim to pay $18,000/year at end of seven (7) years until Jane's graduation from college or 23rd birthday, whichever event is earlier

College Costs
Daniel Durkheim to pay college tuition, room, and board for four (4) years
Maria Meiklejohn to pay books and other expenses

Ordinary Alimony or Spousal Support
Daniel Durkheim to pay $60,000/year to Maria Meiklejohn for seven (7) years from signing or terminating event
Terminating events: remarriage; Maria Meiklejohn has a salary of at least $50,000

Rehabilitation Alimony
Daniel Durkheim to pay $30,000/year to Maria Meiklejohn for three (3) years in law school tuition at Mather Law School, or $14,000/year for three (3) years at the University of Narragansett Law School
Terminating event: nonattendance at law school

Reimbursement Alimony
No reimbursement alimony

Medical Insurance
Maria Meiklejohn to pay $3,200 for COBRA account on Daniel Durkheim's policy
Terminating events: alternative health insurance coverage available from law school or employment

New Offer: Comparison with Counteroffer

Account	New Annual	Counter Annual
Child Support (HS; 7 years)	$60,000	$72,000
Child Support (college)	$18,000	$24,000
Alimony	$60,000	$60,000
Rehabilitation Alimony	$30,000	$30,000
Reimbursement Alimony	0	$10,000

October 1, 1999

SANGER & BOOTH
Maria Mather Meiklejohn and Daniel E. Durkheim
New Settlement Offer: Retirement Funds, Investments & Property

Daniel Durkheim's TIAA-CREF Retirement Accounts: $600,000
Counteroffer: Daniel Durkheim to receive $300,000; Maria Meiklejohn
to receive $300,000
New Offer: Daniel Durkheim to keep $600,000

Daniel Durkheim's 401(k) Plan: $300,000
Counteroffer: Daniel Durkheim to receive $150,000; Maria Meiklejohn
to receive $150,000
New Offer: Daniel Durkheim to keep $300,000

Stock Market Investments: $700,000
Counteroffer: Daniel Durkheim to receive $350,000; Maria Meiklejohn
to receive $350,000
*New Offer: Daniel Durkheim to receive $100,000; Maria Meiklejohn to
receive $600,000*

Treasury Bills: $90,000
Counteroffer: Maria Meiklejohn to receive $45,000; Daniel Durkheim
to receive $45,000
New Offer: Daniel Durkheim to receive $90,000

Joint Savings Account: Originally $80,000; Now $16,000
Counteroffer: Maria Meiklejohn to receive $32,000; Daniel Durkheim
to receive $48,000
Equal Division with recognition of Daniel Durkheim's $16,000 inheritance
New Offer: Daniel Durkheim to receive $16,000

Family Residence: Current Value: $525,000; Net Equity: $240,000
Counteroffer: Daniel Durkheim to receive $120,000; Maria Meiklejohn
to receive $120,000
Maria Meiklejohn to receive her share from stock market investments
if house kept by Daniel Durkheim
*New Offer: Daniel Durkheim to receive home; Upon sale or at end of 7
years, Maria Meiklejohn to receive $120,000*

New Offer: Comparison with Counteroffer

Account	DD New	MMM New	DD Counter	MMM Counter
TIAA-CREF	600,000	0	300,000	300,000
401(k) Plan	300,000	0	150,000	150,000
Stocks	100,000	600,000	350,000	350,000
T Bills	90,000	0	45,000	45,000
Savings	16,000	0	16,000	0
TOTAL	**1,106,000**	**600,000**	**861,000**	**845,000**

The total amount in retirement funds and savings is $1,706,000. In the original offer, Dr. Durkheim would have received only $16,000 more than Ms. Meiklejohn. Under this offer, Dr. Durkheim would receive $506,000 more than Ms. Meiklejohn, and $245,000 more than under the original offer.

October 1, 1999

TRAYNOR, HAND, WYZANSKI

222 CHURCH STREET
NEW SALEM, NARRAGANSETT 06555
(393) 876-5678

MEMORANDUM
Attorney Work Product

From:	Joe Salerno
To:	The Firm
RE:	Farrow Allerton
Date:	October 4, 1999
Attachments:	Notice of Farrow Allerton's Two New Partners

Listen up, folks, Farrow Allerton is on the move. Three new women partners in the last month, providing the firm with gender and ethnic cover, not to say talent and brains. We should have hired Caroline and Susanna (and of course retained Fiona). I bet we could have gotten them. Who's in charge of recruitment here, anyway? Anyone? I believe Caroline is Jim Rosental's sister-in-law. We're not going to make it in the new century if all we do is cosset the Octopus.

TRAYNOR, HAND, WYZANSKI

222 CHURCH STREET
NEW SALEM, NARRAGANSETT 06555
(393) 876-5678

MEMORANDUM
Attorney Work Product

From:	Sophie Diehl
To:	David Greaves
RE:	The Durkheim Separation Agreement
Date:	October 7, 1999
Attachments:	Letter from Mamie Booth, October 1, 1999
	New Durkheim Settlement Offer: Custody & Support
	New Durkheim Settlement Offer: Retirement, Investment,
	Property
	Draft Letter to Mamie Booth

Dr. Durkheim's new lawyer, Mamie Booth, has put forward a reasonable offer. I met with Ms. Meiklejohn this afternoon, and we came up with a response. Please look it over and let me know what you think. I don't know that he'll keep paying alimony and support once Jane has gone to college (always dicey, so Felix tells me), but we should be okay for the next seven years.

Fiona Redux

From: Sophie Diehl   10/8/99 3:24 PM
To: Maggie Pfeiffer <mcp15@mather.edu>
Date: Fri, 8 Oct 1999 15:24:19
Subject: Fiona Redux

Dear Maggie,

I was having lunch with two friends from the AG's office at Golightly's (always a mistake, I now think), when who should drop by the table, on her way out, but Fiona, all glammed up. She must have gotten a whopping raise; her clothes were beautiful and expensive. Louboutin shoes. Bottega Veneta bag. Great haircut too, not a local job. "Sophie," she said, "I understand you're now the lead lawyer on the new Octopus bond offering. Just kidding. Please give my best to everyone." She winked and was gone. My friends looked at me in amazement. I just said, "Inside joke."

I wonder if she's going to keep ambushing me every time we run into each other. I wish there was someone at the firm I could talk to about it, but there isn't. Even Joe has told me to suck it up, though of course he puts it in terms of "knocking Brearley out of me." At least he's consistent. He doesn't mind women behaving badly. David, on the other hand, has trouble with it; he doesn't like being challenged or crossed by a woman, all the apologies and expressions of regret to the contrary. He wants us to suck it up like men and suck up like women. I may have to tell him one of these days. It's not a good way to be. So 20th century.

I'm going out for an ice cream.

xoxoxo
Sophie

Pettigrew Flowers
350 TEMPLE AVENUE
NEW SALEM, NA 06555
(393) 876-2363

October 9

Dear Sophie,

Maybe <u>we</u> can have lunch sometime at Golightly's,

Fiona

You Won't Believe This

From: Sophie Diehl   10/9/99 5:14 PM
To: Maggie Pfeiffer <mcp15@mather.edu>
Date: Sat, 9 Oct 1999 17:14:16
Subject: You Won't Believe This

Dear Mags,

You won't believe this. I just got delivery of two dozen white roses. From
Fiona. Isn't white the sign of a truce? Flowers are never ironic, are they?
The thorns don't appear to be dipped in poison, and the note mentioned
"lunch sometime." I think she was sorry for her jab at Golightly's the
other day. I can't tell you how much they lifted my spirits.

Speaking of Fiona, her new firm, Farrow Allerton, hired two more
women partners, bringing their total to 5, out of 15. Joe sent a caustic
memo about it to everyone, partners and associates. David must be
steamed. We are falling behind. Maybe Judge Howard was right about
Fiona being warped by Traynor, Hand's patriarchy. I always thought
Farrow Allerton was stodgier than THW, but maybe not. They don't
do any criminal work, not even white-collar, which is of course a strike
against them, but they do represent several big foundations. What am
I doing? Being an idiot, that's what. As if they might recruit me. I have
no experience and no connections in this town. Shoulder to the wheel,
Sophie girl.

I think I'll go cook something; it will make myself feel a productive
member of society. Did I say the flowers were from Pettigrew and
perfect long-stemmers?

Love and kisses,
Sophie

TRAYNOR, HAND, WYZANSKI

222 CHURCH STREET
NEW SALEM, NARRAGANSETT 06555
(393) 876-5678
ATTORNEYS AT LAW

October 11, 1999

Mary Booth
Sanger & Booth
300 Church Street
New Salem, Narragansett 06555

Dear Mamie,

I write on behalf of Maria Meiklejohn. She has asked me to make a counteroffer offsetting some of the skimpier provisions in the new offer your client Dr. Daniel Durkheim has put forward, including: (1) reducing the proposed child support by $12,000 a year; (2) reducing college child support payments by $6,000 a year; (3) cutting all reimbursement alimony ($10,000 a year); (4) imposing college costs in excess of tuition and room and board on Ms. Meiklejohn; (5) postponing payment of Ms. Meiklejohn's share of the net equity in the family residence for seven years without including future value or paying interest; (6) removing the escalator clauses for alimony and tuition; and (7) retaining all of Dr. Durkheim's retirement funds.

Ms. Meiklejohn proposes: (1) In return for waiving her interest in the family residence and her share of its current net equity ($120,000), Dr. Durkheim will release to Ms. Meiklejohn the $16,000 in the bank account and pay her $100,000 on the signing of the agreement. The latter amount can be taken from Dr. Durkheim's proposed share of the stock funds or from another non-retirement (i.e., liquid) source, his choice. (2) Dr. Durkheim will pay all of Jane's college expenses, including books, fees, and living expenses, as well as tuition, room, and board. Ms. Meiklejohn will pay all of Jane's school costs until she finishes high school. (3) Dr. Durkheim shall provide and pay for medical insurance for Ms. Meiklejohn as long as she is receiving alimony. (4) Dr. Durkheim shall purchase life insurance of $740,000 (twice his current income) payable to Ms. Meiklejohn until Jane completes college. The rest of Dr. Durkheim's offer is accepted with one condition.

Ms. Meiklejohn's counteroffer is premised on Dr. Durkheim's agreement, in the event of Ms. Meiklejohn's death prior to Jane's 18th birthday, that he and Jane's maternal grandfather, Bruce Meiklejohn, will share legal custody and that Mr. Meiklejohn will have physical custody, with Jane living with her grandfather on the same terms she lived with her mother. This condition is nonnegotiable and conforms to the recommendation in the evaluation conducted by Dr. Rachel Fischer of the Mather Child Study Center at the request of Jane's parents. Ms. Meiklejohn will not sign an agreement which doesn't have this condition; she is prepared to litigate the separation and dissolution if agreement is not possible, and she is prepared to ask the court to appoint legal counsel for Jane. Let me know whether these terms are agreeable to Dr. Durkheim. If so, I will draft the agreement.

Yours,

Anne Sophie Diehl

Anne Sophie Diehl

Narragansett Statutes
Title 33 of the Narragansett Code, Sections 801ff.
Dissolution of Marriage, Annulment, and Legal Separation

Sec. 808. Counsel for minor children. Duties.

(a) The court may appoint counsel for any minor child or children of either or both parties at any time if the court deems it to be in the best interests of the child or children. The court may appoint counsel on its own motion, or at the request of either of the parties or of the legal guardian of any child or at the request of any child who is of sufficient age and capable of making a reasonable request. (b) Counsel for the child or children may be appointed in any case before the court when the court finds that the custody, care, education, visitation, or support of a minor child is in actual controversy.

Papa

From: Sophie Diehl

To: Maggie Pfeiffer <mcp15@mather.edu>

Date: Tue, 19 Oct 1999 01:47:16

Subject: Papa

Dearest Mags,

Long long day. Papa came up to New Salem to see me. He looks fine, not like someone dying, though he's thinner and limps a bit. He needs a new knee. The old one has never been quite right since his car accident, or as we say in the family, his alleged accident. I took him around the office and had him meet David and Joe and anyone who went to Columbia College. Turns out, we've got three of them, including, unbelievably, Proctor, who went there during WWII, as part of Naval Officer Training. If ever there was a Yale or Mather man, it was Proctor (viz, the Proctor Observatory at Mather). They were very sweet together. Proctor's very proud that Columbia employs the last great English Marxist historian and makes all its students read Thucydides. Intellectual independence is a big thing with him even though he has trouble voting for a Democrat. Papa didn't wear a tie, but he did wear his navy suit.

Afterward, I took him down to the court. I had a motion to argue in my never-ending Trilling case. Fruit of the forbidden tree. Somebody must have spread the word that my father had come to see me in action. Everyone teased me, including a sort-of-old colleague from my clerking days, Will Jacobsen, who's now an assistant U.S. attorney; he was hanging out with the ADA (pal? girlfriend?) who was arguing against me. When I clerked for Judge Howard on the 13th Circuit, he clerked for Judge Lintilhac. He's improved with age. I thought he was a bit of a dork then; not anymore. During the argument, Judge Stuessy kept calling me "Counselor"; then he'd wink. I almost laughed out loud. As you well know, no one who's ever known me for more than 10 minutes has ever called me anything but Sophie. The ADA, Lily Dion, wasn't too pleased, but hey, she had all the law on her side. Papa said I was first-rate, even though he could see I had a desperate argument. He doesn't know the half of it. Mr. Trilling is going down for a long time. I can't get him to plead. "So what if he's dead," he always says. "No one misses him. I did the world a favor." I keep trying to explain to him the disgraceful lack of gratitude in the criminal courts.

Off to lunch at Golightly's (there's no place else to go!). I told him that I had a divorce client who'd been served there. "That is reprehensible," he said. He then wanted to know how I'd got roped into "so low" a case, so I gave him a rundown, right down to Fiona's sudden (or at least unannounced) flight last month and our war of the roses. I asked him if he remembered a student back in '68 or '69 named Daniel Durkheim. "Ah, Sophie girl," he said, "I don't remember anyone from those years. All I did those springs is take garbage out of Low Library. I don't even think we had graduations in those years."

I had to work that afternoon, and he had made plans to see a colleague at Mather. We met up at my place for dinner. I cooked. Spaghetti carbonara. "Like Maman's," he said, an undeserved compliment. We drank a bottle of wine, and he talked about his cancer, his work, his marriage. He was not exactly frank, but he wasn't dishonest. Gran has leukemia, but the doc assured her she'll die of something else. I love English doctors. No icing the cake.

We walked to the station so he could catch the 10:18 train. It was the best time with him in 15 years. I went home and cried, and then watched *Two for the Road*, so I could cry some more.

Did you get a part in *The Rivals*?

Love,
Sophie

P.S. Word back as I was leaving the office at 6 pm from Ms. Meiklejohn's husband's lawyers. WE HAVE A DEAL. I am now a bona fide divorce lawyer.

The Rivals

From: Maggie Pfeiffer   10/20/99 10:14 PM
To: Sophie Diehl <asdiehl@traynor.com>
Date: Wed, 20 Oct 1999 22:14:37
Subject: The Rivals

Dear Sophie,

I've had two callbacks for *The Rivals*, and I'm Languishing like mad.
I do hope I get it. It's a delicious play. I like comedy better than
tragedy or, in an era without tragedies, drama. It's more difficult,
more complicated—it's harder to make someone laugh than cry—
but so much more satisfying. I'm not funny myself, but I think I can
play funny.

I'm so glad you had a good time with your father. He can be wonderful when he puts his mind and his back into it. It was easier for your
mother to be a good parent, even though she's French. She was
determined not to be her mother. Your father, on the other hand,
took the lessons of bad parenting differently. He simply wanted his
mother dead. Both your grandmothers were/are godawful. In some
way, both your parents are miracles.

What's this about Will Jacobsen? I remember him. Good-looking but
not too good-looking.

Love,
Maggie

P.S. I've been meaning to tell you this for ages but keep forgetting;
all men drop their underpants on the floor until they're 30, unless
their toilet training was too rigorous.

Sarah Littlemore Diehl
405 RIVERSIDE DRIVE
NEW YORK, NY 10025

22 October 1999

My darling Sophie girl,

I've appropriated Sally's stationery. I used to take Maman's too. Hmmm. I could give a Freudian interpretation, but I always get in trouble when I move in that direction with you lot. The great Unanalyzable One speaks. But this is all noise.

I write to say what a wonderful time I had with you on Tuesday. A perfect day. You are a class lawyer, my girl, and everyone in the firm and the courts knows it. I know I'm a difficult parent, bruised and bruising. I regret it. Don't take it personally (a ridiculous thing to say to one's child, but true). I'm unpleasant to most people, except of course waiters, taxi drivers, nannies, and panhandlers. The curse of the U-Marxist. I digress again. You are a class person. That's what I meant to say.

I shall come again to visit you if I may. History shows I'm better on your territory than the home ground.

Will Jacobsen likes you. Believe me. I know the look. The father of beautiful daughters learns early on to recognize it. Next day, he buys a shotgun. Give him a chance. He strikes me as wholly plausible.

All my love,
Papa

TRAYNOR, HAND, WYZANSKI

222 CHURCH STREET
NEW SALEM, NARRAGANSETT 06555
(393) 876-5678

MEMORANDUM
Attorney Work Product

From: Sophie Diehl
To: David Greaves
RE: Meiklejohn/Durkheim Separation Agreement
Date: October 27, 1999
Attachments: Separation Agreement

I am back from Sanger & Booth with the signed and notarized agreement. Felix was a godsend. I couldn't have done it without him. As you know, I've never drafted a separation agreement before. And I never will again, though if I had to do a divorce, this one was the one to do. I will miss Mia Meiklejohn. She was the smartest, most interesting, most humorous client I've ever had. She was badly behaved in a way I like. And it was a collaborative relationship, which it rarely is in criminal cases; your criminal clients mostly think of you as a patsy or a tool, and they never tell the truth. Maybe I'm developing a taste for civil litigation. I sometimes wish we didn't have to specialize.

The meeting went well. Ms. Meiklejohn was civil; Dr. Durkheim was surly. I don't blame him. The custody clause is a tough one, but Ms. Meiklejohn wouldn't budge. She urged him to write a letter to Jane explaining why he went along. He didn't say anything.

The parties agreed to waive the Parent Education Classes. I know Ms. Meikle-john was tempted not to, but she swallowed hard and went along.

Is there anything else I have to do? There are no escalators in the agreement; Felix says their only use is as a bargaining chip to give up. No one pays with-out being sued, he said, and by the time you've won, you're back in court suing for the next increase. "Frontload, frontload," was his advice.

I'll do my hours and send them to you. I'll let you decide which are billable and which are not.

Commonwealth of Narragansett
Family Court

County: Tyler   **Docket No:** 99-27

Separation Agreement

Daniel E. Durkheim   **Plaintiff**

v.

Maria M. Durkheim,   **Defendant**
a.k.a. Maria M. Meiklejohn

I. Parties

Agreement, made this _____th/st day of _____, 1999, by and between **DANIEL DURKHEIM, HUSBAND**, residing at 404 St. Cloud Street, New Salem, Narragansett, 06556 (hereinafter referred to as the "Husband"), and **MARIA M. DURKHEIM** a.k.a. **MARIA M. MEIKLEJOHN, WIFE**, residing at 404 St. Cloud Street, New Salem, Narragansett, 06556 (hereinafter referred to as the "Wife").

II. Recitals

A. Marriage
The Husband and Wife were married in New York, New York, on June 21, 1982.

B. Children
There is one (1) Child of the marriage. Jane Mather Durkheim (hereinafter referred to as the "Child"), born April 23, 1988, who is a minor and is dependent upon the Parties for support and maintenance.

C. Agreement to Separate
Serious and irreconcilable differences have arisen between the Husband and Wife, and Husband and Wife acknowledge that there has been an irretrievable breakdown of the marriage on or about January 3, 1999. Both parties desire to settle their financial, property, and other rights and obligations arising out of the marriage.

D. Restoration of Wife's Name

In any judgment of dissolution of marriage, it shall be ordered that Wife's name shall be restored to Maria Mather Meiklejohn.

III. Covenants

A. Effect of Agreement

The Husband and the Wife shall live separate and apart from one another, and each shall be free from interference, harassment, molestation, authority, and control, direct or indirect, by the other as fully as if single and unmarried. The Parties shall each have the right to dispose of his or her property by will or otherwise, in such manner as each may in his or her uncontrolled discretion deem proper, and neither will claim any interest in the estate or property of the other, except to enforce any obligation imposed by this Agreement, which shall be enforceable against the estate of each of them. The Husband and the Wife each warrant that he or she will not hereafter contract or incur any debt, charge, or liability whatsoever for which the other or his or her legal representative, property, or estate will or may become liable. The Husband and Wife further warrant to hold each other free, harmless, and indemnified from and against all debts, charges, and liabilities hereafter contracted or incurred by the other in breach of the provision of this Agreement.

B. Full Disclosure

Each Party warrants that he or she has made full disclosure of his or her income, assets, property, liabilities, and financial prospects.

C. Child Custody

The Wife and the Husband shall share legal custody of the Child and the Wife shall have physical custody of the Child, the Child residing with the Wife. The Husband shall have the right to visit with and be visited by the Child at reasonable times and for reasonable durations upon reasonable notice to the Wife.

The Husband and the Wife shall consult together in an effort to mutually agree in regard to the welfare, education, religious observance, and development of the Child to the end that, so far as possible, they may pursue a mutually harmonious policy in regard to her upbringing.

Neither the Husband nor the Wife shall attempt nor condone any attempt to estrange the Child from each other, or to injure or impede the respect or affection of the Child for the other, but on the contrary shall at all times encourage and foster in the Child respect and affection for both parents.

If for reasons of employment or other exigency, the Wife seeks to relocate with the Child more than 50 miles from New Salem, she shall notify the Husband prior to the move and arrange a reasonable schedule of visitation. Reasonable transportation expenses for the Child visiting the Husband under these circumstances shall be paid by the Wife. If the Husband seeks to relocate more than 50 miles from New Salem, he shall notify the Wife prior to the move and arrange a reasonable schedule of visitation. Transportation expenses for the Child visiting the Husband under these circumstances shall be paid by the Husband.

In the event of any serious illness of the Child, the parent with whom the Child is then staying shall immediately, if reasonably possible, notify the other parent, and that parent shall have the right to visit the Child during the illness.

Upon the death of the Husband prior to the Child reaching the age of 18, the Wife shall assume sole legal custody and retain physical custody. Upon the death of the Wife prior to the Child reaching the age of 18, the Husband and the maternal Grandfather of the Child, Bruce Meiklejohn (hereinafter referred to as the "Grandfather"), shall share legal custody and the Grandfather shall have physical custody, the Child residing with the Grandfather. The Husband shall have the right to visit with and be visited by the Child at reasonable times and for reasonable durations upon reasonable notice to the Grandfather.

D. Child Support

The Husband shall pay to the Wife for the support and maintenance of the Child the sum of $5,000.00 a month, beginning the first day of the month, following the execution of this Agreement, for seven (7) years. Thereafter, the Husband shall pay for the support and maintenance of the Child the sum of $1,500.00 a month, due the first day of the month, until her 23rd birthday or her graduation from college, whichever event occurs first.

E. Spousal Support / Traditional Alimony

As spousal support for the Wife, the Husband shall pay to the Wife the sum of $5,000.00 a month, beginning the first day of the month, following the execution of this Agreement, for seven years. Spousal support will cease upon the Wife's death, remarriage, or employment at an annual salary of $48,000 or more.

F. Rehabilitation Alimony

The Husband shall provide the Wife with rehabilitation alimony up to the sum of $30,000.00 a year for three (3) years, in payment of law school tuition. The actual payment, up to the sum of $30,000, shall be the tuition cost of the law school the Wife attends.

G. Child's Education

The Husband shall be responsible for payment of all college expenses of the Child, including tuition, room and board, fees, books, and living expenses, for four (4) years of college. In recognition of the Husband's obligations for spousal support, the Wife shall be responsible for all of the Child's primary and secondary education school fees at the Peabody School or other school she may attend.

H. Real Property

The Husband and Wife have resided together at 404 St. Cloud Street, New Salem, Narragansett (hereinafter referred to as the "Marital Residence"). On or before the 30th day following the signing of this Agreement, the Wife shall vacate the Marital Residence and the Husband shall be entitled to exclusive occupancy. The Wife shall convey to the Husband all her right, title, and interest in the Marital Residence; and upon conveyance, the Husband shall be solely responsible for the payment of all mortgages, loans, taxes, and insurance. The Husband hereby releases the Wife from all claims made by the bank holding the mortgage on the Marital Residence, the bank providing the Home Equity Loan, and all other liabilities arising out of the Husband's ownership of interest in the Marital Residence. The Parties' current net equity in the Marital Residence is $240,000 (current valuation of $525,000 less mortgage, Realtors' fees, and closing costs). The Wife releases her claims to her one-half interest in the net equity ($120,000).

I. Personal Property

The Parties have divided their tangible personal property to the satisfaction of each. The Parties agree that all furniture and household furnishings located in the Marital Residence shall be the exclusive property of the Husband, except for the items identified below, which shall be the exclusive property of the Wife. The Wife shall remove such items from the Marital Residence at a time or times mutually convenient to the Parties. The Husband will keep the Persian rug. The Wife will keep the original works by Cindy Sherman, Jenny Holzer, Ephraim Rubenstein, Robert Sweeney, Boris Chaliapin, and Ray and Charles Eames; all flatware, china, pottery, cooking utensils, and table linens; the Ian Ingersoll dining table; the Thonet chairs; the quilts and other antique bed linens; and all other personal property given by or inherited from her family with the exception of the Persian rug.

J. Automobiles

The Wife will retain the 1997 Saab, which is two years old and has two years left on its loan. The car is registered in her name. Its original cost was $32,000; its current value is $22,000. The Wife will make all loan payments. The Husband will retain the 1999 Audi, which was leased under a four-year Agreement. The car cost $68,000. It is now worth $60,000. The lease is in the Husband's name. The difference in value of the two cars recognizes the Husband's inheritance of $16,000 in 1968 from his mother.

K. Pets
The family pets, Tito the cat and Fido the dog, will live with the Wife
and the Child. The Husband will have reasonable visitation, which
includes having the pets stay with him in his residence.

L. Bank Accounts
The Parties have a joint savings account with Federated Central Bank,
New Salem, with $16,000 on deposit. This sum shall go to the Wife.
The Parties hereby waive all claims with respect to funds previously
withdrawn from the joint bank accounts of the Parties.

M. Investments
The Parties have investment accounts with the firm of Ira Lowenstein:
stock market account (Account Number: 04-0042-91) and Treasury
Bills (Account Number: 04-0042-93). As of March 31, 1999, the stock
market account had $700,000. The Husband shall convey to the Wife
his interest in the stock market account and release all claims to any
interest in it. The Husband and Wife jointly own $90,000 in Treasury
Bills. The Wife releases all claims to the Treasury Bills and conveys to
the Husband her interest in the Bills.

N. Pension Plans and Retirement Accounts
The Wife releases all claims to the Husband's TIAA-CREF Accounts
(TIAA Contract Number: ZZ 88567342-3; CREF Certificate
Number: ZZ 88567342-8; Premium Remitter: Mather University)
with a value of $600,000 as of March 31, 1999, and his 401(k) Plan
with the firm of Ira Lowenstein (401[k] Plan Account Number:
04-0043-92) with a value of $300,000, as of March 31, 1999.

O. Medical Insurance
The Husband will maintain medical and hospital insurance for the
Wife for seven (7) years from the signing of this Agreement. The
Husband will maintain medical and hospital insurance for the Child
until her 23rd birthday or her graduation from college, whichever
event occurs first.

P. Life Insurance
Until the Child's 23rd birthday or her graduation from college, the Husband shall carry a life insurance policy on his life in the face amount of $740,000 (two times his current annual salary), naming the Wife as beneficiary.

Q. Income Taxes
The Parties shall execute and file joint tax returns for the calendar year 1999. Any refund payable with respect to any joint tax returns shall be remitted to the Husband. If there is any deficiency or tax liability assessed on any jointly filed tax return, such deficiency or tax liability, with any interest or penalties thereon, shall be paid by the Husband.

R. Mutual Release and Discharge of Claims in Estates
Each Party shall have the right to dispose of the property of such Party by last will and testament in such manner as such Party may deem proper in the sole discretion of such Party, with the same force and effect as if the other Party had died. Each Party, individually and for his or her heirs, executors, administrators, successors, and assigns, hereby waives, releases, and relinquishes any and all claims, rights, or interests as a surviving spouse in or to any property, real or personal, that the other Party owns or possesses at death, or to which the other Party or his or her estate may be entitled.

S. Legal Representation
In connection with this Agreement, the Wife and Husband have had the advice of independent counsel of his and her own selection. Both Parties acknowledge that this Agreement has been achieved after competent legal representation and honest negotiations. Nothing herein shall be construed as a waiver or denial of the right of either Party to secure payment of attorneys' fees as provided by law for any breach by the other of any provision of this Agreement. Each Party acknowledges that all of the matters embodied in this Agreement, including all terms, covenants, conditions, waivers, releases, and other provisions contained herein, are fully understood by him or her; that he or she is entering into

this Agreement freely, voluntarily, and after due consideration of the consequences of doing so; and that this Agreement is valid and binding upon him or her.

T. General Provisions

This Agreement is entire and complete and embodies all understandings and Agreements between the Parties. No representation, warranty, Agreement, or undertaking of any kind or nature has been made to either Party to induce the making of this Agreement, except as is expressly set forth herein.

This Agreement shall not be amended, modified, discharged, or terminated except by a writing executed and acknowledged by the Party sought to be bound. It is the intention of the Parties that the division and transfer of property provided for in this Agreement shall be final, unless the Parties hereto shall hereafter agree to the contrary in writing.

This Agreement and all rights and obligations of the Parties hereunder shall be construed according to the laws of the State of Narragansett. If any provision of this Agreement should be held to be invalid or unenforceable under the laws of any state, country, or other jurisdiction, the remainder of this Agreement shall continue in full force and effect. Each of the rights and obligations of the Parties hereunder shall be deemed independent and may be enforced irrespective of any other rights and obligations herein.

The final decree for divorce, the decree nisi, shall issue 90 days from signing.

This Agreement shall be binding upon the Parties hereto, and their respective heirs, executors, administrators, successors, and assigns.

In Witness Whereof, the Parties hereto have executed this Agreement on the date first above written.

The Plaintiff   The Defendant

_____   _____

Then personally appeared the above-named David E. Durkheim and acknowledged the foregoing to be his free act and deed before me.

_____

Eve Charles, Notary Public

My commission expires: 10-18-02

Then personally appeared the above-named Maria M. Durkheim, a.k.a. Maria M. Meiklejohn, and acknowledged the foregoing to be her free act and deed before me.

_____

Geraldine Morris, Notary Public

My commission expires: 10-18-02

TRAYNOR, HAND, WYZANSKI

222 CHURCH STREET
NEW SALEM, NARRAGANSETT 06555
(393) 876-5678

MEMORANDUM
Attorney Work Product

From: David Greaves
To: Sophie Diehl
RE: Meiklejohn/Durkheim Separation Agreement
Date: October 27, 1999
Attachments:

You should be very proud of the work you did in this case. It was a first-rate job. Well done. I know you never want to do a divorce case again, but what about other civil litigation? What about employment law, say, sex discrimination or harassment? What about a right-to-die case? Those sides of our practice are growing, and I bet you'd be terrific at it. Give it a thought. You wouldn't have to give up the criminal work. And you could work with me or Felix. It's one of the great benefits of working in a small firm in a midsized city. You don't have to specialize if you don't want to. Civil, criminal, plaintiffs, defendants. The right kind of stew for someone like you. It's always worked for me. I've never been bored.

November 1

Dear Sophie,

Daniel came through like a mensch. He wrote Jane exactly the right letter. It made me teary, but then almost everything does these days. Here's a copy. Now maybe you can understand, or almost understand, why I married him.

I'm off to Rancho La Puerta over Veterans' weekend. Jane will stay with Daniel. We'll see how that goes. We're moving out on December 1. I've rented an apartment around the corner from Jane's school, 90 Germyn Street. That's the tiny street that runs between St. Cloud and Church near the Racquet Club. My father is just around the corner too.

Thanks for everything. You are the best lawyer ever.

Best,

Mia

October 28

Dear Jane,

Yesterday, your Mom and I signed a separation agreement. I want you to know about one part of it, the part about custody if your Mom should die before you are 18 years old. This isn't going to happen. (I promise and your Mom promises, but still, I know you worry about this.)

Your Mom and I have agreed that you will live with Poppa if that impossible event happens. Poppa and I will work things out so we both get to see lots of you. But this is never going to happen. Your Mom is going to live a long time, until 80 at least.

I would love you to live with me, and if you ever change your mind, you can always do it. Call at any time, or just drop in. My house is your house. I always want you around, even if I'm busy. You're my Musketeer.

I put in long hours at the hospital, and I know you sometimes think my work is more important to me than anything else. It is important but you are more important.

I love you. You are a fantastic person and great runner.

Love,
Daddy

Will Jacobsen!

From: Sophie Diehl
To: Maggie Pfeiffer <mcp15@mather.edu>
Date: Fri, 5 Nov 1999 21:42:11
Subject: Will Jacobsen!

11/5/99 9:42 PM

Darling Mags,

Life is picking up. Papa wrote me the best letter. You won't believe it.
I don't believe it. I'll show it to you when we have supper tomorrow.
He was his old wonderful self. I don't like to think about why he's
so changed, so I don't. I also got my annual postcard from him
reminding me it was Guy Fawkes Day, the 394th anniversary. Is there
a better holiday for an English Catholic Marxist? Made for him.

But there's other good news too. I'm finished with the Meiklejohn/
Durkheims. They signed the agreement. I'm sort of proud of the work
I did, but I daren't tell anyone at the office because they'll draft me
to divorce duty. Too much business in that line of work.

And then there's Will Jacobsen. I ran into him again this morning in
court (another one of my hopeless Trilling motions), and we went
out for coffee. He is, as Papa would say, plausible. We had a lively
conversation about the Clintons. I'm more of a fan, probably because
I'm more forgiving of bad behavior. He was disapproving of the
Monica shenanigans. He's probably not neurotic enough to go for
me, but I'd like it if he did. We've got things in common, including—
sound the trumpets!—European parents. I don't know if that's good
or bad. Probably bad. No Russian Jews lurking in his background per
Maman's instructions. His dad, Anders Jacobsen, is mixed Danish-
Norwegian, and teaches Northern European history at Rutgers; he
is not a Marxist, only your garden-variety Scandinavian socialist. His
mother, an Italian Jew (Giulia Levi), teaches Con Law at Penn. Distant
relation of Primo. Will (who is a Willem) said all Italian Jews were
related. He wants to go into state politics. Maybe he's my route to
the Court of Appeals. His favorite book is *Infinite Jest*. His favorite
writer, David Foster Wallace. I can't hold that against him. He's a guy

after all. He's only been to the Mather Rep once the whole time he's lived in New Salem. *That* I can hold against him. He's a movie person. Loves the first two *Godfather*s. Another guy thing. Did I mention that he's gotten much better-looking since you last saw him, with his very dark hair, blue eyes, good strong nose, like an axe, which of course is a pre-req, *un grand beau nez* as Maman used to say of Papa's honker. I think he's got a sense of humor—at least he laughed at my snappers—and he seems to like my looks too. He broke off at one point, when we were talking about our bullyingly intellectual fathers, and said, "You have yellow eyes. I've never seen that before." And then he smiled at me, a kind of Gatsby smile that made my toes curl. Am I to be loved not for my yellow hair, but my yellow eyes?

I guess you could say I've won this week's lottery. I've got to know my luck better, like little Jane Durkheim, whose parents worship at the shrine of "knowing your luck." I don't know. Is that a better family motto than "pulling up your socks"?

I know you have rehearsal tomorrow afternoon, so you and Matt should come at 8. I've laid in four bottles of wine. And they each cost more than $10.

Love,
Sophie

The Rivals

From: Maggie Pfeiffer   11/7/99 5:07 PM
To: Sophie Diehl <asdiehl@traynor.com>
Date: Sun, 7 Nov 1999 17:07:04
Subject: The Rivals

Dearest Sophie—

Dinner was wonderful; you're getting to be a very good French cook; your bourguignon was meltingly delicious. Have you cooked for your mother? Better, have you ever cooked for Grandmere? That would put her in a proper quandary. In my hearing, she's never praised anyone's cooking, not even Bocuse's. I remember her saying she couldn't understand how he'd gotten three Michelin stars, one maybe, two a stretch, three an outrage, another sign of the decline of France, since de Gaulle died. Yet she is always telling you everything you do is the best (especially if your mother is in the vicinity). I wonder if your sturdy ego is in part owing to her and her adoration of you along with your sibs. She never veers, even when your mother isn't around.

The wine was velvety. I suspect it was seriously more than $10. Were we the beneficiaries of your father's largess as well as yours? We walked home very slowly, practicing walking the crack on the sidewalk. I figured out a trick. Don't look down, look straight ahead. You have a much better chance of keeping on the crack. I do love good wine, good food, and good company, in ascending order. A perfect evening.

Congratulations on finishing the divorce. I know it's been hard on you (and on all of us who love you). Don't do another. I can't see David asking you again. He saw the toll it took, however good a job you did.

Your father's letter was wonderful. Dear old John Diehl. When he's good, he's very, very good . . .

As for Willem Jacobsen, he sounds more than plausible. Maybe I'll run down to the courthouse next week to scope him out.

Still boning up on *The Rivals*. They still haven't picked the cast. What are they waiting for?

Love,
Maggie

November 18, 1999

Dear Sophie—

Isn't Jane wonderful? Helen's a pip.

Best,

Mia

Dear Mia,   November 15, 1999

I understand from Tom that you and Daniel have signed your separation agreement. It only gets better, I promise. And if you marry again, the second divorce won't be so painful. You'll know you can survive it. Divorce makes optimists.

I have to tell you about a conversation Tom reported to me. He was up visiting Daniel over the holiday weekend when you were in Mexico. It was a full house. Tom, Jane, AND Dr. Roth. A bit awkward, you'd think, but then Daniel doesn't notice anything's wrong unless someone under 10 is running a temperature of 105°.

On Saturday night, they all went to dinner at the Plimouth Club (when did Daniel join? I know you refuse to go). Jane saw that Dr. R was wearing a necklace with a Jewish star. She said to her, "I'm Jewish, but Christian too." Daniel laughed and said Jane was nothing, just a little pagan. "She doesn't go to Sunday school or services, she only celebrates holidays, Christmas, Passover, Thanksgiving, and birthdays." They all then had a short discussion about

God. Dr. R declared herself a believer. The Durkheims were none too sure. "I pray sometimes but it's really wishing," Jane said. "God isn't going to get my mom and dad back together again, is he?" Silence fell upon the table. Not being a Durkheim, Dr. R couldn't take it; she spoke up: "Maybe he has a different plan, better than that." Jane shot back at her, "Better for who?" Dr. R turned beet red and looked to Daniel. Daniel said nothing, he just tousled Jane's hair.

Dr. R did not stay in Daniel's room. Welcome to the prurient world of the divorced.

all the best,

Helen

ELISABETH DREYFUS | 480 RIVERSIDE DRIVE, NEW YORK, NY 10027

November 19, 1999

Chère Sophie,

I've been reading Louise Glück's newish book of
poems, Meadowlands. Our conversation the other
night made me pick it up again. It's about her
marriage and divorce and also The Odyssey and
Odysseus and Penelope. I thought you'd like this
poem, a son's take on his difficult parents.

> Telemachus' Detachment
>
> When I was a child looking
> at my parents' lives, you know
> what I thought? I thought
> heartbreaking. Now I think
> heartbreaking, but also
> insane. Also
> very funny.

She's very good, Glück. A new favorite.

with love,
Maman

Will

From: Sophie Diehl   11/22/99 9:45 PM
To: Maggie Pfeiffer <mcp15@mather.edu>
Date: Mon, 22 Nov 1999 21:45:19
Subject: Will

Magster,

I have a date! With a lawyer! Will called and invited me to a movie on
Sunday. I said I'd like to see the new Almodovar, *All About My Mother*.
(The choice, of course, of the badly behaved.) He was listing toward
American Beauty. He said that Denby had been luke on *Mother* but
high on *Beauty*. I said Denby was very good but sometimes just plain
wrong. "Are you always this definite?" he asked. I said I was afraid so.
"Good," he said. Imagine that.

I do like him. He has the look and feel of a decent human being. I just
hope I won't be tired (i.e., cranky). I'll be coming off Thanksgiving
with the family, which is always a test of my character no matter that
I love them all madly. There's always one to-the-death argument per
visit. I can see us all getting hot under the collar over who's worse:
Bush or McCain? Or: why is Al Gore such a jerk about Clinton? Doesn't
he want to win? You know what it's like. We throw ourselves into
these debates, as if they mattered. And we all want to win, except
of course Jake, who privately roots for Maman (for sentimental
reasons, d'accord) but publicly assumes a dignified position of analytic
neutrality.

Love,
Sophie

P.S. Maman sent me a poem by Louise Glück, "Telemachus'
Detachment." Do you know it? I'll show it to you. I think she's giving
me advice. Or maybe permission.

November 23

Dear Mia,

Jane is a gift of a child. First Atalanta, now Maisie, taking in everything her parents say and do. Wait till her first novel comes out!

You were very lucky in your husband's first wife. As his third wife will be in you. I don't think Dr. Stephanie cuts the mustard. Daniel wrote a very good letter.

I'll tie up all the loose ends shortly.

Regards,
Sophie

TRAYNOR, HAND, WYZANSKI
162 CHURCH STREET, NEW SALEM, NARRAGANSETT 06555 (393) 876-5678

Shrinkage

From: Sophie Diehl   11/24/99 12:17 PM
To: Maggie Pfeiffer <mcp15@mather.edu>
Date: Wed, 24 Nov 1999 12:17:53
Subject: Shrinkage

Dear Maggie,

I've taken a big step. I've decided to grow up, now that I'm 30. This
morning I called Rachel Fischer, a professor at the Child Study Center at
Mather, and asked her if she could recommend a shrink. I apologized
for calling her—conflict of interest (?): she was a Durkheim shrink—but
she couldn't have been nicer. I told her who my stepdad was and asked
if she could find someone who didn't know him, or at least hadn't
trained with him or under him. And no NY Psychoanalytic. I said it
didn't have to be a psychiatrist, and it couldn't be Isabel Stokes, another
Durkheim shrink. She gave me a name, a psychiatric social worker who
was trained at New Salem Psychoanalytic, Antonia Phelps. I called her
and have an appointment next Tuesday. I had to do it. I sent some
confessional emails to David Greaves that were inappropriate (to put
it most generously to myself) as communications between boss and
underling. It's time I paid someone to spill to, like a proper grown-up,
and stopped leaking all over the place. You must be weary of my spilling.
I am. And I'm worried that I'll never have a decent relationship (with Will
or anyone) unless I talk through my bad boyfriend jones.

My plan is to keep this venture to myself (and you, of course) for now.
Jake would want to vet her. And of course, Papa will think she's a
quack. He always says he doesn't "believe" in therapy (and has said it
increasingly since Maman married Jake), in exactly the way he says he
doesn't "believe" in creationism.

Have a great Thanksgiving. I'm going for the good-enough.

What would I do without you?

xoxoxo
Sophie

P.S. I forgot to tell you. A headhunter for Farrow Allerton called me yesterday and asked whether I might be interested in talking to them about their new criminal practice. Apparently, one of their partners heard me arguing my latest Trilling motion. I wonder if Fiona knows, if she's behind this. It's too soon for me to move, even if I wanted to move (no?), but it certainly was an ego booster. I said I would seriously consider the offer. I suppose the manly thing to do is to tell David and see what he has to offer. I think I'm a very good negotiator when it comes to my clients, but I hate hate hate doing it for myself. WWFWD? Talk to Joe first and have him do the negotiating for me!

Thanksgiving and Therapy

From: Maggie Pfeiffer   11/30/99 11:03 AM
To: Sophie Diehl <asdiehl@traynor.com>
Date: Tue, 30 Nov 1999 11:03:55
Subject: Thanksgiving and Therapy

Dear Sophie—

I'm so glad Thanksgiving was an unmitigated success. It was lovely of all of you to call and sing "La Marseillaise." I don't know what my in-laws thought. They seemed dumbfounded. They don't understand my relationship with the Diehl clan. They don't socialize outside the family. Matt and his sisters always found it confining growing up but thought, until they went to college, that everyone's family spent every weekend with family. I told Howard and Linda that from the time I was 8 until I went to college, I spent every weekend at your place. "But didn't your parents mind?" "Nope, they thought it good for me," I said. Did they notice I was gone? "And your grandparents, didn't you want to see them?" That I could answer safely, they all being dead. At the wedding, I could see they were perplexed that your parents, and not my parents, gave toasts, but I decided I wouldn't explain if they didn't ask. And they didn't ask. My parents had cleaned up for the wedding pretty well, but toasting was not something they could do, unless it was "down the hatch," or "Cheers." When my mother took my father home immediately after dinner so he couldn't get falling-down drunk there, the Davidoffs didn't think it odd; they thought it was Catholic. Theirs is an insular world, but there's no malice in them and they're kind to their children and to me.

I think therapy is a good step. And I agree that you shouldn't say anything to your parents now. You're right to think Jake would want to vet the therapist, and your mother would probably be skeptical. She wouldn't be hostile, like your dad, but she's too French to think it useful, unless, of course, it was Lacanian. She can't help herself. The French regard psychoanalysis as acceptable as a kind of graduate school experience, good for one's intellectual growth, but "therapy" they think *infra dig*, only for the weak-minded or undisciplined, a.k.a. Les Americains.

Saving the best for last, I'm so glad you had a good time on Sunday with Will. I think, like your mother, you're happiest when you have a man you can argue with. Did you really think he would be as liberal as you? No one's as liberal as you and still aspires to political office. You're unelectable in every state, even Massachusetts.

Love,
Maggie

P.S. I got the part in *The Rivals*. At the rep. I just got the email. Oh bliss, oh rapture.

MARIA MATHER MEIKLEJOHN
90 GERMYN STREET
NEW SALEM, NA 06556

December 8, 1999

Dear Sophie,

Jane and I moved out of the St. Cloud Street house on the 1st and are now very cozily ensconced in our apartment on Germyn Street. We took Tito but left Fido. I know Daniel and I skirmished over that, but this place is too small for a dog, and without a proper backyard I'd have to walk him morning and night, which in the clear light of a new day did not seem attractive.

I'm a bit embarrassed about the stationery, the third monogrammed version in less than a year, but it's so ingrained, having it and using it, that not having it and not using it would be like going outside without underpants. Maybe that's an exaggeration. But I would feel undressed without it, or at the very least badly dressed, stationerily speaking. I still confess to you.

Which brings me to the real point. Can a divorce lawyer and her client ever be friends? I know I've behaved badly in front of you, but then I've behaved badly in front of many of my friends—and relations too. I can also behave well. I'm hoping now, with this all settled, I'll settle too. Maybe we can have a drink sometime. At Golightly's, for auld lang syne?

Thanks for everything,

Mia

P.S. Don't forget to send the bill. I must owe you money.

You Won't Believe This, Part II

From: Sophie Diehl   12/9/99 7:44 PM
To: Maggie Pfeiffer <mcp15@mather.edu>
Date: Thu, 9 Dec 1999 19:44:20
Subject: You Won't Believe This, Part II

Dear Mags,

I just tried calling you. Where are you? I had a jaw-dropping moment
this evening, in Good Foods. I still can't wrap my mind around it. You
won't believe it. I don't believe it. But, of course, I do. I was there.

As I was standing in front of the ice cream freezer, trying to decide
between Narragansett Dairy's Compton Salted Caramel or New Salem
Nougatine, I felt someone tap me on the shoulder. I wheeled around,
almost expecting Harry. But no. It was Daniel Durkheim, the almost ex-
husband of my divorce client. "Hello," he said. "I thought it was you."
"Oh," I said. "Hello." I started to turn back to the freezer. He spoke
again: "I was hoping I'd run into you." He paused, smiling slightly. "Oh,"
I said, not knowing what to say, not knowing what to think. How would
Emily Post handle this situation? He went on. "I was wondering if you'd
like to have a drink sometime?" I must have looked as astonished as I
felt. "Are you serious?" I asked. "Of course," he said, "why wouldn't I
be?" "Well," I said, taking a deep breath, "you're the man who forever
ruined Golightly's for me. Why would I want to have a drink with you?"
He flushed scarlet, then turned and walked away.

I will never ever understand men, not as long as I live. I bought both ice
creams and am now, as I sit in front of the computer, eating alternately
out of the two cartons. Next up, I'm going to make myself a stiff gin and
tonic and watch at least three episodes of *Tinker Tailor*. I worship Alec
Guinness.

Love,
Sophie

P.S. Yesterday Will and I went to see *Mansfield Park*. When I told him earlier in the day I wanted to see it, he had no idea what it was. I was so taken aback. "Haven't you read Jane Austen?" I asked. Shamefacedly (well, sort of, he doesn't shame easily), he admitted he hadn't. "Not even *Pride and Prejudice*?" I asked. He shook his head. "How can that be?" His response: "I wasn't an English major." I was aghast. "What has that to do with it? Didn't they make you read any novels at Penn? Didn't they have gen ed courses?" He went on the offensive. "You haven't read any David Foster Wallace," he said. "He's the greatest writer of his, our generation." I told him I had tried but came a cropper. "He's like Bellow," I said. "So many words." He gave me a kiss. "I'll give the old girl a try," he said. And he's doing that. He just called to say he picked up a copy of *P&P*. In a spirit of reciprocal good sportsmanship, I am reading one of DFW's essays, "Neither Adult Nor Entertainment," about the porn Oscars. It's very good, funny too. All the women are called "starlets" and the men "woodmen." Who else would think to write about this, besides, of course, Hunter Thompson?

P.P.S. Joe came through. David gave me a $25,000 raise (not a bonus!) for turning down Farrow Allerton. Joe said David was at first stunned. Who goes recruiting raw associates? Then he got alarmed. Good. He first offered to raise me $10,000. Joe told him to get serious. The negotiations went two more rounds. Joe is the best. The next day, David asked me why I didn't come to him myself. I'd prepared for that, not wanting to look craven. I quoted the old saying that any person who represents herself has a fool for a client. David raised an eyebrow, then congratulated me. He's the next best.

TRAYNOR, HAND, WYZANSKI

222 CHURCH STREET
NEW SALEM, NARRAGANSETT 06555
(393) 876-5678

TIME SHEET
Attorney Work Product

Client: Maria Mather Meiklejohn
Attorney: Anne Sophie Diehl
Date: December 10, 1999
Rate: $150/hour

Date	Item	Hour(s)
6/3/99	Letter to RK on Restraining Order	1
6/9/99	Review of 4M's Will	
	Consultation with Proctor Hand*	2
6/18/99	Consultation with MMM	
	RE: Child Evaluation; 4M's Trust	2
7/7/99	Conference with DED, RK at RK Office	2
7/9/99	Review of 4M's Trust	1
	Email to MMM, summing up	1
	Letter to MMM on Trust, MV property	3
7/16/99	Draft of Revised Settlement Offer	3
7/21/99	Letter to RK on 4M's Trust	1
	Rules on Necessary, Emergency Invasions	3
	Revised Settlement Offer to DED, RK	2
9/7/99	Review of Child Evaluation	2
10/5/99	Review of New Offer from S&B	2
10/7/99	Consultation with MMM on New Offer	1
	Draft of Counteroffer	3
10/11/99	Letter to S&B with Counteroffer	2
10/20/99	Review of Narragansett Divorce Code	3

10/21/99	Draft of Separation Agreement	4
	Consultation with Felix Landau*	2
10/27/99	Signing Agreement at S&B	2

Total Hours   42

Bill $6,300

* Proctor Hand and Felix Landau will charge $150/hour for 2 hours of consultation each in accord with the Fee Agreement.

TRAYNOR, HAND, WYZANSKI

222 CHURCH STREET
NEW SALEM, NARRAGANSETT 06555
(393) 876-5678

BILL FOR SERVICES
Attorney Work Product

Client: Maria Mather Meiklejohn
Rate: $150/hour
Period: 6/3/99 to 10/27/99
Date: December 10, 1999

Attorney:	Anne Sophie Diehl	
	42 Hours	$6,300
Attorney:	Proctor Hand	
	2 Hours	$300
Attorney:	Felix Landau	
	2 Hours	$300
Secretarial Support:	30 hours at $40/hour	$1,200
Reproduction Costs, Postage, Messenger:		$400
Subtotal:		$8,500
Previous Bill:		$5,700
Total:		$14,200
Retainer Paid:		*$12,000*
Total Due:		$2,200

TRAYNOR, HAND, WYZANSKI

222 CHURCH STREET
NEW SALEM, NARRAGANSETT 06555
(393) 876-5678

MEMORANDUM
Attorney Work Product

From:	Sophie Diehl
To:	David Greaves
RE:	Maria Meiklejohn/Daniel Durkheim
	Last Shot Across the Bow !?!?
Date:	December 17, 1999
Attachments:	

I just got off the phone with Mia Meiklejohn. In the move, the movers
took an ancient 17" cathode-ray black-and-white television that sat on
the kitchen counter. It was supposed to stay with Dr. Durkheim at the St.
Cloud Street house; he protested, formally, through Mamie Booth. Ms.
Meiklejohn called him to tell him he was the most pathetic person she
knew but, sure, if he wanted it, he could get it when he next took Jane out
to dinner. I asked her not to kick it in. She promised.

New Year's

From: Sophie Diehl   12/19/99 7:28 PM
To: Maggie Pfeiffer <mcp15@mather.edu>
Date: Sun, 19 Dec 1999 19:28:48
Subject: New Year's

Dear Mags,

I'm so glad you and Matt can come for New Year's. Will is taking charge. I am sous-chefing, which is a real test of our relationship. He is a tyrant in the kitchen. His older sisters toughened him up and made him a feminist, but there's no escaping he's the family baby and his mother dotes. Can you imagine a Jewish Mother who is also an Italian Mother? He explained (instead of apologizing) when I complained about his kitchen bullying: "I can't do anything about it. You've met my younger sister. Well, my older sister is Stella squared. Mom made each of us cook one meal a week, and I became very belligerent in the kitchen (and highly skilled) because they were so critical. An 8-year-old doesn't exactly have a wide repertoire." I suppose I'm feeling with him in the kitchen the way Francoise feels with me all the time.

He's planning to make a fish stew, though not a bouillabaisse. "Nothing French," he said, in a preemptive strike against any criticism I might make. I will do dessert. I'm dying to try a galette. He thinks that's too chaste, after fish. He wants chocolate. All this negotiation. I think I have a real boyfriend.

Shrinking is going . . . After our third session, Ms. Phelps said, "Your editing function seems to be on the fritz—I'm not talking about here, in this room, but out in the world. You know, you don't have to say everything you think." I'd say her diagnosis was dead on. Will says the same thing. So does Maman, so do you, David, the Judge. I just never really heard it clearly before she said it.

I'm almost happy.

Don't bring anything. Just yourselves. Maman and Jake sent a mixed case of wine and champagne to celebrate the New Year's. I think they know something's going on.

xoxo,
Sophie

December 20

Dear Mia,

I'd like to meet for a drink, but not Golightly's. Let's do it in the new year and start with a clean slate. How about Frank's Bar and Grill? It's no better than it should be.

This is all I can manage in the way of monogrammed stationery right now. My mother, who's always used it, is threatening to get me some for Christmas, as a sign I've grown up.

Are you ready for the new millennium? I'm hopeful.

Merry Christmas and Happy New Year,

Sophie

TRAYNOR, HAND, WYZANSKI
122 CHURCH STREET, NEW SALEM, NARRAGANSETT 06555 (393) 876-5678

2000

HAPPY NEW MILLENNIUM

December 31, 1999

Stephanie,

Keep an eye out for Catherine Strand, a postdoc in Daniel's lab and the first author on a recent paper in "Pediatric Oncology." She's a blond WASP with a trust fund, the Durkheim trifecta.

Mia

P.S. He did it with you; he'll do it to you.

MARIA MEIKLEJOHN and JANE DURKHEIM

From the desk of Sophie Diehl

1/4/00

Final decree to issue 1/25/00

Send note to Mia Meiklejohn

TRAYNOR, HAND, WYZANSKI
222 CHURCH STREET, NEW SALEM, NARRAGANSETT 06555 (393) 876-5678

THE DIVORCE PAPERS (Page 461)

ACKNOWLEDGMENTS

Like Jane Durkheim, I know my luck. Special thanks go to five women, the *sine qua nons* of this novel: my daughter, the writer Maggie Pouncey, for her readiness to read every iteration of the manuscript and her unflagging confidence in it; the novelist Karen Thompson Walker, for her early reading of the final draft, which encouraged me to look for an agent; my agent, Kathy Robbins, for her editorial skills, her gift for negotiation, her discretion, and her friendship; my editor, Lindsay Sagnette, for her commitment to the novel, which gave it life and put me in such good literary company; and publisher Molly Stern, for her belief in the novel, which allowed me to imagine a different third act, and for her talented design team.

Others, too, have helped me along the way. My thanks to: my son-in-law, Matt Miller, for his unblinking assurance that the book would be published; my stepsons, Christian Pouncey, Max Denby, and Tommy Denby, and my daughter-in-law, Victoria Pouncey, for their generous notion of family; Katherine DiLeo of the Robbins Office, for her staunch defense of Sophie when she behaved badly; Jane Booth, Becky Okrent, Nancy Dunbar, Barbara Fisher, Joanne McGrath, Carol Sanger, Jean Howard, Niki Parisier, and Jill Cutler, for their advice and stories; and Joanna and Jonathan Cole, for their bedrock support.

I want to acknowledge a particular debt to Carl Hovde, who died in 2009. I appropriated a line from a letter he wrote when he was dean of Columbia College (1968–72) and ascribed it in the novel to Judge Anne Howard; it is the line about fencing unicorns and foddering wolves. I know the line because I typed the letter. I was Carl's secretary. Carl tossed off lines like that effortlessly.

The odds against this novel getting finished, not to say published, were long. I came to fiction late in life; I adopted an irregular genre, Epistolary 2.0; for many years I worked on it only intermittently. Early in our relationship, my husband, David Denby, read a very raw draft. He gave me criticism I wasn't interested in hearing, let alone accepting. Years later, I realized he had made good points. David took me seriously and made me take myself seriously. He gave me the freedom and room to write.

ABOUT THE AUTHOR

Susan Rieger was educated at Mount Holyoke College and Columbia Law School. She was a residential college dean at Yale and an associate provost at Columbia, and she has taught law to undergraduates at Mount Holyoke, Hampshire, Columbia, and Yale. She has written frequently about the law, her articles appearing in publications including the *Berkshire Eagle*, the *Hartford Courant*, the *Boston Globe*, and the *New York Times*. This is her first novel. She lives with her husband, the *New Yorker* critic David Denby, in New York.

THE DIVORCE PAPERS

EXTRA LIBRIS

ESSAYS,
READER'S GUIDES,
AND MORE

A Reader's Guide

The questions and discussion topics below are designed to enhance your reading group's discussion of *The Divorce Papers*.

QUESTIONS AND TOPICS FOR DISCUSSION

1. Is Sophie a good lawyer? Why? Why not?
2. At the beginning of the novel, Sophie feels she's "treading water." Why does Sophie seem to be having so much trouble finding her way? How does this change as the novel progresses?
3. Both of Sophie's parents are European. How has that influenced who she is?
4. Why does Maggie put up with Sophie? Would you?
5. Is Dr. Durkheim the book's "villain"? Why do you think he wanted a divorce? Do you think he knew about Jacques? Did your opinion of him change over time?
6. Mia confesses she initially withheld some information from Sophie. She also has a flair for the dramatic and loves to tell a good story. Do you believe her version of events? In an epistolary novel, how do you decide who is a reliable narrator?

7. Are Mia and Daniel equally to blame for the failure of their marriage? Do you think their marriage could have been saved?

8. Mia loved living and working in New York City, but she moved to New Salem for Daniel and his job. What were the trade-offs at that time? Do they seem worthwhile in retrospect?

9. What do you think was going on at the firm with Fiona? Why was she so hostile toward Sophie at the beginning? Did you agree with Fiona that her reprimand was unfair? Sexist?

10. Will or Harry?

11. There are three father-daughter relationships, all difficult: Mia and Bruce Meiklejohn; Sophie and John Diehl; Jane and Daniel Durkheim. Do they change over time? If so, what makes the change happen? If not, what is the sticking point?

12. There are two mother-daughter relationships: Elisabeth and Sophie and Mia and Jane. In what ways are these stronger than the father-daughter relationships? Weaker?

13. What do you think of the decision to give custody to Bruce in the event Mia dies before Jane is eighteen? Was Mia right to insist on that? How do you think Daniel felt?

14. Is the separation agreement fair and reasonable? Who came out better, if anyone?

15. What's next for Mia? For Sophie?

A Conversation with Susan Rieger

Q. You've taught law at Columbia and Yale. You've written about law for newspapers and magazines. And now you've written what one critic called a "brutally comic" and "extremely clever" novel about a lawyer. What about law so fascinated you that you've dedicated your life to it, and what do you hope to achieve with a novel that you didn't with your previous professional work?

A. At an impressionable age, I saw *A Man for All Seasons*, Robert Bolt's wonderful movie about Thomas More, Henry VIII's doomed chancellor. At one point More gets into a testy argument with his son-in-law, Will Roper, who says he'd "cut down every law in England" to get the Devil. More answers him: "And when the last law was down, and the Devil turned 'round on you—where would you hide, Roper, the laws all being flat? This country's planted thick with laws from coast to coast—man's laws, not God's—and if you cut them down—and you're just the man to do it—d'you really think you could stand upright in the winds that would blow then?"

After that speech I was a goner for the law, *but* I was very young and I didn't know any women lawyers. That all changed, of course, and ten years later I went to law school.

It took me much longer to screw up the courage to try to write a novel, to shake myself loose from the fact-based world of law and make things up. In 1999 I had a kind of now-or-never moment. I wanted more play in my life, more imagination and invention. It took another twelve years, and I didn't know until 2010 that I'd actually finish.

Q. You mentioned that you've been divorced once. How did your own experience of divorce influence the writing of this novel?

A. Getting divorced made me see the drama in the experience, not only for the couple and any children they might have, but for their whole world: their parents, friends, colleagues. For a first novel, this seemed a good place to start—with what I knew. Then I made things up. That was the most fun—and the most work.

Q. The women in *The Divorce Papers* are powerhouses in their own way: brilliant, witty, dynamic. Did you have any influences in mind while writing these characters?

A. My mother was smart and funny. The only piece of marital advice she ever gave me was this: Marry the man who makes you laugh; they all make you cry. That's true, as far as it goes, but I might have benefited from some additional instruction. Still, I passed it along to my daughter, who is also smart and funny. Then there are my good friends, who are smart and funny. I had all those voices in my head.

Q. There is a slew of literary and film references throughout your novel, sure to delight voracious readers. Were any references particularly important or essential to you?

A. I have three favorite quotes in the book. The first is from *A Man for All Seasons*. Mia is telling Sophie about "the other woman": "Do you remember that scene in *A Man for All Seasons*, when More confronts Richard Rich for betraying him in exchange for being made Chancellor of Wales? More says to him, 'I can understand a man giving up his soul for the world, Richard, but for Wales?' That's how I feel. I can understand Daniel leaving me, but for Stephanie Roth?"

My second favorite is the poem "Telemachus' Detachment" by Louise Glück, from her book *Meadowlands*. It's for grown children who are having trouble freeing themselves from the thrall of difficult or unhappy parents. Short and powerful, moving and funny.

My third favorite is a longish quote from Tom Stoppard's play *The Real Thing*. It's a quote about the possibility—and only the possibility—of another person. I've never believed in soul mates. I've always thought there were at least a hundred people out there for each of us. The Stoppard quote is about one of those hundred, unpursued but acknowledged.

Q. Main character Sophie loves criminal law and is only very reluctantly pulled into this divorce case. What are your preferred (and least favorite) areas of law, and why?

A. I like law when it intersects with daily life, with family life and working life. So much of our lives is shaped by law, from putting a dad's name on a baby's birth certificate to forbidding gramps from burying granny in the back garden. Outside the domestic realm, my favorite areas of law are civil rights and criminal rights—free speech on the one hand, the right to remain silent on the other. In law school, the course I disliked the most was on the Uniform Commercial Code. The only thing I remember was the professor's economical, cynical, and, I believe, accurate statement on Chapter IV, the section on banks: "The bank never loses. That's all you need to know."

Q. Do you envision writing more fiction and, if so, what's your next project?

A. I do want to write more fiction; I'm working on a second novel now. I'm not quite ready to talk about it. I worry that I'll talk about it and not do it. I don't want to jinx it. It's hard work writing a novel. And I'm not taking twelve years this time around.

Recommended Reading:
Favorite Novels of Marriage and Divorce

Aside from Henry VIII's wives, until the twentieth century, divorce was not a real possibility for women in bad marriages.

If death (either his or hers) didn't deliver a woman, she might trudge on in bitter resignation, seek a dignified separation, or, more often than you think, commit adultery.

In fiction, adultery offered engrossing plots, to wit, the great French and Russian novels of the nineteenth century, *Madame Bovary* and *Anna Karenina*. (The great American novels of the nineteenth century, *Moby-Dick* and *Huckleberry Finn*, have no women at all to speak of. What does that say about us?)

The twentieth century brought a sea change in laws, customs, and literature. Divorce no longer necessarily meant desperation and destitution for women, not in art or life. While nineteenth-century novels of adultery lent themselves to tragedy, divorce novels of the twentieth and twenty-first centuries lend themselves to comedy.

As a reader, I love both. As a writer, I'm firmly in comedy's camp: sadness, anger, worry, sleeplessness, they're all acceptable, but no rat poison, no throwing yourself under a train. Here are some of my favorite literary works on marriage and divorce.

What Maisie Knew, Henry James, 1897

Young Maisie's divorced parents are uncaring, cruel, selfish, and unscrupulous. Her stepparents are not uncaring, but they are weak, self-involved, and manipulative. The novella might have been written yesterday: the child nobody wants callously fought over. It's a great story, chilling and memorable.

The Twelve Pound Look, J. M. Barrie, 1910

J. M. Barrie's short play, often revived, is a sly riff on the importance of financial independence for a woman who wants a divorce. This is still true. In Barrie's play, twelve pounds buys his heroine a typewriter. The twelve pound look is a Eureka moment.

The Maples Stories, John Updike, 2009

This book, a series of linked stories about a couple, Joan and Richard Maple, takes them from their first date in a hospital to their last kiss on the day of their divorce, some twenty years later. I'll let Updike make his own case, in a brilliant distillation of why a marriage endures and why it ends. " 'I hate your ego,' [Joan] said, 'and our sex is lousy, but I've never been lonely with you. I've never for an instance felt alone when you were in the room.' "

Heartburn, Nora Ephron, 1983

Ephron's book, by turns heartbreaking and hilarious, is a highly entertaining read, as well as a wholly satisfying act of revenge against her philandering ex-husband. And even better than a pie in his face, it was a bestseller.

Perfect Reader, Maggie Pouncey, 2010

Before I was a novelist, I was the mother of the novelist Maggie Pouncey. At first reckoning, Maggie's novel is the story of a young woman, Flora Dempsey, coming to grips with her father's sudden death and secret life. At second, it is the story of Flora coming to grips, after twenty years, with an earlier death, the death of her family, brought on by her parents' contentious divorce when she was seven. At once moving, painful, and funny, the novel lays bare the shattering blow divorce delivers to children and the wrenching sense of loss, never fully expunged, they carry with them.

Dept. of Speculation, Jenny Offill, 2014

Written in a spare, glancing style that is the un-Knausgård, but as compelling and as mysterious in its achievement, Jenny Offill's novel tells the story of a marriage under duress and the struggle by the wife to hold it together. It is a great and haunting work.

For additional Extra Libris content from your other favorite authors and to enter great book giveaways, visit ReadItForward.com/Extra-Libris.

ESSAYS, READER'S GUIDES, AND MORE